The Mysterious Miss Mayhew

HAZEL OSMOND

Quercus

First published in the UK in 2014 by

Quercus Editions Ltd
55 Baker Street
7th Floor, South Block
London W1U 8EW

Copyright © 2014 Hazel Osmond

A CIP catalogue record for this book is available
from the British Library.

PB ISBN 978 1 78087 371 8
Ebook ISBN 978 1 78087 372 5

10 9 8 7 6 5 4 3 2 1

Printed and bound in Great Britain by Clays Ltd, St Ives plc

Typeset by Hewer Text UK Ltd, Edinburgh

For anyone who has put two and two
together and come up with five.

CHAPTER 1

Thursday 8 May

It seems to me that a car which is more or less the colour of a ripe tomato is not the best vehicle to drive when you are trying to keep a very low profile indeed.

The man in the hire place informed me that it is the only automatic they have.

'No call for them, pet,' he said. Or he might have been saying, 'I need to call my pet.' I haven't quite got my ear attuned to the accent yet, which is weird after all those years in Scotland – you'd think I could pick my way through something this gutsy.

I did understand him later, though, when he said I had the same colour hair as his 'gran'.

Nice to meet someone as tactless as I am.

Apart from that, he is a sweetheart – very chatty and he's made me a cup of coffee while he's gone off to check over the car.

I could sit and twiddle my thumbs, but I've 'borrowed' a piece of his paper because I always find paper comforting and writing on it stops me feeling quite so alone in this part of the world where I've never been and where I know absolutely no one.

Although I suppose that's not strictly true.

Mr Friendly seemed very enthusiastic about Tynebrook. Said he and his girlfriend often had a run out there and although he wasn't quite sure of the date, he thought the county show would be taking place quite soon. He looked almost misty-eyed.

When I mentioned I was going to be staying in a cottage, he made a noise that suggested I had all the luck and he didn't.

I can't disagree with that. So lovely to imagine getting there and sitting in a cosy, chintzy sitting room, looking out over a garden brimming with old-fashioned flowers and feeling a bit like I'm coming home. I wonder if it has inglenooks inside and roses around the door.

So . . . I'm still thinking about that chattiness of his. I'll have to watch it if that's a widespread trait up here. Coming straight from London where they might as well put 'Do not have eye contact with strangers' notices on the walls, it wrong-footed me rather. Found myself offering information I hadn't meant to.

Had a moment's unease when he asked me if I was up here on holiday. In the end I just said 'Yes' and made sure I had my fingers crossed behind my back.

After all, it wasn't a black lie, it was one of those social ones that keep everything moving along instead of the conversation grinding to a halt. I mean, even someone as chatty as he is might have found it hard to carry on if I'd said, 'No, not a holiday. I've come to find something I didn't even know I had until I lost someone I obviously didn't ever really know.'

Looks more like gobbledygook when it's written down than when I say it.

But then that's the thing about the truth. It's often stranger than fiction. Harder to believe.

CHAPTER 2

Tom Howard didn't want to look down at the llama spit on his shirt; the smell of it was horrible enough – masticated cabbage with top notes of vomit.

'Bad, Salome. Very bad,' the woman holding the llama said as she tried to advance on Tom with an antiseptic wet wipe. Her progress was impeded by the way Salome, teeth bared, was rearing back as if there was more spit coming. The woman kept hanging on, but as Salome was about twice her size, Tom wouldn't have been surprised to see her being whirled around and launched over the county showground like a human discus.

He leaned forward to retrieve the wet wipe, freeing up the woman to administer a jerk to Salome's halter that would have snapped a lesser neck. Salome simply continued to glare at him. Those hostile eyes and that long neck reminded Tom of his wife – although, to be fair, she had never spat at him.

He dabbed at his shirt. Great, gobbed on by an overgrown draught-excluder on legs. Perhaps he could pass the sludgy stain off as something Paul Smith had intended – *My signature look for summer: Irish linen with a hint of hockle.*

'She's taken against the crowds today,' the woman announced, whisking the soiled wet wipe from Tom's hand. 'Never seen it this busy.'

Tom had to agree with her. He was forced to plant his feet to avoid getting jostled back into Salome's spit line.

'OK,' he said flipping his notebook shut and shoving it deep into his trouser pocket, 'I think I've got all I need for now, but I'll send Derek, our photographer, over to take some shots too.'

Very slowly, so as not to spook Salome, Tom put his sunglasses back on. He caught the sharp way she swivelled her head, like some malignant periscope, but this time she was glaring at a guy waving his ice cream about as he talked. It looked like he was about to get an unusual topping on his Mr Whippy.

Tom pushed out into the crowd and attempted to make some headway. Big contrast to last year when it rained from first light and it was just the locals and farmers who'd turned up to slip around in the mud. He'd watched the rain bead and run off the wax jackets before seeking warmth in one of the marquees. Bit like Glastonbury, but without the music or the drugs.

Today, everyone else was following the British tradition of exposing as much skin as possible because it might never be sunny again – he could feel the back of his neck starting to burn, but his mind was taken off the discomfort of that by the public address system. Its broadcasts generally had all the clarity of Esperanto being spoken through a sock full of wet sand and, right now, whoever was holding the mic was experiencing particularly trying technical difficulties.

'In the main arena at 2.30 . . .' whistle, squeak, 'the popular . . .' dip to voice-from-beyond-the-grave volume, 'trained ferrets . . .' surge of power before an ear-splitting whine, followed by a voice saying, with perfect clarity, 'Well I didn't know I had to keep my finger on the fucking button all the time.'

Tom joined in the spontaneous cheering at that before skirting around some hen houses and bee hives. He was avoiding a woman putting the dry into dry stone walling, when his phone rang.

'Sorry, took longer than I thought,' he said when he answered it. 'Nearly there . . . Yeah, I see you.' He raised a hand in greeting and by the time he'd put his phone away, he had reached his brother. Rob was cradling a tray of tomato plants on his stomach and carrying a blow-up hammer under one arm.

'You planning some DIY?'

'Yeah. Gonna buy some blow-up nails in a minute. Works though, look.'

Tom took the thwack that Rob gave him in good part. 'Nice touch, that squeak.'

'Reminds me of that blow-up woman you brought to my stag party. Miss Flatulence. The one with the faulty vulva.'

'Valve, you pillock.'

'Oh, aye. Tricky sods, vowels.'

Despite the different routes they'd taken since school, Tom and his brother had now reverted to the roles of childhood – Rob playing gormless and making the rude jokes, Tom reeling him back in. Tom suspected that Rob was aware of this too, judging by the way he was grinning at him.

'Git,' Tom said with affection, before asking, 'OK, what have you done with Hattie?'

'Toilets. Baby's pressing on Kath's bladder. Hattie went to keep her company in the queue.' Rob's expression suggested that they had been gone a long time. He nodded at the tomato plants. 'They should have just peed on these to bring them back to life.'

'Lovely. Remind me never to have salad at your house. So, has she behaved herself?'

A laugh. 'Usual wall-to-wall questions, especially when Kath and I took her in to see the bulls.' Rob lowered his voice. 'Well-endowed lads. And Hattie wanted to know what, well, what those big rugby ball type things hanging down were.'

'Oh God, tell me, you didn't run through every word you know?' Tom moved so he could look at his brother without the sun shining in his eyes.

'Nah. You'd have been proud of us. Well, of Kath. She just said, "They're testicles. All male mammals have them." Hattie seemed happy with that and we moved on.'

'No doubt it's gone into her memory bank to be hooked out at some inappropriate moment. But thanks.'

'No bother.'

They watched the crowd for a while.

'Bloody busy,' Rob said as if it was a novel observation. 'You got to schmooze anybody later? Hand out the magazine?'

'Hey, I'm the editor, not the delivery boy. And no, no schmoozing. Mrs Mawson's hired some promotion people. "Let us, Tom," she said, "keep the show for pleasure and the day for families".'

'Very good. Closed my eyes there for a minute and thought it was her.'

'Yeah. I'm the spitting double. Speaking of which.' He pointed at the stain on his shirt. 'Llama didn't like the way . . .'

His attention was taken by a woman whose primary thought when she got dressed that morning had obviously been, 'To hell with chafing, you can never have your shorts cut too high or too tight.'

'The sights you see when you haven't got your gun,' Rob said and whistled softly.

Tom waited.

'Speaking of hot women.' Rob's tone was a study in innocence.

'Here we go,' Tom said, struggling to hide his irritation.

'You remember Suzie, that woman who works with Kath?'

Tom crossed his arms. 'No.'

'Yeah you do. Well she's single again.'

'Leave it, Rob.'

'Hate to see you in limbo, mate.' Rob's tone was sincere, and that made it worse.

'I'm not in limbo—'

'Had any contact from her, recently? I mean since that parcel?'

His brother rarely uttered the name 'Steph', as though if he didn't name her, Tom's wife would fade away.

'It'll get sorted,' Tom said, firmly. 'And stop trying to fix me up with someone. I've only just recovered from the shit storm that was the last blind date you lured me into.'

Rob looked so sheepish Tom could have entered him in the show.

'That wasn't me,' he said. 'I never liked that woman.'

'Yeah, but it was me who had to put up with her necking best part of two bottles of wine and then, when I had to drive her all the way back to Carlisle, her trying to grab my penis.'

'Some men would pay for that.'

'I'm not interested, Rob. Work, Hattie and not beating my brother to death with his own blow-up hammer keep me really, really busy.'

Rob put the hammer behind his back, but carried on, all at a gallop, 'Look, I know you're not after anything permanent . . . but sex . . . we all need it. You'll wear out your wrist.'

Tom hoped his expression conveyed that, this time, a line had definitely been crossed. Being endlessly grateful that his family helped him juggle work and Hattie didn't mean he had to let them into every part of his life.

'If you don't stop talking . . .' Tom began, but there was Hattie running towards them and he had seconds to take off his sunglasses and brace himself before she connected with him. He saw how her fishtail plait was fraying, how the shirt was out of her shorts and her socks sagging. She had a bag of cinder toffee clutched to her chest and she was chewing and trying to talk at the same time.

'They . . .' chew, chew, 'they tickle them . . .' More chewing.

'Hats, finish what's in your mouth,' he said, getting down to her level and trying not to kneel in anything nasty. 'I'll have a go at putting you back together.'

Kath was making her slower way towards him and he saw her raise the back of her wrist to one of her cheeks and then the other, as if she could blot away the heat.

'Sorry took so long. A right queue.'

Rob was by her side. 'Not feeling dizzy or anything?'

'No, love. Could do with a sit-down, though.'

Hattie, toffee-free, powered up again. 'They had tickling sticks,' she was saying, tugging at him so hard that he had to put a hand on the grass to stop from toppling over.

He looked to Kath for an explanation.

'The guys leading the cattle have these metal sticks and tickling them on the belly makes the animals stand still. Means they can show them off better.'

'Ah. Right. We should get one for you, Hats.' He tickled her with his fingers instead, till she danced away from him. 'And, Kath, thanks for the . . .' he mouthed the last bit, 'biology lesson.'

Hattie came within range again. 'Want a piece of cinder?'

He barely got out, 'Only if you haven't sucked it first,' before the hard edges of a piece of toffee made contact with his lips.

'So, early lunch?' Rob asked. 'Something roasted that failed to get a rosette? Hey, wonder what llama tastes like?'

Kath patted his stomach affectionately. 'Even you couldn't eat a whole one.'

Rob gave her bump some gentle attention in return and Tom got to his feet. He disentangled the last bits of toffee from his back teeth.

'Come on, Hats, we'll go bail Granny out of Home Baking Hell. Meet you two in the beer tent, fifteen, twenty minutes' time?'

Hattie was off and running and Tom just had a moment to fling a wave behind him and hear his brother's, 'See if you can get the Rev. George to break cover and join us.'

Tom called to Hattie not to get too far ahead and tried to ignore how scratchy he felt. Most of the time he was able to gloss over the way his life had gone in a loop and not a straight line upwards. But Rob's assumption that he understood Tom's needs completely made him feel as if he wasn't just going over the same old ground again, but that he'd never been away. He was growing into the landscape.

'Slow coach,' he shouted, running past Hattie and giving her plait a swipe. Her skipping and bouncing speeded up before she back-tracked to look at a stall selling garden tools. She studied a hat someone had dropped. She talked to a dog.

He watched her sparking out energy, socks falling down once more, and wondered what sex Kath's baby would be. He was betting on a boy, which would please Hattie who didn't have much truck with girls. She particularly didn't like ones who looked as if they'd been ironed along with their clothes, or who already owned their own handbags. Give her a boy who could fart though and she was in heaven.

He hoped she'd grow out of that.

They made good progress until they reached the Cumberland & Westmorland Wrestling ring. Tom thought it looked like crabs trying to fight; the low-holds, the shuffling round and round. In the centre of the ring were two teenage lads, dressed in vests and shorts.

The guy commentating sounded almost poetical. 'And Rich here wrestles out of Rothbury.'

An 'Oooh' from the crowd and one of the boys was on his knees and then up again to shake hands.

And now there was someone tapping Tom on the shoulder, a guy from the furniture store who was one of their biggest advertisers. He obviously wanted to talk business, so Tom tuned out the wrestling and soon they were discussing whether Tom would be interested in doing a four-page spread to celebrate the store's tenth anniversary. Tom heard the last bout of wrestling finish and a new one begin before he said, tactfully, 'Perhaps something smaller?' but the cheering from the crowd was making it hard for him to get his point across. There was laughing too. Tom turned to check on Hattie.

No Hattie! Clammy, disembowelling fear got hold of him. He quickly scanned the crowds. She could be anywhere. But she wouldn't leave the ground, would she? His breathing was suddenly all over the place. 'Sorry, sorry,' he gabbled. 'Got to go—'

'Yeah. Think you better,' Furniture Man agreed. 'Before that lad gets hurt.'

It made no sense to Tom until he turned and looked into the wrestling ring.

CHAPTER 3

'But you always say ladies can do anything,' Hattie grumbled as he hustled her away.

'I know I do, but you can't just barge in because one of the boys didn't turn up to fight.'

Tom thought about the way she'd been clasping that poor teenager. It had been like a koala attacking a tree. Her grip had been so firm, Tom had had difficulty prising her off.

'Look, I'm not angry,' he said, slowing down. 'It's just you need to be entered for these things properly—'

'So next year I can do that? Can I? Can I?'

He was backed into a parenting cul de sac. 'Maybe. We'll see.'

'Yes!' She punched the air before telling him how she was going to flatten the opposition. He didn't doubt it. At least one lad would see her name on the programme and decide to take up a less dangerous sport. Like running with the bulls at Pamplona.

Would it be an easier life with a demure little girl? He'd never know, he'd got a paint-chipper, as his mother put it.

They were nearly at the entrance to the Home Crafts marquee when Tom spotted the distinctive white hair that belonged to the Rev. George. He was balanced on a shooting stick.

'Hello, George,' Tom said, 'we're about to collect Mum and go for lunch. Like to join us?'

George looked as uncomfortable as if he was sitting on the wrong end of his stick. 'Most kind,' he said, his hand worrying away at his clerical collar, 'but I . . . I was just leaving.'

'Why doesn't Granny's friend want to eat with us?' Hattie asked, in a not very whispery whisper as they passed out of the sunshine and into the tent.

'I think he's trying to pretend he isn't Granny's friend. Well, not her special friend.' Tom squeezed her hand. 'But don't ask Granny about it, Hats. OK?'

It pained him to say that because Rob and he were desperate to know what was going on and perhaps Hattie's way of simply asking the same question over and over again might be more effective than their own efforts.

George seemed to be popping up more and more regularly at the same social events as his mother. Yet both he and Tom's mother pretended nothing was going on. And, if they were an item, how did that work? His mother had never had any truck with religion, an attitude that had hardened when his father had dropped dead while out jogging, having decided to take more care of his health. If God existed, she had said, he had a bloody cruel sense of humour. Only eight years old at the time, Tom had agreed.

Inside the tent, it was cooler and much less crowded. Hattie and he had already paid it one visit to see how her entry for 'Vegetable Wildlife, age group five to seven years' had gone down. To Tom it looked as if a potato had been cloned violently with a courgette, but Hattie had been gutted that her 'Shark Attacking a Whale' had been beaten to the top prizes by a porcupine, a lion and a badger.

His mother was standing with the other ladies who made up the baked goods' judging panel. What they had been judging was displayed on trestle tables that ran along one side of the tent.

Although he had known most of the panel's individual members since he was a boy, collectively they unnerved him. He felt they were assessing and marking him: *Attractive appearance but rather a stodgy middle.* And, possibly, his parenting style: *Needs to be firmer to avoid collapse.*

'Had a good wander, love?' his mother asked, and then, 'What's that on your shirt?'

'Something that came out of a llama.' He made sure he

had her directly in his sights. 'And guess what? I saw George outside and invited him to lunch, but he's off somewhere else.'

'George?' *Evasive shift of eyes.* 'Oh, he was here? Hattie, could you get that bag for me?' *Yup, definitely diversionary tactics.*

He gave up. 'So, how's it gone, the judging?'

His mother tutted. 'That *Great British Bake Off* has a lot to answer for. Record entry this year and some you wouldn't give to your dog. We've had the marks of cooling racks clearly visible on items; artificial colourings . . .'

Tom tried to look shocked.

'And we've also had . . . No, Hattie, the blue bag. Yes, that's it. We've also had . . . an incident. That Mrs Egremont. Only class she hasn't won is ham and egg pie on a saucer and she's querying our marks for it.' His mother was sounding ever more indignant. 'She's only asking for a recount. We've told her "No". So now it's a stand about.'

'Do you mean stand-off?'

'Yes, a stand-off.' His mother's gaze drifted past his shoulder and he turned to see Mrs Egremont stationed near the contentious pie. A terrier of a woman, she might just go for your ankles if you annoyed her.

'Nasty,' he agreed, quietly. 'But come on, it's lunchtime.'

His mother was hunting in her bag. 'I'll be two minutes.

I need to warn the Secretary of the Show there might be a formal complaint. Right, pen, paper . . .'

He knew she'd be more than two minutes, so when Hattie asked if she could go and have a look around, he let her. He scanned the marquee for anything of interest and saw a woman bending to inspect the plates on the first trestle table of baked goods. Her distinctive grey-blonde hair looked good against the faded mauves and pinks of her summer dress. Nice touch putting the grey suede bag and sandals with it too.

Being married to Steph had left him with an interest in fashion that he rarely voiced to his own family. Rob, whose greatest accolade was 'That's a nice dress, Kath', would certainly rip the piss out of him.

He spent a few seconds wondering in which European capital Steph was currently matching underfed models with overpriced accessories, and then pushed her away again.

The woman was looking towards the judging panel, but they were still in a huddle, so she turned back to the scones, frowning. Another glance around and she caught his eye. She was much younger than he'd first thought. Must be the hair that had wrong-footed him.

'Excuse me,' she said.

He was bored and she didn't look dangerous, so he wandered over. It was only when he arrived that he realised he'd put his hand over the stain on his shirt. Awkward. It looked as if he was about to take the pledge of allegiance, but if he moved it away again, she would see he had tried to hide the llama spit.

'I'm sorry to be a pain,' she said, 'but do you know anything about these scones?' Her delivery was clipped, but not unfriendly. There was a glance at, and then away from, the hand marooned on his shirt.

'Anything in particular you wanted to know?' He checked on Hattie, who was mooching about near the flower arrangements.

'Fruit oven scones,' she read from her programme. 'But why did these get the first prize? All the entries look perfect to me.'

Her tone was earnest and he did a quick assessment of her straight back and came up with *Slightly odd, possibly humourless, but points for the hair.*

'Well, the scones must have a good colour, and . . .' He used his free hand to draw her attention to the finer details. 'They should have a definite seam around the middle.'

Being so close to the baking was making him feel hungry. It was tempting to filch one of Mrs Egremont's prize-winners, but that would mean spending the rest of his life in a safe house with a new identity.

'Fascinating.' The woman was nodding as if she meant it. She gave him, and the hand on his shirt, another look. 'Ah,' she said, smiling. 'I know why you seem familiar. You're the man who was wrestling those children earlier. Did you hurt your arm?'

He had to check to see if she was joking. Evidently not.

He ignored her question, but she didn't appear to notice. 'Well, thank you for the information on the scones. You've been most kind.'

Most kind? He looked around to see if they were still in the twenty-first century.

She had moved along to the next table and was frowning again.

'Problem?' he said, joining her mainly to see how much odder she might become.

'Well, sorry to repeat myself, but why has this sandwich cake, unfilled, been selected over the others?'

'More even bake,' he pointed out. 'Better texture.'

He appeared to be channelling Mary Berry. Mind you, he had an excuse; he'd reached the age where he was beginning to think Radio 4's *Money Box Live* might be worth listening to. But *she* couldn't be more than twenty-three, twenty-four.

Another frown. 'This Mrs Egremont seems to win a lot. I expect she's some rosy-cheeked farmer's wife.'

He tried to keep his face absolutely neutral, but she laughed and said, 'Oh that look speaks volumes. The opposite of rosy-cheeked, then.'

'Uh . . . I didn't say that.' He wished she'd keep her voice down.

She walked a little further, looking at the rosettes. 'Yes, she's won this and this and, oh, wait a minute. She hasn't won *this* one.' She peered at the offending pie. 'Why is that?'

Mrs Egremont turned to look at him as if to say, 'Yes, you bastard, why is that?' Her elbows looked particularly sharp today, as if she had whittled them on purpose.

'Is it,' the young woman said helpfully, 'because that bit of crust is slightly burnt?'

Mrs Egremont looked as if she'd been Tasered and Tom figured they had ten seconds at most before she snapped out of it and started biting people.

'Hello,' Hattie said, appearing next to the young woman. 'Your hair's nice, is it real?'

Before he could tell her off for that, the young woman said, 'Well, that's an interesting question. It's real hair, but it's not real in the sense that this is my natural colour. I dyed it.'

'Don't even think about it,' he said when Hattie looked at him. 'Not till you're older.'

He checked on Mrs Egremont. She had recovered the power to blink.

'Do you have a tattoo as well?' Hattie was asking.

'No.' The tone was regretful. 'I really don't like needles.'

'Me neither.' Hattie looked at him as if he was always poking her with them. Then her face brightened. 'Would you like to see my vegetable sculpture?'

'I'm sorry . . . your?' The woman was consulting her programme and he was going to say, 'Hattie, enough,' when it occurred to him that getting this completely tactless woman away from Mrs Egremont might not be a bad thing.

'It's just over there,' Hattie said and they all set off, which gave him time to process that word *tactless*. He thought about it some more when Hattie covered up the card that explained what the sculpture was.

'Can you guess the animals?' Hattie asked and Tom wondered how badly this was going to go. Odd Woman seemed as if she had limited experience of dealing with children – possibly humans of any kind. So when she failed to guess what the courgette was doing to the potato, she might be brutally honest about Hattie's artistic skills.

The woman gave the sculpture a good look over and said, 'Well, it's pretty obvious. That's a shark attacking a whale.'

'It is! It is!' Hattie squealed, taking her hand off the card to prove it.

How the bloody hell . . .

That frown was back. 'Great White or Tiger?'

'Tiger,' Hattie said and the woman nodded as if some-body had confirmed that the masterpiece in front of her was a Cézanne and not a Seurat.

She barely glanced at the winning entries. 'And you did yours by yourself?'

'Yes,' Hattie said, proudly. 'Dad didn't give me any help at all.'

It made him sound like a lazy, uninterested git.

'Only one suggestion, though.' A finger was being held up.

Uh-oh, here we go.

'To really pep it up, you could roast a red pepper, take off the skin and then mash the insides to suggest blood and gore.'

The impressed 'Cool!' from Hattie was accompanied by a look that suggested she might like to ask the woman home for a sleepover.

'Hattie, could you go and hurry Granny up a bit?' he said, feeling sidelined.

Hattie went off reluctantly and the young woman sud-denly announced, 'Ah, stick dressing,' and veered off towards the carved shepherd's crooks. 'Oh they're lovely. Look at the detail on this.' He reluctantly joined her to see that she was pointing at a carved brown trout which formed the handle of one of the sticks.

'Oh, and this,' she said, singling out an otter. 'How long do you think it takes to carve one?'

He looked around for one of the old boys who made them.

'Not sure,' he said. 'And, to be honest, these are good, but you should have seen the ones Charlie did.'

'Charlie?'

'Charlie Coburg. He was a "real" artist, could turn his hand to all kinds of things; drawing, painting, carving. Used to win this every year. The others said he should be barred to give them a chance.'

'Was he?'

'No. Nobody would dare to ban Charlie from anything. Big character, plus his family, well, they're one of *the* county families. Died before Christmas.'

'A big character?' She was studying one of the less successful handles, a sheepdog that looked as if its mother had been intimate with a pig. Over near the judging table he saw his own mother give her *I'm ready now* wave. Best wrap this up.

'There are all kinds of stories out there about Charlie,' he explained. 'Armour-plated liver. Bit of a lady-killer in his younger days. A devil at parties.' He remembered

Charlie at the office Christmas bash, baring his arse at the window.

'You don't make him sound very attractive,' the woman said. Her back looked even stiffer.

That irked him. Even worse, he was irked by the way he was suddenly using the word *irked*.

'That wasn't my intention,' he said. 'Charlie was a real life-enhancer. People loved his illustrations and his pieces on wildlife. We've never really filled the gap he left.'

'We?'

'The magazine. *The Place, the People.* He was a contributor. I'm the editor.'

'So you have a hole in your parties and your magazine?' She turned a page in her programme as if making a point.

'No, that's not what I—'

'Really?' There were no more jolly hockey sticks in her tone.

'Now, hang on . . .' He realised that, in his agitation, he'd taken his hand off his shirt.

She wrinkled her nose when she saw the stain. 'You haven't hurt your arm wrestling at all.'

'I never said I—'

'In fact, you appear to have dropped some of your lunch down your shirt.'

'I haven't had my lunch yet.'

'Somebody else's lunch then, perhaps.'

'It's actually llama spit,' he protested, wondering, even as he said it, why he thought that was preferable. Her expression told him it wasn't.

Hattie reappeared. 'Granny says she's hungry. So am I. Do you want to come?' This to the woman.

'No thank you,' she said primly. 'But . . . Hattie, it is Hattie, isn't it? You're very kind to ask me. And I meant to say how much I enjoyed *your* wrestling.'

He was trying to think of a smart come-back to that, but she was unnerving him by the way she was looking at the stain again. 'Were you antagonising it? The llama?' she asked.

Subtext – like you're antagonising me.

'No, I wasn't antagonising it.'

'Well something must have caused it to spit.'

She lifted her chin and regarded him gravely and again he searched for just the right phrase to convey that he thought she was weird and bloody ungrateful after he'd taken the time to explain baking and sticks to her. That he was a grown-up with a daughter, a man of the world, while she was obviously a tight-arse who couldn't understand how you could think someone like Charlie was a piss-head, but still admire him. He almost had the perfect thing when he became aware that Hattie was studying him with a strange expression.

'Dad,' she asked, 'can I have a look at your testicles?'

Tumbleweed blew through the tent, first one way and then the other, before he was trying to explain how Hattie had just been taught the word . . . not by him . . . and not about him . . . about mammals . . . bollocks, no, he didn't mean bollocks, he meant bullocks . . .

The young woman gave Hattie a sympathetic look before walking purposefully to the entrance of the tent. She paused only to wipe off something that had adhered to her sandal.

He had no doubt she was thinking about him when she did it.

CHAPTER 4

Sunday 11 May

Well, I've made a start and dipped my toe in the water.

Actually, in those strappy sandals, I dipped my toe in quite a lot of other stuff too.

And the heat took me by surprise. The entire Internet led me to believe the essential item of clothing for summer in Northumberland was a polo-neck jumper, but I was boiling, even in that dress. It's still warm now, sitting here in the last of the sun and slowly filling up the first page of this notebook.

And it has to be said, sitting outside my 'cottage' – cue hollow laughter – is better than sitting inside. My fond imagining of inglenooks and roses around the door was dashed on arrival. 'Cottage' obviously means a red-brick bungalow stripped of all original features and decorated by the dead hand of a gorilla. A gorilla who may have been incontinent, judging by the damp on the bedroom wall.

But I digress.

Back to the notebook.

I can't help smiling when I see the title on the front of it: *Things I have learned today.* One of my mother's bargains – three boxes of them bought from an educational materials supplier who was going out of business. I remember helping her carry them to the car and worrying if the suspension would take the weight.

They weren't meant to be scribbled in, I had to make them last. 'Just write your main impressions at the end of every day,' she said, 'ten points, maximum. That will ensure you focus on the important things.'

And the notebooks did last. Out-lasted my mother anyway. Probably because life got too busy for me to keep writing in them.

A very good discipline though, keeping it simple. Perhaps that's why I slipped this notebook into my suitcase. I fear that life is about to get messy – and if I start writing about emotions, I'll wallow. And wallowing isn't a family trait.

Or is it?

Whether I'll write in it every day, I doubt. But now is a good day to start. A day that was busy and quite, quite bizarre.

So . . . I have learned:

1) Northumberland doesn't seem to be much of a melting pot, although today a lot of it did look as if it were melting. The faces I saw were mainly pink or red.

2) One should never wear strappy sandals to an agricultural show.

3) Getting animals ready to be judged involves a huge amount of shampooing and brushing and even the rubbing of talcum powder into hides. The last time I saw so much care with grooming was at a gay fashion show. Even I know that would not be a good thing to say out loud here.

4) People in the countryside seem very thirsty and as I was leaving, police were heading towards a beer tent. The whole thing is a bit Gay Pride meets the Wild West.

5) Mrs Mawson is formidable-looking. Her grand-daughter, who is obviously keen on show-jumping, resembles her horse. Called Mabel – the granddaughter, not the horse. (Oh, I'm not proud of that *resembles her horse* comment, but perhaps writing it will stop me blurting it out when I'm nervous.)

6) A good scone should have a seam around it.

7) Some women like to wear shorts that will not only give them a camel toe, but probably cystitis too.

8) Ferrets are not attractive, even when jumping through hoops.

9) Just because a man appears friendly and is handsome in a chunky, middle-aged way, it doesn't give him the right to be extremely free with his objectionable views about people. It's his poor daughter I really feel sorry for.

10) It's hard to eat a lamb burger when there is a lamb looking at you.

CHAPTER 5

Tom wondered why that damn bird sitting on his window-sill sounded like a telephone. Until he realised that it *was* the telephone.

A flurry of eye rubbing, leaning over and picking it up; half-formed fears about his mother. Or Kath, gone into labour early. Brain prepared for Rob's voice in either case, and so Steph's 'It's me' was like a bucket of cold water hurled at his chest.

A check on the clock before he said, 'It's quarter to five.'

'Not here it isn't.' And then silence. Classic Steph. Was he meant to apologise that they didn't have the *proper* time in Northumberland?

He sat upright, the back of his neck feeling sore where the sun had caught it yesterday.

He waited. He'd had to learn how to stay quiet as well, otherwise he was always the one asking and placating – like a hostage negotiator desperately trying to stop a call from ending. Anything to stave off that moment when

Steph said, 'I'm going,' and, yet again, he hadn't got any decisions from her.

He looked at the curtains, already bright-backed by the sun. It was going to be a beautiful day out there, but in this bedroom there would be a deep depression later. And that was just in his brain.

The cheery red numbers on the clock told him it was 04.55.

'I expect you think I've just got in from a party, don't you?'

'No,' he lied, 'I expect you're just going out to work.'

'Well . . . Yes, I am . . .'

He could hear she felt cheated out of being able to tell him that he always thought the worst of her, and he should have felt glad he'd wrong-footed her, but he'd had nearly three and a half years of this crap dance and he was bone tired of it.

'I'd like to talk to Hattie.'

'She's asleep, Steph. I get her up at seven-thirty for school. If I wake her up now she won't go back to sleep and she's going to be knackered.'

'If you wanted to wake her up you could.'

'It would have to be something pretty urgent.' He just stopped himself from saying *important*.

'So that's the only time I can speak to her, is it? When you decide it's urgent?'

'Steph, whenever you ring, I put her straight on.' *Because it's such a bloody rarity.*

'All right, stop proving you're Father of the Bloody Year.'

In his head, he kicked things and swore violently. He had a go at tuning into the dawn chorus again, but now the birds were just irritating him. Didn't they know any other bloody songs?

'Look,' he said, 'compromise. Ring back at seven and I'll get her up.'

'All right.' Pause. 'If it makes it easier for *you.*'

More kicking and swearing.

'Did she get my parcel?'

'Yes, she did. She thought it was all lovely. She'll tell you that when you have a chat.'

She'll tell you because we've rehearsed her saying 'Thank you' and not saying 'I don't really like floaty things to wear, Mummy. Or handbags. Could you send me some dungarees next time? With one of those loops on them for tools?'

'I suppose it would be too much to ask you to send me a photograph of her wearing the dress? With the handbag?'

'But where would I send it *to*, Steph? And even if I did, maybe that inability to open envelopes that you have would strike again.'

Silence once more and in it he imagined trying to cram Hattie into the Fendi dress after they'd prised it off Monty, the brown bear who was currently modelling it. Next to the camel in the shorts with marabou trim. Hattie had some of the best-dressed soft toys in the county. The Juicy Couture handbag was full of toy dinosaurs, under the bed.

'I'm in Milan at the moment with Alessandro. He's seeing his folks while I work.'

Why was he being handed that piece of information? And what was with the change of tone? Almost chatty.

'And we were thinking . . .'

'You were thinking?'

'We're coming back to Milan for Christmas. He has one of those big Italian families, lots of children around . . .'

Ah, and you don't have the essential accessory to show off.

'So Alessandro said, why don't we get Hattie to come out? More the merrier.'

'He said that, in Italian? More the merrier?'

A pause as if she was biting her tongue. 'Come on, Tom, it would be lovely for her. We could take her skiing.'

'Good idea. I'll look into flights.'

'You will?' she said unsteadily, as if not sure she'd heard him correctly.

'Yup. We could come out, say, Christmas Eve, stay in a hotel.'

He could hear her thinking how to say, that's not what I mean. Not you with her. Her on her own.

'Wouldn't it be easier if you just put her on a plane, Tom?'

'Like a parcel?' He waited for the explosion. The fact that none came told him she really wanted this.

'No, not like a parcel. They have people who look after children on flights. And she's not *that* young, only a couple of years younger than I was when I went away to school.'

He could have said many things in response to that, but they'd all been said so many times before.

05.15.

Time for a change of tack. 'I sent your parents a letter to forward to you. Yet again. I need you to look at it, Steph, and get this all sorted legally. Stringing this out makes no sense; neither of us wants to get back together so—'

'I haven't seen the letter. But . . . but I could ring Daddy. Ask him to forward it . . . If you let Hattie come out for Christmas.'

He shouldn't be surprised at the way that screamed naked manipulation with overtones of blackmail. Steph was a mistress of naked manipulation. Literally; it was one of her skill sets.

'Not going to happen, Steph. And you know why it's not going to happen.'

Silence.

'And, quite apart from that, I've no bloody idea what Alessandro or his family are like. They could be the Corleones, for all I know.'

Nothing.

Perhaps he'd gone too far with that Corleone comment. 'Listen,' he said, in a more conciliatory tone, 'you can see Hattie any time, we've been through this. I'm not stopping you. I just want to be nearby.'

A sudden, 'You know what? You're a fucking control freak, Tom. And I really, really hate you.'

'Then divorce me.'

And she'd gone. He gripped the phone. The same arguments over and over again like some German existentialist remake of *Groundhog Day*.

05.30.

He'd never get back to sleep now. He thought of ringing Steph's parents to see if they *had* actually forwarded the letter, but imagined them lying stiffly in their single beds, like a medieval knight and his wife cast in stone. No. Too early, too old, too much afraid of antagonising Steph.

He went to look in on Hattie. She was on her back, a dead-to-the-world starfish with her mouth open. He thought of her out in Milan at Christmas. Was he jealous of the idea of her having fun without him? Please God he wasn't turning into one of those creepy fathers – 'Oh, don't mind me sitting in the seat behind you and your boyfriend. Go right ahead and enjoy the film.'

No, it was lovely to think of Hattie in a glow of candlelight and Italian hospitality, a mug of hot chocolate in her hands. But he knew with certainty that Steph would, somewhere along the line, get bored with playing mamma and irritated that Hattie wasn't keeping to the script of darling, delicate daughter. Then she'd lose her temper or sub-contract responsibility for her to some relation of Alessandro's. *Hey, Hattie, you hold the horsa steady while I cut off hees head.*

He saw Hattie feeling rejected, Hattie trying to make it work. He saw, oh God, Hattie left behind on a ski run because nobody thought to check.

He straightened out Hattie's duvet and tucked it around her. No one was going to leave her anywhere.

He returned to his room and decided he might have a go at getting back to sleep. There was no way Steph would ring again this morning. She'd punish him by punishing Hattie and he felt guilty about that – more guilty than Steph did, no doubt.

He picked up the clock and reset the alarm – Mondays were good – school uniform and sports kit all clean, any letters from school answered. They could have an extra fifteen minutes' sleep and still be out of the house in good time.

He closed his eyes. The wood pigeons were chiming in now; restful, lulling . . .

'Dad, am I going to school? Only they said I could change the date on the calendar and if I miss my turn, I have to wait another twenty-two whole days to do it.'

'I'm sure they'll let you do it sooner than that,' he told the pillow before his brain went 'hang on a mo'. He jerked his head up to look at the clock.

08.15.

He stared at Hattie standing by the bed, still in her pyjamas.

'Oh, fu . . . fu . . . fudge with another fudging lump of fudge on top,' he shouted, translating it in his head to the full bellowing Anglo-Saxon version.

'Eight-fifteen, it can't be eight-fifteen.' He picked up the clock and shook it as if that would help. Damn, he'd nudged the hour on as well when he'd altered the minutes.

'Right, Hattie. Listen to me.' He was trying to wrap the duvet around his bottom half and get out of bed at the same time, which was making him flail about like a demented, partially hatched butterfly.

'We have fifteen minutes, Hattie, just fifteen minutes to dress, grab something to eat and get out of the house.'

Hattie was looking at the clock. 'It says 08.16 now.'

'Yeah, time does that, keeps right on fudging moving. Come on, get dressed, the quickest you've *ever* got dressed.' Hattie did not look galvanised. He thought about that and changed his tone. 'OK, Midshipman Howard,' he bellowed, 'we're holed below the waterline and we only have minutes to abandon ship.'

Hattie was suddenly fuel-injected. 'Yay,' she shouted, hurtling from the room. 'Can I wear my eye-patch?'

'Long as you've got your school uniform and all your underpinnings on too, yup.'

He plunged around the room, grabbing items of clothing and shoving himself into them. Damn Steph. Damn the clock.

He hated arriving at school as if they were being chased by demons. It was what people expected of single fathers. 'Poor Mr Howard. He tries, doesn't he?'

He worked hard to make sure it rarely happened and had the drive to Hattie's school in Lowheatherington and then back along the valley to work precision-planned. But not today, today he'd be bringing up the rear with the woman who delivered her kids to school still in her dressing gown.

Hattie was at the door – dressed and with eye-patch in place. 'Ready, Captain.'

'Brilliant! I mean, very good, Howard.'

'Permission to take on supplies,' she said and he mouthed 'What?' and she whispered 'Breakfast' and they were back on track.

'Good idea,' he boomed, hustling her down the stairs. 'Suggest cereal bars and box of juice. Permission to dispense with teeth brushing. I have mints in the glove compartment.'

He went to the loo, glugged down a large glass of water, gathered up his papers, his bag, the car keys. Hattie returned from the kitchen, her arms full.

'I don't recall mentioning Tunnock's tea cakes,' he said.

Her expression was serious. 'We could be drifting for days.'

He laughed and combined a hug with getting her nearer the door and thought, what the hell, it's free dental treatment till she's eighteen.

Her reading bag was scooped up, along with some suntan cream and her hat in a plastic bag.

'Well done, Midshipman. Eight-thirty exactly,' he said as he helped her into the car. She was pointing at the house and shouting, 'Look, it's sinking, it's sinking,' so convincingly that he was beginning to worry that a sudden attack of subsidence might mean it was really going down with all hands.

'Pipe down or I'll ping your eye-patch,' he told her as they set off. At the gate he stopped. 'Got Gummy?'

He watched her root around in the book bag and hold

up the blue gum shield. Rob had bought it for her for Christmas and she'd spent the entire holidays looking like an extra from *Planet of the Apes*. But one night he'd checked on her in bed and it was still in, so he'd confiscated it. Cue a run of fretful evenings. Which is when he realised it was a more grown-up version of the yellow cot blanket with the silky edging that she worried between finger and thumb when going off to sleep. They'd brokered a truce which allowed her to mess about with it while he read a story and then it had to go on the bedside table next to the lumps of plasticine and the photo of Steph.

When it appeared at other times, he knew something was up. And that something usually involved Steph. A phone call promised that didn't come. Another parcel of stuff that didn't fit Hattie's body or her character. Sometimes it would also be popped in after she'd talked to Steph, even if the call had appeared to be a good one. Those times he made a point of going back over the old mantra: 'Mummy loves you very much, it's just that Mummy and Dad don't love each other any more. And because Mummy has to work and travel, she wouldn't be able to look after you. Dad can. Mummy sees you whenever she's able to and she's always thinking about you.'

At those moments he thought how funny it was that you told your children not to lie, and yet from the word go you did it – even if it was only to preserve their belief in something they thought was magical. Was he any different to all those parents who chose not to say 'It's your dad, a little pissed, who puts the presents in your stocking on Christmas Eve'?

Gummy back in the bag, they were off along the lane, and when he wasn't concentrating on where he was heading, he was looking at Hattie in the rear-view mirror as she tucked into a breakfast that would have sent Jamie Oliver ballistic.

'Gorgeous day,' he said, 'you're going to need that sun hat.' She pulled a face, having a natural aversion to hats unless they were pirate ones.

He slowed down at the speed camera and checked his watch. On time and back as Dad in Control. Past the farm on the left, take the tight corner, just this long stretch with trees either side before the descent into Lowheatherington. Easy peasy.

'Dad, I really, really need a wee.'

Nooooo.

He looked at her in the mirror.

'Can't it wait? We're only a few minutes from school.'

She was pressing her lips together and shook her head. He had ignored a look like that once before and had to have the car valeted. Steam wash, top of the range.

'You didn't go before we came out?' It was the kind of stupid question parents asked where it made no difference what the reply was. Her bladder was full *now*.

'I didn't think we had time,' she said, adding guilt on to the newly resurrected panic.

Pull on to the verge. Get out of the car. Help her out. She was hopping around, with a look that screamed 'Don't take too long, I won't be able to hold it in'. He yanked some tissues out of the box on the back seat and gave them to her.

They looked at the verge, the traffic going by. No good. He grabbed her hand and she did a little running limp that made him feel even worse about hustling her out of the house.

They headed for the small track leading down to fields and the river.

'Here we are,' he said, trying to jolly up the situation. 'That's it, that's right.'

They stopped just round the corner. 'This do?' he asked doubtfully. She shook her head and he agreed. 'What about this?' he said, pointing to the red-brick bungalow, empty and stuck on the market for months. They ran towards the gate. Yup, good overgrown garden and a hedge that came up to his chin. 'Nip in there, Hats. I'll stay right here. Find a flat bit and take off your shoes and socks so, you know, you don't splash them.'

He looked back up the track. He hoped the car was all right parked on the verge.

'OK, Hats?' he shouted and got back a relieved-sounding 'Yes.'

Dealing with Hattie's full bladder had set up a sympathetic urge in his. Ignoring it didn't work. Turning his back to the gate so that Hattie wouldn't see if she came out, he started to pee into the hedge, not managing to avoid the 'For Sale' sign that had fallen into it.

A noise made him turn his head and he almost ruined his shoes. The odd woman was striding up the road, a bunch of wild flowers in her hands. She slowed when she saw him, and as she was wearing sunglasses he couldn't see her full expression, just her mouth opening into an 'O'. He turned back round quickly, trying to look as though it was the most natural thing in the world to be standing there peeing into a hedge, dressed in his suit.

'Morning,' he said brightly, hoping it would mask the noise he was making, and then ran out of anything to add. It seemed a long time until he was ready to fumble himself decent again.

Her sunglasses were now pushed up on to her hair and he saw a face that didn't know what emotion to settle on. Confusion? Bewilderment? Disgust? She said nothing, only speeded back up and, with horror, he watched her heading for the gate.

The relevance of the 'For Sale' sign in the hedge hit him just as she disappeared. He would have put his head in his hands, but he remembered where they had just been.

Everything was quiet before he heard Hattie and the woman talking and they came out at the gate. Hattie skipped towards him completely unfazed. He did a quick check that she had on her socks and shoes and wondered what stage of undress the woman might have found her in.

Oh God, she's still wearing her eye-patch.

'It's this lady again,' Hattie said.

This lady wasn't holding the flowers any more. That back was very straight. When he went to speak, she eyed him warily.

'Your bungalow?' he asked.

'Just renting, they couldn't find a buyer.' She dropped her gaze to his shirt as she spoke, presumably to see if it was stain-free this morning.

'I know this looks bad,' he started, 'but Hattie was desperate for the toilet—'

'I was,' Hattie joined in, 'because we overslept, which meant I didn't have time for a wee. AND I had to eat my breakfast in the car. Dad let me have a whole load of Tunnock's tea cakes and he says I don't need to bother brushing my teeth as he's got some mints in the glove department.' Big smile to finish, showing chocolate-specked teeth.

'Uh, when you take it out of context like that . . .'

He got the same look he'd received after the 'testicles' comment and decided to stop making the large hole of mortification he was currently standing in any bigger.

'Well that explains everything,' the young woman said, briskly, smiling only at Hattie. 'Lovely to meet you again.' Still only to Hattie. 'And . . . and perhaps if I could give you these.' He realised that last bit *was* directed at him and saw her open one of her hands and proffer the tissues Hattie had taken into the garden.

And obviously used.

CHAPTER 6

Monday 12 May

Unbelievable. Only 9.30 and I already have enough to fill today's page.

I have learned that:

1) When you see a man you barely know weeing in your hedge, you immediately jump to the conclusion that because you have had an altercation the day before, he is getting his own back.

2) Your second thought is that he might be carrying out some ancient Northumbrian ritual along the lines of, 'She's one of us now, lads, let's go round and pee in her garden'.

3) You wonder if the suit the man is wearing is one specifically reserved for this purpose.

4) Urine falling on a 'For Sale' sign makes a very loud noise.

5) Only one thing is more bewildering than a person using your garden as a public convenience. And that is two people. Particularly if the second one is a child wearing an eye-patch.

6) Helping put a child's socks back on is trickier than it looks.

7) You do not need a licence to have a child. You do not even need an alarm clock.

8) Mints are, evidently, an effective alternative to toothpaste.

9) I will not be sunbathing on the lawn for a while, even though I spent some time clearing that patch.

10) Gripping wild flowers too tightly bends the stems.

CHAPTER 7

Liz intercepted him before he'd reached his office.

'I should really be carrying a scythe,' she said.

Liz had *cojones* of steel; she was the kind of sub-editor who would be sorting out the kinks in copy while flames were licking the building, but she did like everything served with a side order of drama.

'Nothing wrong at the printers'?' he asked, quickly. June's edition of the magazine had only been put to bed on Friday and they were in that hiatus between it being at the printers' and delivered neatly wrapped in plastic.

She shook her head, but didn't seem inclined to tell him what was wrong.

'OK, give me a couple of minutes,' he told her, 'I need to wash my hands.'

'Planning to operate?'

'Ha, very good.' He nodded towards his office. 'You want to go on in and wait for me?'

In the toilet, he tried not to revisit the twin humiliations

of the peeing incident and his walk into the school playground under the judgemental gaze of the mothers already
returning home. Even Mrs Dressing Gown had looked
superior.

Heading back through the main office he said some
quick 'hellos' to the few people already in. The calm atmosphere bore no relation to how frantic it had been last
week.

Derek the photographer was at his computer, peering at
the photos he'd taken yesterday. He was doing it in his
usual dreamy way.

Tom often wondered whether Derek did in fact live in a
flat in Hexham or just wrapped himself in a cobweb and
lay down in a bush to sleep. He could have been on Derek's
case all the time, trying to gee him up, but with his big,
soft body and features that looked as if someone had
smudged them while still wet, there was something fragile
about the guy.

They chatted about the show, or Tom did because Derek
rarely finished any sentence he started.

'Photos turned out to be really . . .' Derek offered.

Tom started to look through them himself, knowing it
was probably the only way he'd find out what Derek meant.
A Texel ram. A bull looking as if he wanted to nut the judge
who'd put such a fey rosette on his snout, and then he

almost took a step back, because there was a photo of the woman whose hedge he'd just watered. And another one. And another. Yup, and a fourth one.

He looked at Derek for explanation.

'Just liked her colouring,' he said. 'That hair, the dress. . . She's kind of . . .'

Tom could think of some good words to finish that sentence, but he let it hang as he continued to scroll through the photos.

'Great one of the llama,' he said, trying to imagine how Mr Dreamy had got on with Miss Spitty. 'And good job on the show-jumping shots. Nice and subtle, like you just happened to catch Mrs Mawson's granddaughter and her horse. Nothing that screams "this photo is only here because Mrs Mawson owns the magazine".'

'Horses,' Derek said. 'They're my . . .'

Undeclared love? What I eat when there's nothing else in the fridge?

Tom would never know. He nodded briskly and walked away.

In his office he shut the door behind him, or would have done if, over the life of the building, the door had not swelled. He needed to persuade it to become intimate with the door frame. Second attempt he got it right – sometimes it took him three goes.

The Place, The People ranged over the top two floors of a listed building that ran along one side of the village of Tynebrook's market square. It was a building that was past its best and Mrs Mawson, who not only owned the magazine but also the building, seemed disinclined to spend money working with the authorities to refurbish it sympathetically. Tom was worried that he'd turn up for work one day and find his two floors had shifted downwards and crushed the art gallery below.

Sometimes he found the building's rough walls and slightly off-square rooms charming, other times, as the roof leaked, or yet more of the plaster moulding in his office fell off, he yearned for the soulless steel and glass hutch of his office in London. Hattie unreservedly loved the place, particularly the great galleon-type windows that allowed her to stand on the sills and pretend she was a pirate surveying the ocean.

Liz had assumed her customary position next to his desk. He spotted the art portfolio leaning against the legs of her chair and sensed that was where the bad news lay. He also spotted the cup of coffee on the desk. 'This for me?'

'Yeah. I *am* Anne Hathaway to your Meryl Streep.' She didn't quite get to the end of the sentence before they were both laughing at the comparisons.

Despite Liz's tendency to tell him regularly that the sky

was falling in, he overlooked it because she was funny. And she worked like a pit pony. On a magazine with 160 pages to fill every month and only a limited number of core staff to fill them, both he and Liz had to get involved in a lot of things that weren't strictly in their fancy job specifications.

'Here's to the havoc of mornings,' she said, raising her own coffee cup. The smile she gave him was a sympathetic one, being a single parent herself.

He raised his cup in response before taking a tentative sip from it. Liz's coffee was terrible, the kind that removed the enamel from your teeth and came back to haunt you as heartburn. Everybody suspected she made it like that on purpose, but nobody had ever raised the issue with her. Liz was a woman who held grudges very, very tightly.

When his throat had stabilised he said, 'OK. Bring out your dead,' and let her enjoy her moment.

She put down her cup. 'You know Felix mentioned this illustrator who might be just what we're looking for?'

'Yeah. The website looked promising.'

'Well, he dropped his portfolio in first thing this morning. So . . . Felix and I have had a look. We drew lots to see who should show it to you because we both wanted to see your reaction. I won, obviously, as Felix knows everything about design, but f*** all about cheating.' The portfolio was hauled up and opened with something of a flourish.

'Holy crap,' he said when he saw the illustration in the first plastic wallet. It was as if Toad of Toad Hall had mated with *Reservoir Dogs* to produce an intensely disturbing vision of the English countryside that was all fangs and scything claws.

He flicked quickly to another illustration. A fox ripping off a chicken's head.

'This doesn't bear any relation to the stuff on his website.'

'No. He told me he's "moved on".'

'No kidding.' Tom flipped the page again. 'Oh, hang on, this is better. Badgers play-fighting. Bit dark, but perhaps Felix could lighten it up.'

'Shall we ask him to rub this bit out too?' Liz was pointing at something on one of the badgers.

Tom looked closer. 'Ah, not fighting then. Perfect. That's going to have Outraged of the Shire foaming at the mouth.'

He gave the portfolio a shove. 'Why is it so bloody difficult to find someone who can draw wildlife? And cobble together a bit of description? Get back to this guy, would you please, Liz? Tell him we think he's too . . . challenging for us.'

The brisk way Liz was zipping the portfolio back together indicated that she was even more frustrated than he was. 'Don't know how much longer we can keep regurgitating

Charlie's stuff and pretending we're doing it as a homage. The readers won't be happy, Mrs Mawson won't be—'

'Yeah, thanks for pointing that out. But they'll be even more unhappy if I flash Armageddon in Ambridge at them. Right, anything else? Good.'

He was on his feet trying to shepherd Liz out of the room before she had time to answer that last question, but she had applied the brakes and had her Cassandra voice on again.

'Did I mention I think it's time we sacked that tosser who writes the book reviews?' she said. 'He only just got them done last time.'

'Yeah, you mention it every month. So *that* tosser has upped his game.' He went to his bag and with as dramatic a flourish as she'd used earlier, extracted his laptop and opened it. 'He got through one of the books this weekend, I'll forward the review to you now. And . . . while we're throwing insults about, that woman who fannies about with the films needs a kick up the backside as well.'

'Hey!' Liz looked aggrieved. 'If that poor woman has to see another zombie film, she may kill herself because, after all, if you can't beat them, join them.'

With no dedicated editor for the Culture section, the two of them had to carve it up between them, fifty-fifty. The only thing Tom had stipulated was that he wanted to do the theatre reviews, even though it meant getting a babysitter every couple of weeks. When Liz had accepted his explanation that he was passionate about drama of all kinds, it made him feel ashamed that he was such a good liar.

'I'll see you in the boardroom in a minute,' he said, finally steering her to the door. He wrenched it open. 'So fly, little bird. Go dump your cheer on some other poor sod.'

He was aiming for a swift door-in-door-frame scenario to underline that he'd had the last word. And, by some fluke, he managed it. There was a satisfying clunk, followed some moments later by a thud as more plaster grapes fell from the wall.

Outside the door he heard the unmistakable sound of Liz laughing.

'Liposuction, breast-enhancement, dead-heading and blossom end rot . . .' Across the boardroom table, Victoria paused in her shuffle of press releases. 'Oh, not a beauty treatment – this must be for the gardening section. But you need to watch out, Kelvin, blossom end rot sounds like something you might be prone to.'

The man opposite gave her the smile Tom supposed someone had once told him was devastating. The same person who probably said, 'You, Kelv, my son, have a way with the layyyy-deees.'

Victoria was still reading the press release. 'Ah, it's actually a very nasty disease that afflicts tomatoes,' she said, 'so there you go, first it'll affect your blossom end, then spread to your tomatoes.'

'Look forward to that.' Kelvin was going for a smoulder, but as Victoria was half-trophy wife, half-Teflon, she snuffed it out quickly. All that was left was the lingering smell of Kelvin's aftershave, commonly known as 'Eau d'Erection'.

'OK,' Tom said, tiring of the entertainment, 'on we go. Anything else, Victoria?'

'Thought we could follow up June's article on safe tanning with one on after-sun products.'

'Good. And . . .?'

'And double-page spread on packing light for holidays? Three different kinds of trip – show what you should take. We can make a big thing of the right luggage, too?'

Kelvin was nodding, eyes closed, and then – ping – they were back open again and his expression suggested Victoria was a genius. 'Yeah, might get a tie-in with a store – link with an ad. Half-page landscape, probably.' Kelvin was in Ad Manager mode, but under all that business talk was the suggestion that Victoria might like to reward him for supporting her so enthusiastically.

Victoria's smile was very expensive and she didn't waste much of it on Kelvin. It was Tom who got the full veneer treatment. He smiled back, partly at the deflated expression on Kelvin's face and partly because he found it hard not to be amused by Victoria's blend of balls, enthusiasm and blatant toadying.

She was someone he'd brought in to add some much-needed 'bigger thinking' to a Fashion and Beauty section that had previously been marooned in the 1990s. Her only fault was that she sometimes needed to be reined in. And not just from teasing Kelvin's groin and then slapping it back down again.

She had a tendency to forget their readership was canny with its money and that their eyes would bleed if presented with a pair of shoes she called 'reasonably priced'.

Tom glanced towards Liz to see if she wanted to add anything.

'Seems OK,' she said, not looking up from the notes she was making. 'What happened about that spa article?'

'Thought nearer Christmas. Kelvin's in negotiations with them about a review and a reader's offer.'

'Yup, I am,' Kelvin said. 'I'm very optimistic.'

Sub-text: And hopeful that my fantasy involving me, Victoria and a jacuzzi will finally, finally come true.

Tom wondered whether Kelvin had noticed that he was no longer an up-for-it lad, but a dad in his late forties. Or was it only Tom feeling his age today? Probably. Kelvin was still as shiny as his suits – a guy who could talk someone up from a quarter to a full-page ad and make them think *they'd* got the best of the deal.

Tom thanked Victoria for her ideas, but because she looked a little too smug, added, 'Just remember, no banker's bonus stuff.'

Her hand went over her own, very flashy, watch.

'And careful with the colours – none of the acid greens and yellows I'm seeing in the style mags.'

As he finished speaking, he checked on Stan, the Men's Editor. He was looking as if he suspected that, under his suit, Tom was wearing a tutu and hold-ups. Stan was not someone at ease with his own or any other man's feminine side. He was married to a doughty woman who had only fingertip contact with her own.

Pre-Tom, the Men's section was stuffed with all things sporty and anything that had an engine. Fashion, if it was tackled at all, was the odd V-neck jumper or some slacks from the local men's outfitters who Kelvin had persuaded to buy a quarter-page ad. Once, shock horror, they had featured a blue mackintosh. With. A. Red. Scarf.

Since Tom's arrival, Stan had been forced to raise his game and he grumbled regularly about having to arse around with 'dressing-up clothes'. Yet when Victoria had suggested he hand men's fashion to her, the answer had been a loud 'No'. Since then, Stan had gone on the offensive and started writing all his own fashion copy. It had to have extensive snark surgery from Liz, who kept his worst efforts in 'The File of Shame'. Recently slotted in had been his review of men's satchel bags:

If you like to carry around something that most of us grew out of when we were nine . . .

Tom decided to make Stan wait till later and went to the portly man sitting next to him.

'So, Flat Plan Meeting, Monty.' (To remind Monty *where* he was.) 'Give us your ideas for July's issue.' (To prompt him into remembering *why* he was there.)

Monty usually needed a lot of spoon feeding (which was apt as he was the Food and Wine Editor). And the amount he needed depended on how good a time he was having outside work. As he freely admitted, he had slid a long way down the food chain from a glossy supermarket supplement to *The Place, The People*. That slide had included a couple of divorces, a stint in rehab and a failed attempt to run his own restaurant.

'Monty?' Tom said again, knowing that if it was down to Monty his pages would be plastered with photos of him in vineyards knocking back wine or eating in Michelin-starred restaurants. On Tom's budget, he was more likely to get a voucher for Wetherspoon's.

Monty was opening his mouth. 'I was thinking a couple of pages on Prosecco. Great alternative to Champagne. Could tie it in with a plug for local wine merchants. Right, Kelvin?' He didn't wait for Kelvin's reply. 'Got some nice bits of puffery about a pink bubbly being produced this year – should be able to cobble together an article from that.'

Monty smiled, which made his eyes close to slits and his already wide face appear wider. 'I'd like to spotlight some local food producers and I've sounded out someone for asparagus.' He was flicking through his notes. Notes! Monty had notes. Astonished expressions around the table.

'And, last page, soft drinks. Cordials. Home-made lemonade. There.'

'Very good, Monty,' Tom said, trying to keep the surprise out of his voice.

'Well, I've been laid up all weekend, nothing else to do. Waterworks,' he added, doing a very unpleasant mime with his hand.

'Thank you, the patron saint of bladders,' Liz said, drily.

Tom speeded up the meeting with a quick trip around Stan's ideas, although he did pause for a discussion about whether sarongs for men were making a comeback, just to hear Stan say the word as if he had faecal matter under his tongue.

'Right,' Tom said, finally. 'Let's hear what the rest of you have to suggest for your sections, fifteen minutes each and try and remember what your budget is and who your readers are. No titting about . . .'

As they got stuck in, Liz passed him a note. *Ooh, you're so masterful, Meryl.*

CHAPTER 8

Monday 12 May (Part 2)

My mother would not approve of a second page for the 12th. She'd call it cheating.

Which is ironic really.

Anyway, more things I've learned today:

1) A person, namely the estate agent, can be as charming as anything until you bring up the fact that the reality of the 'cottage' differs greatly from the description in the paperwork and that you'd like a reduction in the rent.

   Then that person gives you what I believe is called 'grief'. I think what I've just witnessed is some kind of highly ritualised display of aggression.

2) The local library keeps records of all its old newspapers on microfiche.

3) Microfiche and the machines used to read them are the work of the devil (as my mother would say).

4) The only good thing about reading a newspaper on microfiche is that you can eat biscuits without getting the pages greasy.

5) I have started at 1940 (of course) and reached 1960. By 2013, I will need spectacles. And a tumbrel to transport me around as I will have eaten over seventy years'-worth of biscuits.

6) I was right about the colour of the car. The only way it could be more conspicuous is if I painted 'Fran Mayhew, digging for information' along the side.

7) I may be using this research as a means of putting off the day when I have to actually *do* what I came here to do.

8) No matter how long you look at a photograph in a newspaper, the person in it won't talk to you.

9) There is no 10.

CHAPTER 9

As Tom left the office, he recalled the high spots of this Monday. Tasty pesto and Parma ham roll for lunch. Good cup of coffee, not made by Liz. Yup, that was it.

The crinkled gusset in this underpants of a day had been his trip to the Finance department, during which he'd had to listen to the Finance Director tell him once again that the magazine industry had never had it so bad. On balance, Tom preferred the Finance Director's second-in-command, Linda – he had never heard her say anything.

He unlocked his car and had one final think about whether there was anything he had forgotten to do and then pushed his job to the back of his brain.

Unless he had something to write, or some proofs to check, he left work at work. He wasn't that guy any more; on his mobile in the car, or sitting with one eye on the TV, the other on his laptop. If he thought about his life in London it was like looking back at some over-eager high-achiever who he vaguely recognised.

Even his social life had seemed like a competition to get the best table and the premium tickets.

Yet it all went, more or less overnight.

Whether he missed that stuff was immaterial. Whether his life was richer or poorer now was off the point. He'd just been irrevocably changed. When a small child looked at you with absolute trust as you were about to get a splinter out of her finger, the idea of getting worked up about a table by the toilets seemed more than a bit fuck-witty.

He drove across the stone bridge over the river, past the showground where the marquees were nearly all down and the rugby posts back up, then climbed the hill. Right again and he was on a lane of a few houses with his at the end.

Hell of a commute.

He stopped to look down at the view and could see the roof of the magazine building. At least it was still standing.

There were a couple of new estates changing the shape of the village, but really it hadn't altered much since he was a child. The Roman site was still trying to attract visitors by dressing some poor tit up in a centurion's uniform. The river still got uppity in winter and ran amok in the low-lying car park. There was still a butcher's and a baker's and a fruit and veg shop. The thought of all that unchanging life wasn't driving him mad this evening as it had at the show. Stupid to feel grouchy when the swallows were diving and everyone was out in their garden with their shoes off.

Correction, when everyone was in *his* garden with their shoes off. He came down the drive to see Rob's car tucked behind his mother's and as he pushed open the side gate, Hattie was shouting, 'Look, Dad, Uncle Rob's ready to put up a wall!' She was jiggling about on a wooden platform built into the horse chestnut tree. It was the floor of her tree house and Rob pulled her leg that Tom and he had made it out of the sawdust Rob smuggled out of work down his trousers. As his company took huge swathes of conifer forest and converted it into chipboard, Hattie had believed him for a while.

Rob wanted to crack on while the weather held and it looked as if he'd come straight from work. He had his back to Tom, but from the way he was kneeling and his shoulders moving, he was obviously fixing some brackets into the floor.

Kath was sitting in one of the canvas chairs, a pair of barbecue tongs hanging from her hand. 'Won't be long,' she said. 'Your mum's already given Hattie a snack, but we thought there aren't many days you can do this.' She pointed towards the barbecue with the tongs. 'Had to fight someone for these sausages.'

Tom used his laugh as cover for a surreptitious glance at Kath's ankles to see how swollen they were. He wondered if he could subtly bring something out from the house for her to rest her feet on.

'Hey, stop with the jumping,' he heard Rob say, 'it's like working on a trampoline.'

'Come here, you,' he called to Hattie, knowing that 'stop jumping' was as effective a command as 'stop breathing'.

When she was down the ladder, he got a partial hug, her head turned back towards the tree house, amid a long stream of chatter about Rob letting her screw in some of the bolts.

She looked like an unmade bed as usual, but he was pleased to see she was in her oldest clothes. He guessed her school dress would be festering away on her bedroom floor, complete with lunch/paint/soil decoration.

'Behave at school?' he asked the back of her head.

'A bit,' she said, skipping away, and he didn't know if she meant a bit of her had behaved, or she'd been on her best behaviour for nanoseconds.

'Just fix this last one in place, then you can give me a hand getting the wall panels out of the garage,' Rob called back over his shoulder.

A laugh from Kath. 'Tom's helping? So . . . finished by Christmas, then?'

Hattie was back round his legs. A tug on his trousers. 'It won't take that long, will it?' Her most appealing look; huge green eyes, freckles as if someone had flicked them on from a paintbrush.

'Auntie Kath was joking, Hats. If the weather stays like this, it might be up by the weekend.'

'No might about it,' Rob cut in, one hand reaching behind him blindly and then obviously finding what it was searching for.

Hattie was climbing up the ladder again.

'What's the view like up there?' Tom shouted to her.

On her tiptoes, scanning the horizon through the branches and leaves, she shouted back, 'I can see the Spanish fleet.'

That would be a sight, the Armada heading up the Tyne.

I was down the quayside, completely mortal, and these Spanish gadgies came right up to the bridge in a boot, like, and I swear they were lush. I come home with a bra full of doubloons.

Rob stood up. 'That's that done.' Tom saw his eyes immediately seek out Kath. 'All right there?' he called to her and she raised the tongs as if to say, 'Don't fuss'. She stood up, probably to underline that point, and started moving the sausages around on the barbecue.

'Can Auntie Kath climb up?' Hattie asked and Rob's 'No' was too abrupt, which he must have realised the minute it left his mouth. He put his hand on Hattie's shoulder. 'Sorry, love,' he said. 'It'll take a lot of weight, but not that much.'

There was a 'charming' from Kath, but Tom knew she wouldn't have been fooled by his brother's attempt to hide behind humour.

He wandered over to her.

'Good day?' she asked him.

'Had better, but the main thing is it's over. You OK?'

'What, apart from feeling like a bit of china?' She glanced towards Rob. 'Start our classes at the hospital tomorrow. He's a bit nervous.'

'You want me to try and talk him down? From, you know . . . Not the tree, obviously.' He took the tongs from her and pushed a couple of sausages to the edge of the barbecue and moved the burgers to the middle.

'No. Think he's got to work through this himself. And why do men always do that?' She was looking at the tongs. 'They *have* to take over the barbecue. Is it a phallic thing? You know, the sausages? Here,' she took the tongs from him, 'you'll get fat on your suit.'

'Phallic thing? Sometimes you make less sense than my

mother. Hang on . . .' He looked towards the house. 'Where is she?'

When Kath looked evasive, he pulled her chair nearer to the barbecue. 'Plonk yourself there. I'll be back.'

One quick scan of the kitchen and the sitting room confirmed his suspicions and when he got upstairs, he tracked his mother down to the bathroom. She was bent over, cleaning the bath.

'Step away from the cleaning products, lady,' he said and regretted it as he saw her shoot up straight.

'Oh, bugger me,' she blurted and then rounded on him, 'Tom, don't do that. My heart's come out of my mouth.'

'That's going to make a mess on that newly cleaned bath.'

'What?'

'You said . . . Oh, never mind.' He put his hand on her arm. 'Sorry, I didn't mean to scare you. But it's the only way to catch you at it.'

She was looking as if she'd been discovered rooting through his wallet. 'I just saw the cloth,' she said. 'Thought I'd give it a bit of a . . . freshen-up.'

'And what about downstairs? The hoover just happened to leap into your hands?'

She moved to the sink and started wiping around the taps. 'New teaching assistant at school. Looks about twelve. Can't be, I suppose.'

'No, Hattie says she's twenty-five, and she's only covering for Mrs . . . Wait a minute . . . you've changed the subject. God, you're good.' He took the cloth from her. 'Don't expect you to do this, Mum. Picking up Hattie twice a week is enough.'

'You're working all day.'

'You've worked all your life.'

'Aw, get away with it.' She tried to get the cloth back, but he wasn't letting go. She gave it up and started dabbing her hands on the towel. He half expected her to pick it up and smell it. Perhaps she already had.

'While I think on,' she said, 'I put Hattie's karate kit and her school dress in to wash.'

'Mum . . .'

'Oh now, it's nothing.' She straightened up the towel to her satisfaction and as they went downstairs said, 'I don't mean anything by having a quick tidy-up.' She put her hand on his shoulder. 'You keep it lovely. For a man.'

Pointless explaining to his mother how sexist that was – she'd only just got used to that nice Clare Balding being a lesbian.

Two walls and twelve sausages later, they waved goodbye to Rob and Kath and he wondered whether he should tell Hattie that her mother had rung that morning. He always told her about any contact, believing it was her right to know. But the timing was crucial. Too near bedtime and he was afraid she'd lie awake in the dark.

No, not tonight, it was too late. And he couldn't tell her in the rush and tumble of the morning and then leave her at school to think about it on her own.

Whenever that conversation was going to take place, he wasn't looking forward to it. He knew how unsettling it was for Hattie to have Steph zoom in and out of her life and then disappear as if she'd been abducted by aliens.

Sometimes miracles did happen, though. Like on Hattie's first day of school, a phone call from Morocco and all the right things said. Easter, when Steph had arranged to Skype her. And actually done it.

He walked around the garden, packing away the chairs while Hattie had a few more minutes in the tree house.

It was the bats swooping and darting now and, at times like this, he was glad they were the end house in the row, with nothing between them and the fields.

'Come on now,' he shouted to Hattie. 'No arguing.'

While she had her bath, he sat on the stool and she made a beard out of bubbles and they chatted about Josh, her best friend in the world, and how hot water came out of taps. He felt a drawing sadness that one day the bathroom door would be closed on him. Even now, it was probably more acceptable to say you owned a sub-machine gun than admit that the favourite part of your day was sitting chatting to your daughter while she had a good soak.

When she got out, he wrapped her in a towel as if she was something precious. Definitely not a parcel.

'Put your pyjamas on, choose a story and I'll go and get you some water.'

'And Gummy.'

Yeah, the little bugger. 'And Gummy.'

Downstairs he filled up a cup with water, but could not find Gummy in Hattie's reading bag. He saw it had fallen under the table and when he reached for it, cracked his head on the wood. By the time he'd stopped cursing and was aware the phone was ringing, he was also aware that Hattie had padded into his bedroom and picked it up in there.

'Mummy!' he heard her say and the happy glow of the evening went fizzle, phut. Two phone calls in one day? Damn, he just knew what was coming now.

He went up the stairs softly and stood outside his bedroom door, hating being an eavesdropper, but unable to stop himself.

Hattie was talking fast about the tree house and he imagined her face, alight with the fact that Steph had rung. There was an expanse of silence, he could hear his own breathing in it. Then, 'Yes, it was lovely, Mummy. And the bag.' Good girl. More silence and his stomach tightened. Hattie getting more excited, 'Yes, yes! Please. Will it be deep snow? Do they have reindeer?'

Steph hadn't got him to agree, so had brought in the heaviest gun of all on her side.

More gabbling from Hattie before, 'Nun-night. I love you too. Bye, Mummy. Bye.'

It felt as if his heart was being scrunched up by the longing in that 'bye'.

The door swung back and there was Hattie, face like it was Christmas already. 'Dad, Dad! I'm going to Italy. Mummy says I can. We're going skiing.'

Lying on his side on the sofa later, he felt almost too weary to raise the bottle of lager to his lips. Bloody Steph. She'd come out of this looking fantastic and he was the villain for nipping all that joy in the bud.

He had a tear-stained five-year-old lying upstairs in her bed, clutching her gum shield. Or more likely lying with it defiantly in her mouth.

They had argued—

'But why can't I go?'

'Because I want to be there and Mummy doesn't like that.'

'But I could go on my own. Mummy said you could put me on the plane.'

'No. You're too young.'

'Mummy says I'm not too young.'

Round and round they went, Hattie getting more and more frustrated. And all the time he had his hands tied because there was no way he could say, 'I don't trust your mother with you. She'll lose it at some point.'

'I want to go skiing,' she had cried finally and he'd watched the tears stream out, snot too, and tried to put his arms around her. She pushed him away and turned her back on him.

He'd sat in the chair by her bed and asked if she wanted a story, but her silent antagonism felt like another presence in the room, forcing him out and down the stairs after a fumbled kiss on the top of her head.

He took a sip of lager. He had already tried to ring Steph back, but only got her message service. Lying low, no doubt.

He thought of how he'd let her parents off this morning and not rung them. (My God, was that only this morning?) Well, good old Tom wasn't feeling so kind right now.

He imagined Geoffrey blinking awake, nose and ear hair akimbo.

Striped pyjamas, concave chest. Caroline in the other bed. Another concave chest.

'Yes!' Geoffrey's bark was hoarse this late.

'Tom here. How are you doing?' Geoffrey's eyebrows would be having a field day. He could hear Caroline saying something and pictured the waving-down-a-car movement she employed to get her husband's attention. 'Just thought I'd let you know I've had a call from Steph.'

A growly 'Anything wrong?'

'I won't bore you with the details. But I'm not having her upsetting Hattie like this. Not after I've been so bloody reasonable—'

'Upsetting? What? I . . .'

'So . . . I am asking you yet again to help me stop this long, lingering death with Hattie being used as leverage for God knows what.' Tom took a breath. 'That envelope I left with you. She said you haven't passed it on to her?'

'Yes I did. I gave it to her when she was . . .'

'When she was over here?' Tom asked. 'That's what you were going to say, weren't you? When was that?' He wished he could reach down the phone and pull Geoffrey up it by his nose hairs.

There was what sounded like a skirmish and it was Caroline on the phone. 'What seems to be the problem?'

She appeared to be reading from a 'How to handle a belligerent customer' handbook.

'Usual one, Caroline. I'd like to divorce your daughter. I'm trying to be civilised, but she's still blocking me.'

Silence for a while. He knew where Steph had learned her communication skills.

There was an arrogant whine to Caroline's tone when she spoke. 'I don't know what you expect us to do? We didn't know Stephanie was coming over until she rang from the airport. We've tried never to interfere in the lives of any of our children.'

That's because you'd have to get emotionally involved. Emotions are messy and you're very tidy people.

A longer pause, before she asked, 'And how is Harriet?'

If they were down to platitudes, he might as well give up.

He finished the call feeling that he'd achieved nothing. Why should he be surprised? These were the people who had never asked, not once, why Hattie had ended up living with him. Was it because they were too frozen in the ice of good breeding to enquire? Or had they always had their suspicions about how volatile Steph was?

He looked at the lager bottle. Unfair really to criticise them for not asking. His family had, plenty of times, and he'd always side-stepped telling them everything.

He just had to cling on to the fact that Geoffrey and Caroline, in their own frigid way, loved Hattie. But Steph, jeez, he couldn't believe she'd been to see her mother and father but not her daughter. It was nearly four months since their last, fraught meeting in York.

He got up and checked on Hattie again. Gummy was still in her hand, but she wasn't asleep, he could tell. There was an echo of his earlier position on the sofa in the way she was lying on her side, shoulders stiff.

'I love you, Hats,' he said, feeling needy, and got a little squeak back, but when he sat on the bed, she shifted on to her front and pulled the covers up over her head.

Back downstairs he lay down on the floor and cried out the way he felt trapped and manipulated and how someone, with one phone call, could sweep away all that warmth between him and Hattie. It would come back again, but for now he felt miles away from her. Stupid the way the tears went straight from his eyes into his ears.

There was the sound of a text arriving and he wasn't going to check it, but there was that niggling worry about it being something to do with Kath.

When he looked at the message, he smiled despite the gloom.

Yes please he texted back. *Usual day?*

He waited for the response before signing off with: *Grietje. You're a bloody lifesaver.*

He lay back down and texted Natalie the babysitter. There was always the reserve team of Rob and Kath, but they asked too many questions when he returned home afterwards.

As he took himself off to bed, he thought that he might just forgive Monday because of this late present. But he sure as hell wasn't going to forgive Steph.

CHAPTER 10

Monday 12 May (Part 3)

Yes, here I am again. And it turns out there is a number 10.

10) It would appear that flinging oneself around and grunting is not a display of aggression, but some kind of courtship ritual. Estate agent has just invited me for a drink tomorrow lunchtime to 'discuss a possible reduction in the rent'.

10a) (See what I did there?)

Agreeing to have a drink with a man who is probably only going to give you something if you offer him another thing in return, is not necessarily a good thing.

For the man.

CHAPTER 11

Tom got back into the car after dropping Hattie at school feeling that he'd been snapped so rapidly from one emotion to the next, he probably had whiplash.

In bed the night before, he'd lain awake, alert to what was going on in that little brain in the bedroom over the other side of the landing. Then, all of a sudden, that little brain and the body that carried it about were climbing into bed with him. He just let her hunker down next to him and felt pathetically grateful for that. The next thing he knew, the birds were waking him up and he was on the edge of the bed, only the bedside table stopping him from falling on to the floor, while Hattie occupied the rest of the mattress in a horizontal arabesque.

They hadn't talked much over breakfast. No point in pushing it. But that silence from her was . . . torturous.

On the journey to school, he had tried to think of something to chat about. He'd had stand-offs with all kinds of people in his life – irate printers, stroppy writers, a couple of drunk players from an opposing team in a back street in Carlisle, but this was the worst. It made him feel unmanned.

He could only suppose that was because this incident wasn't about him managing to placate someone enough to get what he wanted (and in the case of Carlisle, not losing his teeth). This time it was about trying to give Hattie what *she* wanted. But what she wanted was the one thing he couldn't deliver.

He had parked further away from school than he normally did, hoping that during the walk to the playground, he could think of the right words to prevent them parting with this awful thing wedged between them. But he'd only just taken the key out of the ignition when she said, in an un-Hattie-like voice, 'Will you ever let me see Mummy again?'

It was as if someone had put their hand flat on his stomach and pushed it as hard as possible towards his backbone. Undoing his seatbelt he had turned quickly and seen that she was really scared of the question she was asking. Not caring that it was a struggle, he had clambered into the back of the car and sat beside her and got hold of her hand.

'Hattie, sweetheart, please don't ever think I won't let you see Mummy. It's just you're too young to travel to Italy on your own.'

'But Mummy says I could. And that she can look after me without you over Christmas. Why can't she do that?'

It was a question she hadn't asked the night before. Her face told him that he wasn't going to be able to fob her off with not answering it.

'Because Mummy will have to work some of the time and you'll be looked after by people who I don't know and you don't know. And sitting in this car here, with me, you think that will be OK, but just try and imagine going to bed without someone you know to tuck you in, or if you fell over and hurt yourself and you wanted a bit of a hug . . .'

He hated this, not least because he was putting fears in her mind on purpose. It would serve him right if she was still living at home in her forties.

Her face, as he'd been talking, had been scrunched up, as if she was imagining the scene he'd just outlined.

'I wouldn't like that,' she had said, so earnestly that he had wanted to hit his head on the window for being such a horrible manipulator. 'I would be really sad.'

He'd felt her hand turn in his and gave it a squeeze.

Some serious swallowing had been necessary before he'd replied, 'I wouldn't like it either, Hats.' And then he heard himself say, 'How about if I see whether you and I can go skiing over Christmas? Just the two of us? And then, either on the way there, or the way back, we can pop in and see Mummy.'

He wished he'd thought about that a bit more before he'd opened his mouth. Hattie's face was no longer scrunched up. 'Yes,' she said on a breath out. 'Yes. Us skiing. Yessss. I'm going to tell Josh.' Slipping her hand from his, she had struggled to get out of her seat.

He was powerless to stop the onrush of enthusiasm that he'd started. Steph was going to go ballistic. And how to tell Rob and Kath they wouldn't be around for the first Christmas with the new baby? How to tell his mum?

In the end, he'd decided not to worry about that now. Hattie had stopped dwelling on the pain of missing her mother and they'd swerved round the tricky nature of reality once again.

He drove away from school, watching it recede in the rear-view mirror.

Lies and bribery. And possibly a scheme that wasn't going to work anyway. Fantastic fathering skills. Well done, Tom. Top of the class.

Liz was standing in exactly the same spot as yesterday.

'Bloody hell, you look like crap,' she said. 'And what I've got to tell you isn't going to help.'

Until she'd spoken, he didn't realise how much he

needed to shout at someone. He clamped his mouth shut, but couldn't keep the emotion off his face. In his office, he took it out on the door before checking again to see if Natalie had replied to his text from last night about babysitting.

He sent another.

The phone on his desk rang.

'I'd leave you alone as you're obviously pre-menstrual,' Liz said when he answered it, 'but you're going to get a visitor in about ten minutes and I thought you'd rather know about it than have her just appear.'

'Her?'

'Mrs Mawson.'

'Did she say what she wanted?'

'Nope. Probably going to sack you or something.' The phone was put down.

He put his down too and went to the window to see if he could spot Mrs Mawson's car. No, just a bright-red one trying to go the wrong way out of the square and having to reverse in the face of a bus.

Bit worrying that Mrs Mawson was visiting the office. Now and again she would ring to congratulate him when circulation figures showed a particularly large hike. Four times a year he was invited to schmoozing suppers that she held for advertisers and directors at Mawson Towers (a name he found easier to remember than the real one). But normally she trusted him to get on with it.

The phone rang again. 'And not that I bloody care, but there's nothing wrong with Hattie, is there?' The concerned tone of Liz's voice made him start to feel shabby about his truculence.

'No, nothing wrong with Hattie. Just her mother.' He paused. 'Thank you for asking, though. And Liz? Look, you stop waylaying me before I've even got into my office and I'll stop acting like a diva.'

'Point taken.'

'Excellent. And . . . could you arrange for some coffee when Mrs Mawson arrives? I don't mean make it yourself,' he added hastily. 'Send out for some.'

There was a laugh that was almost a cackle. 'Oh no, the woman has never acknowledged I exist. *I'll* make the coffee.'

Mrs Mawson did not look as if she owned approximately one-eighth of the county. She looked as if she owned all of it.

It wasn't to do with the way she dressed. That was in the understated, confident manner of old money, where nothing had to be proven or slavishly followed. Even though she was only in her early fifties, she favoured suits teamed with a subtly coloured blouse. At social events she always wore black. When relaxing it was jeans and cashmere. If he bumped into her then, looking so casual, it felt wrong. Like spotting one of his teachers in town on a Saturday night when he was younger.

Almost as wrong as addressing her as 'Deborah'.

No, it was something to do with how her head sat on her neck. Most people Tom knew maintained a rough ninety-degree head-to-neck relationship; Mrs Mawson took a right angle as merely her starting point. Which meant Tom was often looking up her nostrils.

He watched her contemplating the colour of her coffee, her face too well bred to exhibit distaste. Her trusty handbag, what Liz called 'a right Thatcher', was near her feet. She had another accessory with her today too – Jamie, her younger boy.

'Jamie graduated last summer,' Mrs Mawson was saying, 'he's done some travelling, but now it's time for him to show us what he's made of.'

Her smile inferred that Jamie was already a disappointment to her. It wasn't a smile Tom ever wanted to see on his own mother's face and, fair play to her, he hadn't – even when he'd returned like a homing pigeon, one small daughter under his wing.

Jamie was smiling too, but it was apologetic and aimed

towards Tom. The smile was on a very handsome face. Jamie had the compulsory upper-middle-class floppy hair and rugby physique – a touch of Ralph Lauren via Hollister – but something about him also suggested sensitivity. Not a trait that would get him very far in the Mawson world.

Tom had last seen him at Charlie's funeral, turning away as if hiding the fact he was crying. He had been the only Mawson displaying any emotion that day.

And before that? At least ten years ago at Newcastle station, a glimpse of an awkward lad dressed in school uniform. Tom added that to the list of things making him feel ancient. Right up there alongside *Geordie Shore*.

The more Tom studied Jamie, the more he suspected he was the softest of the Mawsons. Certainly his brown eyes did not have that unblinking way of looking at you that made you wonder if you'd been entered into some kind of staring contest that you couldn't win. Jamie was a world away from his brother, Edward, a man born with a sneer who spent vast tracts of time offing wildlife.

'We feel it's beneficial,' Mrs Mawson continued, 'for Jamie to gain some practical experience in each of the family businesses, before he decides on which one he wishes to specialise.'

Tom struggled to imagine a world where you didn't need to go outside your family to find career opportunities.

'So, work experience?' Tom clarified.

'Quite. And I'd like him to actually *do* something while he's here. Not just spectate.'

There was only one possible reply. 'We'd be delighted to have you, Jamie. Have you got any newspaper or magazine experience?'

'No. Although, I did, you know, go out with a girl at university who reviewed bands . . . but . . .'

Mrs Mawson's smile reappeared and Jamie trailed off, like a bouncy dog suddenly pulled up sharp on his leash.

'Not a problem,' Tom assured him. 'After all, that's what you're here for – to learn how we operate—'

'And how to *manage*.' Mrs Mawson said the word as if it was interchangeable with *how to rule*. Tom suspected that, for Jamie, it was more about learning what was expected of the 'spare' when the 'heir' was running the big, pointy-ended, serious stuff.

'Well, Tom, it's been good to see you again.' Mrs Mawson was getting up and he did too. 'Oh, and thank you, I appreciated the photographer taking some shots of Mabel and her horse at the show.'

Tom had to resist the urge to bend his knee when she was gracious like this, because however you looked at it, their relationship had distinctly feudal overtones. He wasn't sure where he ranked in the pecking order of the many people who worked for her. Probably slightly above the manager of her farm shop, but way below her game-keeper.

'When would you like Jamie to start?' he asked and she said, 'Why, now, of course.'

He got to the door before her and had his usual tussle with it.

'I don't suppose . . .' he began and he sensed that she knew he was going to raise the issue of the state of the building because she said sharply, 'Any luck with a replacement for Charles?'

Tom was never quite in tune with Charlie being referred to as Charles. But then, he still couldn't believe the old goat had been Mrs Mawson's father. She definitely took after her mother. Another woman who liked to show you her nostrils.

'Not yet,' he said. 'Charlie is a hard person to replace.'

'Yes.' Emotionless. The relationship between Charlie and his daughter had been glacial on her part, tepid on his.

He heard her sigh as if she was using it as a thick-nibbed marker to underline her point. 'It is rather tiresome to see his work rehashed issue after issue.'

Great, landed with babysitting her son and rapped over the knuckles. He was irritated enough not to walk her down the stairs to the street.

'Sorry, you know, about me being dumped on you,' Jamie said when she was gone. Tom had never heard a Mawson apologise for anything – not even Charlie over the flashing incident.

Jamie was looking at his shoes, his hand skimming up over his forehead and then pushing back his floppy hair in that movement that got handed out at birth with the investment bonds. When he looked up, a message passed from those brown eyes to Tom's green ones along the lines of: *I have no interest in this, but I'll try my best to pretend I do.* And the message Tom attempted to convey back was: *Just make sure you pretend really well, otherwise when it gets busy, you're going to find yourself out on a windowsill with half my staff urging you to jump.*

Feeling they'd reached some kind of agreement, Tom said, 'Come on, I need some help with the travel pages – the guy who usually does them is on long-term sick leave and as you've just been travelling . . .'

Jamie looked slightly more animated and Tom shepherded him towards the door and braced himself for what was sure to be a fine display of sucking up from Victoria.

CHAPTER 12

Having failed to get a reply from Natalie all morning about
the babysitting, Tom went out at lunchtime to buy a sandwich and spotted her by the bookshop. She was doing a
one-legged dance as she tried to put the brake on a pram
with her foot. Her arms were full of bawling baby.

'Want a hand?'

'Thanks!' She shoved the baby at him and he walked
around on the pavement jiggling it in his arms, one hand
lightly on the back of a downy head, the way that he'd used
to do with Hattie. Natalie bent down to apply the brake
and he looked away. God, he must be getting old if he was
beginning to feel uncomfortable about how short skirts
were.

The baby seemed to be calming down.

'Not lost your knack, then?' Natalie said when she
straightened back up. 'And sorry, Tom, I know you've been
trying to contact me, but he's been a right little bugger this
morning.' She rooted around in the pocket of her little

leather jacket and pulled out her phone. 'Thursday as usual? Yeah, no problem. Course.'

He felt the baby become more of a dead weight against his chest.

'He's going off,' Natalie said, as if he were a bottle of milk.

Tom got out of the way of a man with a dog who seemed disinclined to vacate the pavement for a pram or someone holding a baby.

The tourist season was already gearing up and the square was busy. A group of walkers, taking a break from tackling Hadrian's Wall, were sitting on the steps of the market cross licking ice creams.

'Ignorant git,' Natalie said to the man's back. He turned and, in doing so, stumbled off the edge of the pavement. Natalie laughed and, just for an instant, she was a cheeky little girl before she returned to being a twenty-year-old. In many ways, she made Tom think of a glammed-up pixie with her short hair and delicate features. But it was doubtful whether many pixies were as determined as Natalie. Or as tough. And inside that neat little head of hers was a brain the size of a planet. Bucking the family tradition of attending school only sporadically, she'd turned out to be a star pupil. Now she was studying Law and making ends meet with a variety of part-time jobs. It annoyed him when people assumed her chosen profession might be something that involved gyrating round a pole.

'How come you've got Karl?' he asked, giving the baby a gentle hike up in his arms. 'Your mum not well?'

'You could say that,' Natalie replied in a way that did not encourage him to ask anything further. She was looking towards the bookshop. 'Don't suppose you could hang on to him while I go in there, could you? I'll be dead quick.'

All went well until the church clock clicked round to 1 p.m. and there was a loud BONG. Karl's eyes shot open and he reared back and hiccupped some partially digested milk on to Tom's shirt before his eyes closed again.

Tom squinted down at the lumpy stain. It smelled worse than the llama spit. When he looked up, coming towards him was the odd woman. Of course she was. Perfect.

She was in another of her shabby-chic dresses, this time with a thick blue fisherman's jumper on top and espadrilles on her feet. Her hair, in two plaits, made him imagine her striding across a high meadow like some demented Heidi. Yodelling.

She slowed when she noticed him and then, like two heat-seeking missiles, her eyes locked on to his shirt. He saw her press her lips together.

'Go on,' he said, 'get it over with.'

'I'm sorry.' She stopped a few feet from him. 'I was going to make the obvious comment that I see it's not only llamas that you antagonise. But it seems a cheap shot.' A pause and a frown. 'Although, of course, I have said it, cheap or not.'

'Well done.'

She was peering at the baby. 'It seems calm enough now.'

He didn't like the inference that she was amazed he wasn't juggling the baby with some live tigers.

'It's a he,' Tom snapped, 'not an it.'

'Yes, yes, of course.' More frowning. 'It's just I've had some terrible incidents where I've called a he she and vice versa.'

'Well that's fascinating. And it's not actually *my* baby.'

He had no idea why he'd said that, it only made her look at the pram in a worried way.

'You mean you just decided to pick him up?' She sounded appalled. 'Well, you must put him back, immediately.'

'What? No. I'm looking after him for a friend while she's in the shop. Why would you think I'd steal a baby?'

'I didn't say you'd stolen it . . . him. I just thought you might be one of those people who couldn't pass a baby without picking it up.'

He was saved from having to ask her what bloody planet

she lived on where people would chance doing that these days, when Natalie came out of the shop carrying two thick textbooks.

'How's he been?' she asked.

'Fine, except when he was sick on my shirt.'

'Yeah, he does that sometimes.'

'Ah, I see.' Odd Woman's face looked as if a lot of light bulbs had just come on in her head. 'The baby is—'

'Natalie's brother,' Tom leaped in, just stopping Miss Tactless from annoying Natalie by making the all-too-common assumption that she was a young mum.

'Bit jittery there, Tom,' Natalie said, raising her eyebrows at him, before she turned to focus on the woman. 'So, what's going on here, then? A bit of secret chatting up?'

'Oh he wasn't . . .' The woman trailed off as she realised Natalie was teasing.

'No, you're right, I wasn't,' Tom said abruptly. Somewhere along the line this woman was going to tell Natalie that he and Hattie had used her garden as a toilet.

Natalie moved the books around in her arms. 'Well, I'll introduce myself then. Hi. I'm Natalie.'

'And I'm Fran,' the woman said. 'Fran Mayhew. It's very good to meet you.'

'Moved here?' Natalie asked.

'Visiting. Maybe with a view to . . . settling later on.'

'That'll be nice,' Tom said to the top of the baby's head in a tone that implied the opposite. He knew if he glanced up, Natalie would be giving him an admonishing look, so he kept on concentrating on Karl.

'I'm in a red-brick bungalow between here and Low-heatherington,' Fran explained. 'Off to the left, down a narrow track.'

Natalie was laughing. 'That dump! Poor you.'

'Yes, it's pretty bad. But I'm meeting the man from the estate agent's for a drink later. I'm working on getting a reduction in the rent.'

She seemed unaware of how bad that sounded.

'Estate agent guy?' Natalie was frowning. 'That wouldn't be Greg Vasey, would it?'

'Yes, do you know him?'

'Everyone knows him. He's a creep.'

Tom knew that Natalie could have used at least one of her sisters to illustrate that character assessment. And, possibly, her mother.

'Oh he is,' Fran said, enthusiastically, 'an utter creep. But they are often the easiest.' There was a pause while a cat's cradle of looks passed between Tom and Natalie. Still oblivious, Fran was off again. She peered at the books in Natalie's arms.

'My boyfriend at university read Law. How are you getting on with it?'

'I'm just finishing my first year at Newcastle. Yeah, it's great. Whereabouts was he?'

'Warwick. We both were.' Fran did a mock shudder. 'Not my boyfriend any more, thankfully. I imagine he'll be using what he learned to keep himself from ending up behind bars.' She paused. 'He went into the City.'

Tom wondered if this was a skill she had – to put her foot right in it up to her thigh? He waited for nice Natalie to be replaced by tough Natalie and so was surprised to hear her laugh.

'Yeah, good one,' she said, 'that lot make my dad look like a bloody saint. He's doing time at the minute. Bit sticky-fingered.'

There were a couple of seconds during which Fran's face was a blank and then both hands went to her mouth. When she moved them, she said, earnestly, 'I am so, so sorry. That must be really hard for you and your family.' She shook her head as if exasperated with herself. 'I have this unerring ability to say exactly the wrong thing. Always have.'

Natalie waved Fran's discomfort away. 'Forget it,' she said. 'It's not like you knew.'

'Well, that's really generous of you. Has he . . . I mean, is he in for long?'

'He's been in thirteen months so far. Bit more to go.'

Tom could only be thankful that Fran did not ask how old Karl was.

Natalie bent to stow her books under the pram. 'So you and Tom just met today then?' she asked.

'No, we met at the show. And then . . .' Fran darted a quick, mischievous look towards him, 'he came round with his daughter to water my garden.'

'Didn't know you offered that as a service, Tom.' Natalie reached out for Karl and Tom passed him over, glad to have a reason not to answer. He watched Natalie strap the baby in the pram and cover him up and then there was a quick dip down again to retrieve something.

Tom only spotted the pack of baby wipes as Natalie came towards him. 'Hold still,' she said, while she dabbed at the baby vomit.

His life was going around in a circle with wet wipes and body fluids as the unifying themes.

Jamie, ambling into view, saved him.

'Uh, Liz told me I could take a break to get something to eat.' He spoke as if he expected Tom to tell him off.

'So, what's got you up before lunchtime?' Natalie asked.

'He's joining us to find out what we do.' Tom sensed Jamie's discomfort, and added, cheerily, 'Getting your hands dirty, aren't you?'

'That'll be a first for a Mawson,' Natalie said and Jamie blushed deeply and looked at the display of books in the shop window.

'A Mawson?' Fran was staring.

Natalie nodded. 'Yeah, owns most of this village and a lot of Northumberland. Jamie Mawson, this is Fran Mayhew. Fran, Jamie.'

'Jamie Mawson.' Fran spoke the words as if trying them out.

'Yup, second in line to the throne, aren't you?' Natalie teased.

Fran was still staring at Jamie as if she'd never seen anyone as handsome in her entire life. Tom wondered if he was the only one who noticed.

'The things I could tell you about Jamie's bedroom,' Natalie was saying. 'Some really dirty stuff I've found in there.'

'Please, Natalie . . .' Jamie gave up with the shop window and concentrated on his shoes.

'Oh, stop looking so embarrassed.' Natalie tapped Jamie on the arm. 'I'm joking.' She turned to Fran. 'I clean at the Mawson house and he's a buggar for leaving his coffee cups in his room. Although . . . that's a hell of a guilty face. Perhaps there are some shocking secrets hidden away in your room?'

Jamie flushed an even darker shade of red and did the best squirm Tom had seen for years. Of the three people in front of him, Natalie currently seemed the most grown up – Jamie was an embarrassed schoolboy and Fran a lovesick teenager. How old did Tom feel? Way older than all of them.

'I have to go,' Fran said, suddenly, still looking at Jamie. 'Sorry to take off so abruptly, but there are some things I need to get before . . . before, well, before I see Mr . . . Mr . . . um . . . Vasey. It's been lovely meeting you. Goodbye. Goodbye.'

And then she was striding away, which should have been a physical impossibility in espadrilles.

'Now that is one weird woman,' Tom said when he was sure she wouldn't hear.

'Really?' Natalie was still watching Fran. 'She wasn't that bad. Bit intense, but I liked how direct she was.' There was another tap on Jamie's arm. 'Took a shine to you, dream-boat.'

Ah, so Natalie had noticed.

Tom left them not long after that, Jamie still looking down at his shoes.

As he went back to the office, sandwich finally in his hand, he saw Fran loading some large sheets of coloured paper into her car outside the art shop. It was the red car he'd spotted tussling with the bus earlier. Figured.

He tried to walk past, but she noticed him.

'Ah, I'm glad I've caught you,' she said, turning around, 'I wanted to say thank you for saving me from that faux pas I nearly made about the baby and Natalie.' She looked disgusted with herself. 'That's on top of the one I made about her father.'

'Don't mention it.' He started to move away.

'Oh, I see,' she said, her tone less easy-going. 'That's how it works, is it? I say thank you for some decency on your part, but you just gloss over me being kind to you?'

He took a step back. What the hell was she gabbling on about now? *Walk away, Tom.*

'I'm sorry?' he said.

'I think you heard me quite distinctly, Mr Man with no name.' She was looking very fierce, which Tom thought was quite a major achievement for somebody sporting plaits.

Half-turning towards the car, she slammed down the boot before saying, with exasperation, 'What a difficult person you really are!'

'Hang on—'

'No I will not. I skirted around the weeing in my garden incident in what I thought was a delicate way . . .' Tom glanced at the people going by. 'And what do I get for that? Any thanks?' She tutted theatrically. 'No.'

Her eyes were very wide, her colour up. Heidi gone feral.

'And, to top it all, you don't even have the rudimentary manners to introduce yourself. I can only presume you're on some kind of Witness Protection scheme?' She had raised her arms for emphasis, but the movement looked awkward and jarring and she suddenly lowered them like a conductor who had just suffered a loss of confidence.

'Do you get into many fights?' he asked her. 'I mean, apart from with buses when you try to go the wrong direction up a one-way street?' She opened her mouth, but he talked on. 'I imagine you do. And I'm Tom. Tom Howard. And, whoopee, I am so grateful you didn't actually draw a full picture of what happened yesterday morning, but here's a thought – how about you hadn't mentioned it at all?'

By the end of the speech he was actually annoyed. He also thought he might have damaged his sandwich.

He looked down. Yes, squeezed to buggery.

He expected a tirade of words back, but from what he knew of her facial expressions, she appeared to be distracted.

'Yes. You're right,' she said, quietly. 'I could have done that.'

It was as if a balloon that you expected to pop had suddenly deflated itself.

'That's it?' he said. 'Nothing else you want to berate me about?'

'No. Absolutely nothing, thank you.' She gave him a tight smile.

He wanted to move, but now felt that he had been the unreasonable one and needed to make amends.

'You know how to get to the pub, do you?' he asked.

She nodded briskly. 'Yes. Absolutely.'

'OK . . . Well, I'll probably see you around then.'

'Quite possibly.' She gave him a wave as if shooing him away.

He looked at how she was standing.

'You've shut your jumper in the boot, haven't you?' he said.

She sighed. 'Yes. Yes I have.'

CHAPTER 13

Tuesday 13 May

1) Unless I calm down, I am likely to:
    A. Crash into a bus.
    B. Put my foot in everything right up to my thigh.
2) Jamie Mawson is a very, very attractive man. Attractive and shy – a devastating combination.
3) Greg Vasey is neither of these things. He is, however, related to a many-armed octopus. Or do I mean a slug? There's certainly a high level of slime.
4) Adopting your best 'Joanna Lumley fights for the rights of the Gurkhas' persona appears to be the perfect way of dealing with both octopus and slug tendencies. The rent reduction is agreed, but not secured. His need to 'draw up a new contract and drop it round' is, I fear, shorthand for 'I'm going to have another go at you under the pretext of presenting the contract to you for signature.' Joanna Lumley is going to have to wear big knickers with a reinforced gusset.

5) Natalie is a very friendly pixie with a backbone of steel. Probably how she has triumphed over what seems like a very 'interesting' background.

6) In the next life I would like to come back as Natalie (especially if I can have her legs).

7) I do not know much about babies. What I do know leads me to suspect that Natalie's mother is not pining for Natalie's father.

8) 'Tom' as a name has always seemed to me to belong to the type of man who is kind and honourable (if I can use such an old-fashioned word). Not to someone who veers between being friendly and open (explanation of baking, help with removal of jumper from boot) and bad-tempered and deranged (sarcastic backchat about me to Natalie, weeing in hedge incident).

9) Point 8 either means I am wrong about the name or there is something wrong with the person.

10) Some men should always wear a bib.

CHAPTER 14

Thursday evening and Tom knew that the closer he got to Newcastle, the more his mind would empty until, by the time he parked his car, there would only be one thing left gnawing away at it. And very soon after that, even this one thing would go and he would stop thinking completely. He would just do. And be.

He laughed. *Do be do be do.*

But still some way from the dual carriageway to Newcastle, his thoughts were anchored firmly at home. Had he locked the back door? Had he told Natalie to check that damn gum shield was out of Hattie's mouth before she went to sleep? Of course he had and, even if he hadn't, Natalie was capable of sorting it all out herself. She had looked after more children than he had.

Those questions he was asking were like worry beads – to be rubbed between his fingers and let go. Unlike the other fears that, now he had reached the slip road, sidled into his consciousness. First came fire, all-consuming. Next a madman with a knife and, lastly, the chunk of biscuit lodged in the windpipe.

He speeded up and, in the slipstream of a lorry, got on to the dual carriageway and headed east. The unrealistic fears diminished as he reminded himself again that Natalie was on watch – a non-smoker, fierce, good at first aid.

And then 'Steph' flashed across his brain as if a car travelling on the opposite carriageway had just signalled the word with its headlights. He pulled into the next lay-by.

'Natalie,' he said when she answered the phone, 'one thing I forgot to mention, and can you just listen without saying anything? You'll understand why in a minute.' In the background he could hear Hattie telling Natalie she was going to be red and he hoped she was laying out a board game and not planning to experiment with body paint.

'OK,' Natalie said.

'Thanks. Just . . . if the phone rings, can you check who it is before you answer? If it's an international call or a mobile other than mine or Rob's, please leave it. Steph rang twice on Monday and, complicated story, but I wouldn't want her to call while I'm out and stir everything up again. Oh, and when you put Hattie to bed, could you take the handset out of my bedroom? Hats has a habit of going in and picking it up when it rings.'

Anyone other than Natalie might have asked for a fuller

explanation, but in the light of her own home life, it must have seemed dull.

Back on the road again, he didn't waste a minute wondering whether, in this instance, preventing Steph talking to Hattie was the right thing. Hattie was still high on the promise of going skiing and seeing Steph and he was damned if that was going to be taken away from her. He had done what he'd promised and got on the computer to suss out suitable ski resorts close to Milan. The prices were boggling, so much so that when he looked at the notes he'd made and saw 2043 written down, he couldn't remember if it referred to the time of a return flight into Manchester, the price of a half-board package without ski-pass or the date when he'd actually pay off the loan he'd need to take out.

By the time he got to the sign telling him Newcastle was only ten miles away, Steph and Christmas and skiing had drifted away and now his mind was skimming through his earlier phone call to Kath. He'd wanted to check how the pre-natal class at the hospital had gone and had hoped to get her alone, but Rob was there. Kath seemed her usual calm self, but his brother had repeatedly shouted out comments until eventually Kath handed him the phone. He gave the impression that after just one session, he had become an expert on childbirth, but all that excitement seemed just a shade away from hysteria to Tom.

Five miles to Newcastle, and he was thinking of his mother. That was bad, she was the last person he wanted in his brain right at this moment. He forced himself to stop thinking about Rob's sighting of the rev.'s car outside her house that afternoon and focused instead on how good June's edition of the magazine had looked fresh out of its plastic yesterday. After that, he shoved work away to mull over whether Newcastle was going to sack yet another manager. That took him to the outskirts of the city where the traffic was so heavy he couldn't think of anything else.

As he pulled into the multi-storey car park, he wasn't a father or a brother, a son or an editor. He wasn't even a football supporter. He was Tom Howard.

He took the lift down to ground level, in his hand his mobile phone, a couple of files and a notebook. Already his heart rate was speeding up. Heading down to the river, he arrived at the theatre. A quick check on the posters outside and he was walking on past, the excitement in him building.

He got another surge of adrenaline as a text arrived and he smiled when he saw it consisted of just three numbers: a 3, a 4 and a 1. Brief and to the point. When he thought about that single-mindedness, he felt the familiar tightening of his stomach, the nagging sense of need in his groin. He crossed the road, ran up the steps of the hotel and walked purposefully through to the lifts. If he bumped into anyone he knew, he could nod at the files and the notebook and say he was here for an interview.

It was about now that anticipation usually tipped over into something else – it felt like a hunger so strong that it scared him to think what would happen if anything prevented him from knocking on that door with those numbers on it. By the time he stepped out of the lift on the third floor, the adrenaline was in charge of him, not the other way round, and his blood felt thick and sluggish, his brain dissatisfied with everything until he could feed this need he had.

He arrived at the door and laughed at himself. He was sure he could have knocked on it with his cock, it felt hard enough. He used his hand instead, remembering not to thump, although it was pointless trying to act cool. She'd known him long enough to understand how up for it he would be. And he knew she would be feeling the same.

'How lovely to see you again,' she said when she opened the door, even those innocuous words sounding heavily exotic in her Dutch accent.

He went inside. Four hours, to do anything.

'You look wonderful, Grietje.' The compliment came out without effort, because she did – dark-blue dress this time, linen, fitted at the bust and hips, ending where it showed her legs to best advantage. Bare arms, tanned this time of year. Bare legs too by the look of it, although he couldn't always tell until he touched them. Whenever he saw her he was struck by how blonde her hair was – that flaxen blonde of northern Europe that came with blue eyes and a clear complexion. She'd had it cut into a shaggy bob a few months ago and although he missed the way he could lose his mouth and his hands in her longer hair, this suited her better.

He liked the way she enjoyed being looked at. There was none of that 'I wasn't sure about the length of this hemline', or 'My arms, can I still get away with having them bare?'

A woman at ease in her own skin.

She offered her cheek for kissing. It always felt so formal this bit, so foreign, the turning of the head first one way and then the other for one, two, three kisses, but he knew she loved the build-up, the sense that they were strangers even though there was little about each other's bodies they did not know.

He had her perfume on him now, something from a bottle that was unfamiliar and smelled like old wealth and exotic travel, and something from her that smelled completely and utterly of sex – uninhibited and unabashed. Tom didn't know if all Dutch women were like her, but

Grietje understood what she wanted and was never afraid to ask for it. To her it was like making sure you got what you fancied in a restaurant and that it was cooked exactly the right way. Why be embarrassed?

He liked the directness of 'More slowly there, Tom. I like this and *this*. Now, what would you think if I . . . ?' Perfect English, even when she was being filthy.

She was appraising him, her eyes shining. The large pupils told him she was turned on too.

'Ah, but you look so well, Tom.'

He saw the knowing smile when her gaze loitered at his groin.

'Time to stop talking, I think?' he said, hoping that he didn't sound too desperate. She laughed – the type that made his stomach tense because it contained the command to wait and the promise that the wait would be worth it.

He watched how she moved towards the two glasses of red wine poured before he arrived. *Moved.* He couldn't really describe it as walking, something too languorous about it. That turned him on even more.

She only picked up one glass and returned to him, raising it in a toast and taking a sip. She leaned forward and placed her lips on his. As he opened his mouth, he took her and the wine in and got an instant hit from both – an extra layer of fuzz to add to the sexual static in his brain. Her tongue was warm and felt obscenely alive and he wanted to put his arms around her and grind himself into her, but she was pulling back. Another slow sip, another deep kiss. No touching.

'Grietje, please. My erection is killing me,' he said when she pulled away again.

A slow, wide smile and then, 'I don't understand, Tom, you need to say it in Dutch. Say it in Dutch and there may be a reward.'

Could he still think, looking at the way her lipstick was smeared, tasting it on his own tongue?

'*Mijn erectie* is killing me,' he dredged up. An easy one, the last three words particularly.

'Wrong pronunciation,' she said, frowning, 'last three words especially. "Muh" not "meeee".'

He tried again and obviously got it right because her hand was on his chest, pushing him towards the chair. He sat as well as he could, but his erection really was killing him.

Down went the wine glass, off came her earrings, her shoes. She bent and lifted up the hem of her dress and stripped that away too.

No stockings and no knickers, but a thing, he couldn't remember just at that moment what you called it. Sheer and cupping. Two of his favourite words in any language. He could see her nipples through the gauze. It made them look black but they were more a caramel colour. He had to stop himself thinking of the way they would change under his mouth, how she liked him to rake his teeth across them.

A body – that was the name. How the hell could he have forgotten that? Probably the sight of the flesh and blood one under it.

She went to the bed, reached under the pillow and placed the things she pulled out on to the bedside table, making a show of touching them, running a finger along the length of one of them. It should have looked over the top, but it was winding him up even tighter.

'Are they for me, or you?' he asked, his mouth suddenly dry. He reached out for the wine glass and took a large slug of the contents, knowing she would have seen the way his hand was unsteady.

'Depends,' she said, leaving the toys behind. 'Let's see if you deserve them.' She dipped her chin and looked up at him with a hint of a smirk. 'Or maybe I'll see if you misbehave enough.'

He tried to calm himself, but she was moving to the desk and making a big show of bending to move the files and papers on to the floor. He looked at the beautiful shape of her buttocks and the view of her breasts from the side, and knew she'd be enjoying the way he was studying her.

A lovely body, not dieted into shape but muscular and capable. He imagined her swimming at her summer home; easy, confident strokes.

'Jakob sends his regards,' she said as she finished clearing a space and he replied, 'And I send mine back,' although in truth he didn't want to talk about her husband now and it was the one part of her utterly straightforward approach to her sexual needs that he, old-fashioned little Englander that he was, would never get used to. He didn't want to talk about her other lovers either, those men who met her in hotel rooms around Europe to take her mind off venture capital and another night apart from Jakob.

'So,' she said, leaning her backside against the desk. First one strap was pushed down from her shoulders and then the other. She lowered the whole top to reveal her breasts, and however many breasts he saw in his life, that thrill never went. He had to will himself not to hurl his mouth towards them.

A smoulder of a look from her and then she was undoing the fastenings on the material between her legs.

What did his face look like at this minute? Yearning?

He thought of that first time he'd met her, when he had *really* been interviewing her – a woman whose bank was bringing jobs to the region. Had he looked like he looked now? Is that what had made her, when all the questions were over, reach under the table and put her hand high up on his thigh? He remembered the shock of realising that he'd stumbled on a woman who could provide him with something that, up until that minute, he hadn't been aware he needed. Someone who didn't want to get to know his family or the intricacies of his job or what had happened to his marriage, but who would love to have sex with him, vigorously, imaginatively, often.

He revelled in the fact that she was a secret and what he was doing seemed daring. That Grietje could never be fully his or even fully known.

'What would you like, Grietje?' he asked, trying to hurry her along to the moment when she'd let him touch her.

She thought about that. Licked her lips, he guessed, on purpose. 'This,' she said and gave him a little demonstration of what she meant, although you couldn't call it a dry run. 'And then again with your mouth.' She arched her back. 'Then however you want it, Tom. Rough. Gentle. Play a bit first.' He followed her gaze to the bedside table.

'So many choices.'

A soft, low laugh. 'So, what are you waiting for? A written invitation?'

Standing up, he felt lightheaded because every drop of blood in his body seemed to be in his groin, burning and bubbling and driving him to stand between her legs and kiss her deeply and roughly on the mouth.

He pushed her back on the desk and she flexed her hips, trying to rub herself against him and then he was moving away a little so he could lower his head.

'So many choices,' he repeated, 'a real smörgåsbord,' and then he was taking a nipple into his mouth and sucking and tonguing it. Smooth, then tightly budded. He brought up a hand to help him and felt her breathing quicken as he scraped his teeth gently back and forth. Everything about him felt hard and taut now – thigh muscles, stomach, cock, resolve.

'Not smörgåsbord . . . Wrong country, wrong country,' she said in little gasps. 'Smörgåsbords are for the Swedish, you stupid Englishman.' He could hear her need to come in the irritation running under her words, as if by making them harsher she could goad him into getting her there quicker.

'Wrong country?' he said. 'Really?' and moved his other hand between her legs. He slipped his fingers into the heat and the wet of her and those two sensations together made him close his eyes in an effort to pace himself. Slowly he slid his thumb to the place he wanted.

He stroked, slowly.

'The wrong country?' he asked again. 'And am I in the

wrong country now, too?' A push that sent his fingers deeper into her and caused a sharp pull in of her breath. 'Strange . . . feels like the right country to me, Grietje.'

Him in control now, her under him and responding. Wonderful to be able to do this with a woman again.

'*Niet stoppen,*' she said, urgently, and she was grabbing hold of his shoulders and pulling herself up so she could grind against his hand . . . '*Niet stoppen, niet stoppen . . .*'

'I'm never stopping,' he assured her, feeling wildly alive.

He didn't catch her reply, too busy concentrating on his thumb, on her and on that moment when he got to fall apart as well.

CHAPTER 15

Thursday 15 May

1) Four days in a row looking at microfiche leaves you with a pain behind one eye. Perhaps I could borrow Hattie's eye-patch. But it was the uninterrupted time I needed to reach the finish line. What a lot I learned along the way.

2) 1962 was an interesting year – although studying other people's wedding photos is not always an uplifting experience.

3) 1963 was another interesting year – and at least now I know how old Mrs Mawson is. And that she is an Aries. This does not surprise me.

4) Charlie Coburg and his wife, Penelope, did not seem like a matching pair. She was carved out of granite while he looked as if someone had squidged him together with their hands.

5) Jamie resembles his maternal grandfather. He definitely

has his mouth and, like him, appears to be the only one in the family who can move the muscles around it to make a smile.

6) Jamie's brother, Edward, likes to kill things. Things smaller than he is.

7) Tom's father died when he was very young – Tom and the father.

8) Tom does not look that different now from how he looked at seventeen in his rugby kit. Except he is about twenty years older, twenty pounds heavier and goodness knows how much more pre-occupied.

9) Charlie Coburg went missing from the newspapers during 1989/1990. Perhaps he was hibernating. (This is a joke, although not the funny kind. And a riddle to which I already know the answer.)

10) The library was very quiet. I suspect that the graveyard, when I can face it, will be even quieter.

CHAPTER 16

'What about a newt, then?'

'No. They're wild, they belong outside.'

'A parrot? All pirates have parrots.'

'Definitely not a parrot.' Tom accompanied the reply with a stern look into the rear-view mirror. It was completely wasted on Hattie who was staring out of the window, no doubt imagining striding over a quarter-deck off the coast of Jamaica with a parrot on her shoulder.

'Python?' she said.

'No. I'd find you missing and the python with a Hattie-shaped lump in it.'

'Terrapins?'

'Too snappy.'

'Rats? Baz keeps rats in his shed.'

'No. Baz *has* rats in his shed – as in, it's overrun. Come on, Hattie, guinea pigs are my best offer. And not till your birthday. And you have to clean them out and feed them.'

Hattie looked unimpressed. Guinea pigs were nowhere near exotic enough.

'Tarantula?' she tried, ending with a melting smile.

'Not in a million years.' He slowed the car. 'I did put your PE kit in the boot, didn't I?'

She nodded vigorously. Good, no need to execute a U-turn and hare back to the house.

Hattie was now practising her karate moves as much as she could while being strapped in, which seemed to signal the end of this particular episode of *Pets I Want and You Won't Let Me Have.*

As he parked the car outside school, he was a bit heavy on the brake and a large brown envelope fell from the dashboard into the footwell. It was addressed to his in-laws and contained two sets of photographs – one for Caroline and Geoffrey and one for Steph. There were some of Hattie holding the de-dinosaured bag and wearing the dress (cut down the back and pinned to a vest to make it look as if it fitted and to keep it in place). And some of Hattie in shorts and T-shirt. Tom liked the ones where Hattie was being herself, but he knew Steph would prefer the ones where she was trying to be someone else.

Also winging its way to Steph, via her parents, was a letter asking her, once more, to get divorce proceedings restarted and a briefer note setting out his plans to bring

Hattie to Italy in December. He wasn't looking forward to the phone call he was going to get when she read either.

When he arrived in the office, Liz had taken to heart his plea not to leap on him as soon as he got in. It gave him the opportunity to turn on his computer and trawl for information on the play he was meant to have seen in Newcastle the evening before. He made some notes from the theatre's website and scanned their Twitter stream to make sure Benedict Cumberbatch hadn't made a surprise appearance. With some judicious knitting, no one would be any the wiser that he'd had a really, really obscured view of the performance.

He didn't allow his mind to roam back over that room or Grietje – he wasn't that man here, although his muscles kept reminding him something spectacular had happened to them.

Liz, having obviously decided that it was safe to disturb him now, was standing in the doorway holding what he thought of as her little paper hand grenades.

'You look perky,' she said, coming in and sitting down. 'Obviously enjoyed the play.'

He kept his eyes on the computer screen. 'Yes. Very interesting. Very . . . challenging.'

Liz made a noise that could have meant anything and he stopped looking at the screen.

There seemed to be something sluggish about her this morning. Even her curls looked less bouncy.

'Rough night?' he asked, and she screwed up her face.

'Waited up for No. 1 to come in.'

Tom wondered how someone with as keen a sense of humour as Liz could refer to her daughters as No. 1 and No. 2. Still, that was less wince-making than how she referred to her ex-husband.

She might have said more if Victoria had not appeared. She leaned against the door frame, all bright-eyed and wide-smiled.

'Got some lovely pieces from that new jeweller who's going to move in next to the post office.' She must have seen his expression, because she added, quickly, 'It's OK, she does a range of prices.'

'Great. Good work.'

Victoria pushed herself off from the door frame, did an elegant turn and was gone.

Liz was able to convey the words 'brown-noser' in a variety of facial expressions. Today she chose to let her mouth drop open and cross her eyes.

Tom looked past her out into the office where he could see Monty. He actually appeared to be typing.

'See Monty's out-of-body experience is continuing,' he said.

Liz turned to look. 'He's finished one of his pages. It's on my desk now.'

'That's very worrying.'

Liz faced him again. 'Yup, and you know what else is worrying . . . ?' One of the pieces of paper was handed to him. It was headed up *Thailand for all budgets* and he guessed it was something Jamie had written.

'Hard to believe English is his first language, isn't it?' Liz said as Tom scanned through it. He could only agree.

'You got time to help him?'

Liz's look suggested she didn't. 'I've given him some old copies of the mag and told him to read, learn and rewrite.'

Tom put that problem to the back of the queue and turned to the more pressing one. 'Any breakthrough on the illustrator?'

'Felix is interviewing the last one now. Said could you pop up and discuss options. Half an hour or so?' She stood up and put her hand over a yawn. 'Other than that, things are peachy.'

'Peachy and perky, what a great team we make,' he said brightly, knowing it would get Liz out of the office like a shot. He followed her, noticing how Kelvin was, as usual, in orbit around Victoria's desk like some priapic moon.

Upstairs, he could tell by the expression on his Creative Director's face that the interview had not gone well. The polar opposite to Liz, Felix was unerringly upbeat – from his cheery T-shirt and jeans, to his face like a big-eyed open book with spiky cartoon hair on top. Felix's section was like a playpen; a couple of young designers, noses to Apple Macs, bright posters on the walls and silly gadgets on the desks.

'No go then?' Tom said, perching on the edge of Felix's desk.

Felix's earring danced with the ferocity of his head shaking. 'His work was great.' Tom was shown a photocopy of a drawing of a red squirrel.

'But?'

'But you would not believe what he wanted to be paid.' He named the figure and Felix was right, Tom didn't believe it.

'What did you tell him?'

'To stick his drawing of a squirrel where it'll always be near some nuts.'

'Good man. So . . . our options are . . .?'

Felix held up his index finger and thumb in a big 'O' shape and Tom went to the window and looked out into the square as he tried to think of a way through this problem. He watched the woman from the art shop cross to the post office and he was still standing at the window when she came back out. Something prodded at his sub-conscious.

He turned back to Felix. 'Borrow your computer a minute?'

He typed a name into the search engine. A quick double-click and he was looking at a website.

'Now that,' Felix said, peering over Tom's shoulder, 'that's more like it.'

CHAPTER 17

As Tom turned down the track, he saw the white four-wheel drive squatting there like a puffed-up Imperial Stormtrooper. It had Greg Vasey written all over it, literally. *Greg Vasey Estate Agent.*

Greg Vasey was nowhere near his favourite person and Tom hadn't yet managed a conversation with Fran that ended well. Put the two together and he saw only irritation ahead.

And what if they were *together* together? Going for a drink with Vasey was one thing, inviting him back to where you lived was something else. Maybe Fran was the kind of woman who could grit her teeth and shag someone she thought was a creep, just to get a bit off her rent.

And even if she agreed to do a piece for them, could they afford her? She'd worked for some pretty heavyweight magazines and book publishers.

Come on, Tom, where's your fighting spirit?

He got out of the car and thought about his fighting

spirit. That was actually the problem where Greg Vasey was concerned. He rarely bumped into the guy these days, but if he did, the years since school melted away. Shaggy's 'Boombastic' was in the charts, his mother was being embarrassing about Colin Firth's white shirt and Tom was dragging Vasey across the Tarmac behind the Science Building by his school tie.

Pathetic. Nearly twenty years had passed. Rob had let it all go; so should Tom.

He could hear the sound of a lawnmower, but there was no one in the front garden and no reply when he knocked, so he went around to the back of the bungalow. Which was where he saw a sweating Greg Vasey pushing an ancient petrol mower, wet patches under his arms and his shirt open to show a damp-looking chest. His hair, which was normally strand perfect, looked as if something large and spitty had licked it to his head. Tom was pleased to see all these things. If Greg could actually run over his own toes with the mower, he'd have been even more pleased.

Back at school, Vasey had looked like an undernourished weasel, complete with sandy hair and overbite. His role had been to stand beside the school bully, supplying encouragement. He'd filled out a lot since then, muscle mainly by the look of it.

Vasey stopped pushing the mower and gave Tom an unfriendly, shifty stare that showed he still harboured a grudge about having his nose rubbed, literally, into the school Tarmac.

Tom knew that he not only had to ignore all signs of hostility, but also fight his own impulse to deliberately wind Vasey up. So he did not ask, 'This a new skill of yours? Selling and renting properties *and* sweaty lawn-mowing?'

'What do you want?' Vasey said, as if Tom were trespassing, and turned off the mower with a showy twist of his wrist.

'I'd like to see Fran. She in here?' Tom indicated the back door and started to move towards it, but his question was answered by the appearance of Fran carrying a glass and bottle of beer. He did a quick scan of what she was wearing – another of those 1940s-type dresses, no shoes. Her hair was loose. Was it bed-head hair?

She made an 'Oh' sound and he waited for her to ask him if he had come round to pee in her garden again.

'Lovely day,' he got in before she could speak.

'Isn't it?' she replied with a smile that had a bit too much width to it, as if she was forcing herself to be jolly. Her eyes didn't look fully engaged with that smile either.

'That for me, doll?' Greg walked towards the beer and

Fran's smile solidified. She held the bottle and the glass out – really held them out, as if she wanted to keep Vasey as far away from her body as possible.

'You two know each other, I expect?' she said.

Neither of them answered and she looked quizzically at Tom. He figured that saying, 'Yes, I know him, he's the bastard who helped make my brother's first year at senior school a nightmare,' was not going to get the visit off to a relaxed start.

Vasey suddenly said, 'Still running that little magazine?'

Tom let it lie and turned to talk to Fran, but Vasey was speaking again.

'Suppose you saw in the paper, I'm about to open my second branch? Newcastle.'

Tom let that bit of one-upmanship lie too. He even, when Vasey went on with, 'Your Rob *still* at Wheatley's?' ignored the sneering undercurrent.

'Yes,' he simply said, 'my brother's done well. Thank you for asking.'

The urge to vomit in his own mouth because he'd been pleasant to Vasey was offset by the satisfaction of seeing the sly bugger realise that his efforts at baiting had failed. Perhaps he'd also heard echoes of the past in Tom's 'my brother' – as in 'touch my brother one more time and it won't just be your face I'm smearing over the Tarmac'.

'Any chance of a chat about the magazine?' he was able to finally ask Fran.

She led the way to the house and only on the threshold of the kitchen did she turn to Vasey. 'You're doing a wonderful job, Greg,' she called and, by the time they were in the kitchen, the mower had started up again.

Natalie had called the place a 'dump', and there *was* a frowsy air to the room. Everything looked shabby, although an effort had been made to brighten things up with jam jars and jugs full of wild flowers. The only plus point was the view over the back garden to the fields beyond and even that was ruined when the figure of Vasey, trudging along with the mower, cut across it.

'Come through to the sitting room,' Fran said. 'It's no more palatial, but at least it's away from that noise.'

As he followed her, he noticed a cooling rack bearing two sunken halves of a sandwich cake. 'Been baking?' he asked, remembering he was meant to be buttering her up.

'Yes. I was inspired by the county show, but it's harder than it looks. Especially in that brute of an oven.' That earnestness of hers was suddenly lightened by a laugh. 'Although a bad workman always blames his tools, doesn't he?'

The sitting room looked over the front garden and the old-fashioned three-piece suite had been pushed back to make space for a square table in front of the window. On it sat a board and some coloured paper, a ruler and a scalpel. There was more paper piled up in one of the corners of the room. Propped against the legs of the table were a number of box frames and Tom guessed they contained some of the work he'd seen on the website.

'Would you like to sit?' she asked, while she perched on the arm of the sofa.

He noticed that she didn't offer *him* a beer.

'So . . .?' She folded her hands in her lap like a child waiting to be told a story.

'Well . . . do you remember I told you about Charlie Coburg?'

'The gentleman who used to do nature drawings and notes for you?'

'Ye-es,' he said, trying not to stumble over Charlie being called a *gentleman*. 'And I think I told you that we haven't been able to find a replacement for him? Which is a big shame because our readers loved his stuff. The countryside plays a huge part in people's lives round here, so a magazine without a proper nod to the wildlife feels out of balance.'

'Very nicely put,' she said and then frowned and tilted her head. The noise of the mower had suddenly got louder, as if Vasey had also moved to the front of the bungalow.

Tom tried to ignore it. 'Anyway, I remembered seeing you come out of the art shop with all this paper and so I had a dig around on the Internet and saw your pictures.' He was having to raise his voice over the sound of the mower. 'Is it pictures or sculptures? Sorry, I don't know how to describe them.'

Vasey walked past the window and turned and peered in. It would have been comical if it wasn't getting in the way of Tom's mission.

Tom got up and walked over to the box frames. 'May I?'

Fran nodded, and as he bent to pick one up he saw she had turned her face back towards the window. It looked as if she was sucking in both her cheeks.

The frame he was holding contained a paper sculpture of a fox, the different shades of paper cut and layered so beautifully that you felt you could reach through the glass and stroke fur. The snout had a delicate fold to suggest the skull underneath and the thinnest of tendrils were whiskers. The fox was standing in a forest where the trees and even the brambles were cut from paper. Tom could imagine disappearing into the picture. To get such intricacy and depth from something that had started out flat seemed incredible to him.

'This really is beautiful,' he said.

'Thank you.' A tone in her voice made him turn and he

saw that she was beaming. Her eyes were definitely caught up in this smile.

He put the fox back and picked up a grey seal in an even greyer sea. The markings on its skin, the ripples of the water, all done in paper. There was a rock with tiny limpets off to the seal's left; the grey sea bleeding into the many blues of a horizon off to its right.

Even the readers who usually flicked past the nature pages would stop and linger over this.

Tom ignored yet another reconnaissance trip by Vasey and said, tentatively, 'I know you've done work for magazines before, so I was wondering—'

'No. Absolutely not.'

The sharpness of that response made him blink. 'No? Just like that? Before you've even heard what I was going to ask?'

'You were going to see if I'd produce something for your magazine?'

'Yes, but—'

'There you are then.'

'Can I just ask why?'

'Not really.' She paused as the noise of the mower stopped. 'I'm sorry that I can't help you and your readers, but it would be . . . difficult.'

'Because we've had some sticky conversations?'

'Literally,' she said, looking at his shirt.

Yup, she was starting to irritate him again. He tried to remember that he was an editor desperate to solve a problem.

'Look, you wouldn't be working with me,' he said, 'it would be our Creative Director, Felix . . .'

Tom trailed off as Vasey had appeared in the doorway, flicking some grass cuttings from his arm. He might as well have been wearing a T-shirt with I *am checking up on you* written across it. Tom tried to find the fact that Vasey considered him a threat amusing. Until Vasey said, 'How long did you work in London, then?'

'About twelve years.' Tom knew where this was leading.

Vasey nodded. 'Travelled all over, didn't you? Where did you live?'

'Yes, I did travel all over. And Fulham. That was the last place I lived.'

'Good part?'

Tom nodded and waited.

'Divorced yet?' Vasey jabbed at him.

'Not quite. Takes time.'

There was a snort from Vasey. 'Wouldn't know,' he said and, with a smile, left the room again.

A few moments later, the sound of the mower started up once more.

'Oh, really!' Fran crossed to the table and looked out of the window. 'Such an annoying man. Look, shall we go through to the kitchen? It's so hard to hear oneself talk in here.'

So, she *was* just playing Vasey for what she could get. Good luck with that.

In the kitchen, Tom had one last try at persuading her, ending with, 'And Mrs Mawson would see it as a huge favour.'

'Oh?'

'Definitely. She's Charlie's daughter – you probably weren't aware of that.'

Fran was looking over at the cakes on the cooling rack.

'I think,' Tom went on, 'she finds it painful to see Charlie's work every month when he's no longer around.'

He really had to watch these lies; that wasn't even a white one.

Fran was still staring at the sad-looking cakes and it seemed to be making her sad too.

'No, I'm sorry,' she said, finally. 'It wouldn't be wise.'

'Wise?' he asked and then couldn't help adding some swear words as the noise of the mower grew louder again. Vasey had obviously discovered they had moved from the sitting room.

'Oh, for goodness sake,' Fran said, closing the back door.

'Not only an annoying man, but such a difficult one to get rid of.'

'Perhaps you should have thought about that before you invited him round to cut your lawn,' Tom shot back, the discontent at her point-blank refusal to help him finally spilling over. 'Now he's going to want some kind of payment.'

He opened the back door again, even as her, 'I did not invite him round, he just turned up,' bounced off his back.

He kept on walking, watching Vasey travel the width of the lawn. When Vasey spotted that Fran and Tom had emerged, he changed his route to get closer.

'Are you listening to me?' Fran was behind Tom. 'He just turned up. Un. In. Vited. And why wouldn't I ask him to cut the lawn? It should have been done before I moved in. Goodness me! I'm surprised at your suggesting that making a simple request to mow a lawn is asking for trouble. I had no idea you'd be one of *those* men. Not a very nice message to be sending your own daughter.'

'I'm sorry,' he said slowly, turning to face her. He felt he was being told off by someone much older than he was. That back was as straight as an ironing board.

'It seems to me,' she started again, 'you're peddling that sexist rubbish about a woman being the one at fault if a man decides to make a nuisance of himself.'

'That's not what I meant.'

Vasey had stopped and looked as if he was trying to work out what was going on.

'What *did* you mean, then?' Fran asked. 'And, before you answer, can I just point out that you have, yourself, turned up uninvited, too. Is that also my fault?'

'Now hold on. First, I resent being lumped together with all those prats who think just because a woman accepts a drink, or dresses in a certain way, it's an invitation to . . . to . . .' Looking down into her face he was unable to say the word 'sex'. It was too fresh, like something just picked off a tree.

He tried a different approach, 'And stop acting as if this has just dropped on you out of the sky. Haven't you tried to manipulate Vasey to get your rent reduced?' He shook his head like an irritating know-it-all because he figured it would annoy her even more. 'Well, you have no idea who you're dealing with. Vasey sees a weakness and exploits it. You've poked a wasps' nest and now you're moaning that the wasps are trying to sting you.' He wasn't quite sure that was the analogy he wanted, but it certainly stirred *her* up.

'I see.' She waved a hand towards Vasey. 'So, if they find my dismembered body tomorrow, it will be my own fault?'

'Dismembered body?' He laughed. 'Oh he's not likely to

dismember you. Not unless you decide it's less horrendous to throw yourself under the lawnmower than him.'

The sound of the mower died. Fran closed her mouth and there was a shift of her eyes towards Vasey.

'Well, it's been a pleasure as always,' Tom said. 'Hope you have a good plan B.' He walked away, ignoring Vasey lumbering in his direction and skirted back round the bungalow and to his car. He felt the rush of heat as he opened the door and gave it a couple of minutes for everything to cool.

He still wasn't getting in the car. Should he really leave her on her own with Vasey? The guy was a bully, he treated women like a Neanderthal.

Not his problem.

He fast-forwarded the years and saw Hattie walking home one night by the side of the road, nobody kind bothering to stop, just leaving her for the psychopath to scoop up.

It was his problem. Every good man's problem.

With a sigh he closed the car door again and retraced his route to the back garden. Nobody about. He went towards the door and heard Vasey grunting. A groan. Fran's voice, urgent, a pleading tone.

And that was it, all the anger still sloshing around from 1995 was sending him charging through the door, hurtling through the kitchen, screaming, 'LEAVE HER ALONE, YOU GREAT BIG FUCKING BULLY . . .'

Two faces looked up at him, expressions astonished. And then they turned back to what they had been doing before he careered in on them.

It took a moment for Tom to work out that Vasey was lying flat on his back, mouth an open clench. Fran, kneeling by his side, appeared to be trying to persuade him to sit up. 'Come on, lean on me.'

'Aah, ahhh, ahhh,' Vasey went with every tiny movement towards a sitting position.

'Could you just push that chair behind his back, Tom?' Fran asked, and Tom did so as if in some kind of dream where he was a hospital orderly and Fran was Florence Nightingale.

'There,' Fran said with satisfaction when Vasey was propped up. She kept her hands on his shoulders and lowered her head to look in his eyes. 'Just keep breathing in, slowly and rhythmically.' Her voice was calm and reassuring. 'You went down with quite a thump, probably winded yourself when you fell.'

'Over what?' Tom looked around. Had Vasey fallen over his own feet? Or some stray air?

'Who knows?' Fran replied as if the whole thing was a mystery. 'The important thing is that he doesn't try to get up too soon, isn't it, Greg?'

Vasey looked up from under his brows at Fran and nodded and she smiled at him as if rewarding a good boy. 'Five minutes and you'll be as right as rain,' she assured him.

It was more like a quarter of an hour before Vasey could be helped to the car.

There was now more than a hint of ambulance about the Imperial Storm Trooper and Tom had to give Vasey a shove to help him up into the driver's seat.

Vasey was very subdued, and Tom sensed it wasn't just because he was in pain. When Fran said, 'Ah, is that the new contract there?' Vasey gingerly reached out for the papers on the passenger seat. A pen was located and first Vasey signed both copies, using the middle of the steering wheel as a rest, and then Fran signed them. When she handed him back the top copy, he didn't even look at it, just let it drop into his lap and started up the car.

After he had driven away, not in a particularly straight line, Tom asked, 'What did you do to him?'

She was still looking up the track. 'I could show you, but it's a manoeuvre I can only do properly when cornered. And absolutely livid.'

'Does that happen a lot?' He was remembering the dis-agreements they'd already had.

She turned to him and her eyes were infused with light,

as if she wanted to laugh but was being polite. 'Do you realise that's the second time you've asked me if I get into a lot of fights?' she said.

'And you've avoided answering the question both times.'

The light in her eyes was animating her whole face. 'No, Tom, I do not get into a lot of fights. That is only my third.'

He didn't know what to say to that and because she might at any minute bring up his embarrassing re-entry into the bungalow, he thought it best to go. This time he didn't wait for the heat trapped inside his car to dissipate, but he did put on his sunglasses because she was watching him and they made him feel less self-conscious.

As he drove away, she continued to watch him.

'No, don't thank me for trying to help,' he said as he speeded up and couldn't work out if he was relieved or aggravated that she hadn't.

CHAPTER 18

Friday 16 May

1) That saying is right. Men *are* like buses and you can wait and wait and then two turn up at once. Except I do not recall that I was waiting for a man this afternoon. Or a bus.

2) It is surprisingly difficult to make a Victoria Sandwich cake.

3) I need to be careful how I use the words 'please mow my lawn'. It is obviously as provocative as asking someone to 'come round the back and trim my lady garden'.

4) You can fit an awful lot of testosterone in a small room. Especially when there appears to be 'history' (unspecified) between two of the people in that room.

5) Tom is not a very good liar – I cannot imagine Mrs Mawson being pained by anything. Other than socialists running the country. It will take more than that to persuade me to break cover.

6) Some people have no manners.

7) Some people should not attempt to touch your breasts unless expressly invited to.

8) Mr Yakamito would be pleased to know that I remembered everything he taught me about unarmed combat. Shame I can't say the same about chemistry and maths.

9) It is annoying when a man has almost Victorian views about how women should behave.

10) It is not annoying when the same man does an extremely spectacular re-enactment of a knight trying to rescue a damsel in distress. It is, in fact, quite touching. Almost as touching as his embarrassment.

CHAPTER 19

Tom was meant to be looking at the proofs on his desk, but his mind was still kneading away at the problem of Charlie's pages. When the phone rang, he was glad of the interruption.

'Just wondered if you fancied some lunch?' his brother asked.

'Yeah, why not? A change of scene might give me some inspiration.'

'Thought we could have some sandwiches. I've already bought them . . . Got you something cheesy. Couple of bottles of water . . .'

There was a pause, during which Tom instinctively got up and wrestled the door shut. If he had to pick one word to describe Rob's voice, it would be 'wobbly'.

He kept his own tone light. 'So, where do you want to meet?'

'I'm in the cemetery.'

Tom's light tone went out the window. 'You're in the cemetery?'

'Yeah. Nice and cool here. Trees.'

Did that make any kind of sense?

No it didn't. Who had their lunch in the cemetery, besides flesh-eating zombies?

'I'll come straight away.' He looked at his watch. If he took the car, could he get there quicker? Probably not, traffic lights on the way, streets full of tourists . . .

'No need to rush,' Rob said. 'I'm talking to Dad.'

Tom nearly dropped the phone and had to do some juggling to prevent it from falling on to the desk.

'Dad?' he repeated, the phone back to his ear. 'Dad? Rob, what are you talking about? Dad's not there.'

Silence. Tom took the phone from his ear to confirm what he already knew; Rob had ended the call.

Tom should have seen this coming. First there was Rob's barely concealed hysteria after the visit to the hospital, then his reaction when Tom had broached the subject of skiing at Christmas. As usual Kath and his mum thought Steph had a nerve stirring everything up, but they understood the compromise Tom was trying to reach. Rob hadn't said much, but later he'd come up to Tom out of hearing of the others and said, 'It would have been good to have a child round the place at Christmas.' When Tom had shot back, 'You will have – your own,' Rob had screwed his mouth up and walked away again.

Tom managed the quickest exit from the office ever, barely stopping to give Liz a garbled outline of where he was going.

Talking to Dad! Their father's ashes had been scattered in the sea up the coast, over fifty miles away. If he could hear Rob from up there, he must have pretty good hearing in the after-life.

Outside in the square, the heat was building and the message coming off the tourists trying to find some shade was that they'd rather flop and forget the sightseeing.

Tom turned for the bridge and, as he crossed, looked down at the river to take his mind off what he might find in the cemetery when he got there. At this time of the year the water was wide and placid and dotted with small islands you could wade out to. On the one directly below him, a couple of women were sitting on a rug, a picnic spread around them while an assortment of children, some just in underwear, paddled and splashed and screeched. He remembered similar picnics with Hattie and a day much further in the past when he and Rob had jumped in with their school uniforms still on.

Thinking about Rob jumping in the river made him speed up. He was over the bridge and past the car park and could already see the village cemetery, bordered by a low wall. Today, in this heat, it seemed much further away than he remembered.

He realised he was doing a kind of half run, half walk and slowed down. No point in looking as if he was panicking.

He went in under the massive stone arch and passed between the two small chapels. Yes, definitely cooler here, with the trees creating great blocks of dappled shade. He scanned from left to right, his gaze snagging on the showy obelisk adorning the Mawson family tomb, before making progress past weeping angels and rugged crosses.

Rob was over by the far wall on the seat that faced away from the tombstones and looked out to the hills.

'Here you are,' he said, cheerily when he got nearer and Rob gave a start as if he had been somewhere else in his head. He scooted along the bench to make way for Tom.

'You look a bit hot,' Rob said. 'Here, have some water.' The bottle and some sandwiches were handed over.

Tom took great slugs of the water and tried to let the tranquil mood of the place get inside him – the sound of the breeze in the sycamore trees, the odd car going past just on the edge of his hearing. But he felt his brother's face didn't look right, as if he was working hard to make it appear normal, but bits of it kept drifting out of his control.

'Nice spot,' Tom said, unsure if it was better to talk or stay quiet.

'Aye,' Rob replied. 'Gives you space to think.' He put his half-eaten sandwich down on the bench between them.

'And what are you thinking about?' Tom asked, looking at the sandwich.

'I'm thinking: I can't do this. I just can't do it.' Rob was swallowing as if some of the sandwich hadn't gone down properly.

If this had been Hattie looking so sad and lost, Tom would have simply put his arm around her shoulders and pulled her in close. That probably wasn't going to work with Rob – a manly punch on the arm was the closest they got to bodily contact if they weren't the wrong side of a couple of beers. He pushed the remains of the sandwich on to the grass and chanced closing the gap between them.

'Has something in particular made you feel like this?' he asked, lowering his voice so that Rob would look at him. 'I mean, other than the worry over how Kath's getting along? The consultant hasn't said anything?'

Rob shook his head and appeared to be concentrating on the hills as if his sanity depended on it.

'The trip to look round the hospital . . .' Tom tried. 'Has it . . .?' He was avoiding saying "scared you?"'

Rob filled in the missing words anyway and shrugged.

'Bit, maybe. But I can see it's a good set-up they've got there. She's going to get the best care.'

Another period of hill watching.

'The classes then?'

Suddenly Rob was pressing his lips tightly together and then they were opening and he said, all in a gabble, 'So much to remember. Pain relief, breathing through contractions, the after-birth, stitches . . .' Rob's own breathing sounded not only too fast now, but wrong. As if he was taking in too much air and not pushing it all back out again.

'Hey, take it easy.' Tom did actually put his hand on Rob's leg then. 'Look, Kath's history means she'll get a lot of attention. And the medical staff will help you with all that stuff.'

There was nodding from Rob. 'I know, I know,' he said, 'but it's not just that. It's about seeing Kath in pain. About needing to be strong for her. And then what about afterwards? How will I know what to do about anything?' Rob's voice had been getting steadily louder, his breathing more ragged and on 'anything', Tom felt the muscles in his brother's leg bunch and he was struggling to his feet. 'Me and Kath, we've never got this far before,' he said, and it came almost like a wail and the sadness of it got inside Tom and scrabbled about in his chest.

Sod it.

Tom got up too and before Rob could object, pulled him close. He tightened his grip, feeling his brother's belly against his own and not caring. There was a small flare of resistance from Rob, before Tom felt him slump into him, and if Tom hadn't been the bigger of the two of them, they might have ended up half on the ground and half on the bench.

'There's so much to go wrong,' Rob said into Tom's shoulder, sadly. 'Do I lie the baby down on its front? On its back? How do I tell a cold from something more dangerous?'

'You learn as you go along.' Even as he was speaking, he registered that his brother's hair smelled of sawdust. 'You'll be fine. You just need to be there for Kath.' What did that platitude mean? He tried to be more direct. 'She doesn't need you to be strong. Bloody hell, she's a strong woman herself and you know she doesn't like to be fussed over. All she needs you to do is stay calm and not give her anything else to worry about.'

Was he getting through to Rob, or just smothering him?

'And just remember, everyone's hopeless at the start.' Tom discovered he was now rubbing Rob's back with one hand as if *he* were some oversized baby. 'I've told you what happened when I had to bathe Hattie for the first time in hospital?'

He repeated the story in the hope it would calm Rob.

'The nurse said to me, "Mind your watch," and I said, "It's OK, it's waterproof." And she said, sharply, "Mr Howard, I was *not* worried about damaging your watch, I was worried about the baby getting scratched." See, that's how hopeless I was.'

Rob started to push away, not violently, but with enough determination to make Tom let go. 'I know all that, mate,' he said, 'but what if Kath's brilliant at this and I'm not and she starts resenting me?'

'Kath? I don't think so. And listen, Rob, you and her are rock solid, you'll find a way through together. The pair of you are potty about babies and look how brilliant you are with Hattie.'

He'd lost Rob somewhere in that speech. He was peering over Tom's shoulder into the cemetery. Suddenly he said, 'Oh, hell,' his eyes widening, and he jerked back his head in an involuntary movement that looked like fear. Tom turned round and had almost exactly the same response. Something black was moving between the tombstones in the middle of the cemetery.

He felt Rob's hand on his arm. 'Jesus. It's not the phantom black cat, is it?' he whispered.

From time to time there were sightings of a large black

cat reported in the local paper, usually accompanied by a blurry photo and a vague eye-witness account.

The black shape all at once stopped being scary and became understandable. 'No, it's a person not an animal,' Tom said and then shouted, 'Hey!'

The shape stopped moving and a head appeared from behind one of the gravestones.

Grey-blonde hair.

As the rest of Fran rose up and into view, Tom could see that she not only looked embarrassed, but had obviously been crying. When she was standing upright, she gave him an awkward wave.

'Who the hell is that?' Rob asked.

'Woman called Fran Mayhew,' Tom said, not taking his eyes off her. 'Artist. Does paper pictures . . . sculptures. Wanted her to create something for the magazine. She's . . . she's a little unconventional.'

'You don't say.' Rob did an exaggerated mime of someone looking amazed.

Tom saw Fran glance towards the entrance as though she wanted to escape, but perhaps she realised that would seem weirder than the weirdness she was already involved in. She started weaving her way towards them through the tombstones. She appeared older today, more sophisticated in a sleeveless black dress and with her hair up. Black bag slung over her body and black shoes too, as if she'd been to a funeral. That would explain the crying.

'Is she dangerous?' Rob asked, out of the side of his mouth.

Tom thought of Greg Vasey lying on the floor. 'Possibly.'

Well at least that had taken Rob's mind off the baby.

Fran stopped a few feet away, smoothing down her dress as though she was deliberately trying to avoid eye contact.

Tom did not ask her if she usually crawled around in cemeteries – he sensed that it would not take much to make her cry again.

'This probably looks a bit . . . bizarre,' she said, as if choosing her words carefully.

'A little.' He'd wanted to add 'even for you', but let the better man in him rise to the surface.

'Well, the thing is,' she said, hesitantly, 'I did spot you both earlier and I was going to come over and say hello, but I didn't want to interrupt your . . .' She was struggling for words. 'Your embrace. It seemed so very intimate, that I—'

'We're brothers,' Tom said quickly at exactly the same time as Rob did. Rob was also pointing from his own chest to Tom's and back again repeatedly, just in case the words hadn't explained things enough.

Fran's smile animated the whole of her face so that for an instant the old her was back. 'Oh, you're brothers! Well, that's lovely. Not that it would have mattered if you hadn't been, but I would have felt I was interrupting something a bit . . . um, you know. Anyway. Brothers. Marvellous. Yes, I can see that now.' She stepped towards Rob with her hand held out and it was almost comical the way he looked at Tom as if to check it was safe to take it.

'I'm Fran Mayhew, by the way,' she said. 'You must be Rob. Your name came up when Tom was talking to Greg Vasey.'

Rob let go of her hand and Tom wondered how Fran managed to step unerringly on the mines in conversations like some demented sniffer dog. While Rob was philosophical about being bullied at school, it wasn't something he needed to be reminded about. Tom tried glaring at Fran, but she was focused on Rob, as if trying to work out why he'd let go of her hand so abruptly.

'I think it's an overstatement to say I was talking to Vasey,' Tom said, still glaring. 'He was talking *at* me while I did my best not to strangle him.' As Rob was still looking confused, he added, 'I went round to talk to Fran about the magazine and Vasey was there. He's her landlord. He was cutting her lawn. I was hoping he'd cut his toes off.'

Rob snorted. 'He's not worth even thinking about, mate. Tosser. Being himself is his own punishment. Shall we talk about something else?'

Tom wanted to hug Rob again. He didn't – twice in one lifetime would have been too much, so he just said, 'Good man,' and punched him on the arm.

He was waiting for Fran to mention that Vasey had ended up on the floor, but when he checked her face, her expression reminded him of how Hattie looked just after she'd said goodbye to Steph and before she put the phone back on its stand. He couldn't work out what it meant, possibly because at the same time, he was also appreciating the way the black of her dress looked against her skin.

'You been to a funeral?' Rob asked and Fran's expression solidified into one of misery again.

'No,' she said. 'I was much too late for that.'

Rob gave him a perplexed look and Tom batted it right back. Again he wanted to ask her what she was doing. Had she been hiding in the cemetery the entire time he'd been there? Or just walked in when he and Rob had been holding each other and plummeted immediately to the ground?

She appeared to have gone into some kind of trance and then, suddenly, she was saying, 'Well, this has been lovely, but I'd better go now. Goodbye, Tom. Goodbye, Rob.'

She had got as far as the gateway when he saw her stop, turn and walk back towards them and he waited with unease for the next weapon of mass tactlessness to be dropped on them.

Please God she hadn't heard them talking about babies and wasn't going to offer Rob some of her blunt advice.

She was doing that look again. 'Tom,' she said, gently. 'I've had a rethink about creating some work for the magazine. Do you think I could come in tomorrow, talk it through?'

She was gone again so quickly that he wasn't sure he'd given an answer, and that brisk pace of hers reappeared to carry her right to the gateway. But once there, her posture sagged and it was obvious that she had stopped pretending everything was all right with her.

CHAPTER 20

Tuesday 20 May

1) The graveyard was not quieter than the library.

2) Words on stone are much more upsetting than words on newspaper. There is something so final about them; a name: some dates, a trite piece of verse, that's all you get for a whole life.

3) Being really, really hollowed out and sobbing buckets does not stop you from noticing a thrusting obelisk and thinking how apt that is. It does stop you noticing that a man has come into the cemetery and is sitting quietly on a bench.

4) Hiding among tombstones is not an uplifting experience and may actually be against some kind of religious law. Also, crawling along the ground gives new meaning to the phrase 'maintaining a low profile'.

5) Two heterosexual men can look very jittery when you suggest they may have been involved in a gay tryst.

They are so busy telling you they are not gay or trysting that most of the questions you thought you'd get asked, don't materialise. Such as: where were you crawling away from?

6) I still have a monumental ability to put my foot in it – although perhaps in the cemetery context, monumental is an unfortunate choice of words.

7) With regard to point 6, it is obvious that Greg Vasey has hurt Rob in some way in the past and Tom still feels protective towards his brother about it. I wish that I had not only executed Mr Yakamito's Striking Cobra with Half Twist on Vasey, but also Charging Rhino with Full Flex.

8) Tom either has a squint or a thing about black dresses.

9) It is amazing how the sight of Tom gently holding his brother, and his efforts to protect him, can make you understand that he does have the right name (see entry for May 13). It also makes you even more intrigued about what life has done to him.

10) It is easy to reverse a decision you thought was watertight, because:

    A. The hardness of a monument and the sharpness of words are enough to convince you that it's vital to make a favourable impression on the person you came to see – before they know that you are you.*

B. Seeing siblings looking after each other (in a manly way, obviously) makes you feel that you're privy to something very tender, but also utterly, utterly alone. In this frame of mind, spending hours in a 'cottage' with only a scalpel for company is a bad idea. Getting out in the world is a better one.

* This may in fact be gibberish, as I am halfway down a bottle of Merlot. It is my second one.

CHAPTER 21

'This is absolutely wonderful, just like being in a galleon as it sails down Middle Street.' Fran was in the bay window of Tom's office, bending so that she could fit and running her hand over the surface of the glass as if it was precious to her.

He was watching Liz's expression. It was shouting, FRUITCAKE ALERT! FRUITCAKE ALERT!

'You're so lucky to have such a beautiful place to work,' Fran said, lowering herself into a sitting position and then jumping down from the windowsill. 'So *simpatico*.'

As she walked back to her chair, Tom could see she had plaster dust on her bottom. And that it was a very good bottom. He diverted his attention back to her face.

Fran had enthused about everything from the moment she'd entered the main office. She'd done it so fulsomely that he'd heard her before he saw her.

Liz, still looking wary, was asking Fran if she would like a coffee. To Tom the question sounded like a challenge being thrown down. Liz didn't like what she called *affected* people and he could tell that Fran, with her plaits and her cardigan with big multi-coloured buttons, was irritating Liz merely by existing.

'A coffee?' Fran asked. 'You have time to do that? But I thought you were the sub-editor – you more or less run the magazine, don't you?'

Liz glanced towards Tom as if she suspected some sarcasm hidden beneath those words. 'Yeah, well, I can do a lot of different tasks at the same time. No room here for prima donnas.'

Fran was oblivious to the way that last phrase had been aimed at her. 'Goodness,' she said, 'you muck in with everything? I do hope Tom appreciates that.'

'Of course I do,' he said, defensively. He got a big smile from Fran and a 'patronising git' look from Liz before she started moving for the door.

'I'll be back in a minute,' she said, grimly, and Tom found himself feeling sorry for Fran and what was about to come at her in a cup.

'So,' he said, trying to get Fran's mind back on to business. 'You said that you'd had a change of heart . . .?'

Fran studied him for long enough without replying to make him wonder if she'd heard him, but just as he was about to rephrase his question she said, 'Yes. A change of heart. Exactly,' and did a strange little smile before looking down at her hands.

'Great. I'll get Felix, the Creative Director I mentioned, to pop down. I'd also like Derek, our photographer, in on the discussion.' He glanced at Fran's website which he had brought up on the screen in front of him. 'I guess you might want to have your agent involved too? We can set up a conference call—'

'Oh, that won't be necessary.' Fran frowned. 'To be honest, Tom, my website is a teeny bit out of date. I'm what you might call "between agents" at present.'

'Between agents?'

'Yes. My last one was excellent at getting work, but I was beginning to feel a little like I was on a galley ship.' She grinned. 'Not a galleon. No sooner had I finished one commission than I was off on another. Did you see the sculptures for the shopping mall in Singapore?'

He found the huge waves with tiny boats riding on them. Just packaging all the pieces up and sending them off must have been a nightmare.

'Two months' work,' she said and grimaced. 'And then straight on to the Christmas windows for a store in Glasgow. And things change, don't they?' She peered at him as if expecting him to confirm that. 'I wanted to slow down for a while . . . and he wasn't very sympathetic. The only work I'm doing at the moment is to please myself. I suppose it's a kind of sabbatical.'

Tom wondered why she'd wanted to slow down, but guessed that was too personal a question to ask, so went instead for, 'Any particular reason why you chose North-umberland?'

She looked blank before saying, quickly, 'Castles . . . and . . . sheep. I heard there were a lot of sheep here. And beaches . . . Oh, goodness!' She suddenly got up. 'Is that an original ventilation grille?'

She was off to peer at what looked like a very dull piece of metal high up on the wall behind his desk. He took the opportunity to find the autobiography section of her web-site again. It told him practically nothing apart from the fact that she had lived in a variety of locations around the world and studied at Central St Martins in London.

'It says here that you studied in London, but I'm sure you told Natalie that you'd—'

'Been at Warwick?' She was still looking at the ventila-tion grille. 'Well done, Tom, you're very observant, I've noticed that. Which makes me very observant too, I sup-pose.' She laughed and sat back down. 'I started off studying Classics and Ancient History at Warwick. My mother's choice, but I hated the course. So I left and went and did what I wanted to do.' Another laugh, but not an amused one this time. 'Goodness. I had no idea you'd be checking my background. Are you worried I'll run off with the tea money? Or that I'm an imposter? So many questions, Tom.'

'No, it's just—'

'You think I'm a little strange?'

It was a direct question delivered with a direct gaze, and he didn't have enough warning that it was coming to deny it.

'Silence speaks volumes,' she said. 'But don't worry, lots of people think I'm strange.' She was leaning forward. 'But I'm going to say two words, Tom, that will help you understand me better.'

What, 'escaped inmate'? 'Alien life form'? No, that was three.

'Go on,' he said, liking the way her pale-blue eyes seemed to spark at that instruction.

'All right,' she said. 'Here they are: *home-schooled.*' She laughed. 'Ah, there it is, *that* look. The one I always get when I tell people. A mixture of amusement and pity.'

He couldn't deny what his face had been doing. 'Home-schooled,' he repeated, 'I'd never have guessed.'

'Very funny, Tom.' A quick flick of her gaze towards the ceiling and then right back at him. 'And before you ask, no, I did not have to be taken out of a conventional school for my own safety. We moved around a lot, my mother and I, and home-schooling provided me with continuity. And when we did settle somewhere, it was very remote, so being educated at home still seemed like the best solution.'

He wanted to ask why they moved around a lot, but Fran was sitting back in her chair with her arms folded. He remembered how much he needed her to solve the problem of Charlie's pages.

'I see,' he said, blandly.

'I doubt it.' Her tone was dust dry and she turned her head towards the window as if she needed time to gather together what else she wanted to say.

'While it meant I got a very good education,' she went on, 'I spent too much time with adults. And, of course, it made me a late starter with the social niceties. Where others can hear the conversation *under* the one that's actually going on and stay quiet, I tend to blunder in.'

'I hadn't noticed.'

She twisted her mouth out of the smile she might have been going to give in response to that. 'Hilarious, Tom. You would have got on well with my friends at college. They were always pulling my leg about how tactless I can be. Luckily my lovely personality won them over.'

'I've no doubt.'

'Of course the other thing I do is ask inappropriate questions. For example, is your brother all right? He seemed panicky yesterday and I could see you were worried about him?'

He hadn't seen that coming either. 'It was something and nothing. He's fine now,' he trotted out.

More lies. After Fran had left them in the cemetery, Rob had said he felt better, but Tom was one hundred per cent unconvinced.

Fran looked equally sceptical about his reply, so he said, sharply, 'Talking of inappropriate questions, what were you doing crawling around in the cemetery?'

He was especially eager to know since a quick scout around the tombstones had failed to reveal any new graves, any old ones with fresh flowers on them or, indeed, anything bearing the name Mayhew at all.

A dig around on the Internet had only brought up her site, a Facebook page dedicated to her work and about a million other people called Mayhew.

He expected Fran to be evasive, but if anything, her gaze was more intense. She kept staring at him and so he stared back. He was determined that here in his own damn office it wasn't going to be him that broke away first. Even when she said, 'Touché,' he kept looking into her eyes. But it was starting to get embarrassing. Did she realise that too or was that another social nicety not covered in home-schooling?

At that moment, she reminded him of one of the Mawsons with their impromptu staring competitions – the kind you only realised you were in when it was too late. He desperately wanted to blink. How the hell could anyone with plaits and a retroussé nose be so focused?

It was with huge relief that he heard the door open and he made a big show of being surprised that Liz was back so that he could escape from those blue eyes without looking as if he'd backed down. He wondered if Fran felt as relieved because, when she saw the cup Liz was carrying, she seemed to leap at the chance to be enthusiastic about it.

You won't be so bloody enthusiastic when you taste what's in it.

He was looking forward to this – he might have sailed close to defeat in the staring event, but Liz was going to walk it in the poisoning finals.

'Here you go,' Liz said, putting the cup in front of Fran. It was, even by Liz's standards, vile-looking. He watched as Fran took a sip and waited for the normal effort not to gag. The sudden lowering of the cup to reveal a smile that took in the whole of Fran's face was completely unexpected.

'Oh, Liz,' she said, 'you make coffee just like my mother used to. It's rare to find someone who has the knack. Thank you so much.'

Liz was peering at Fran as if she suspected the piss was being siphoned off in industrial quantities, but that delighted expression was unmistakably guileless. As they watched, it settled into something that had a slug of sadness mixed in with it – Fran was swallowing more times than she was sipping.

Tom was embarrassed all over again, but this time because it felt too intrusive to be an observer. He wondered whether that need to slow down that she'd talked about earlier had something to do with her mother?

It was likely Liz was thinking the same, as her combative expression was fading. 'That's all right. Glad you like it,' she said, resting her backside against the desk just along from where Fran was sitting. She watched her face for a while, before adding, 'So, you're going to help us out with the nature pages then? What did you have in mind? Tom says you've got a seal and a fox stashed in that bungalow of yours.'

There was one more deep swallow from Fran. 'It sounds funny when you put it like that.' She handed back the coffee cup and Liz peered into it as if checking it really was empty.

'You want me to go and get Felix and Derek?' Liz asked, one eye still on the cup, and when Tom said he did, she went off without a murmur.

That left Tom and Fran alone again and, even with the door open, Tom felt weird about it. He couldn't think of a thing to say. Fran appeared to be self-conscious too and started to look through her handbag as if hoping to find something to fill the silence. She pulled out a tissue and wiped her nose.

'Comforting to have your daughter with you while you work,' was the only thing that she did say, just before Felix bounded into the room. She was staring at the paperweight on his desk. 'Quite right too,' she added. There was a brisk nod of her head and a further application of the tissue.

Tom looked at the glass dome with a photo of Hattie at the base and was left with the impression that he'd passed some kind of test, but didn't know what it was.

Felix wanted to go for a three-page spread and ideally feature another animal along with the seal and fox.

'Ah, that's easy,' Fran said, 'I'll do a red squirrel to give it a real Northumberland flavour. If I can track one down and finish sketching it by the weekend, I should have the actual sculpture completed towards the back of the following week. Does that give you enough time for the photography, Derek? Felix?'

'It'll be quite . . .' Derek said, doubtfully, before Felix chipped in with, 'Do-able.'

'And what about the copy?' Liz had on her Eeyore voice.

'I'll see to that too,' Fran said, brightly. 'A tiny little bit about me – and then a lot about the animals – where to find them in the area, their habits etc.'

'Sorry to sound rude.' Tom made sure he looked it. 'But we need someone who can write to a high standard – plus the piece has to show a real knowledge of the area. And what with you not being a local—'

'Oh I've made quite a study of this part of the world, Tom. I'm sure I can give it the Northumberland flavour you want. And yes, I can write to a very high standard.' She paused. 'Although I use a slate, obviously . . .'

'A slate,' Derek repeated, 'why do you use a . . . ?'

'I was just pulling Tom's leg,' Fran said, patting Derek's and making him jump. Tom wondered if a woman had ever patted anything of Derek's before.

'But joking aside,' Fran carried on, 'would it be acceptable for me to come into the office to work? It's always nice to feel part of something.'

'She could have Charlie's old desk,' Liz suggested.

'Charlie's old desk? No . . . I . . .'

'It's a dumping ground for all sorts of crap. I'll get Jamie to clear it for you.' Liz stood up. 'And, if you're going to be part of the furniture, let's get you introduced.'

The meeting broke up then and Tom re-applied himself to checking the ever-increasing pile of proofs on his desk. When he looked up, he saw Victoria standing by Charlie's old desk, talking to Fran. He wondered what the two of them would make of each other.

Next time he glanced up, Fran was chatting to Jamie

with the same look on her face as she'd had outside the bookshop. Smitten.

He re-applied himself to the proofs.

He'd moved on to something from Monty when there was a knock on the door frame.

'Look at you,' Natalie said, 'captain of industry.'

'Yeah, thanks. Have you come to babysit one of my staff?'

She glanced back over her shoulder. 'That'll be Jamie then.'

Behind her, Tom saw Jamie bend over his keyboard, his face already going red.

Natalie came into the room. 'I'm here to pick up Fran. Thought I'd pop my head in, say hello, and ask if you wanted me to pencil in next Thursday for babysitting?'

He looked back down at his work, avoiding Hattie's eye in the paperweight. 'It'll depend how next week pans out – whether I can get away.'

Code for: it depends on when Grietje texts me.

'No problem.' Natalie had moved over to the bay window and was running her finger over the sill. 'What are you paying your bloody cleaner?'

'I've no idea . . . You said you've come to collect Fran?'

'Yeah. Off into town, see a couple of bands. Ah . . . here she is.'

Fran was in the doorway.

'Ready to go?' Natalie asked.

'Yes, all set. And, Tom, I've given Liz my mobile number if anyone needs to contact me. I'll let you know how I'm getting on.'

Tom wanted to ask what bands they were going to see, but was afraid he wouldn't have heard of them and would look even older than he already felt. And he wanted to ask how the two of them had got together again after that initial meeting outside the bookshop.

And would calling it a 'concert' mark him out as a real old fart?

He heard Natalie winding Jamie up one last time as she passed by and then it was Victoria loitering about near the door. 'She's a one-off,' she said, obviously feeling she didn't need to explain who she was talking about.

'Certainly genuine,' Liz said behind her. The barb was not lost on Victoria, who did that elegant pirouette of hers and went back to her desk.

'Liz,' Tom said, 'easy on the loaded comments.'

Liz snorted and did a parody of Victoria's pirouette, which was ruined by having to steady herself on the door frame as she came to a halt. 'I think I'm going to like her, Fran. Mad as a box of frogs, obviously, but a lifeboat kind of person.'

'Lifeboat?'

'Yeah. She'd help you catch fish and collect rainwater. Whereas Victoria would club you to death and eat you.'

Tom got up when Liz had gone and looked out of the window. Suddenly Kelvin was at his elbow, standing on tiptoe to get the last possible glimpse of Fran and Natalie before they turned the corner out of sight.

'I would,' he said, 'wouldn't you?'

When Tom ignored the question, Kelvin added, 'Very sexy – pert, hell of an arse.'

'You want to stop dribbling down my arm, Kelvin? And can I just remind you, that's my daughter's babysitter you're talking about. Told you before, I don't like the sexist stuff.'

'I wasn't talking about Natalie. Her family's trouble. I was talking about the one in the dress. She's like a posh Debbie Harry.' Kelvin was screwing up his face as if considering that and added, 'How she was in the eighties, obviously, not like she is now. Don't tell me you didn't knock one out every time Debbie was on the telly?'

'Well done, Kelvin. Ageist and sexist in one disturbing parcel.' Tom moved so that the desk was between them. 'Anyway, you're ten years older than me and Debbie Harry was white-blonde. Now, bugger off.'

Fantastic. Not only did he have an image of Debbie Harry in his head, but also a much worse one of Kelvin as a teenager.

CHAPTER 22

Wednesday 21st May

1) Acting strangely can be a result of being frightened (see point 2) and/or because when you walk into an office, you are aware that you are walking in the footsteps of ghosts.

2) On first meeting, Liz seems blisteringly scary. It is only later that you realise she is a woman who wants to be:

    A. Taken seriously

    B. Not taken for granted and

    C. Freed from having to babysit people who might be weird or hopeless at their job or both.

3) You can have a bottom covered in plaster dust that nobody notices until your friend points it out to you on the street. Even Kelvin did not notice because I'm sure if he had, he would have tried to brush it off for me (see point 9).

4) When I am nervous, I not only blurt out tactless things, but seem to have developed a love of architectural

detailing. Especially creaking floorboards and dusty old plaster grapes which you leap on as if they were the Holy Grail (or should that be grille? – sorry, poor joke). I could not work out if I was inhabiting the soul of Kevin McCloud, or in the case of Tom's window, Johnny Depp. (Window is magnificent, though, can imagine Hattie and her eye-patch take up position there on a frequent basis.)

5) No amount of telling yourself beforehand that you will *not*, repeat, *not* tell anybody that you are home-schooled, will work in the face of Tom's nosiness. Tom's ability to ask questions and remember the answers is worrying.

6) Tom is not easily stared out, but I think another minute and I would have done it.

7) It is amazing how the taste of over-stewed, too-strong coffee can make you want to put your head down on a desk and weep.

8) It is also amazing how your reaction to the taste of old, too-strong coffee can make a woman who you thought was going to be very tricky indeed become someone you would very much like to have by your side in an emergency.

9) Tom has an interesting mixture of staff and it is too early to say what I have learned about any of them.

Except for Kelvin. I have learned not to stand too close to him or to bend forward without first putting your hand modestly to the neckline of your dress. He made the lads drinking three shots for five pounds in town later seem very well behaved – although that could have been because I was a 'friend of Natalie's'. This is not the same as being a 'friend of Dorothy's'.

10) There are worse people to have a staring competition with than Tom Howard.

CHAPTER 23

He was beginning to think that the bookshop was some kind of magnet for people he knew. This time it was the unmistakable shape of his mother that he saw standing outside with her trusty wicker basket over her arm.

'You do know they don't sell cleaning products in there, don't you?' he asked, coming up behind her and making her jump. He should stop doing that.

'Idiot,' she said, swiping his arm with the back of her free hand. 'And don't be so cheeky, I can read. I can even do it without moving my lips.'

He looked into his mother's basket for some clue to what she might have bought, but was distracted by an A4 envelope with her name on it.

She must have seen him looking. 'Just been to a meeting with the Secretary of the Show to discuss the Mrs Egremont incident,' she explained. 'We've all been given new guidelines.' There was a pull down of his mother's mouth.

Tom nodded in what he hoped was a sympathetic way.

'Anyway, enough of that,' his mother said. 'I'm meeting Kath in a minute. So tell me quickly, what's going on with your brother?'

'In what respect?'

'Stop playing the fool, Tom. You know what I mean. I understand that he's worried about Kath and the baby. Why wouldn't he be? But it seems to have got worse recently. Are you telling me you haven't noticed?'

Tom found it relatively easy to lie to his mother about the massive things in his life – the state of his marriage when it was dying; why he had brought Hattie north – but he had never been able to lie to her about his brother. It would have felt as if he was betraying the tightly knit, triangular relationship that had been the bedrock of their lives after his dad had died.

He told her about the latest conversation he'd had with Rob, but omitted to say it had taken place in the cemetery, or the comment about 'talking to Dad'.

Patting things into a less worrying shape didn't count as lying, did it?

'I'll have to have a chat with him,' she said when he'd finished. 'Oh, don't worry, I won't drop you in it. He's going to suck all the enjoyment out of this for Kath. I mean, she's nervous too, but *she* just gets on with it.'

'To be fair to Rob, he realises that.'

A brisk nod. 'Leave it with me. Slowly, slowly, khaki monkey.'

She shifted her basket from her left to her right arm as if to underline the truth of that statement and Tom was thinking that was a good mash-up of words, even for his mother, when he noticed that the contents of her basket had shifted too. The envelope had slipped over enough to reveal a steak, all snugly wrapped in its plastic tray.

His mother had been a vegetarian since she was a teenager.

'You know what we need for Rob,' Tom said, looking pointedly at the steak, 'someone with good listening skills. A counsellor, say, or a *vicar* . . .'

His mother raised her chin and gave the basket a jiggle, perhaps in the hope the steak would get covered up again. It didn't.

'They have a good choice of books in the shop,' she said, turning to look in the window. 'I might bring Hattie—'

'Or,' Tom went on, 'what would be even better, would be one of those retired vicars who has more time to devote to him.' He moved so that he was in his mother's sightline again. 'Hey, just had a brilliant idea – someone like Rev. George would be perfect. He's retired, isn't he? Now . . . if only we knew how to get in touch with him.'

His mother looked as if she was losing her patience and

then her expression changed to a smug one. 'Oh,' she said, 'here's Kath. Just when I was getting a headache . . .' There was a hawk-like stare at him before she was all smiles for her daughter-in-law.

To Tom's eyes, it seemed as if the baby was ready to come at any moment and there was definitely a trudging look to Kath's walk, but she said, 'Playing truant?' cheerily to Tom and gave him a big kiss on the cheek. Her skin felt hot, even though the sky was mostly overcast today.

'Hope you're ready for some serious shopping,' she said to his mother. 'I want to get a couple more sleepsuits and take a look in that shop near the estate agent's. They've got some lovely little knitted hats.'

Tom never failed to be touched by Kath's optimism. He just wished his brother would catch some of it.

'Sounds expensive,' he said.

'It's my treat.' His mother put her hand up as if she knew Kath would remonstrate and the basket over her other arm wobbled.

He saw from Kath's face that she had spotted the steak.

'That's really kind of you, Joan,' she said, 'but only if you let me treat you to lunch.' There was a cheeky look Tom's way. 'The cafe on the corner does a nice steak and onion pie.'

Tom nodded his head. 'That'll get you revved up, Mum.'

He saw Kath press her lips together and look away.

With what she probably thought was a great amount of subtlety, his mother rearranged the contents of her basket so the steak was no longer visible.

'Sometimes,' she said, giving them both a sour look, 'you two talk complete gibbonish. Now come on, Kath, I'm sure Tom has to be back at the office.'

Tom was still wondering if his mother's mangling of words was going to be completely primate-themed from now on, when he pushed open his office door to find Liz sitting in his seat.

'You're breaking our agreement,' he said. 'It still counts as leaping on me as soon as I get in even if you're sitting down.'

'*Verbal* agreement, Tom. And I had my fingers crossed behind my back when I said it.' She stood up and, with a grin, thrust a piece of paper at him. 'Thought you'd want to see this as soon as possible. It'll cheer you up.'

Jamie's copy. Tom's irritation slowly changed to surprise as he read. This was good. Interesting. Punchy.

'How has he suddenly improved so much?' Tom looked towards the open door where he could see Jamie sitting at his desk, slowly and methodically eating a bar of chocolate and staring at the far wall. The way he was swivelling his chair made his fringe flop. It suggested he was feeling more light-hearted than usual when faced with a keyboard.

'You didn't help him with this, did you, Liz?'

She made a 'Did I bollocks?' face. 'Fran was in this morning. Said she'd had a brainwave about how to make her feature look even better – drop flowers over the page and fit the copy round them. Should have heard Felix and her, like they were going to orgasm together.'

Tom wished Liz hadn't placed that image in his brain. 'Not sure where this is going, Liz?'

'Where it's going is that after she finished talking to Felix, she came down here. She wanted to do some research about red squirrels. That's where she is now, up at Slaley Forest, just finishing off her drawing of one of the little buggers. Anyway, I got stuck into something else, and Jamie and her were chatting away, heads together. When she leaves, Jamie hands over the wundercopy.'

They looked out at Jamie again. He was trying to tie the empty chocolate wrapper in a knot. One particularly energetic swivel of his chair brought him round to face them. He saw them looking, might even have seen the paper in Tom's hand. He was soon eyes front, hands on his keyboard.

'Guilty as charged,' Liz said smugly, 'he knows we know.'

'Thanks, Miss Marple. OK, we'll see how he gets on with

his next couple of articles. Right . . . shut the door after you.'

He settled slowly back to his work, but he was disquieted by an image of Fran and Jamie's heads in such close proximity, blonde against dark.

When the phone rang, he thought at first it was Kelvin taking the piss with some heavy-duty heavy breathing. Then he realised it was someone panicking and trying to talk at the same time.

'Tom,' Fran said, 'oh, thank goodness you're there. I'm so, so sorry, I know how busy you are . . . but I didn't know who else to trust. I've had an accident. A terrible, terrible accident.'

CHAPTER 24

'Yes, definitely dead.' Tom stood up and brushed the soil from the knees of his trousers, noting again the way the radiator grille was buckled. 'That doesn't look so good either.'

'I know both of those things, Tom.' Fran glanced at the body under the wheel. She no longer sounded panicky and he supposed that she'd had time to calm herself as she'd waited for him to arrive.

Through the window of the car he noticed the large sketch pad on the back seat.

'When Liz told me you were finishing off a red squirrel, I had no idea she meant it literally,' Tom said. 'So, did you *get him* before you *got him*?'

'Tom!' she said, sharply. 'How can you make a joke at a time like this?'

Hard to believe someone could open their eyes so wide.

'It's a squirrel, Fran. You haven't mown down a child or a pensioner.'

'But it was so beautiful. Its bushy tail, its little tufted ears.' She was bending down to peer at what was left of the squirrel – which didn't include the tufty ears or very much of the tail.

He gave her a couple of seconds before asking again, 'Well, did you get it?'

She was still looking down, so her 'yes' was only just audible.

'One way to look at this,' he said, trying to cheer her up, 'is that he'll get a permanent memorial. In paper. He'll live on in—'

'Don't patronise me, Tom.' She jerked back up straight. 'If I'd swerved the other way when it ran across the road, I'd have missed it and the tree. I could blame the sun . . .' She gave it an accusatory squint. 'It blinded me at the crucial moment. But really this is no one's fault but mine.' Her shoulders rose and fell and he looked at the sun too, slanting through the trees like so many diagonals of light and making the forest seem more secluded and secret.

No sound, not even a breeze in the leaves. Everything at peace.

Especially the squirrel.

He watched how the sunlight caught her hair and brought out the silver, and then he saw her hair move as she shook her head.

'The poor reds have a hard enough time as it is against those lumpish grey things,' she said. 'Fighting over food, getting the pox from them.'

To Tom it sounded like a typical Friday night round the kebab vans on Newcastle quayside, but he kept that joke to himself and offered her the platitude, 'Accidents happen.'

She looked unconvinced. 'But the reds are getting rarer all the time, and I've made them even more so.'

'Well, how about you run over a grey on your way home and even things up again?'

Her admonishing look was back. 'Have you no heart?'

He was about to reply when she became businesslike. 'No good moping. I'll just have to report it.'

'What?'

'I saw on the Internet that they monitor them – numbers, geographical locations, that kind of thing.'

He could feel his patience begin to stretch. His desk was full of work and standing on the edge of a forest discussing a dead red squirrel with a woman in a floral dress was not on his To Do list. 'They aren't pin-point accurate studies,' he said. 'They don't give them names – it's not a case of "Come in, Red October, your time is up".'

How could he possibly have entertained the idea that she was in any way normal?

'But—'

'For God's sake, it's a bloody squirrel – a *really* bloody squirrel. Just reverse off it and drive home.'

She pulled back her shoulders and Kelvin's comment about her being 'pert' drifted across his mind.

'You know when you were home-schooled?' he asked, to take his mind off the pertness.

'Ye-es?'

'Was it in a cupboard? Totally away from how the world really works?'

Fran was sucking in her cheeks as she had done when irritated by Vasey. When she did speak, it was in a clipped, formal fashion.

'If you've quite finished, Tom, I agree that I believe things matter when they don't. I can find myself weeping at the sight of a dead cat as I think of its owners, waiting vainly at home for—'

'We're not talking family cats here, we're talking squirrels.'

She studied him. 'Yes,' she said, finally. 'You're right. All we need to do is bury it.'

'What! In a forest? Where, unburied, something bigger would simply eat it within minutes of you driving off?'

'This is not about being practical, it's about doing the decent thing,' she said firmly. 'Oh, and *driving off*? That was the other reason I called you. The car won't move. I think I've done some serious damage to it.'

'Not as much as to the fucking squirrel!' he shouted, his patience finally going 'ping'.

During the ensuing silence, he realised he had plonked his hands on his hips and quickly moved them.

'Very funny,' she said, when he was just beginning to think she was not going to talk to him any more. 'Very funny, but also quite cruel . . . and, Tom, I have no idea why a person who *can* be kind is choosing to be difficult. It doesn't do you justice. And, if you turn your back on me now, well, I'm not sure how our working relationship will survive unscathed.'

Was she blackmailing him – help me bury this squirrel or you won't get the paper one? He didn't feel blackmailed, he felt like a naughty boy hauled out in front of the class.

The sun was still slanting down, the forest was still green and dark and quiet. All at once he was aware how big the trees were and how he felt dwarfed by them. Yet standing here, out of his office and out of his car, he was inextricably linked to them. Him, this woman, even that damn squirrel.

He couldn't look at Fran. Easier to focus on the trunk of the tree damaged by the car.

'Have you called the car hire company?' he asked, still looking at the tree.

'Yes, they're sending someone out with a breakdown

lorry.' Fran's tone softened. 'But I'd still like to bury the squirrel before they arrive. What do you think, Tom? Help or hinder?'

'I really, really do appreciate this,' Fran said, looking down at the mound of leaves and twigs that marked the squirrel's last resting place. 'I know how hard it was to get anywhere in this soil.' She looked up at him and there was one of her big smiles. 'Inspired using the corner of that file as a scraper.'

He was trying not to engage with that smile. 'So. Do you want to say a few words over him?'

'Good Lord,' she said, her eyes widening, 'even I'm not that strange.'

He wasn't inclined to correct her because he was feeling very strange himself. At first he thought it was the exertion of pushing the car off the squirrel. Later, that it was a reaction to having bits of squirrel on his hands. Now he didn't know what it was, not with that smile blazing away at him. Or that look that suggested he'd done something monumentally wonderful for her.

It was like sea-sickness without the nausea. Then again, his head felt as if it was packed with wadding, so perhaps he was getting an ear infection and it was affecting his balance.

He walked towards his car, his thoughts sluggish but his senses in overdrive. The bright light was hurting his eyes and every rustle of a leaf and snap of a twig sounded too loud.

Perhaps he was dehydrated. He turned to Fran to ask her for a drink, and glugged down the water she got from her car, hoping it would cure everything. As he lowered the bottle, he heard the noise of something heavy approaching along the road.

'That will be the truck,' Fran said. 'I'll be fine from here on in, but before you go, Tom . . .' She put her hand on his arm and he looked down at it, wondering why he wanted to simultaneously draw away from her *and* roll up the sleeve of his shirt to reveal his skin. He felt her press down on his arm and knew that she would also be pushing herself up on her tiptoes and leaning in to him. In places their bodies touched and he knew how this dance, which was hard-wired into everyone, would end. He would first feel the heat of her, then her breath and then her lips on his face, and he would need to turn his head right now if he was going to ensure he felt all that on his cheek and not, more intimately, on his mouth.

He wasn't turning his head. He still wasn't. No, not even now. And then, at the last possible moment, he did and felt relief before disappointment came surging after it.

He heard her whispered 'I'm really touched that you put yourself out so much for me.'

He was in the car after that. Had he said goodbye? All he knew was that he was driving and then stopping again in a lay-by.

It wasn't an ear infection or the sight of squashed squirrel or even dehydration that was making him feel strange. It was the fact that he'd started the day knowing irrefutably that someone was not and never could be his type, never mind how hot they looked in a black dress. And then, somewhere between her irritating the hell out of him and burying a dead squirrel, he had discovered that her face, the way she looked into the sun, her determination to do the 'decent' thing, had all become lovely and sexy and the kind of fascinating that you just wanted to spend more time with because without it you felt you were simply sitting in a dusty room waiting for life to begin.

'Oh God. Oh God,' he said to the windscreen. 'Oh God. I have lost my bloody mind. I am a sad, middle-aged git who has lost his mind.'

But what if it's not your mind you've lost? What if it's your heart?

'Shut up,' he said, also to the windscreen. 'Shut the hell up.'

CHAPTER 25

Friday 23 May

1) It is possible to start the day in an office and end it in a breakdown truck.

2) The only sound more distressing than that of red squirrel meeting tyre, is red car meeting tree.

3) Tom's irritation comes with personal comments and cruel humour. His anger comes with shouting and a way of putting his hands on his hips that looks very camp.

4) A lot of men would have given up trying to dig a shallow grave in a forest. It takes a certain kind of man who would elicit the help of a stationery product to complete the task.

5) I have just reread point number 4 and feel I should make it clear that the grave was for a squirrel. I would hate anyone to arrest Tom on suspicion of burying his wife.

6) I have just reread point number 5 and feel Freud would have a fine old time with it. 'Vy, Miss Mayhew, did your mind immediately go to Tom's wife and the getting rid of the same?' Hmmm.

7) Tom is squeamish. He looked particularly queasy after burying the squirrel and me kissing him did not help. The only way he could have looked more uncomfortable was if I'd been wearing a barbed-wire hat. Perhaps it is not the custom to kiss people as a sign of friendship and gratitude in Northumberland? The poor man was completely rigid (not in that way, you dirty devil, Freud). He could barely move his neck to offer me his cheek.

8) It is possible to be both disappointed by a man's reaction to a kiss and relieved. Disappointed? It's always gutting to know that a man thinks you have all the allure of a used pan scourer. Relieved? Because the only man I should be concentrating on having a relationship with is Jamie. (Trying to have a relationship with his brother may be tricky bearing in mind our differing views on dead wildlife.)

9) It is impossible to look at Jamie without thinking:
   A. You are very, very attractive.
   B. You are very sweet.
   C. You should have paid more attention in English lessons.

10) Crying over a squirrel is all very well, but soggy paper is impossible to cut.

CHAPTER 26

'It's a bottle. But it's made of chocolate. It's made of chocolate, but it's a bottle.' The clear window of the large cardboard box Hattie was holding was steaming up under her enthusiasm.

'Think we got the idea, Hats,' he said, 'but haven't you forgotten something?'

He gave her his special stare, accompanied by a subtle jerk of the head towards Natalie.

Hattie finally twigged. 'Thank you, thank YOU, THANK YOU, NAT-LEE.' Two seconds later, she was pressing her nose to the see-through window again.

'Well that looks like a hit,' Natalie said, shrugging off her jacket and throwing it on to the kitchen table next to the folder and text books. 'I thought, seeing as that tree house will spend so much time being a ship, it needs to get launched. You got time to hang around, see us do it?'

'Yes, if we're quick. And you, Natalie, are a genius.'

Natalie gave him a look which suggested that was self-evident, before sniffing the air. 'What was it for tea then, Hattie, curry? Save any for me?' The questions were accompanied by a lunge and some enthusiastic tickling during which Hattie tried to defend herself while still clinging on to the box.

Perhaps it was a day for good things: this impromptu launch, Grietje later; she would sort out whatever kinks in his libido had made him go weird up in that forest, kinks he'd been trying to ignore despite Fran appearing regularly in the office and insisting on looking gorgeous. And, just before he'd got the curry out of the oven, there had been a phone call from Caroline and Geoffrey. They'd been out for lunch, a long and fairly liquid one he guessed. They'd said all the right things to him and Hattie about the photographs and, unprompted, had also told him they'd forwarded the envelope for Steph.

'Can I take the chocolate bottle out of the box?' Hattie asked when the game had run out of steam.

'Not yet,' Natalie said. 'Take it out too soon and the heat of those hot little paws of yours will start to melt it. We'll get the box unsealed and ready though. Fran's getting your other present out of the boot.'

Tom hadn't really tuned into the conversation until he heard 'Fran' and suddenly went from happy anticipation of the evening ahead to a state of pins-and-needles anxiety.

'Fran?' he asked, just before the door opened.

'Uh-huh.' Natalie was helping Hattie get the Sellotape off the end of the box. 'She wanted a break from making that ginger rat with a tail. Going to keep me company and test me on some employment law. You know Fran, don't you, Hattie?'

'Yes. She let me wee in her garden.'

'Ri-ight.' Fran's entrance stopped Natalie from asking any more.

Tom knew he had to do the best impression of normal that he could. 'Hello there,' he said cheerfully, and set about putting his shoes on and tying the laces while surreptitiously checking out what Fran was wearing.

For once it wasn't a dress, but a blue-and-white striped T-shirt and those trousers that stopped at the calf. Capri pants. Bloody figure-skimming Capri pants.

'Hello there,' she said, enthusiastically, 'I've come dressed as a pirate. You don't mind me crashing your launch party, do you, Hattie?'

Tom saw Hattie glance towards the large carrier bag Fran was holding. 'You *can* stay,' she said, seriously, 'but I don't know about the crashing. I know you crashed into that other tree . . . but mine's got a house in it.'

Fran looked at Tom as if to say, 'Oh no, you didn't tell her?' and he found that he hadn't quite managed to tie one of his shoes properly and had to start again.

'Crashing in this case means coming along to something without being invited,' Natalie explained.

'Oh, that's all right then,' Hattie said. 'And you let me wee in your garden, so it's only fair.'

When Tom heard Fran and Natalie laugh, he understood that he should too, but he had gone into a time loop where he was forever untying and re-tying his shoes.

'I'd better head off,' he blurted.

'But you said you'd hang around.' Natalie's expression was going to have grown men wetting themselves in court.

'Are you giving me that present, then?' Hattie asked and Tom's scold got lost in Fran's response. 'Of course. Here you are . . .' She had put her hand in the bag but took it out again, empty. 'I mean, I know you probably have plenty. And I wasn't sure about the size, because, well, children's heads are—'

'Fran, just get it out,' Natalie said, 'before Hattie bursts with anticipation and I have to clean it up.'

Fran pulled a paper hat out of the bag, but it was unlike any paper hat Tom had ever got from a cracker. Navy blue and tri-cornered, it might have belonged to Nelson. It had an ornate silver-coloured star that looked spiky and solid and a great deal of gold piping.

'Is it all made of paper?' Hattie asked, poking it tentatively.

'Yes, I'm not sure it's historically or militarily accurate, but it is indeed made of paper. And glue.'

'It's FANTASTIC!' Hattie exclaimed, suddenly coming to life. She lifted the hat from Fran's hand. 'Look, Dad. A pirate's hat. All made of paper. And glue. Look!'

He watched as Hattie placed the hat on her head.

'Ah, Cinderella, you shall go to the ball,' Fran said. When it was obvious no one knew what she meant, she busied herself folding up the carrier bag. 'I mean . . . it fits . . . like the glass slipper.'

She trailed off and Tom wanted to put his arm around her, but instead reminded Hattie of her manners.

'I'm never going to take it off,' she said. 'Thank you.'

Another child might have found a mirror to check what the hat looked like, but Hattie raised a hand and shouted, 'Full steam ahead,' before making for the door.

'Yeah, tally-ho!' Natalie said. 'A hat made of paper and a bottle made of chocolate. It's all kicking off here.'

Both Tom and Fran arrived at the back door at the same time.

'After you,' he said, 'and . . . um . . . the tree house is over there.'

Why had he felt the need to point that out; it was a ruddy great house stuck in a ruddy great tree, but Fran's face immediately looked like Hattie's had done when she'd seen the hat.

'You built this all yourself?'

He felt as if he'd constructed one of the great pyramids at Giza. 'Well, me and Rob,' he said, modestly.

Hattie had already climbed the ladder to the tree house and Natalie followed.

'Dear Natalie,' Fran said. 'You can almost see what she had for breakfast, that skirt's so short. She has *such* confidence.'

He did a pathetic laugh. *Pathetic.*

Standing on that part of the platform not taken up with the house, Hattie was finally being allowed to get the bottle out of the box.

'Don't shake it whatever you do,' he heard Natalie say.

'So what play are you going to see tonight?' Fran was saying and he wondered how had he failed to notice during those first meetings how completely and utterly lovely she was. And smelled like . . . God, what did she smell like? Cut grass. No. Lemons. Scrambled eggs. Possum's breath. God, he didn't bloody know. What day was it?

'The play, Tom?' Fran said again, as if he were a younger child than Hattie.

Do I know the name of the play? Yes!

'*The Bricklayer's Bequest*,' he said, and had enough confidence to add, 'it's about a workman who wins the Euro lottery—'

'And spends it to help his friends sort out their lives.'

'You know it?' he asked, politely, while his brain bellowed, 'Arrrrggghh.'

'Yes. I went to see the preview. I'm extremely keen on drama, particularly from new playwrights.'

Of course you are.

He was going to have to do some homework before he came back tonight.

'How's the squirrel?' he gabbled.

'Nearly done. Planning on delivering it—'

'Are you going to get up here, Fran?' Natalie shouted. 'And Tom, take some video and photos, will you?'

'So bossy,' Fran said with obvious delight. 'She'll make a wonderful lawyer. Oh well, up I go.'

Tom made a meal of getting his phone out of his jacket so that he would not be tempted to watch Fran climbing the ladder. When he did chance looking up at the platform, he saw Hattie was holding the bottle like a club.

'OK,' he shouted.

'I declare,' Hattie announced, 'the *Jolly Howard* launched!' She swung back the bottle and smashed it against the edge of the house where it shattered into pieces and released a shower of chocolate beans which fell on to the platform and rolled about, some falling down on to the lawn. Natalie and Fran clapped and cheered.

'That's why I didn't want you to shake it, Hattie,' Natalie said, bending down and picking up a chocolate bean. 'Or you'd have realised they were inside.'

'A chocolate bottle,' Hattie squealed. 'A chocolate bottle with more chocolate hiding in it.'

Tom didn't say anything. He was too busy holding the camera steady and looking at Fran's sweet, sad smile as she watched Hattie and Natalie trying to throw chocolate into each other's mouths.

He was thinking of that smile as he walked along the corridor in the hotel. Room 432 this time. By now his mind should be free of anything but the prospect of abandoning himself in Grietje.

He looked at the numbers on the door. The 4, the 3, the 2 – like some truncated countdown for which he didn't seem to be prepared. One particular part of him certainly wasn't ready for take-off.

Trying to clear his brain of everything but who was on the other side of that door, he pictured Grietje in nothing but that sheer body and felt the draw of lust start in his belly and move down. Grietje running her fingers over whatever little surprises she'd brought with her this time. His need intensified and hardened. That was better.

'Come,' she called when he knocked on the door and he smiled.

That was exactly what he intended to do.

Hair still wet from the shower, he was on his knees, bending to kiss her between her legs. He took his time, enjoying how his tongue travelled over the roughness of hair to the smoothness of the folds within. Gently he pushed her thighs wider apart and slid his hands round her backside and buried himself deeper in her slipperiness, the taste and the scent of her hiking up his desire. Ah, there was the place he was after. He started to lavish all his attention on it and waited for her hips to rise and fall, the signal he was getting it right. He focused more intently – his lips, her lips, mouth, tongue.

He was thinking that usually this was more tricky because he had to keep pace with her movements, when suddenly there was a lot more movement than he expected and a dragging pain in the back of his head. Grietje was sitting up and she was pulling his hair to drag him up with her.

They were face to face when she disentangled her fingers. If this was some new game, he didn't like it. Through watering eyes he saw that she did not have that heavy-lidded look she normally had when seriously turned on.

'What are you doing, Tom?' she said, her accent not sounding exotic, but harsh and accusatory. When he didn't reply because he didn't understand the question, she repeated it.

'Trying to give you an orgasm?' he said.

She clicked her tongue and muttered something in Dutch that obviously wasn't complimentary, before saying in English, 'I did not mean literally. I mean, what are you doing in this room?'

He looked around as though the bathroom might tell him.

'Oh, for goodness sake,' she said, and swivelled away from him and stood up.

'No . . . look.' He was scrambling to his feet too. 'What? I don't understand.'

'Shall I put it in the simplest English for you? Why do you and I get together?'

He went for the simplest answer. 'To have sex?'

'Well done. To have sex.' Her smile was patronising. 'We come together to enjoy each other. Free of any emotions from our lives outside this hotel. But you . . . you have brought something in here with you.'

He felt so exposed that for the first time ever in her company, he wanted to put his clothes back on.

You know what she's talking about. You've known since that day up in the forest.

Grietje shrugged, doing magnificent things to her breasts, and he tried to concentrate on them. If he said he was really, really sorry, would she let him cup them in his hands again . . .

She crossed her arms as if she'd heard what he had been thinking.

'Tom,' she said, almost conversationally, 'I don't mind that you have another lover. Why should I? But I do mind that you can't leave her behind. Believe me, if I wanted a threesome I would ask.'

Without bidding, Fran walked into his head and into the room and he imagined her looking at Grietje and at him and probably finding the architectural detailing on the far wall more fascinating.

'It's not like that—'

'Really, Tom, if you knew you couldn't give me your full attention, we should not have met this evening.' She walked out of the bathroom and left him with his thoughts scrambled.

Had his brain been sabotaging his body? Stupid brain and even stupider body – didn't they both understand how much he needed Grietje and what went on here? How this thing with Fran could only ever be a mid-life crush?

He followed her, trying not to look desperate. She was already pushing her arm into the sleeve of the flimsy robe that only recently he had taken off her and thrown on the floor. There was something very decisive about the way she was fastening the ties. Double knots, not bows.

'Grietje, come on,' he reasoned, 'I don't know why you felt I was distracted. I didn't *feel* distracted.' He chanced moving closer. 'I felt right there in the moment trying to give you pleasure.' He reached out and tentatively ran a finger down from her shoulder to the crook of her elbow and let it lie there. 'Come on, forgive me. Or if you like, really punish me. Do your worst . . . make me pay.'

He saw that heavy-lidded look come back and a little cruel upturn of her lips. She studied him.

'Maybe I will,' she said slowly, the hint of a threat under the words. 'Yes. You have treated me with disrespect, Tom. You have asked for this.' She reached for his face, her hands grasping it roughly and kissed him hard on the lips. That tiny layer of wispy material between her nipples and his chest was really turning him on.

'Perhaps you thought you could make me jealous, huh?' she whispered before kissing him again, even more roughly. He fell gladly into the kiss, bringing his arms up around her and pulling her in. She was grinding herself against him and he thanked the argument for this added spice. The kissing was morphing into something almost obscene in its own right, her tongue demanding so much of his mouth. He knew she wanted to take the lead and he had to let her, but it was all he could do not to rip that bloody robe off her shoulders again and damn the knots.

She surfaced from one of the kisses with her mouth wet and her eyes barely open and, slowly, tantalisingly, ran a nail down his belly to scrape tortuously along his hairline before she was wrapping her hand around his cock. 'Oh God, Tom. So hard. So turned on. Me too. Feel.'

He did as he was told and wanted to put himself where his fingers had just been.

'So tell me,' she hissed into his ear.

'What? Tell you what?'

'Tell me what you and this other lover do. How do you have her? Does she take you in her mouth? Do you—'

'Stop it,' he said, sharply, and stepped backwards.

As she was still holding him, it really hurt.

There was no thought driving what he had just said or done, only the need to stop Grietje talking about Fran in a way that was wrong, wrong, absolutely bloody wrong.

Grietje could look very frightening when she tried and she was definitely trying now. She pushed her hair back and stared at him. She didn't blink – there was no respite from those eyes.

'I see,' she said, 'that's how it is. Well, it would appear that you have become the kind of Englishman who bores me.' She looked past him to the window as if to prove how bored she was. 'Provincial, Tom. And I thought you had no hang-ups.'

She raised one hand and ran her little finger along her bottom lip, first one way and then back, before rubbing her lips together. He didn't know what it meant – perhaps she was underlining the fact there would be no more kissing. She moved towards the bathroom again and now her speech was matter-of-fact, as if she was winding up a business meeting. 'Perhaps when you feel more . . . European,' she said, 'you will contact me. And please,' she paused at the door, 'when I come back out, do not be here.'

He didn't try to stop her, but dressed quickly, fumbling with buttons and stuffing himself back in his pants. He had a fight with his socks before getting them sorted and putting on his shoes. At least concentrating on dressing meant he didn't have to go back over what had just happened. That took place out in the corridor.

Why couldn't he have pretended and just said anything? Yes, we have sex on the traffic island in the middle of town. Anything just to get through that moment.

At the lift, he jabbed the button to summon it. Would Grietje ever want to see him again? His body had a panicky response to that. How could he cope with the homework, the housework, standing in the school playground, the hours in the play park pushing the swings, reading the same bedtime story over and over again. With being bone tired, but still having to explain wrong from right and why wars happened and what rainbows were made of.

It was only when he was in the lift that he allowed himself to think about Fran properly. He knew next to nothing about her, yet she was making him feel grubby about all this skulking around and lying to everyone. Grietje was right, he was a hidebound, provincial guy with hang-ups.

Usually in this lift he felt exhausted but elated that he'd made love with a beautiful, vibrant woman and no one but Grietje and he knew about it.

And Grietje's husband.

Oh God. Now he was feeling guilty about her husband.

'I am bloody well entitled to a private life,' he said out loud, just before the doors of the lift opened again. 'I have nothing to hide.' He stepped out into the reception area still fighting the misery in his head, but it abated long enough for him to notice the two people facing the reception desk. They looked incredibly like his mother and the rev. Holy Crap! It was his mother and the rev. As he watched, he saw the rev.'s hand move to rest on his mother's bottom. It was a movement that said, 'We are checking into this hotel to have sex.'

And Tom should know.

He staggered back into the lift and hit the button to close the doors and, as they came together, he flattened himself against the wall and selected a floor number, any number, just to get the lift to move. When it set off, he took in a huge gulp of air and allowed himself, very slowly, to slide to the floor.

CHAPTER 27

Thursday 29 May

1) It is not possible to choose your relations. If it was, I would have chosen Natalie as my sister – a woman who can climb in high heels and a pelmet and also knows a great deal about the impact of a possible reduction in maximum compensatory claims.

2) For a thirty-eight-year-old man, Tom has terrible trouble tying his shoe laces.

3) Tom has very good taste in socks.

4) Putting a small child to bed is exhausting – they can make it last for hours, especially if you are under the impression that you have to 'do' all the voices in their bedtime story.

5) You can listen to a young child telling you about their mother and know you should change the subject, but find yourself failing to do so – possibly because it is less stressful than having to field a raft of questions about

your own mother and childhood. I think Hattie has inherited her questioning skills from Tom. Or maybe in a previous life she was a member of the Spanish Inquisition.

6) One can look at a photograph of a child's mother and see how glamorous she is, but know without doubt that she is the kind of person who would blow cigarette smoke in your face and smirk out a 'Sorry'. (Or perhaps say, like Victoria, 'Not everyone can wear vintage' – as though there's some quota enforced by law.)

7) Actually, point 6 isn't strictly accurate. Natalie's stories of promised visits not made and ranting phone calls might have influenced me before I even saw the photograph.

8) Hattie has the most bizarrely dressed soft toys. I did not think it was possible to make a stuffed bear look so much like a hooker.

9) When a man is extremely evasive about the play he is going to see, it makes you wonder what he is really up to in Newcastle. Particularly when, on his return, it becomes obvious that he has only watched the end of that play.

10) Also in relation to point 9. If you are going to go in for distinctive socks, you should make sure that when you return home, one of them is not inside out.

CHAPTER 28

'I cannot believe you have done this, Hattie,' Tom said as they walked down the school corridor lined with paintings of castles, some of which even looked like castles. 'You know, absolutely know, that stealing is wrong.'

Hattie looked ashamed of herself. 'I didn't know it was *real* stealing.'

'*Real* stealing? What does that mean? And have you any idea how inconvenient it is for me to have to drop everything at work and come into school to . . .' He stopped talking, having spotted the young teaching assistant lurking at the far end of the corridor.

'How did it go?' she said when they got closer. She was a study in sympathy and bent down to Hattie's level with her hands on her knees. 'How are you feeling?'

Hattie shrugged and the teaching assistant said, 'I know, I know,' and straightened up. Turning to Tom she lowered her voice, 'If it wasn't part of a county-wide initiative, it wouldn't be so bad.' She raised her voice again. 'Good to go home early, eh? Give everyone time to cool off over the weekend.'

Thirty-eight years old and getting called to the head's office felt worse than when he was a teenager. Then it was only his own bad behaviour he was responsible for, now it was Hattie's too. Shame was clinging to him like a damp jacket.

Out in the playground, he knew his parenting skills were about to get another bashing when he saw one of the women who belonged to a group he had nicknamed the 'Smug Maternals' tanking towards him.

Whereas he and Hattie's friend Josh's parents happily admitted to having lost the instruction manual for their children, this woman knew everything about perfect parenting.

In her eyes, her son Sebastian was not only a genius whose potential was unacknowledged by the school system, but he never misbehaved either. She unnerved Tom more than the mothers who were Plastics (always in full make-up and neat clothes, married to company men, only using the state system till the Common Entrance Exam came around) and the Power Tools (dads who made tits of themselves at sporting events by being too competitive).

He waited for the opening salvo.

'Ah, I see you're here,' she said and Tom heard the unspoken 'that's no surprise'.

'Well, looks like you've been called in too,' he shot back. 'I saw Sebastian waiting in the corridor.'

There was a patronising smile. 'Sebastian is not an instigator, he's a peacemaker. He will merely have gone along with the dominant character to avoid confrontation.' There was a stare at Hattie to underline who that dominant character was.

Tom was boiling to say any number of things in response to that, ranging from 'You do know Sebastian trades in his fruit for Cheesy Wotsits, don't you?' to the less reasoned 'You're a sanctimonious cow', but he figured that saying any of that in front of Hattie would yet again prove what a very bad father he was.

By the time they got to the car, Hattie had Gummy firmly in place.

They drove in silence before he remembered that he needed to ring Kath and tell her she didn't have to come to school to pick up Hattie. Perhaps he could take her directly to Kath's? That way, he could leave Hattie there and return to work.

Was that fair on Kath though – an out-of-sorts Hattie? He decided to cancel Kath altogether and take Hattie to work – really hammer home the punishment.

He pulled over and as he retrieved his phone, it rang.

'How did you get on?' Liz asked.

'Tell you when I get back. I've got Hattie with me. She can sit and wait for me to finish.'

A glance in the mirror told him what Hattie thought of that.

'OK. Sounds serious. I'm thinking arson in the quiet corner or—'

'What was it you wanted, Liz?'

'Oh, like that, is it? Right, well, had a call from Fran. She's finished the squirrel and I thought as you have to come right past her place, you could bring it in. She's not got a car at the moment. You still there?'

He was, but frantically trying to devise an escape plan. 'Nobody else who can come and pick it up? Or couldn't she bring it along on the bus?'

Liz came right back at him. 'Tom, strap on a pair, will you? Believe me, I understand the embarrassment of getting hauled into school, but you're driving right past. You really want Fran to sit on a bus? What if the bloody thing gets damaged? If we can get it here this afternoon, Derek can book some studio time and get it photographed over the weekend. You trying to give me more to worry about?'

He had no counter-argument – other than a dread of

making a complete tit of himself and adding 'man in the throes of a mid-life crisis' to the other roles he'd been playing since the evening before. So far they included 'thwarted lover', 'appalled son' and 'shamed parent'.

He started the car reluctantly, yet if anyone had appeared to say, 'OK, forget about going to see Fran,' he would have knocked them out of the way to get to her.

As soon as Fran appeared round the side of the bungalow, he knew this was going to go badly. She had the dress on that she'd been wearing the first time he'd seen her and her hair was loose. Bare legs. Nothing on her feet. Like she'd just stepped out of bed and thrown the dress over her head and possibly had nothing on underneath it.

She was getting tanned and seemed so full of life and vitality that he wondered if he put his arms around her, would some of that energy transfer to him? His body would feel her warmth and it might, just for a minute or two, make him forget what it felt like to be alone and stuffing up as a parent.

But then the torturous conversation he'd had with her when he'd returned home the night before started playing in his head again.

He'd tied himself in knots about the play and it seemed obvious to him that she knew he hadn't seen it all, even though for most of his spiel she'd been looking down at his feet.

It was only when he went upstairs to bed that he realised one of his socks was inside out.

'Oh, and Hattie's here, too,' Fran said. 'How lovely to . . .'

She had obviously caught sight of Hattie's mouth, with gum shield.

'I've come for the squirrel,' he said, abruptly.

Fran jerked her head back and blinked. 'Well hello to you too, Tom.' And then her attention was back on Hattie. 'Have you been stung on the mouth?' she asked.

Hattie took out the gum shield, said 'No', put it back in again and then almost immediately removed it once more to add, 'You've put a paving stone where I had a wee.'

'Ye-es, I have.'

Had that been there on his last visit? If it had, Vasey must have mowed around it.

'Think of it as X marks the spot,' Fran said cheerily. 'Like pirates do with treasure.'

Hattie nodded morosely and re-positioned the gum shield and Tom saw the sideways look Fran gave him.

'The squirrel?' he reminded her.

'Yes, yes, of course. Come along in, round the back.'

'We won't, thank you.' Tom was quite definite about that. 'We'll just take the squirrel and go.' If he stayed here any longer, he'd start thinking about Fran's bare legs and whether there was anything separating them from the material of the dress which he was sure he could hear making a seductive 'slip, slip, slip' noise whenever she moved.

Had he been too abrupt? 'We don't want to disturb your work,' he said, less brusquely.

'But I've finished my work, that's why you're here. Come on.' Short of refusing to budge, he didn't see what he could do. Hattie was already trotting along and he followed, absolutely not looking at Fran's backside or the way the dress swished at the hem.

Since his last visit, a delicate metal table and matching chairs had been put out on the grass and he guessed they must belong to her. Too stylish for Vasey.

'Sit down and don't move,' he told Hattie. 'And don't pick anything and eat it.' She plonked herself down on one of the pale-lilac cushions, folded her arms and lowered her chin.

Fran gave him another one of her out-of-the-corner-of-her-eye looks before saying, brightly, 'What would you like to drink, Hattie? I'm not really sure what children—'

'She'll have water,' he said before Hattie could even get a hand to the gum shield.

'Water?' Fran repeated, as if unconvinced, and when

neither he nor Hattie added anything further, she said, under her breath, 'Right, water it is, then.'

Tom followed her into the kitchen and watched her open the fridge and take out a jug of water before pouring some into a glass.

'Tea for us,' she said, and he looked around the kitchen because it hurt less than looking at her. There were more wild flowers in jam jars than last time and the cooling rack was full again.

'See you've been making biscuits,' he said.

'Actually, they're scones.'

He didn't know what to say to apologise and she kept moving around the kitchen, picking up plates and cups, and that dress of hers going 'slip, slip, slip' over her breasts and her hips.

'I . . . I need to get Hattie's sun hat from the car,' he said, heading for the back door.

When he returned, Hattie already had the glass of water in front of her on the table. Gummy was next to it. 'Here,' he said, holding out the hat, and she took it without a word and plonked it on her head.

Back in the kitchen he asked, 'Mind if I look at the squirrel?' and didn't wait for Fran's reply.

Since he'd last seen the sitting room, it had become even more of a workplace. The piles of paper had multiplied and been joined by tins and tubes of glue, a jumble of tools with metal tips, an old baby-milk tin filled with scalpels and large sheets of the foam board Fran used to make the boxes for keeping her sculptures safe. There was one sitting on a chair and he carefully lifted the lid and looked inside.

It was Mr Tufty. He looked more lifelike than last time Tom had seen him. Also, none of his intestines were showing.

Tom had expected a classic sitting-up pose, with it gnawing on a berry or a nut, but the squirrel was on the ground, one of its paws lifted. Fran had captured the moment beautifully when it had heard something and was about to skitter off in that distinctive running-stitch bounce.

You could sense the power of the muscles in its hind quarters and jaws and easily imagine the barely there tip of its tail, wafting in the breeze.

'What do you think? Honestly?' She was behind him.

I think you're lovely.

'Amazing. You've nailed him.'

A low laugh that reverberated within him. 'Not a very good choice of words given the circumstances.'

He didn't answer, knowing that he was being weird and uncommunicative, and was saved by a noise from the kitchen. 'Hattie,' he said loudly, 'what did I say about staying put?' He was moving past Fran and found Hattie jiggling about, looking uncomfortable.

'I need to go to the toilet,' she said. 'I could do it outside again, but then Fran would have to get another stone . . . unless I did it on exactly the same spot.' She looked towards the back door.

'Don't be ridiculous. Fran, where's your . . .' He turned and found Fran right there. 'Bathroom.'

She waved Hattie towards her. 'Through here, come along.' Before they both went out of the room, Fran looked at him as if he was an ogre.

When she came back without Hattie, she nodded at the loaded tea tray on the side.

'If it's not too much trouble, perhaps you could carry that out to the table. Or if you prefer, you could just throw it on the floor and grind it under your foot.' There was a click of her tongue. 'Perhaps you were right – you shouldn't have come in.'

He wanted, suddenly, to make her understand that he was not the angry man she saw before him.

'Look, I'm sorry for the bad atmosphere. But I've had to collect Hattie early from school. She's misbehaved.'

'Well, it must have been something terrible,' Fran shot back. 'I've never seen two people so out of sorts with each other. Can I ask what she did?'

He checked Hattie wasn't on her way back. 'She and a group of her friends stripped all the herbs out of the new herb bed. The children who have packed lunches put them in their sandwiches. Hattie, who has a cooked lunch, sprinkled them over her own and everyone else's meals. She was the ringleader.'

He was still watching the doorway so he only became aware near the end of his explanation, of a noise from Fran. She had closed her eyes. Her mouth was closed too, her lips pressed together, but little snorts were escaping that were unmistakably laughs. All at once she cupped both hands round her nose and mouth and let it all come out.

'It's not funny,' he said, sharply.

She moved her hands long enough to wheeze, 'Oh, but it is,' and then she was off once more.

It felt as if she were laughing at him as well as the incident. 'The poor woman had only just finished the beds,' he said. 'And it was a county-wide initiative.'

Another suppressed gale of laughter.

'How would you like it if someone did the same to one of your sculptures?'

'What? Ate it?' She had to turn away and put her hand on to the worktop to steady herself.

He checked the door again. 'Look, can you stop this before Hattie gets back?'

She nodded, but he didn't notice any change, so he went to find the bathroom. 'You nearly finished?' he shouted through the door.

'I'm having a poo,' Hattie called back.

'Wash your hands afterwards.'

He returned to the kitchen where Fran was wafting air towards her face with her hands. Every now and again her chest would convulse and he must be angry, because normally he would have liked to watch her chest convulsing.

'Quite finished?' he asked, when she had taken in and expelled a couple of deep, calming breaths.

'I'm sorry, Tom,' she said, 'really sorry. But it's *such* a middle-class crime.' She took a few more deep breaths. 'Shock horror, the great basil theft! Where *will* we get our pesto now?'

'It wasn't just basil. It was mint and thyme and chives too.'

He saw her press her lips together again.

He looked away. 'The whole thing has been ruined for the others.'

'Except . . .' she said, 'it sounds like the others all got a taste.' She must have seen the look in his eyes, because she went on, quickly, 'You're right, of course. Very bad. Although . . . they actually used them in the way intended. They didn't kick them round the playground.'

As she made him more and more angry, part of him

thought that this was good. He would go off her now. She didn't understand how the real world operated.

He heard the toilet flush.

'Could you just stop talking?' he asked.

'Of course. But . . . how long does the punishment go on for?'

'What?'

'Well, presumably she's been told off at school? She's been sent home, plus I should think you've given her a good talking-to before you got here. So . . .' She shrugged. 'How about you forget it now and we can all have a nice—'

'I'm sorry? *You're* offering *me* childcare advice? Am I giving you advice on your paper sculptures?' He paused to register that she had raised both her eyebrows at that. 'Children need rules and they need to know when they've broken them and let you down.'

He went to pick up the tray, but she put her arm out to bar the way.

'I agree on the rules thing, Tom, but has Hattie really let you down *that* much? Aren't you just being hyper-sensitive about people judging you because you're a single parent and, shock horror, a man? My mother brought me up single-handedly and had exactly the same problem.' She frowned. 'Although, of course, she wasn't a man.'

'I am not hyper-sensitive,' he said in a tone that betrayed

he was and she just smiled knowingly and, as Hattie trotted back into the room, picked up the tray herself.

They drank the tea in silence and he chewed his way through a scone without saying how terrible it was, even though he wanted to pay her back for hitting a nerve with that damn single-parenting thing.

Hattie only nibbled a bit of her scone before it was back on the plate and Fran said, 'Very wise, Hattie. They truly are dreadful. I should have tried the other recipe for cheese and . . . oh.'

'Cheese and what?' Hattie asked.

'Chives,' Fran said and he saw her mouth tremble afterwards. He glared at her and suddenly she said, 'Oh for goodness sake,' and she was picking up the scones remaining on the serving plate and throwing them. They skimmed past his hair and landed in the garden.

'People make mistakes, Tom,' she said, her eyes locked on to his. 'They *just* make mistakes.' She turned to talk to Hattie who was staring open-mouthed at the scones on the grass. 'Shall I tell you one of mine, Hattie? Involving herbs? When I was about ten, my mother left me in charge of putting a whole load of chickens in to roast. All I had to do was turn the oven on and pop them in. But no, I thought what they needed was some herbs to make them more tasty. So off I went and picked some rosemary – I'd seen my mother put it on lamb. And do you know what my mother did when she came back, just before they'd finished cooking?'

'No,' Hattie said, seriously hooked by the story.

Fran's eyes were huge. 'She did her own impression of a chicken with no head. Demanded to know if I'd eaten any of the rosemary and threw all the chickens away. Because, dear Hattie, I had not picked rosemary, I'd picked some yew. And yew is very poisonous. I mean rosemary grows in a bush and smells good and yew, well . . . yew is totally different. That chicken could have been a last supper for us all, which would have been apt as it was a religious community, but there you are you see—'

'Fran, stop talking right now!' Tom said sharply as he watched Hattie's face crumpling.

'Josh was sick!' Hattie said with a cry. 'Have I poisoned him?' She was out of her chair and reaching for him and he had her on his lap. She sobbed into his shoulder and he said, 'No. You have absolutely not poisoned him. All those herbs were ones you *do* use in cooking. Josh just ate too much. Shush now, shush now.'

'Oh dear,' Fran said, her hand going to her mouth, 'I didn't mean . . . That wasn't the lesson . . . I . . .'

It was only when he had managed to get Hattie to a

stage where she was just sniffling, that he noticed Fran going into the house.

'It's all right,' he said to Hattie, and kissed her on the nose and sensed that they were back in touch with each other. She looked up at him, her face tear-washed and gulped, 'I'm really sorry,' and he said he was too, he'd been too fierce, and then, just like that, he was laughing because Fran had reappeared wearing a large, white cone of a hat with a D drawn on the front.

Hattie looked round and stopped sniffing.

'I don't even know if you're allowed to call people dunces any more,' Fran explained, looking very crestfallen, 'but that's what I am. I was just trying to cheer you up, Hattie, by showing that everyone makes mistakes, but . . .'

'Could I wear that?' Hattie asked, wiping her nose with the back of her hand.

'Well, I should wear it for the rest of the day, really, but here you are.' Fran took it off and held it out. 'And perhaps . . .' she glanced at Tom, 'if your father says it's OK, you could come and have a look at some of the animals in my sitting room.'

Tom said she could and off they went and he got up slowly and put his hand on his shirt where it was wet from Hattie's crying.

He thought of that first day and the llama spit. This

woman. This woman. She could take him from anger to sweetness in the course of a few minutes. Like a man sleep-walking, he followed them into the sitting room.

'Look, it's a kingfisher,' Hattie was saying, pointing at a picture, 'made of paper. All its feathers and everything.' The dunce's hat was too big for her and she kept having to push it up off her eyes.

'I know,' he said and he moved the squirrel box and sat down in the armchair and listened to Fran telling Hattie how she worked – first drawing the animal and then trans-ferring it to the wrong side of the paper before cutting out the shape. And then, she said, it was a case of having a practice with tracing paper to see how all the different layers could fit together. There were lots of questions from Hattie, including one about the glue. Fran showed her all the different pots and tubes and said she was always searching for the perfect kind.

'Anyone would think I was a glue-sniffer.'

'What's a glue-sniffer?' Hattie asked.

Fran winced. 'Ah. Moving on . . .'

Hattie's questions kept on coming and Fran kept on answering, and when Tom looked at them together he imagined them like that the night before. Hattie said they'd had a long talk, but he hadn't been able to get much out of her this morning about what was discussed – apart from that Fran had lived on an island. But not one with palm trees. A boring island where it was always windy. And a Japanese man had taught her maths and chemistry and fighting. Fran had lived in hot places too. Italy, France and a bit of America.

He should ask Fran about all that. And what had she said earlier? 'A religious community'?

'Fran . . .' he began, but Hattie cut across with, 'So could I help you fold some paper?' and the look she gave Fran was so endearing that Tom decided to shut up for now.

He went back to picturing Fran in his house, sitting in the low chair next to Hattie's bed and reading to her, and wondered if she'd come back up the stairs later, as he always did, to check she was asleep. He felt the stillness of the bedroom, that sense of being privy to something pure that settled on you when you watched a child deep in sleep. He saw the grave look on Fran's face.

Grave. A good word because that was what was different about her. When she wasn't being overenthusiastic or toe-curlingly tactless, she had a grave stillness about her that made you want to watch her face to see the moment that expression broke.

He was feeling a bit misty-eyed thinking about all that, but then Fran shifted position and he found himself imagining again what she had on under that dress. He wasn't proud of that, what with Hattie being in the room, but there it was.

He might have stayed in that pleasant day-dream, if he hadn't remembered he still needed to ring Kath. He left Fran and Hattie exploring the difference between folding a piece of paper and scoring it, and wandered around the garden with the phone.

Kath said all the right things about the herb incident and when he asked if she and Rob were still going to join them for tea the next day she said, 'Course. Be good to see your mum. She sounded really tired on the phone this morning. I think she's doing too much.'

No. She's doing the vicar.

He rang Josh's mother next.

'Just checking Josh is all right. Heard he'd been sick.'

There was a snigger. 'Serves him right. Basil overdose. And this from the boy who removes anything that remotely looks like a herb when he's at home. Did you get a good telling-off from the head, too?'

He stumbled over something in the grass and saw it was one of the scones. 'Well, it was done politely, but yeah, she's definitely disappointed in me.'

'I felt so guilty, I made a contribution towards some new plants.'

'Damn you,' he said, kicking at the scone and noticing it didn't even crumble. 'Wish I'd thought of that.'

There was another laugh and then, 'Oh, and sorry to add to the bad news, but while you're on the phone I'd better tell you that Josh has got head lice yet again.'

Walking back into the house, he figured he'd have to tell Fran about the lice. She'd had her head right up close to Hattie's today and who knew about when she'd babysat? Have to tell Natalie too, although she'd said she'd had them enough times to be immune. Great, weeks of lathering on the hair conditioner and combing the little sods out.

He thought of Fran washing her hair, it wet on her bare shoulders.

'That's right, Hattie. Gently does it.' He could hear her now, showing Hattie something. He wondered if she'd ever done a sculpture of a head louse.

'Do I have to press harder?' Hattie was saying.

'No,' came Fran's reply, 'the scalpel blade is extraordinarily sharp, it'll make a nice, clean cut with only a bit of pressure. Control is the thing, so you can get . . .'

He didn't hear the rest because his brain was zoning in on 'blade', 'sharp' and 'cut'. He moved quickly towards the sitting-room door and his worst fears were confirmed. Hattie, minus dunce's hat, was holding a scalpel with Fran leaning over her.

A scalpel! In a five-year-old's hand!

This woman wasn't right, she was out of her tree. What was he thinking of leaving her alone with Hattie? What was he thinking of, lusting after her?

All these thoughts travelled through his mind as his body hurtled into the sitting room, shouting and grabbing at the scalpel. He only realised as he did so that it was actually being held between Fran's fingers – Hattie was just resting her hand lightly on top of Fran's, feeling the movement of cutting without any of the danger.

Ah.

He fumbled with the scalpel and dropped it. Which was when he felt a stabbing pain in his thigh. Literally. The scalpel was stuck there and he heard himself shriek, more from shock than pain, before he pulled it out and put his hand over the cut in his trousers.

There was a lot of noise, what with Hattie leaping around and Fran telling him to stay still and him trying to assure everyone he was fine, although blood was seeping between his fingers.

'Will Daddy be all right?' Hattie asked and he noticed she seemed less worried than when she thought she had poisoned Josh.

'Yes, yes,' Fran said, her voice calm. 'These cuts bleed a lot, but they're not deep. I've done the same thing loads of times. Look at my hands.' She held them up in front of Hattie's face. 'I've got lots of little scars. Oh, and a lump on my finger where the scalpel rests. See?' She turned to him with her hands still held out for Hattie to inspect. 'If you just sit down and take off your trousers, Tom, I can have a look at the damage. I don't think there's anything to worry about, that material is quite thick.'

Tom knew if he took his trousers off now, he was going to die of embarrassment rather than loss of blood. Which was weird because earlier he'd been quite happy to fantasise about Fran and taking his trousers off. Now he felt like some terrified adolescent.

'I can look myself,' he said. 'I'll go in the bathroom and do it.'

'Are you sure?' Fran seemed doubtful. 'We don't want you fainting in there, do we, Hattie?'

Hattie agreed, but Tom was already backing out of the room.

Fran was following him. 'Tom,' she said, lowering her voice, 'this is ridiculous. I'm sure there's nothing in your trousers that I haven't seen before.'

At that he turned and speeded up like a sprinting Quasimodo.

He shut the bathroom door and took his trousers right off. Bloody ruined.

'Don't forget to raise your leg,' Fran said outside the door. 'I'll be back in a minute.'

He perched on the bath and put his leg up on the sink.

Fran was right, the cut didn't seem deep, but it was bleeding a lot. He dabbed at it with dry toilet paper and then ran some water into the sink and tried with some wet stuff.

Fran was back. 'How is it?' she asked.

'OK, I think. Bloody sore though.'

'Oh don't be a baby. One of the girls on my course sliced off the tip of her finger and we had to take it to the hospital in a bag of ice to have it sewn back on. Never even whimpered.'

'Thanks for that. What's Hattie doing?'

'Playing in the knife drawer, obviously, while waiting for you to do some of that fantastic scalpel juggling of yours.'

'All right, all right. I thought she was holding it.'

'I said I was a dunce, but even I know you don't give a five-year-old a knife. Well, unless you're running a street gang. Hattie is actually outside eating strawberries and cream. No herbs.' He imagined her laughing on the other side of the door. 'So, is the bleeding slowing down? Or will you need stitches?'

'I thought you said it would be OK?'

'Oh that was for Hattie's benefit. If it's in a place which

gets a lot of movement, you might need a stitch to stop it breaking open. How does it look?'

'Not sure.'

When she didn't answer, he thought she'd gone, but the bathroom door was opening.

'You're hopeless, Tom,' she said when she saw the toilet paper in his hand and on the floor. 'There's cotton wool in the cabinet.'

She was all briskness, getting it for him and tearing off a handful. She wet it and said, 'Come on, lift up your shirt.'

What was he scared of? That he'd have a sudden erection and poke out her eye? This was not how his fantasy involving her and his trousers had played out.

She peered and dabbed at the cut and pronounced it fine and unlikely to need stitches.

'This will sting though,' she said with a sympathetic smile as she reached for the TCP.

She was right, but he didn't mind. As he watched her leaning over his leg, her hair falling forward, he began to feel choked up – the closeness of her, the way she was looking after him. It had been a long time since someone had shown that amount of care over him. He knew he was getting maudlin and hoped she wouldn't be able to read his expression when she looked up.

'Seems nice and clean,' she said, with one last wipe, 'but

if you haven't had a tetanus injection recently, you should trot along to A&E.'

He checked his watch. The timetable for delivery of the squirrel to Derek had taken a knock. Nope. He didn't care about that either.

She was getting a pack of plasters out of the cabinet and selecting a large one.

'Here, I can do that,' he said and took it from her and as he put it on, he told her about the head lice. It should have been embarrassing, but wasn't. He supposed that when you'd stabbed yourself in the thigh and shown someone who worked for you your underpants, your concept of what was embarrassing shifted.

'Goodness, haven't had those for a while,' Fran said. 'They call them *pediculosi del capo* in Italy. Sounds much more exotic. Right. I'll check on Hattie.' She was nearly at the door when she stopped, looking self-conscious. 'Sorry about throwing the scones earlier. You just got me so exasperated.'

'Don't apologise. I was being an arse.'

'Yes you were.' She smiled. 'But I wasn't trying to hit you, just bring you to your senses.'

'Too late for that,' he said when she'd gone.

CHAPTER 29

Friday 30 May

1) The middle classes can be quite draconian when it comes to herbs. Not enough and you're a philistine. Too many and your parents have to be summoned. In Italy they'd give you a medal for eating that much basil in one sitting.

2) There is obviously a force field around this 'cottage' that means Tom and Hattie never arrive on my doorstep looking normal. This time Tom was a thundercloud and Hattie a sad ape.

3) Tom is something of an expert on baked goods, yet he could not tell the difference between a scone and a biscuit. This suggests that with my cooking, there is actually no difference.

4) It is not easy to know the right thing to say to a child. For future reference, suggesting that they may have poisoned their best friend is not it.

5) Hattie reminds me of someone. It came to me today when she asked all those questions and was so determined to have a go at cutting a piece of paper. That someone is me.

6) All you need to know about how protective parents feel towards their children can be learned by watching a man's face as he rushes to remove a scalpel he believes is in his daughter's hand.

7) Point six has made me revisit all those times I felt my own mother was being smothering. Too late to tell her I understand her now, of course.

8) For an ex-rugby player, Tom is surprisingly modest. I thought rugby players were always leaping naked into the bath with each other? I think he may be self-conscious about his legs. He has no need to be.

9) Tom obviously does not have the same problem with his underpants as with his socks. They were not on inside out. I checked.

10) Smells can be very evocative. A whiff of TCP will always make me think of Tom in my bathroom, leg up on the sink while I dabbed at his thigh and he studied me as if he feared I would inflict further pain on him.

CHAPTER 30

Fran's work had obviously inspired everyone. The three-page spread Tom was looking at would not have been out of place in a colour supplement for a national newspaper.

'Makes the rest of the mag look a bit provincial,' Felix said, following up with a sharp laugh. 'You're showing us all up, Fran.'

'No, no.' She looked pained. 'Please don't say that. It's Derek's wonderful photography and your imaginative design that make it so impressive.'

Tom felt a swirl of pride in her skills and her modesty. Ridiculous – there was no connection between them other than the one in his head.

'Do you think it needs . . . ?' Derek started and Fran said, 'No, I really don't think people want to see a photo of my weird face as part of the feature, it'll detract from the wild-life.'

'How did you know he was going to say that?' Felix

asked, looking from Fran to Derek. 'Are you telepathically linked?'

Derek seemed as if he might be giving that question serious consideration, but Fran merely smiled politely before saying to Tom, 'Are you happy with it? You haven't said much.'

Such a lovely face. And so much younger than yours.

'Haven't I?' He bent forward to study some of the finer details of the squirrel and immediately pictured Fran's hands smoothing out the paper and that squinty frown she had when concentrating, which shouldn't have been attractive but . . .

'You've done very well,' he said, gruffly, straightening back up again. 'Especially considering the time constraints. How's the copy going?'

'Getting there,' she said, not looking at him any more, 'I'd better crack on.'

He walked back down the stairs with her and as he did so, found himself operating on so many different levels under the conversation they were having, that it absolutely refuted the claim that men couldn't multi-task. Some of the things he was doing he wasn't proud of, and he blamed them on his sex drive, but that made it sound as if he was an automatic car and wasn't responsible for his own gear changes. Right now he was registering that the dress she had on did great things for her breasts.

And her collarbones. Collarbones! Yeah, he had it bad.

He lied to himself that he wasn't doing full-on leering, but processing snippets of information about how the dress fitted her and the way that the downy hairs on her arm were very sun-bleached. And how her lips sometimes hiked into a little smile at the end of what she was saying.

Would he have noticed the bump on her middle finger if she hadn't pointed it out to Hattie? Yep, he thought he would today – he was like a lovesick scanning machine.

'So where are you off to, now?' he asked, still imagining running his hand down that straight back.

'To buy a sandwich.'

Her back was naked now against his chest. Also naked.

Thinking like that made him feel ashamed and just a little turned on – which made him feel more ashamed.

'Well,' he did an awkward flourish with his hand, 'have a great sandwich then.'

'Yes, yes I will . . . And Hattie? No ill effects from the herbs?'

'No. Har-har-har. She's absolutely fine.'

'Good. Well, I'll see you later.'

He watched her down the remaining stairs until she went into the main office.

Have a good sandwich? Har-har-har. Good God.

He tried not to be too hard on himself – it was tricky talking in a relaxed way when you were pulling in your stomach.

Completely baffling, this 'first you don't see it, now you do' kind of sexual attraction. At least with love at first sight you were reacting to someone fresh and unknown.

Was it a chemical reaction that just needed time to brew like a proper pot of tea?

He thought of Steph. How he'd felt the hook go in the first time he'd seen her chatting at a party. How the loveliness of her face and that air of glamour that hung about her had made him blind to reality and he had, as lovers did, filled in the blanks of what he knew about her with some idyllic creation. He'd given her a beautiful personality to match her face. Who wouldn't?

From the start, it felt like falling from a height into something exciting and more exotic than he was.

But this thing with Fran? It felt like a stumble against his better judgement via a series of misunderstandings and fights. He counted out all the reasons, once again, why he couldn't fall for someone like her – too young, too strange, too tactless, too earnest, not even his type.

So why was he remembering her crawling around in the cemetery, the black of her dress against her skin, and wishing he had placed his lips over the marks her tears had left on her face and kissed them away?

Tom stopped thinking of salt on his lips as he pushed open the door into the main office, because he could almost feel the panic level rising. The usual glitches and log-jams were surfacing. Heads were bent towards screens.

He aimed for a nonchalant walk past Fran's desk, but it came out like a saunter. Good God, he'd be wearing a panama hat next and a cravat.

He went to his office and barely raised his own head for the rest of the day, but when he did, he saw that Jamie had pulled up the empty chair that was next to Fran's desk and was chatting to her.

Was Tom imagining that the besotted look Fran reserved for Jamie had intensified?

'She ought to move that chair,' Liz said, as she came in. 'It's a magnet for time-wasters. Particularly the spawn of Mawson. By God, he loves that chair. Right . . . another load of proofs for you to cast your eagle eye over. Lot more in hand, usual culprits dragging their feet.'

Putting the proofs down, she flipped open her notebook and started to update him, with relish, on the list of potential disasters. 'Also . . .' There was one of her rare, wide smiles. 'Stan has got himself another entry into the "File of Shame" with a totally made-up word. *Manslack*.'

Liz took a moment to snigger. 'He says it's the perfect description for summer trousers. I say it sounds like something that stops you getting an erection.' She raised her hand and moved it from left to right as through indicating a headline: 'Manslack – the trousers that don't come in any colours.'

'You're wasted here,' Tom told her, trying not to think about erections or the trousers that might stop them.

Liz had started looking out through the door again.

'See what I mean about that chair?' she said.

It was Monty now ensconced next to Fran. He had his wallet open.

'What's he up to?' Tom asked.

'Offering her money?' Liz craned her neck. 'No, can't see. Right, if I could have your attention again?'

Liz selected a sheet of paper from between the proofs she'd put on his desk. It was handed to him.

'Jamie's final efforts. And she did it again. Turned Mr Stay Behind to Discuss Your Abuse of English into Ernest Hemingway.'

Tom had been reading as Liz talked. It was Fran's voice running through the piece, her self-deprecating sense of humour.

'Bloody sleight of hand while I was off making her a cup

of coffee. Sneaky woman.' It sounded as if Liz meant it as a compliment.

'Well, at least it's all done,' Tom said, glancing out towards Fran again, but she was no longer there and neither was Monty.

'Yeah, one less problem.' Liz paused. 'They make a good couple, mind, Jamie and Fran. Seem suited, somehow. Hey, where are you off to?'

Tom was out through the door. Jamie was nipping bits off a rubber with his fingernails and forming a pattern on the desk with them.

'A word,' Tom said to him, the logical part of his brain warning him to hold back; the overwrought bit ready to take a pair of scissors to Jamie's floppy fringe.

Jamie came into the office and looked uneasily from Tom to Liz. He was studiously *not* looking at the piece of paper in Tom's hand.

Tom was ready to tear into him about the unethical nature of getting Fran to do his work for him, but there was an almost dog-like cower to the way Jamie was standing. He kept looking at Tom as if waiting for the lash to fall. It made Tom wonder what kind of life Jamie had at home, always on the receiving end of his mother's disapproval. Tom didn't envisage that brother of his was particularly nurturing, either.

When Tom didn't speak, Jamie cut in with, 'Look, Tom. I've never been any good at writing . . . it's never, you know, been my best . . . thingy.'

'Thingy?' Liz said, but not unkindly, and Tom sensed that her parenting genes had also picked up on Jamie's vulnerability.

Tom looked at him again, trying to work out if this beaten-dog stance was an act to save himself from a showdown.

He put the piece of paper on his desk. 'Forget it,' he said, 'time to move you on to something else.'

It was almost possible to see Jamie unwind. He even managed to look Tom in the eye. 'Appreciate it,' he said, colouring high up on his cheeks. 'Really do.'

Such a winning smile. Such a young face.

'I thought you were going to tear his head off,' Liz said when Jamie had lolloped out again. 'You going soft in your old age?'

'Less of the old,' he said, and then had to apologise to Liz as her expression told him that he'd spoken with too much force and way too much feeling.

CHAPTER 31

Tuesday 3 June

In my time in the office, I have learned that:

1) Victoria is a blonde shark who says all the right things and smiles a lot. If I were Tom, I would make sure she was never behind me holding anything sharp. (He does not have a good track record with knives.)

2) If I were Kelvin, I would watch her too – although I should rephrase that, as Kelvin – or 'King Leer' as I call him – is always watching her.

3) Monty is a sinner trying hard to be a saint. I fear it could go either way.

4) Stan thinks the word 'fashion' is synonymous with 'effeminate'. Being macho is important to him. Yet he becomes extremely agitated when things do not look 'just so'. I wonder if Stan is wearing an alpha male disguise most of the time and his real clothes are back in the closet. *Closet* is the important word here.

5) Derek rarely finishes a sentence, Linda from the Finance department barely speaks. Yet I keep getting this idea that both of them would like to chat the other one up. I fear I may be turning into one of those women who likes to pair people off.

6) Tom is largely viewed as a 'good boss'. Nobody seems to notice that some of the time he is either hysterical ('Har-har-har'?) or dismissively gruff.

7) Jamie is a round peg being bashed into a square hole. Or vice versa. But I could stare at his mouth all day, especially when he smiles.

8) The fact that Jamie wants to sit by me and talk, makes me inordinately happy. Perhaps the happiest I've been since coming here. It's hard hiding that happiness.

9) My mother always said I should pay attention to signs (particularly 'No Entry' ones). So, there is an art gallery on the ground floor of the office building. It is badly stocked and poorly run. And the room at the back, currently full of things in bubble wrap, has plenty of natural light.

10) Enthusiasm for my work from two people does not make up for a lukewarm reaction from the third. I think Tom is still angry with me about the scalpel. And the rosemary/yew story. And possibly every incident since we first met. Perhaps our chemistry is just wrong.

CHAPTER 32

If Tom had been acting in a film about a magazine, the day when it got put to bed would have been depicted as a dramatic race against time. And as he and Liz finally solved a terrible last-minute hitch, an office-wide cheer would have greeted the file winging its way to the printer.

In reality, most of the last-minute problems usually got sorted out during the marathon session the night before, where everyone worked late and ate takeaways. It was only Tom, Liz and Felix, just before lunch, giving the magazine the traditional last once-over. They rarely found anything wrong – although, famously, Liz had once picked up a typo – 'Mr Rossiter, a keen strumpet player . . .'

Today there were no such hiccups. July's magazine was sent off without any fanfare and now, as far as the writers and creative staff were concerned, it was August's edition that they were thinking about.

Thinking about, but perhaps not acting on – after working flat out the day before, there was a tradition of having a very long lunch and then sloping off early and Tom tended to turn a blind eye to it.

He wasn't turning a blind eye to Fran though, and when he saw her get up and with her bag swinging from one hand leave the office, he waited a few minutes and went out too. He 'bumped' into her in the market square. Was she going home? No, just for lunch.

Well, in that case, could she spare an hour, just to discuss what the likelihood of her doing some more work for them would be? Possibly over a drink and a spot of food?

In the pub garden, they sat in the shade and discussed some of Felix's ideas and she said they were interesting, but could she wait until after the weekend before she made a decision?

Tom wished she would take off her sunglasses, because they hid too much of her face. He had to settle for guessing what expression there was in her eyes as he watched her talk and drink and eat, and as he did, he felt sad that they couldn't be doing this as a couple. That he couldn't just lean across, whisper in her ear and then they would get up and leave and end up in a bed somewhere.

'Can I ask you a question?' Fran suddenly said and did take off her sunglasses. There was a sideways glance at him that stirred up even more thoughts of being in a bedroom with her, tangled up in each other and the bedding.

'Only if I can ask you some too. Afterwards.' He knew he'd used his flirting voice, although when it had last had an outing he couldn't remember.

'Didn't you ask me enough at my interview?' She grinned. 'Almost as many as Hattie asked when I was babysitting.'

'Ah, but she's an expert, I'm just an amateur. And it wasn't an interview.'

Fran was still grinning, so he grinned back and it felt to him like some kind of connection had been made.

'It's just . . .' Fran was toying with the stem of her wine glass, 'well, tell me to mind my own business, but I can't stop thinking about your brother. In the cemetery. How upset he was. And . . . Natalie did tell me that he and Kath have had a very hard time with . . .' Fran looked at him for help.

'Having a baby?' he said.

Fran winced. 'Yes,' she said, 'and I'm glad Natalie did tell me, what with the way I'm capable of putting my foot in things. So . . . I suppose what I really want to know is, has anything happened? Is Kath OK?'

'She's fine,' he said, 'it's all going well . . . but . . .'

'It's all right, Tom.' Fran moved her hand from the wine glass to put it over his. 'Please don't go on. It's wrong of me to stick my nose into your business like this. Let's talk about something else.'

A group of people passed by them to go to a table further up the garden. Her hand felt soft and warm on the back of his. Suddenly he was telling her everything.

He told her about the babies that Kath and Rob had lost before they'd gone to full term and about Rob's panic attacks – one of which she'd witnessed in the cemetery – and his fears that not only would something go wrong, but that he'd be a terrible father. He told her that the thing that Rob was really worried about was letting Kath down.

Fran listened to it all with a sweet, grave expression. 'So sad,' she said when he had finished. 'I suppose Kath's very nervous about everything and relies on Rob for—'

'No. She's an exceptionally strong person. Picks herself up and goes for it. Never complains. You'd like her.'

Fran gave him a slow smile that made the hook work its way a little deeper into his heart.

'I'm sure I would,' she said and then seemed to remember her hand was on his and moved it back to the wine glass. He tried not to show how sad he felt about that.

'So if Kath is so strong . . .' Fran seemed to be thinking it through as she spoke, 'I would think that all Rob has to do is not give her anything else to worry about?'

'That's exactly what I keep telling him.'

'You do?' she said and seemed happy that they had both

had the same thought. He felt that connection between them deepen, only to be jolted out of it when she added, suddenly serious, 'You're not afraid he's going to bolt, are you?'

'Oh God. I hadn't even thought of that. Rob? No.'

'Sorry. Sorry. My tactless gene kicking in again. It's just . . . Well, some men do.' She sat back in her seat and screwed up her eyes.

'Rob won't bolt,' Tom said again, more definitely. 'He might give himself a heart attack, but he'd have it holding Kath's hand.'

She nodded, looking at a spot on the table. 'You're a good brother, Tom. He's lucky to have you.'

'Well, it might seem like that at the moment, but I'm actually the one who's lucky to have him. And Kath. And Joan – that's my mother. I wouldn't have coped without all of them.'

He didn't feel self-conscious unloading that.

'And Hattie's own mother . . .?' Fran asked, delicately.

'Decided she preferred her job,' he said, not ready yet to extend his urge to tell the whole truth of every aspect of his life. 'She's in fashion and travels a lot. We keep in touch by phone and Skype. And we meet up. It works. Now . . . my turn to ask some questions.'

'Fire away,' Fran said and drained her glass.

'OK. You told Hattie that you'd lived all over the place?'

Fran nodded. 'Yes, Italy, France, America. My mother liked to travel.'

'Must have been disruptive? I mean, not just on the schooling front.'

Fran shrugged. 'Well, she settled down when I was about twelve. We stayed in one place then.' Fran pulled a face. 'More's the pity.'

'The island?'

'Yes.'

'And the religious community you mentioned?'

She did a quick look around to see who might be nearby, before leaning in towards him. He leaned forward too, glad of the excuse. She licked her lips.

'It was more of a sect than a community, Tom. Sharing everything, if you get my drift. No boundaries, no heating, home-grown food, weaving our own clothes.' He saw her swallow hard. 'My mother loved it, but it got too much for me . . . I couldn't take the intensity . . . So I stole a rowing boat one evening and escaped – I spent days drifting before I was picked up by a fishing trawler. Just as well, I was down to my last piece of whale blubber and dry biscuit.'

'You're taking the piss, aren't you?' he said.

He had never heard anyone hoot with laughter, but that was the only way to describe the sound that came out of

Fran's mouth. It should have put him off, but he found he was laughing too.

'Oh, Tom. Your face.' She shook her head. 'Priceless. I'm afraid the truth is less picturesque. The religious community was a very sedate collection of retired Church of England clergymen, academics, a smattering of monks and one or two Buddhists. They spent their time either contemplating God or offering guidance to those who came to the island for retreats. My mother was the housekeeper and cook.'

She was studying his reaction. 'You look a bit disappointed. I'm sorry. Apart from all the travel, I've had a very mundane life.' She picked up the glass and tipped it up again, obviously having forgotten she'd already finished her drink.

'And your mother . . .'

Tom didn't know how to finish the question and he wished he hadn't asked it because Fran twisted her mouth and put down the glass.

'Died at Christmas time,' she said in a flat tone.

Well done, Tom . . . way to kill a good atmosphere.

'I'm sorry, Fran,' he said and would have reached out for her hand if she had not, at that moment, put them both in her lap.

'That's all right,' she said, simply. 'It's just been hard . . . you know. There was just her and me for so long—'

'You've no other family?'

Fran wrinkled up her nose before saying, 'Yes. But we've never been close. Still . . . no good wallowing.' She reached out for her sunglasses. 'We should probably go, do you think? Liz will be sending out a search party. We've had our hour.'

They walked back through the village and he wanted to apologise for the questions and for lowering her mood. But most of all he wanted to put his arms round her.

They passed the place where she had been parked when she shut her jumper in the boot and he remembered how spiky they had been with each other then, yet now, if she gave him the smallest sign, he would kiss her and not give a damn what anyone thought.

Had the question about Steph been a sign? The nice comment about how good a brother he was?

Before they went upstairs again, she stopped in front of the window of the art gallery.

'Do you know who owns it?' she asked. When he said it was Mrs Mawson, she replied, 'Oh, I didn't realise. The whole building?'

'Are you hoping they might stock some of your sculptures?'

'Well, possibly. It was just an idea.'

Was that another sign? One that meant she might be staying in the area?

He asked her straight out about her plans and she said, 'This place is really growing on me, Tom. And the people.'

He was sure her gaze stayed with him for a beat too long, but it was so hard to tell with those sunglasses on. It was all he could do not to take her hand and hold it to his lips.

They had barely been back ten minutes when he called her into his office and handed her the phone.

'Someone would like to speak to you,' he said.

He watched her face as she put the phone to her ear and listened. It was Mrs Mawson, and he guessed she was telling Fran all the things that she'd just told him in an uncharacteristically effusive tone – 'Such original work. My father would have been very proud that his tradition of excellence was continuing.'

He'd sent her a hard copy of the main features as he always did, just out of courtesy. She never usually made any comment at all.

Tom had expected Fran to simply look pleased, but her expression was one of unguarded happiness. He almost had to look away, it seemed so raw.

'Thank you . . . very kind.' she said at intervals and then,

'Goodbye. Goodbye.' before she handed him the phone and with a little closed-lips smile went back to her desk.

Tom was upstairs talking to Felix, but he couldn't get his mind off those signs. Or how bereft Fran had looked when talking about her mother. He remembered her sad smile that evening when she watched Natalie and Hattie throwing chocolate beans at each other. The way Fran had dabbed his leg with the cotton wool.

Suddenly he didn't give a stuff about the reasons why she was so wrong for him. All those doubts were sideshows compared to that connection he felt running between them. He was certain she felt it too.

I'm going to offer her a lift home and ask her out. There were signs, definite signs.

Once the words had come into his head, he couldn't rest until he'd talked to her. Having to stand there and finish his conversation with Felix was torture, but he managed it. And then he was walking towards the door leading to the stairs, feeling light on his feet, and as he pushed it open, he glanced down the stairwell. Fran and Jamie were a flight below him, standing on the landing just outside the main-office door. Their heads were close together and Fran had one of her hands on Jamie's shoulder. It looked as if they were ready to dance. Fran was talking softly and Jamie was nodding.

The intimacy between them was obvious.

This was the reason why Fran might stay in the area. It was nothing to do with Tom, but to do with the man whose copy she'd rewritten.

Tom remembered all those looks Fran had lavished on Jamie – the ones he'd chosen to conveniently forget in the onrush of his own desire for her.

He stepped back through the door, feeling as if he was witnessing something intensely private.

An older man on the outside looking in.

CHAPTER 33

Saturday 7 June

1) Tom is affected by stress like a sailing ship is affected by the wind. Yesterday, with the magazine put to bed, he transformed into *kind* Tom again. *Open* Tom.

2) Sunglasses are very good for hiding behind. Almost as good as untruths. Or should that be half-truths?

3) I don't know much about fashion, other than that most of it seems designed to make you discontented with:

   A. Your body.

   B. Your income.

   This ignorance, I suppose, makes me ill-equipped to comment on a woman who chooses it over her family. My mother used to say, 'Do not judge others, lest you be judged yourself.' But really, things over people? 1½ marks out of 3,000 – that's my judgement.

4) Tom is a hopeless liar. If you're going to say, 'It works',

then you should make sure your face is telling the same story as your mouth.

5) I'd like to meet Kath, she sounds . . . this is going to look patronising to anyone who reads it . . . courageous. The kind of courage that is just about clinging on and refusing to give up. I nearly had to put my sunglasses on again when Tom was telling me about her and Rob and the babies. I wish, too, that I believed in Something as my mother did, so I could pray that all will be right with this one. 'It's the furthest they've ever got,' Natalie said when she told me. Of course the tragic effect of Natalie's words was ruined by her adding, 'Whereas my mother, she's popping them out left, right and centre.' I said I wasn't sure about the left and right bit.

6) It felt lovely teasing Tom. He took it in good part too, which proves that, despite some evidence to the contrary, he does have a fine sense of humour.

7) Mrs Mawson was very kind to me on the phone. Almost warm. It's a comfort that, at this moment, she is having pleasant thoughts about me. I hope she remembers that when I'm standing in front of her.

8) Tom should look at his staff and read the signs. It's as if he is also wearing sunglasses but can't see out of them properly.

9) Stairwells can be the best places – somewhere to be

private for a while and let the world go on without you. Wonderful to be able to tell someone how you feel about them. There's nothing I don't like about Jamie, from his floppy hair to his slightly oversized feet. I'm fascinated too by the way he is quietly getting on with what he wants to do with his life, while all this other stuff is heaped upon his shoulders. He says we're heading for trouble. I've told him to remember he has a strong woman on his side now, one who loves him back.

10) The thought of what I'm going to do tomorrow is terrifying me. But I know that now is absolutely the right time. I've done the homework, I've laid the groundwork. Besides, until I take this step, I can't get on with 'other things'.

CHAPTER 34

Sunday 8 June

1) No matter how gently you tell someone something they do not want to hear, they will not like it.

2) When people feel cornered, they call you names and question your motives. That does not hurt as much as the many things they call your mother.

3) Being ejected forcibly on to a gravel drive does not leave you much opportunity for making a dignified exit.

4) Cruelty takes many forms and all of them seem to be acceptable if you live in a big house.

5) The absence of love and warmth smells of furniture polish and dog beds and horse manure.

6) I am a naïve idiot who does not understand how the world works. I thought it would be a matter of what I could bring to their lives, but they can only think what I might take from them.

7) I have learned nothing in twenty-four years. This book was a waste of time. I can't write in it any more. What's the point? Of anything?

8) See point 7.

9) Ditto.

10) Ditto.

CHAPTER 35

'She what?' Tom asked, not because he hadn't caught what Liz said, but because it might as well have been in Welsh.

'She wanted to know if there was any way we could halt printing.'

'Mrs Mawson?' It was as if his brain refused to absorb what he was being told.

'Rang about twenty minutes ago. Voice like razor wire. Said she'd ring back at 9.30, you've got a few minutes.'

'No explanation?'

'Whatever it is, it's too late to put it right. She said she'd discuss it with you, as if I was too inferior to hear what she had to say. Halt printing! I bloody ask you.'

He recalled how happy Mrs Mawson had been on Friday, and now this. Flicking through the magazine in his brain, he tried to pinpoint what might have blown up in their faces.

'Check out the local news sites, will you, Liz? See if you can find any scandal relating to someone we've featured. Use mine.' He nodded at his computer.

'This is a first, eh?' Liz said, with what seemed like relish. 'You caught the sun?'

'What?'

Liz pointed at her nose, then at his.

'Yeah, probably. We went up the coast to one of those cottages we featured back in April. Buckets and spades, crabbing, fish and chips, you know the kind of thing.'

'Sounds perfect. Now, let's see: *Fashion editor on local magazine caught wearing cheap watch.* Nice picture of Victoria, mind.'

Tom has been halfway round the desk before he realised it was a joke. He must be doing a good job of hiding the fact that he didn't feel like laughing.

What *was* funny, though, was that he'd expected his main problem today to be how to act normally around Fran and Jamie. He had no right to be sulky with either of them – he was the one who'd misread the signs or, more accurately, seen them where they did not exist.

Why was he surprised that Fran fancied a younger, good-looking guy and not an older one with 'baggage'?

Trouble was, that reasonable outlook kept slipping and then he felt as if life was closing down again. It would be work, eat, get rid of head lice, sleep, day after day now. Until Hattie left home.

The phone rang and Liz whispered, 'Do you want me to

stay or go?' As if, even before he picked it up, Mrs Mawson might be listening.

'Stay.'

'I talked to someone earlier,' Mrs Mawson said, with no preamble. 'She told me that halting the printing process would be highly difficult. Is that correct?' It was a harsh voice, a voice that said, 'I own this magazine and you work for me.'

He explained the cost and time penalties involved in stopping the print run before asking her what the problem was.

'I suspected it wouldn't be feasible,' she said, ignoring his question. 'I just needed you to confirm it. Perhaps I should have come straight to you on Sunday evening, but one's never prepared for this type of thing.'

'It wouldn't have made much difference, to be honest. And this problem? Are we in danger of printing something that's going to get us into legal trouble?'

There was silence before Mrs Mawson came back with, 'I wish you'd asked me before hiring that woman. It was a poor decision, Tom.'

Fran. This was about Fran.

He sat down, but had enough presence of mind to say, 'Could we just backtrack a second? A poor decision? When

I talked to you on Friday you were delighted with her work. You rang up especially to tell her.'

Silence.

'Mrs Mawson?'

'I don't want to use her again.'

'Can I ask why?'

'No.'

He couldn't hold back the scratchy anger at the way she was talking to him or her assumption that she could dictate who he hired.

'I always thought you were happy that I had full editorial control,' he said. 'If you're going to change that, I think you owe me—'

'I don't owe anyone anything,' Mrs Mawson said with some force. 'I'd be obliged if you'd tell your staff that no further work will be commissioned from Miss Mayhew. And I do not want her allowed access to the office. There will be no further discussion of this matter. Goodbye.'

'Well, that's the peasants told,' he said, not even checking that she had rung off. He threw the phone on the desk.

'So I gather it's about Fran, then?' Liz put the phone back on its stand. 'What's she supposed to have done?'

'Wouldn't tell me. But whatever it is, I'm at fault for

hiring her, evidently.' He filled Liz in on the rest of the conversation.

A whistle from Liz was followed by the word 'harsh'.

'Bloody harsh.' Tom was so incensed that he couldn't even feign loyalty.

'You don't suppose this is something to do with Jamie, do you?' Liz said, with enthusiasm. 'His mother's got wind of him and Fran getting friendly and she doesn't like it? Hey! You don't think Fran's one of those gold-diggers?'

Liz hadn't said the last bit with any seriousness, but he still wanted to throw her out of his office. 'I wouldn't have thought so,' he said, flatly.

She got up to open the door and then closed it again. 'Thought if Jamie was missing, it might mean something. But he's already in.'

Tom didn't know what difference that made.

Liz was doing serious pacing. 'This is tough on Fran, but it's landed us right in the crap again too. We're back looking for someone decent to take over the nature pages.'

'I'm not being bounced into this, Liz. If I roll over now, she might start interfering all the time – who I hire, what we feature. And I'm insulted that she doesn't trust me with what's really going on. She can't just demand this.'

'She probably can, she's the owner. Just be careful, Tom. Don't get yourself sacked.'

'They can't just sack people – do the words "Industrial Tribunal" mean nothing to you?'

'Do the words "Feudal Overlord" mean nothing to *you*?'

He ignored that. 'I'm going to go and see Fran, find out what this is all about. Then I'm going to try and get an audience with the Mawsons. Until I get back, let's keep this to ourselves. It might all blow over.'

There was no answer when he rang the bell at Fran's, but there was a red car on the drive, a slightly different model from last time.

At the rear of the bungalow, he found the back door open.

Someone was clattering bits of metal about – suitable sound-effects for the jittery feelings in Tom's stomach at the thought of seeing Fran again. He knocked on the door frame and the noises stopped abruptly.

She appeared at the window, holding a baking tin in an oven-gloved hand. She had an apron on over her dress, her hair up, but even seen through the glass, her face looked changed. As if someone had soaked it in water overnight. Every muscle seemed drawn downwards.

She moved to come to the door, but then didn't.

He took the initiative and went in.

'Tom,' she said, as if confirming it to herself.

The kitchen was messy and hot. Dirty bowls and baking trays lay on the work surfaces and were piled up in the sink, and what he could only describe as attempts at baking were arranged on plates, or strewn over the table as if she'd removed them from the oven, but didn't know what to do with them. On the cooling racks sat a handful of singed cupcakes.

As he watched, she wandered over to the table and turned the baking tin upside down and some half-hearted muffins plopped out and landed in a drift of flour.

There was nothing decisive in her movements today – as if everything was too much effort.

'What are you doing?' he asked.

She shrugged, picked up a wooden spoon and started to stir some beige-looking mixture in a large earthenware bowl. Although she was doing it slowly, there was a huge amount of feeling going into her movements, as if she was beating something she hated intensely.

It was no good; even though he knew Jamie was her preferred option, he still wanted to hold her.

He tried to concentrate on business. 'I had a call from Mrs Mawson,' he said and the beating stopped.

'Ah.' She did not look up. 'And what did she say?'

'She wanted us to stop the magazine being printed.'

She did raise her head at this. 'You won't do that, will

you? All your hard work. Everyone's hard work.' She put down her wooden spoon and reached for a roll of paper towels balanced on top of a jar of sugar. Tearing one off, she dabbed at her eyes.

'It's too late to stop it,' he said. 'But she also told me that I shouldn't have hired you and that she didn't want me to use you again. She doesn't even want you back in the building.'

Fran wiped her eyes again before the scrunched-up paper towel went into a pocket of her apron. She resumed her beating, this time with more determination than before. He had no idea what was in the bowl, but it wasn't going to survive.

'Did she say why?' she asked, letting the spoon rest for a moment.

'No. I was hoping you would. She didn't want to discuss it.'

'She doesn't want to discuss anything,' Fran said, bitterly, and started with the wooden spoon again. Tom felt as if the two women were treating him like an idiot. He walked over and took the bowl away, leaving her holding the spoon in mid-air. Carrying it to the sink, he balanced it on a baking tin.

'Right,' he said, back at the table. 'It seems to me that Mrs Mawson knows what's going on and you know what's going on, but I – the editor of the magazine – haven't got a bloody clue. So . . . explain how we've gone from Friday, to this.'

'All I can tell you, Tom,' Fran said in a wobbly voice, 'is that I went to see her yesterday evening about a personal matter. I intended to go in the morning, but courage is a funny thing, isn't it? Comes and goes. Anyway. My visit did not turn out well. Not well at all.' She put the wooden spoon down quickly and retrieved the paper towel from her apron pocket.

'That's all I get?'

She sniffed. 'Yes. I'm sorry. But if Mrs Mawson hasn't told you the full story, Tom, I can't. I don't want to add indiscretion to the many other crimes I'm *evidently* guilty of.' She gave her eyes a more ferocious wipe at that.

'I need to know, Fran,' he said.

'Well you can't, Tom. That's how life is. Some of the things you want you can't have.'

Yes, I know. I'm looking at one of them now.

'Fran,' he tried again. 'Is she upset that you and Jamie . . . seem . . .' He couldn't say it.

'This is nothing to do with poor Jamie.' As she spoke his name, it seemed as if someone had let the air out of her. She fumbled for a chair and sat down heavily. Folding her arms on the table, she laid down her head by the wooden spoon and started to cry.

It was proper crying, noisy and dragged from deep inside her, so that instead of shouting, 'Don't you say "Poor Jamie" to me, he's the luckiest bastard around,' Tom pulled up a chair next to her and sat down too. There was so much pain in the crying – nothing like that manipulative stuff Steph used to turn on.

How to comfort her? Any permutation of a hug would have probably been too much for her and definitely too much for him. He settled for patting her gently between the shoulder blades. She felt soft and warm under his hand and he wasn't sure whether he actually said 'There, there,' lost as he was in his own pleasure at being so close to her.

When the crying lessened and she sat up, he let his hand fall away. She looked a mess, puffy and red-eyed and with whatever had been on the wooden spoon smeared across her chin. He would still have kissed her face off if he could.

'Well, this is embarrassing,' she said, sounding more Fran-like. She had a go at smoothing out the crumpled-up paper towel, but it was too soggy. 'Could you . . .?' She was indicating the roll and he passed it to her. She wiped her eyes and face and he pointed out that she'd missed the stuff on her chin.

'And you have cake mixture on your suit.' There was a sad laugh. 'You always get yourself in a mess. I'll try some water on it.'

As she rubbed at his lapel, he fought the urge to kiss the top of her head.

'Fran,' he said, softly, making her look up at him. 'I can't believe you've done anything so bad that you deserve to be treated like this. Tell me what it is and maybe I can help.'

'Oh, Tom.' She pressed her lips together as if saying anything else was too difficult.

There was more wiping before he said, 'Dry-cleaning job, I think,' and she agreed and offered to pay.

'No, I'll send Mrs Mawson the bill. It's her fault.'

'I don't disagree with that. Oh, if only she were a different kind of woman . . .'

He guessed that made sense to Fran, but knew it was pointless asking her to explain.

She disposed of the paper towel in the pedal bin, saying, with her back to him, 'I'm so sorry about this, Tom. You'll have to start looking all over again for someone to do Charlie's pages. I did so much enjoy working for the magazine. And for you.'

When she turned back to him, her eyes were grave and a few days ago he might have thought that 'And for you' was a sign. Now he knew she was just being polite.

There didn't seem to be anything else to say after that and so he left her and when he got outside and glanced back through the window, she was retrieving the earthenware bowl from the sink, the wooden spoon in her hand.

CHAPTER 36

Everything about the Mawson residence was designed to impress and intimidate.

During the long drive from the gates to the front door, it was possible to catch glimpses of woodland and lake. There were gardeners, mowing and clipping. You passed the sign for the stable blocks – plural. Nearer the house, the drive was gravelled, with a turning circle bordered by large urns filled with spiky foliage.

The building itself was a square property, not pretty enough to be called a manor house, not fortified enough to be a castle.

He was met at the door by the housekeeper and shown into one of the sitting rooms. The massed ranks of the ancient Mawsons and Coburgs looked down from the walls in oils. The more recent ones were gathered on the piano, black and white photos in silver frames. Charlie appeared as both a young and an old man and on his wedding day, it looked as if someone had taken the bride and groom from two different ceremonies and thrown them together.

The clock tastefully chimed two, the hour agreed, and Tom waited.

When the door opened, it was only Natalie with coffee. He saw she had a housecoat on that covered more of her than he'd seen covered for a while. Perhaps Mrs Mawson demanded it.

'What's up?' she asked. 'It's like someone's died.'

He shrugged as answer to that and she took the hint and went out again.

He drank his coffee and knew he was being kept waiting on purpose, a version of the Mawson game where they stared you out. When it got to twenty past two, he went over to one of the bookshelves and picked out a book.

Bleak House – how apt. He was trying to read it when the clock stirred itself to tell him it was now two-thirty, and in came Mrs Mawson and Edward the Sneer. There was no apology for being late and Mrs Mawson's greeting was brisk, her son's non-existent.

Since Mrs Mawson's husband had dropped dead on a shoot five years before, Edward had taken over much of the running of the Mawson Empire. Natalie's take on him was that he only had time for things with four legs. Even then they had to be trained and subservient. Or killed. With most people, including his wife and children, he was short-tempered and very aware of his own superiority.

'I see you've made yourself at home,' he said, staring at the book in Tom's hands.

'Well, I had a little bit of time to kill,' Tom said affably. 'Thank you for agreeing to see me.'

Mrs Mawson inclined her head. 'If we could get on with this? I have another meeting at three.'

Tom got the point that he was barely being afforded half an hour of her time.

'I'll be brief, then,' he said. 'Your phone call this morning has thrown up some . . . interesting issues about my role.'

'In what way?'

'Primarily that I've never consulted you before about who I hire – permanent members of staff or freelancers. I'm the editor, it's my call.'

'Yes it is.' Mrs Mawson's tone suggested she was feeling more conciliatory. 'And I have no wish to interfere in how you run the magazine, Tom. Since you took over, circulation has risen and so have standards. You've proved yourself an able editor.'

'Despite not being the best-qualified candidate for the job,' Edward said.

Mrs Mawson's smile for Edward was different from the

one for Jamie. It was more of a 'Sit, boy. Wait. You'll get your turn' command.

'But in this instance, you *are* telling me what to do,' Tom said. 'You're saying I can't use Fran Mayhew even though her work is, as you agreed, of an excellent standard.'

At the mention of Fran's name, Tom felt the atmosphere in the room change. Something to do with the angle of Mrs Mawson's chin.

'This is an isolated incident,' she said, coldly. 'A response to an unusual situation, and does not indicate any change to your position or my position.'

'I'm pleased to hear that, but I'm still concerned. How do I know that an "unusual situation" won't happen again and once more I'll be kept in the dark and decisions taken away from me?'

'Because my mother has just bloody well told you this is a one-off,' Edward blurted out. 'For God's sake.'

Tom was struggling to stay professional. 'So, even though we've agreed you trust me, you won't tell me what the problem is with Fran Mayhew?'

'No,' Edward said, that small word managing to get across that people like them shouldn't even be asked to give people like Tom explanations. Just orders.

'It's not a question of trust,' Mrs Mawson said after giving her son that smile again. 'It's a question of my right to privacy. This is a highly sensitive issue. I thought I made it clear earlier that I didn't want to discuss it any further? Didn't I make it clear?'

Tom wasn't going to do the first-school question-and-answer shtick, and silence set in until Mrs Mawson said, 'I must go. Edward will see you out.'

She paused en route to the door. 'And, should you *ever* find someone who can do a proper job on the nature pages, check with me first that I'm satisfied with them.'

'You don't look very happy,' Edward said when they were alone. 'Of course, you could refuse to do as my mother asks. I'm sure if push came to shove, the management board would support you rather than her.' He laughed and Tom wanted to practise push and shove with Edward, but knew that was a one-way trip to a P45.

When Tom stood up, Edward nodded at the book, now on the table. 'Aren't you going to put it back?'

'Oh, I'm sorry,' Tom said. 'I thought you had servants for that.'

He got more annoyed as he drove away, not less. That visit had achieved nothing. He should have just knuckled under from the start. Then he thought of Fran crying and cancelled that last thought.

Why was the might of the Mawsons being used to crush

her? Whatever she'd done to produce such an extreme reaction had obviously taken all her courage.

Or did he just want to believe her because he was doing what he'd done with Steph? Creating an ideal woman? He considered that and decided this wasn't the case. Apart from choosing another man over him, Fran had always been kind. And tactlessly honest.

This whole Mawson thing smacked of bullying.

He hated bullying.

He went back over Mrs Mawson's words – 'a highly sensitive issue'.

A family scandal.

The question was, did that mean an old or a new one?

His mother looked alarmed when she opened the door. 'Is there a problem with Hattie?' she said, smoothing down her hair.

'She's fine.'

He waited for her to invite him in, but she said, loudly, 'Oh good, Tom. So, you were just passing?'

'Not really, I want to pick your brains.'

'Right. Tom.'

He wondered if she was starting to go deaf, she was talking much more loudly than normal.

'So . . . shall we go into the house?' he suggested.

'Of course, Tom.'

The way she kept repeating his name was worrying too. He made to move forward, but she wanted to show him how good the clematis on the front wall was this year.

When he was finally inside, they sat in the kitchen and she told him she'd talked to Rob and he'd said all the right things, but she wasn't convinced he meant them.

'If you can keep him busy and occupied, he's fine. If not, he over-thinks everything. Always has.'

Tom moved the conversation along to the Mawsons and asked her if she'd heard any gossip about the family recently.

'Why would I?'

'Because you're on just about every committee in Northumberland. It's like having access to a network of spies.'

'You're not wrong there,' she said, with a laugh. 'But, no, can't say I've heard a peep. Since Charlie died, they've been squeaky clean. Well, really since the younger generation took over – Mrs Mawson, her husband. Edward.'

'So if there's a skeleton, it's likely to be in Charlie's cupboard?'

'It'd be a pretty old one, and who'd be interested? I'm not saying he wasn't a handful. And that wife of his, she was a chilly mare.' There was an almost camp wave. 'Mind you, she had a lot to put up with. Drinking, gambling, growing cannabis in the greenhouses.'

'Cannabis?'

'Oh yes. Women all over the county too.' His mother tutted. 'He'd be besotted for weeks and then on to the next one. I think that's why his wife put up with it – knew none of them were a threat. After all, Charlie was never going to up sticks and leave – the money was all on her side.'

'I'm probably barking up the wrong tree,' Tom said. 'Doesn't seem to fit the "sensitive" and "private" description.'

His mother looked puzzled. 'Am I allowed to ask what this is about?'

He gave her an edited version of what had happened with Fran and how the Mawsons had been with him. Said he'd have to kill her now she knew. Or she could just promise not to discuss it.

She held up her three fingers as if taking the Brownie oath.

'So . . . Fran, have I met her?'

'She was the one interested in the baking at the County Show. She guessed what Hattie's vegetable sculpture was.'

His mother seemed surprised at that, before asking, 'Grey-blonde hair?'

He nodded and she did too, before looking thoughtful.

'So . . . scandal . . . what else can I think of . . . ?' She was drumming her fingers on the table. 'Drink driving? That would have been reported at the time – no secret there. Mooning? That was one of his party tricks, but then you know that. Although, by the time you went to the magazine, he'd calmed down a lot. Had a health scare back in the late 1980s – he was drinking too much. Got packed off to a clinic abroad. Suppose you'd call it rehab nowadays.'

'I can't remember that.'

'Why would you? You'd only have been about thirteen at the time. Other things on your mind. He was away a long while.'

'But he never did knock his drinking on the head – not totally?'

'He was a lot less wild when he came back, believe you me. And he lived to a good old age, didn't he?' His mother went back to drumming her fingers before concluding, 'No. Can't think of anything else.'

He rubbed the back of his neck with his hand. 'Don't worry. It was just a hunch. Might even be something different – like Fran's a hunt saboteur and has it in for them.'

'Well, she's in danger of Edward Mawson shooting her, then.'

Tom felt a bit queasy at that thought and stood up and opened the back door to get some fresh air. He looked out over his mother's garden. It was at its best this time of year – a profusion of what she called 'old-fashioned' flowers; hollyhocks, lupins, nasturtiums, stocks and foxgloves. There were fruit bushes too against one wall and wigwams of runner beans dotted around the flowerbeds.

When he looked at flowers these days, he thought of Fran and her dresses. He remembered how she had been in her kitchen. All that terrible baking. Which got him thinking that even if he couldn't alter Mrs Mawson's attitude, he might be able to help her in another way.

He asked his mother and she laughed and said she'd never made home visits before, but she'd see what she could do and why didn't he come and sit back down.

It was as she was talking, that Tom noticed one of the wigwams of beans had feet. There were legs there as well and all the other bits that made up the rev.

Now he knew why his mother had been shouting and repeating his name and keeping him on the doorstep – buying enough time for the rev. to hide.

'Do you know George is in your garden?' he asked and his mother did a theatrical start.

'Is he?' she said innocently, but when Tom gave her a disbelieving look, she suddenly spat out, 'Oh, I'm sick of this. I'm a sixty-year-old woman and I'm skulking around like a teenager just in case I upset my sons. Yes, I know he's in the garden and yes, he'll probably stay here again tonight and yes . . . he is my Fuck Bunny.'

Tom heard himself gasp. Actually gasp. And then he said, 'Do you mean Fuck Buddy?' and she said, 'That is *so* typical of you, here I am trying to be honest and all you can do is correct my English. And don't look so bloody superior or even surprised. I know you saw us in that hotel, and at least I haven't directly lied about George. I haven't said I was watching a play when I obviously wasn't.'

Rocked back on his heels, Tom replied, like an automaton, 'You're right. I'm sorry. George seems nice and you should bring him round for tea,' to which she said, 'Haven't you been listening? We don't have that kind of relationship. We just have sex and I sometimes cook him a meal afterwards. Really, Tom, what else would I have in common with a man of God, for God's sake, but sex?'

Tom didn't remember saying anything after that and was only aware he was back in the car when he had to stop at the traffic lights just before the bridge in Tynebrook.

CHAPTER 37

'But I thought we were pulling her leg about an OAP romance. Not wild, no-strings-attached . . . um . . .' Even Kath was having trouble getting to grips with the concept.

Rob, looking down at the lawn, mumbled something about: 'Isn't it dangerous for older people to carry on like that?'

'It is,' Kath said. 'Heard about it on the radio. They're more likely to get STDs, apparently. They don't have to worry about pregnancies, see. No condoms.'

'Kaaath!' Rob whined and pulled the collar of his rugby shirt up round his ears.

The three of them sat, each in their own way trying not to think about that, as small plastic figures rained down into the flowerbed next to them. Hattie, in paper hat, was making them walk the plank up in her tree house.

'Would you like a drink?' Kath suddenly asked Rob. 'I'll drive.'

'Do I look like I need one?'

'You do.'

'Come on,' Tom said, getting up, 'it feels like a whisky moment. Fetch you anything, Kath?'

'Just a mind-wipe,' she said, watching a miniature Dr Who come to rest in the lobelia.

In the kitchen, Tom poured them two large measures. Rob had drunk his down before Tom had even lifted the glass to his lips. He didn't know if it was the strength of the whisky that was making Rob screw up his face or the thought of Joan and the rev.

'You should be pleased about Mum,' he said, unable to resist making a point, 'you're always trying to pair people up.'

'Yeah, very funny.' Rob held his glass out for a top-up. 'You not having another?'

'No . . . I was trying to lose some weight.'

Rob looked down at his own large stomach. 'Aye, heard Hattie say she'd been helping you do some sit-ups.'

Tom laughed. 'She just perches on my feet.'

'And you've been going jogging? You thinking of re-starting your rugby career?'

No, I was thinking that a leaner, fitter version of me would make a difference to a twenty-four-year old. Sad old sap.

Rob's whisky glass was drained again and Tom said, blandly, 'Just feel I'm getting a bit stodgy round the middle.

And I need to keep my fitness levels up, Hats runs rings round me some days.'

'Do I?' she said behind him, making them both jump. 'And can I have some of that drink?'

'Yes to the first question and no to the second.' Tom put the bottle back in the only cupboard left that had a fully working child-safety catch. The way his brother watched him do it, he feared it should have a Rob-proof catch too.

'I'm bored with the plank game,' Hattie said, adjusting her hat. 'Could we do a sea battle? You be the Spanish Fleet, me the English?'

Kath sat it out as Queen Elizabeth I, and by the time Hattie was climbing back down the ladder to her to be knighted, he and Rob were knackered and 'imprisoned' in the tree house.

They were planning their escape when there was the noise of a car pulling into the drive. Tom guessed it would be their mother; she obviously had superhuman powers. How else had she spotted him in the hotel when she had her back to him? Now her mega-sensitive hearing must have tuned into him passing on her sex confession.

But it was Fran he heard talking. He was out of the tree house and down several rungs of the ladder before he remembered he was meant to be acting cool.

He climbed back up the ladder.

'Thought I'd better get down there quickly, Kath and Fran haven't met before.'

'Good idea,' Rob said, 'just in case she's being extra weird.'

Fran looked happier than the last time he had seen her, although when she wasn't talking, the grave expression dominated her features.

He didn't care. He loved that grave expression.

'Ah, I see you're being knighted, Hattie,' she was saying as Tom arrived beside her. 'Was it for particularly brave fighting on the high seas?' She held out a hand to Kath. 'Hello, I'm Fran. You must be Kath.'

Kath gave Hattie a quick tap on first one shoulder and then the other before extending her free hand to Fran. 'I am,' she said. 'So, you're the woman who made Tom stab himself.'

Fran's smile died. 'It sounds awful when you say it like that . . .'

'No. Tom's always been ham-fisted. It was only a matter of time.'

Rob arrived breathless, as if he'd sprinted down the ladder.

'Hello again,' Fran said to him.

Kath frowned. 'You two met before? You didn't mention it, Rob.'

Tom knew enough about his brother to see he had no idea what he was going to say next. Tom was having trouble thinking of anything himself that didn't involve the words 'cemetery' and 'meltdown'.

'Oh, it was just a quick hello, goodbye in the market square, when I was talking to Tom,' Fran said cheerily, 'and I'm instantly forgettable. I'm not surprised Rob didn't mention it.' Fran gave Rob a big smile and turned her attention to Kath.

Well, look at that – tact and diplomacy.

Tom wished he could reach out and pull her in to him. And then he remembered someone else had that privilege.

'It's really lovely to meet you at last, Kath,' Fran said. 'Hattie was telling me so much about you when I put her to bed.'

'*You* were putting her to bed?' Rob's gaze went from Fran to Tom and settled on Kath.

'Oh yes. I kept Natalie company, didn't I, Hattie? It was Natalie's idea – I was getting a bit stir-crazy at home, what with my car being out of action. But I suspect Tom told you all about that.'

'He hasn't told us a thing.' Kath's delivery was slow as if she was considering something.

'No? Well, Tom came to the rescue. The second time he's helped me out really. The first time was with Greg Vasey .

. . Although, strictly speaking, I'd already rescued myself with the Striking Cobra with Half Twist. Oh—' Fran stopped abruptly.

Tom could see Fran wanted to apologise for mentioning Vasey, but if she did, that would have revealed that she knew more about Rob than she could possibly have found out during a quick hello and goodbye in the market place.

Hattie, unwittingly, dug her out of the hole by pulling on Fran's sleeve. 'Did I tell you that I defeated a whole Spanish fleet?' she said. 'I put everyone to the sword. Except for two Spaniards who I spared because they fought really well.'

'And because one of them gives you your pocket money,' Tom added.

Fran's laugh felt like a hand trailing over his skin. He was beginning not to care that his soppy smile in response to it would be picked up by Kath.

'Oh! I've left them in the car,' Fran suddenly said and went out at the side gate.

Her departure allowed Rob to say, 'What in hell's name is a Striking Cobra with Half Twist?'

'No idea, but it laid Vasey on his back on her carpet. He's the estate agent letting out Fran's cottage.'

He waited. Kath was looking at the side gate. 'And she works for you, doesn't she?'

'Kind of,' he said, not wishing to go into the Mawson situation.

'Hmmm,' Kath replied and then said nothing more. Her silence was worrying.

Fran came back, carrying a plate of scones covered in cling film. They actually looked like scones.

'I brought you these as a "thank you". Such a kind thing to do, Tom. And . . . I think we've cracked scones.' She tilted the plate. 'See, they even have a seam.'

'We?' Rob asked.

Tom knew he was rumbled.

'Tom's mother and I,' Fran explained. 'Well, she's your mother too, of course. Tom asked her if she could find time to help me get to grips with some recipes. She came round this afternoon.'

'I'll bet she did,' Rob said.

Kath was all wide-eyed innocence. 'That *was* kind of you, Tom. Very neighbourly.'

He tried to ignore them both and watched Hattie. She was touching the cling film with a finger. 'They look nicer than last time. Do they taste better as well?'

Tom tried to apologise, but Fran simply laughed. 'Who am I to take offence at someone saying just what they think?' She handed over the plate. 'Do with them what you will, Hattie.'

'I thought I'd eat some of them.'

Another laugh from Fran. 'So literal. Marvellous.'

Kath put her hand on Hattie's back and started to steer her in the direction of the house. 'Come on,' she called back to Rob, 'let's see if we can find some jam.'

If Rob's head had been facing in the right direction, he would have seen the meaningful look he was getting from his wife.

'Rob!' Kath repeated, sharply. It was as if she'd shouted, 'Heel!' Soon Hattie was being bundled into the house.

'You're very lucky,' Fran said. 'A family.'

She didn't put an adjective in there – no 'lovely' or 'friendly' – and at some level he filed that away.

He agreed that he was lucky.

They could be a lot more bloody subtle, though.

She looked apologetic. 'I'm really sorry about mentioning Vasey.'

'I think you got away with it. Besides, you didn't mention the cemetery, that's the main thing.'

She beamed at that and he decided he wasn't really bothered about talking any more, he would have been happy just standing with her in his garden on a summer's evening. Happier lying naked with her, obviously, but if this was all he could have, it felt great. A kind of bitter-sweet great, with the knowledge that Jamie was waiting in the wings.

'Your mother has a great deal of patience,' Fran said.

'She needed it, with Rob and me as sons.'

'Oh, I'm sure neither of you was much trouble. I was trouble from the moment I was conceived.'

He felt he'd lost her and he didn't know what to say, but seconds later, she jollied up again.

'Nice to see the hat is getting used.'

'I dread the day when anything happens to it. She'll be distraught.'

'No need for that. I'll simply make another.'

'So you're not thinking of leaving?'

The way she glanced at him made him suspect he'd blurted that out, but she went on to say, earnestly, 'No. I still have a tiny bit of hope left that Mrs Mawson will start to feel less threatened by me.'

'Threatened?'

'Yes.' She looked as if she really wanted him to understand her. 'She's lashing out because she's scared that I might take something from her. But if I don't make waves, surely it's only a matter of time before she understands—'

'I wouldn't bank on it. They're hard people, Fran. I didn't get anywhere with them yesterday. And, I'm sorry to tell you this, but when I mentioned you, the atmosphere, well, it didn't improve.'

'You mentioned me?'

'Of course. I don't appreciate being kept in the dark about what's going on. And as you won't tell me anything . . .' He smiled at her so that she would know he wasn't blaming her. 'I had to talk to Mrs Mawson.'

Her hand was suddenly on his arm. 'Tom, don't get yourself into trouble over this. You have a career and a family to think of.' She looked towards the back door.

Tom was really, really glad his family was taking so long to find that jam. He wondered which of the windows Rob and Kath were peering out of. Whichever it was, they wouldn't be able to see how Fran's hand on his arm was affecting him. He was sinking into the warmth of her, his body trying to reach out for hers even though he was standing still.

'Please promise me you won't ask her about me again,' she said, and her eyes were so imploring that he couldn't help staring into them. 'Promise, Tom,' she insisted.

'I promise.' Emboldened by the stillness between them that followed, he wondered whether the world would fall on his head if he just kissed her.

And then the look was broken. She broke it and he remembered the day in the office when she had not looked away at all. It felt as if she was stepping back and made him remember the bitter part of this sweet interlude.

'Maybe,' he said, 'the Mawsons are just afraid that you'll take Jamie away from them.'

She frowned and her hand went from his arm. 'There's no reason I'd do—'

'I saw you, Fran,' he said, gently. 'On the stairs, last Friday. You and Jamie.' It felt like scratching at an old hurt.

He looked at her lips and wished he knew what they felt like against his. After what he'd just said, he guessed he'd never find out – he'd portrayed himself as peeping Tom, spying on her.

Which is why he didn't expect the way her hand came back to his arm. 'Jamie and I have become close, I won't deny that,' she said. 'I won't deny I rewrote his copy too, although you've been too kind to mention that. But Mrs Mawson has nothing to fear from me on the Jamie front. At. All.' There was the slightest pressure from her hand. 'In fact, nobody has anything to fear from me regarding Jamie.'

She was back holding his gaze and he wanted to wallow in her eyes and believe what she'd just said. The more he kept looking at her, the more he felt drunk with the intimacy of it. The way she was smiling, the curve of her cheek, the contrast between the colour of her hair and her tanned skin. He couldn't see the small scars on her hands or that lump on her finger, but he wanted to know what they felt like under his mouth.

Two people standing in a garden with the birds still singing.

He was afraid that if he spoke he was going to break this moment, but it seemed to him that the signs he had been looking for were really there this time. He glanced towards the house.

'Fran,' he said, 'I'm going to take a chance here—'

'Can I just stop you, Tom?' she said quickly, letting her hand drop again, and he did stop because he was confused by her being so very upbeat and reasonable. He had no sense that she was going to kick him into the kerb. In fact, she was leaning closer.

'The thing is, Tom, I've found that being successful with something isn't just a matter of determination. Timing is crucial too. It's essential not to rush the moment for all kinds of reasons . . .' She lifted her arm and swept it through an arc. 'For example, because very soon scones will appear with jam on them. Or the people standing in a garden listening to the birds have had a very rough week indeed, and it's still only Tuesday. Or even – and this will sound like complete gibberish to you, Tom, because one of the people standing in the garden is in shadow.'

'You're right,' he said, still wanting to kiss her, 'that is complete gibberish. Neither of us is in shadow – the sun doesn't disappear until it goes behind that conifer.'

'I know.' She shook her head in that way she had when agreeing that she was really hopeless. 'But, Tom, when the timing is right, it *will* make perfect sense.' She looked towards the house, and he realised that he even liked her profile – that slight lift to the end of her nose. 'What you have to remember,' she carried on, 'is that it's not a case of "Let's never have this conversation again." It's "Let's not have it right now."'

Her smile suggested that was all sorted. 'Right, on to other matters—'

'No, Fran—'

'Yes, Tom,' she said, firmly. The look she was now giving him did not encourage him to try to persuade her. It would have been like throwing a load of bubbles at a cactus.

'So, moving along . . .' she said, talking quickly. 'I want very much to do you a kindness in return for sending your mother to help me.'

He didn't think in a million years that the kindness she had in mind was the one he wanted from her.

'It's about the people who work for you, Tom. You really need to pay more attention to what's going on.'

Was she telling him off now?

'Victoria is . . . Well, she's not as squeaky clean or even as nice as she makes out. Kelvin is completely barking up the wrong tree. And Monty. Now he's the one I'm really worried about.'

That, at least, stirred him to speak. 'Monty? But he's a changed man.'

She smiled, sympathetically. 'Tom. There's trouble ahead there. Oh! Goodness! You took a long time to find that jam.'

Hattie was coming towards them. He guessed that Rob and Kath had been unable to keep her in the kitchen any longer.

He still had a few more seconds of Fran standing beside him and he willed himself to ignore everything she'd said and try again to tell her how he felt.

Too late. Hattie had dropped a couple of scones and Fran was setting off to retrieve them. He watched her move, watched her bend. He couldn't stop watching her.

Rob and Kath were coming out of the back door and Fran was replacing the scones on the plate and smiling down at Hattie – another of those smiles that was merely an approximation of happiness.

Hattie must have picked up on that too, because she said, 'I'm sorry I dropped the scones. You don't have to eat them.'

'Oh I don't mind a bit of dirt and some grass clippings.'

'You sure? 'Cos you looked a bit sad when you put them back on the plate.'

'No, no. It wasn't the scones that were making me sad, Hattie. I'm just not feeling myself at the moment.'

'That's good,' Hattie said, looking up at her. 'We've got a boy in our class – Neale Sutton – he's always feeling himself. Mrs Tucker, our teacher, keeps sending him out to wash his hands.'

The phone was ringing. Which was weird as both he and Fran were naked in the garden and he didn't have his mobile on him. Where, after all, would he have put it?

And then he was blinking in the darkness, pushing up from his dream and realising it was the phone in his bedroom that was ringing.

He grabbed at it.

'You're a complete shit.'

Even in his half-awake state he knew who that was.

'Thanks for that, Steph.' He looked at the time on the bedside clock. 03:09 the cheerful red figures said.

'A complete and utter shit.'

'Guessing you've rediscovered your ability to open envelopes. What did you think of the photos? I particularly liked the one where—'

'Don't try and make small talk with me. It would kill you, would it, to let her come out on her own for Christmas? You always have to muscle in on the act. Well, if you think

I'm going to agree to a quick visit from her and then it's "Bye-bye, Steph, we're off skiing", you're stupider than I thought.'

Tom waited for her to take a breath, but on she went. 'You know what I'm going to do when I put down this phone? I am going to tear up your letter. If you want me to restart divorce proceedings, you send Hattie out here in December. On her own.'

Tom was waiting for his anger to kick in, but it wasn't coming. He couldn't even be bothered to sit up and re-arrange the pillows to make himself comfortable. The clock changed to 03:13 at the same time as a moment of clarity arrived – he didn't care if Steph rang off.

'Know what, Steph?' he said. 'Tear up the letter. Burn it if you want. Eighteen months' time, more or less, and it will be five years since we split up. The divorce can just slide through on a nod. I'm fed up with trying to keep you happy on the vague chance that you might play ball and put Hattie first.'

He stopped to check on his anger levels. Rising but not spiking. 'I'm fed up of being your PR person. Next time you let Hattie down, I'm not making excuses for you. She's getting to an age where she doesn't really believe what I'm saying anyway, she just *wants* to. Do you even think about how heart-breaking that is?'

As Tom had been talking, he had started to think of Fran in the garden, the way she had said, 'It's not a case of "let's never have this conversation again" . . .'

Steph's silence seemed different than usual. As if she didn't know what to say.

'Are you drunk?' she asked eventually.

'No. I've fallen for someone else. Hattie likes her too. So sod you.'

And this time, it was him who put the phone down.

CHAPTER 38

Tuesday 10 June

Yes, I know I threw this book into a corner of the room and said, dramatically, 'What is the point in filling it in? I've learned nothing.'

But I've calmed down a little since then. And I've missed sorting out in ten points or less, what has been important.

So, since my last entry on Sunday, I have learned:

1) Beating cake mix is a very effective way of getting rid of the urge to beat a person.

2) This feeling only lasts for a while – then the urge to lay about Edward Mawson with a wooden spoon resurfaces with a vengeance.

3) Being patted on the back while someone says 'There, there' is no substitute for having him put his arms around you and letting you cry all over his shirt.

4) Tom's mother, Mrs Howard, is very knowledgeable

about baking and an extremely patient teacher. She may also have an 'interesting' private life. When she was putting her apron on and rearranging the collar of her blouse, I saw a love bite.

5) Kath is all those things I thought she was. She also seems like good fun. She is not, however, very subtle about getting a small child from a garden to a kitchen.

6) Tom will not only hurtle into a house if he feels your honour is being threatened, he will also go and fight dragons in their own home.

7) Hattie is as tactless as I am. Which would be a comfort, were she not only five.

8) Tom has no trouble asking questions or spotting things in stairwells, but has failed to see that I am not being one hundred per cent honest about my relationship with Jamie.

9) Tom has also failed to spot that I am not being anywhere near honest about what I feel for him.

10) Points 8 and 9 are beginning to keep me awake at nights. That and the 'other' noises in this bungalow.

CHAPTER 39

He didn't exactly dump Hattie in the playground, but it was one of his quickest goodbyes ever and then he was off like a heat-seeking missile. Sod work and all the little thorns scattered on the floor there – whether to tell everyone that Fran was off the team, having to find someone to replace her, Jamie even existing – he was on a trajectory that led only to Fran's bungalow.

His conversation with her the previous evening seemed unreal. Why had he just stood there and let her stop him talking? Well, this morning he wasn't going to be put off. He parked his car by the hedge and fumbled pressing the button to lock it.

While he was confident enough to think he stood a chance with Fran, he wasn't so sure of himself that he could imagine what might happen next. In his imagination, he'd only got as far as taking her face between his hands and kissing her.

He didn't even bother with the front door today, and as

he rounded the side of the bungalow, he rehearsed in his head how he might begin: 'I know you said yesterday about not having the conversation right now, but is twelve hours later, later enough for you?'

He guessed at this time of the morning, she'd be in the kitchen. Or maybe she wouldn't even be up yet. If so, she might come to the door in whatever she slept in.

He prayed she slept in nothing.

He glanced towards the kitchen window as he walked and stopped so abruptly he felt a jolt as the momentum in the top half of his body carried on. Jamie Mawson was there, just turning away from the sink, a glass of water in his hand. A bare-chested Jamie Mawson.

Tom could see that he had on a pair of striped pyjama bottoms. The first leaden feeling of unease reached his stomach.

Realising his hand was raised to knock on the door, he lowered it and side-stepped out of view. But he could still see anyone who came to the window in the kitchen and here was Jamie again to re-fill his glass. His hair was messed up as if he'd not long raised his head off the pillow.

Tom watched Jamie drink and then roll first one shoulder and then the other. There was not an ounce of bloody fat on him.

Tom felt as if someone had put their hand round his windpipe.

It's all right; Fran might not even be in.

And here was Fran. She had on a nightdress, white with thin shoulder straps and her hair was loose. Tom thought how wonderful life would be if that was his first sight every morning, before the hand round his windpipe tightened.

He wanted to call out to her, 'Don't touch him – if you don't, I can still pretend he's just a friend who's staying over.'

Fran gave one of Jamie's shoulders a pat and Jamie grinned and bent forward and dropped a kiss on the top of her head before peeling away from the window. Almost immediately, Fran was gone too.

He had no doubt where they were both heading.

In addition to the hand around the windpipe, someone had taken a small knife, inserted it between his ribs and twisted it to get to his heart. He slipped away and, by the time he reached the car, he felt breathless as well, as though Fran's duplicity had winded him.

He had trouble getting the car unlocked, before he drove up the track as fast as possible. Half a mile further on, he stopped in a lay-by. Now his breathing sounded like the forerunner of something more emotional and he slammed both hands on the steering wheel. She was a liar. All that crap about timing. All that crap about having nothing to fear from her relationship with Jamie. She'd played him.

But why? Was it all part of the Mawson thing? Get Tom on her side for whatever she was doing here, but don't let him get too hands-on?

A welter of horrible suspicions took hold of him. She'd seemed so honest, so unworldly. All that over-the-top enthusiasm. Yet she was exactly like Steph. How did he do it, pick them like this?

From Peeping Tom to Tom Fool.

He should have trusted what his eyes had seen on the stairs at work.

Well, he trusted them now. That scene in the kitchen came back more vividly than when he was standing just feet away watching it – the fresh-from-bed nature of the pair of them. Her skin on his. That kiss.

He called her a bitch then, out loud. A word he hated for a woman he had come to love. A woman who didn't exist – another idealised version of the real thing.

His phone rang and he ignored it. He remembered with an extra lick of bitterness, how he'd tried to defend Fran against the Mawsons. Well, maybe they were more astute than he was.

A part of Tom knew he was running off into paranoia and self-pity, but this betrayal felt visceral.

The phone rang again. Again he ignored it.

Maybe he'd been spotted and it was Fran. 'Oh, Tom. Jamie just popped round to mend the tap and it's so hot in here he had to strip off . . .'

It was like the plot of a very bad porn film.

The phone had started up again and the word *Kath* managed to shoehorn its way through his bitterness and he checked the screen. Liz. The need to shout at someone reared up and he took the call.

'Thank God,' she said. 'I've got a crisis here!'

'Oh really? What, we're out of photocopier paper? Someone hasn't watered the plants? So you thought, let's dump it all on Tom. His shoulders are bloody broad.'

Tom could almost feel the outrage in the silence that followed and then Liz let fly with, 'Who the hell do you think you're talking to? What's your problem?'

How could he answer that?

'Oh, you've gone quiet now, have you? Well, just listen, then. I'm at the Tap & Badger. Monty is here in a bad way. He's drunk and disturbing the guests. The manager's cutting him some slack, but his patience is going.'

'And what am I meant to do about that?' Tom snapped. The thought of facing anyone seemed beyond him.

'What are you meant to do? Help me drag him out, that's bloody what. If we don't, the police will have to be called and I don't care how pissed off you are with whatever you're pissed off with, I don't want to see Monty in the papers, perhaps in court and definitely in Mrs Mawson's bad books.'

'I don't need this right now,' Tom said.

It was the sound Liz made that brought him to his senses, a cross between a growl and an exasperated sigh. 'Listen, pal. Unless you're actually sitting in A&E with Hattie . . . or Kath, you need to come here now. Or does poor Monty not qualify for help on account of him not being in his twenties with grey-blonde hair?'

Tom found Monty in the lounge of the Tap & Badger – it wasn't hard, he just followed the noise.

Among the wood-panelling and guests having coffee, he was clinging to the back of a sofa demanding a drink. Liz didn't even turn to look at Tom when he arrived.

'I've been a patron of this hotel for years,' Monty shouted. 'I've written reviews for your crappy restaurant. If I were in Spain you'd give me a brandy with my morning coffee, so forget the bloody coffee and just bring me the brandy.'

It being England, everyone in the room pretended nothing was happening, while being covertly, deliciously, outraged.

The hotel manager had cut off Monty's route from sofa to

bar with a legs-apart stance and hands on hips. A teenage waiter with a white cloth over his arm had blocked Monty's other possible route up the stairs to the bedrooms. The cloth made it seem as if Monty was an unusual dish and the waiter was trying to catch and serve him. If he was a dish, it was one that had been steeped in alcohol – Tom could smell it from where he was standing.

It was doubtful whether Monty had slept the previous night, the rims of his eyes were as red as his cheeks and there was an oily sheen to his skin. His shirt, his jacket, his trousers were all crumpled.

'Tell them to give me a drink,' Monty said when he spotted Tom. He lifted one hand from the sofa to make his point and had to swiftly put it back before he slipped to the floor.

'See what I mean?' Liz was still not looking at Tom.

Tom tried to remember how he had handled Hattie during the Tantrum Years. There had not been many – but they had been spectacular.

'OK, Monty,' he said, cheerily. 'I'd rather drink in the Barleycorn. We can have one of their fried egg sandwiches. Come on, I'm paying.'

Tom called it the promise/distract approach. It worked on the theory that it was better to have the fight outside, away from an audience.

'Yes. The Barleycorn,' Monty shouted. 'I'm taking my custom . . . elsewhere.' Although it came out as: 'YER, THE-BARRYCOURT. EMTAKINGMYCOSTUME . . . ELSEWHIRR.'

With the waiter's help, they got Monty outside and propped him against one of the picnic tables.

'To the Barleycorn, *mes amis*,' Monty shouted to the early-morning shoppers.

'What the hell's brought this on?' Tom said.

'Who knows?' Liz shrugged. 'Why do people just start shouting at other people?'

'Liz, I'm sorry. You got me at a bad moment.'

'Yeah? Well, I've been having one of them since 2007.'

'All women are witches.' Monty wagged his finger at Liz. 'Even the ones who aren't women.'

Tom wondered if his own earlier ranting had sounded as insane.

'OK. I'm taking Monty to his flat,' he said. 'You want to keep an eye on him while I get the car?'

Liz already had her hand out for the keys. 'No, I'll go for the car. Then, as I'm putting your Mr Shouty turn down to temporary insanity – I'll ring round his cronies, see if anyone can babysit him instead of you.'

He didn't have time to thank her properly before she had stomped off.

'OK, change of plan, Monty. I've got a bottle of Malt

whisky in the boot,' Tom lied. 'I'm guessing you've had some romantic disaster? Snap! Let's get you home and compare notes over a dram.'

'Is it that wife of yours?'

Tom shook his head. 'No, for once it isn't.'

In the fifteen minutes it took to drive to Monty's flat in a converted agricultural barn, he became maudlin. 'My whole life is a messhh. A big messhh. I'm a fat, old loser.'

Tom had to use all the skills learned on the rugby field to get him from the car into the flat and, on top of getting hammered, it looked as if poor Monty had been burgled. Books and CDs, newspapers and items of clothing were jumbled up on the sitting-room floor. It was only when Monty started to kick out at some of the things, that Tom realised he'd created the mess in the first place.

'Get outa my way,' Monty told a pile of cookery books as Tom lowered him on to the sofa. Once there, he assumed a classic head-in-hands pose.

'My life, Tom. My bloody life. I'm pathetic, pathetic,' he crooned.

It was a soundtrack that was maintained as Tom went to the kitchen to get water. He thought of Fran as he filled the jug. How had she seemed so open, yet wasn't? A neat trick

– a certain degree of eccentricity was useful cover for a lot of things. Look at Boris Johnson.

'Drink up,' Tom said, putting a glass of water in Monty's hand when he got back to the sitting room. He expected Monty to say, 'This isn't whisky,' but got instead, 'Why did it happen?' Monty was spilling a lot of the water. 'She made me try harder. Oh God, Tom. She was lovely, lovely.'

Tom was beginning to wish he did have that whisky. Monty drank some water and shoved the glass back at Tom and scrabbled around in his jacket. Pulling out his wallet, he flipped it open and eased out a photograph. 'So beautiful,' he said.

The photograph was tilted towards Tom and he saw an Asian woman, who was indeed very beautiful. And very young. He wondered if this was what Monty had been showing Fran in the office.

'Met her the last night of my holiday – Bangkok. We connected straight away and talked for hours, right up until I got on my flight.'

'Monty, do you just want to drink some more—'

'We've Skyped constantly since.' Monty stopped tilting the photograph and looked down at it, sadly. 'She was going to come over. I was going to be the man she needed. As hard-working as she is. I've tried, Tom.'

As Monty slurred to the end of his speech, he sobbed.

Tom did some consoling from a safe distance.

Eventually Monty said, 'I'm a fool. Why did I think a young woman who looked like that would see anything in me?'

If Tom couldn't have the whisky, he'd like one of Monty's friends to arrive soon, please, so he didn't have to listen to this version of his own misery.

The photograph was still clamped between Monty's stubby thumb and forefinger.

'Was it the age difference that finished it?' Tom asked, not really wanting to hear the answer.

Monty shook his head. 'We could have coped with the age difference, but I can't cope with her being a man. She told me last night. She didn't want it to change anything, but how would that work?'

Tom found he had sat down next to Monty. How had Fran known there would be trouble ahead with him? Perhaps Monty was right about the witch thing.

'It was the promise of a new start – I've lost that too,' Monty said and Tom could only agree as Monty had another cry, more discreet this time, as though he was sobering up. When he seemed to have got through it, he said, 'I'm going to pass on that bottle of whisky, Tom. Sleep, got to have a sleep.'

Tom went upstairs and brought down a duvet and a pillow and got Monty comfortable.

Monty was mumbling away. 'Should have bloody known it would fall apart . . . I don't ask for much . . . and then some arse like Charlie gets it all . . . a young woman mad about him and what does he do?'

Suddenly Tom was all attention. Was this the skeleton in the Mawsons' cupboard? *A young woman.* Tom did some arithmetic concerning ages and dates, and factored in the way Mrs Mawson had gone on to high alert when Fran had paid her a visit.

Jeez, why had it taken him so long to see? Fran and Charlie. They must have had some kind of fling once – a massive age gap, but not unheard of. Then Fran turns up at the Mawsons', threatens to spill the beans and perhaps asks for a little something to keep quiet.

Tom did another bit of arithmetic to see if he could square pumping a drunk, heart-broken man for information.

He found he could.

'Sorry, Monty, I didn't quite catch that . . . about Charlie?'

Monty gave a start as if he'd forgotten Tom was there. 'What about him?'

'You said, a woman? A young woman.'

Monty screwed up his mouth and frowned and when he

opened it again it was to say, 'Yes, the woman he had in Italy. He hated his wife, you know.'

'I gathered that.'

Monty started to laugh, which turned into coughing and at one stage looked worryingly like it might become vomiting. When Tom had got him stabilised, Monty announced, 'Charlie took off one day, with passport, destination unknown. Wife bloody furious and despatched someone to find him. Took them a bloody long time.' Monty chuckled to himself and closed his eyes.

'But they *did* find him, obviously?'

'Oh yes. In Italy. Along with a young woman.' There was a snort from Monty, during which some snot came out of his nose. He pulled a hand out from under the duvet and wiped it away. 'A pregnant young woman.'

This was worse than Tom thought.

'When was this?' There was no reply and Tom saw that Monty was, as Natalie would say, 'going off'.

'Monty!' Tom said, sharply, and Monty's eyes opened.

'What?' he said.

'This *pregnant* woman. When was this? And what happened to her?'

'I'm very tired,' Monty said, sulkily, putting his hand back under the duvet.

'I know. Just a few more minutes and you can have a

good snooze. So . . . what happened to the woman?'

Another snort from Monty, mercifully snot-free this time. 'Charlie happened to her, that's what. His wife had sent an ultimatum: come home or that's it. Money cut off, whole family disowns you.' Monty pulled the duvet further up around his neck and shifted his hips as if trying to get more comfortable. 'He caved in. Walked out one morning to get bread, never went back. Trotted home, tail between legs.'

That would make you bitter.

Again Tom could feel Monty falling away from him, but he didn't care. Getting down on his knees, he shook him gently.

'The woman, Monty. What was her name?'

'Bugger off, Tom. Sleepy. Never knew a name. Only know all this because Charlie thought he was dying one night, he'd taken something on top of drink. Confessed all, as they say.'

'But the woman, she must have come looking for him?'

'No, Charlie's wife paid her off, or tried to. The cheque came back in pieces. Only thing after that . . . a postcard.' Monty yawned elaborately and a wave of stale drink came Tom's way.

'Which said?'

Monty grumbled something and so Tom shook him less gently this time.

Monty peeled open his eyes. 'What? What? Why don't

you leave me alone? It was just a postcard from San some-where . . . Diego, that's it. Baby born, blah de blah, may God forgive you.' Monty's eyes closed again. 'Charlie got completely rat-arsed that night, told everyone he was cele-brating Nelson Mandela's release.'

Tom stared at Monty's mouth as his Fran/Charlie theory collapsed . . . and then another one started to take its place.

'This happened in the late 1980s, 1990, then? When Charlie was allegedly in rehab?'

Monty grunted. 'Rehab my backside.'

Tom sat back on his heels. He needed one more answer before Monty slipped under.

'This baby?' he asked. 'Was it a boy or a girl?'

Monty didn't respond, so Tom was ashamed to find him-self dabbling his fingers in Monty's glass and then flicking water at him. When there was no response, he cupped his hand, poured some water in it and chucked it at Monty.

He spluttered awake.

'Boy or girl, Monty?'

Tom barely recognised this bullying version of himself and it was a waste of time, anyway. Monty had drifted again, it was going to take a whole bucket of water to bring him round this time. Tom drew the line at that and stood up. And then, softly, as if Monty was dreaming them, he heard the words, 'The pink kind. A girl.'

CHAPTER 40

There was no sign of life, not in the kitchen anyway, so Tom hammered on the back door. That would get them out of bed.

A black stew of emotions had brought him here – the need to tell Fran he knew who she was. Anger that she'd got him involved in whatever she was playing at – which he could only assume was revenge, considering the way she was sleeping with Jamie. And a deep desire to see her and tell her that he despised her.

He might not have been totally honest about that last emotion. It was actually heavier on the desire to see her bit than the despising her part.

She came to the kitchen window, checked who was knocking and then she was at the door. Over one of her dresses, she had on the jumper that she'd trapped in the boot of her car.

'Oh, Tom,' she said. 'I'll just come out.'

'I'll bet you will.'

She frowned but came out anyway, closing the door carefully behind her.

'Good to see you dressed at last,' he said, nastily. 'What happened? Jamie run out of energy?'

When her expression was one of confusion, he was so irritated that he reached round her and pushed open the door again. There, hanging about between the kitchen and the sitting room, was Jamie. He was still bare-chested.

'Oh, for God's sake, isn't it time you put some clothes on too?' Tom shouted through to him.

Jamie looked as if he was trying to disappear by willpower alone. 'Hi, Tom, yeah. Sorry. I had a dentist's appointment . . . but it got cancelled, so I thought I'd . . . I mean . . .' Jamie was pulling at the fingers on one hand with the thumb and finger of the other. 'I was going to set off later, honestly. There was really no need to come and collect me.'

Tom did a great whooping laugh and felt as if he was a pantomime villain. 'That's a good one, Jamie. Think I'm a bloody truancy officer? Add that to the other titles, shall I? Idiot. Sucker.'

'Tom,' Fran said, gently. 'What is wrong with you?'

'Where would you like me to start?' He tried to glower at her, but it was very hard when faced with those blue eyes, so he pushed past her into the kitchen. Jamie took a step back.

Tom looked around; there was a cake on the side sandwiched together with jam and topped with white icing. 'That yours?' he asked.

Fran nodded.

'Well, it's rubbish!'

He saw the look that passed between Jamie and Fran.

'So, Jamie,' Tom said, rubbing his hands together and hating the gesture even as he was doing it. 'Has Fran told you? Has your mother told you? Do you know and don't care? Or are you blissfully ignorant and as big a sap as I am?'

Jamie looked as if he were drowning on dry land.

Tom felt Fran come up behind him and place her hand on his back.

'Don't touch me,' he said, turning on her. 'You're not doing that bloody Crouching Tiger, Flaccid Python thing on me. Well, does Jamie know?'

She seemed as if she was about to say, 'What?' and he couldn't bear it. So lovely, yet such an actress.

'Don't waste your breath with all that "Oh, look at me, I was home-schooled" stuff. I know that you're Charlie's daughter.'

Fran changed the embryonic 'What?' into an 'Ah'.

'Yep. Ah, indeed. You're Charlie's daughter from an affair in Italy. Abandoned by him – which I guess is where all this comes in.' Tom waved his hand about to encompass the kitchen, Jamie and Northumberland.

'Who told you, Tom?' Fran asked. 'Was it Monty?'

Tom pressed his lips together in a dramatic fashion.

'So it was,' she said. 'Well, you got further with him than I did. I knew Monty must have been one of Charlie's drinking pals, but he was very discreet. Oh dear. Don't tell me this means that Monty has twigged about his lady friend in Bangkok and tumbled back into his old ways in spectacular fashion? Poor, poor Monty.' Tom was aware he was being scrutinised. 'And you took advantage of him being drunk?'

How did she bloody do that, make him feel as if he was the guilty one?

She looked pained. 'Well, I'm sure that wasn't your finest moment, Tom.'

'Hang on, *you're* telling *me* off? You're the one at fault. You came to work on the very magazine Mrs Mawson owns and where Jamie just happens to be working—'

'Can I just stop you there?' she said in a reasonable tone. 'I didn't want to work on the magazine. I told you that most definitely.'

'Yeah, played that well but then, lo and behold, you changed your mind. Why was that, Fran?'

'I really don't want to discuss this when you're in such a funny mood.'

Tom realised he had turned his back on Jamie and so spun round in time to see him trying to disappear along the hall.

'And where do you think you're going?' He was so angry now that even he didn't know what was going to come out of his mouth next. 'Did you or did you not know that Fran is Charlie's daughter? You never answered me.' Tom was jabbing his finger in Jamie's direction and Jamie was looking terrified.

'Yes,' he squeaked out.

'Do you know what you've done, then?'

Jamie said, 'No . . . I . . . not really.'

Was he the only one in the room who understood how serious this was?

Tom spelled it out. 'You're sleeping with someone who's your blood relative, Jamie.'

Jamie looked down the hallway. 'Now, Tom . . . that's just not true. There's no way she is.'

'I saw you,' Tom said, 'in the kitchen.'

'Oh dear,' Fran said. 'First the stairwell, now the kitchen.'

That was when he really lost it. 'You heard of incest, Jamie?' he shouted. 'Because I think this probably qualifies. I mean Fran obviously doesn't care who she's shagging, but you, Jamie? For God's sake! You're sleeping with your mother's half-sister. Your grandfather's daughter. Your half-aunt. I could draw you a family tree if you like.'

Jamie looked towards Fran and the expression on his face screamed 'Help!'

'Take a deep breath, Tom,' Fran said. 'Sit down, put your head lower than your hips and take a deep breath.'

'Why? So you can do something horrible to me? What are you trying to achieve here, Fran? Shag Jamie as some kind of revenge on the Mawsons because they tempted Charlie back from your mother? Or is it just a bit of black-mail and Jamie's an unplanned extra—'

Tom stopped talking because he heard a noise and suddenly there was Natalie standing next to Jamie.

She was wearing a striped pyjama top.

CHAPTER 41

He climbed the ladder to the tree house and sat on the platform looking out at the view.

Mortification. That was the word for what he'd been feeling ever since he put the striped pyjama top and the striped pyjama bottom together and made a couple out of Jamie and Natalie.

Not Jamie and Fran.

They'd all tried to get him to stay, but he'd backed out and almost sprinted for the car. His only stop on the drive home had been in the familiar lay-by where he'd rung Liz to tell her Monty was OK and a pal had turned up to babysit him. She was still cool with him, even more so when he said he was knackered and would work from home this afternoon. He had been going to say he wasn't feeling himself but, thanks to Hattie, he was never going to use that phrase again.

Oh. God. All those things he'd said in that kitchen – revenge, incest, shagging. As if they were in some Greek tragedy. What was worse, accusing Fran of sleeping with Jamie or suspecting her of sleeping with Charlie?

Tom looked up into the canopy of the tree and watched the leaves shifting, repeatedly changing the pattern of sunlight being filtered and blocked. It created the illusion that the platform was moving – easy to imagine the tree house was at sea. That's how he was feeling – and he was having to reassess things he thought he'd understood. Including Charlie.

Now he saw the relevance of Fran's question about whether Rob would bolt.

The fact that Fran was so calm in the face of his aggression and stupidity made it all seem worse. He'd come across like a spoilt boy – it must have been so obvious it was all a paranoid fantasy inspired by jealousy.

And poor Jamie. What psychological damage had he done by telling him he was sleeping with his grandfather's daughter?

'If you're going to jump,' Fran called up to him, 'can I suggest something higher?'

Too late to seek sanctuary in the tree house. He peered over the edge of the platform and got a full blast of Fran's face looking up at him. Blue eyes, open expression. General gorgeousness. She was carrying the jumper that she had been wearing earlier.

Should he take it as a good sign that she had come to find him? No, he was sick of signs, they were a big part of the reason he was skulking around in a tree.

He couldn't quite look Fran in the eye and sat back up straight again. He was experiencing what felt like an all-over body wince.

Because he didn't know how to talk about the big things, he simply said, to the leaves of the tree, 'I didn't hear your car?'

'I parked further down the road and I was very careful with the side gate, I know if you pull it open too sharply it squeaks. I thought if you heard me coming, you might run away.'

Why should he be surprised that she was making fun of him? He was a clown.

He chanced peering down at her again. She was, with almost comical slowness, shaking out the jumper and laying it on the lawn. She sat down. The message was, unmistakably, I won't come too close, don't worry. But I'm not leaving either.

'And now what shall we talk about?' she said. 'You up in your tree and me down here?'

'Fran, I don't know how to start to apologise.'

'Then don't, let's talk about something easier to begin

with. How about Natalie and Jamie? Must have been a bit of a surprise?'

'Uh-huh.'

'I didn't twig for a while, what with the way Natalie teased him in public. Been carrying on for months, evidently, right under his family's nose. In between Natalie cleaning and polishing.'

'They look good as a couple,' Tom said.

A laugh drifted up to him. 'Very tactful, Tom. Shorthand for, what does someone as sharp as she is, see in him? But you might think differently when you get to know Jamie properly. Let's just say he's like an iceberg – some bits for public viewing, but below the water, the real him. He's kept it protected so his family can't get to it.'

Tom imagined that faced with someone like Edward, he too might have hidden a huge part of himself.

'That shyness of his,' Fran said, 'it hides how funny he can be and here's the thing, Tom, he can't string a couple of sentences together on paper, but he has a very fine business brain. He can spot where there's money to be made. Would it surprise you to learn that he's already got a good little business going?'

He was surprised, so surprised that he looked down at her and got another fix of those blue eyes.

'Goes to auctions,' she said. 'Looks out for all kinds of

things – mechanical toys from the 1950s, unusual books – hoovers them up for a song, finds a buyer on the Internet and sends them out into the world. I think that's one of the things Natalie likes – he's making his own way, as she is.' There was a noise that sounded like a whistle. 'She really does love him, Tom. Fiercely, and may I say . . . noisily. So . . . she'll go into battle for him when Deborah finds out what's been going on.'

Deborah. It still didn't sound right, even from her half-sister.

Were there any similarities between the two women? Perhaps the straight back, the brisk way of talking, but one of the sisters was closed in, judgemental, whereas the other . . .

'Fran,' he said quickly, 'I'm so, so sorry. All those things I said to you. I could put it down to misreading signs – it's a family trait – but that's a cop-out. I was . . .' He was trying not to say *that* word and looked up into the leaves of the tree for inspiration. All he could see was green. 'Jealous,' he admitted. 'I was jealous.'

The word seemed to plummet out of his mouth straight down to the grass. He'd finally revealed how much he was attracted to her. But then rampaging around her kitchen like a bull elephant had probably confirmed that anyway.

He waited for her to reply and when she didn't he looked

over the edge of the platform once again. She waved up at him. 'Still here,' she said. He saw the way her eyes were scrunched up as if she was thinking hard about what he'd said.

He waited, his heart feeling as if it had slipped out of its regular rhythm.

'Not a *great* fan of jealousy, Tom,' she said at last, as if giving her verdict on gherkins or aniseed balls, 'but I feel that's only part of the reason why you went completely insane in my kitchen. You also have a natural tendency to think the worst of me and I'd suggest that's a learned response to repeatedly negative female behaviour.'

'Have you got a textbook down there?' he joked to cover up how spot-on an assessment of his marriage that had been.

'No. But if I did, I might throw it at you, and this time I wouldn't try to miss. And really, Tom, don't push it. I'm trying to excuse your terrible behaviour. And, for once, I'm being tactful instead of just blurting out that I think you've been treated shabbily and, possibly, stabbed in the back in the past.'

He sat back. 'Yeah, OK, I get the message.'

'Good. And see, I didn't even mention your wife.' There was a pause and a soft, 'Oh! Damn.'

He couldn't help smiling at that, but smiling didn't help

him work out what to say. There was silence until Fran's, 'So . . . not a great fan of jealousy, but the thing I really hate is manipulation. Particularly that brand some women practice – it's as though they're saying "I've run out of logical arguments to get what I want so I'm just going to go for the emotional jugular."'

He may have said, 'Um.'

More silence before Fran's voice, with a sadder tone to it, found its way up to him again. 'But really, all of this is actually my fault, Tom, for being so mysterious. The way I probably seemed to be giving green lights and then holding up stop signs. Crawling around in a cemetery, for goodness sake . . .'

Suddenly her voice broke and there was a strange throaty noise and he saw she had turned her back to him. She was now sitting cross-legged, resting her elbows on her knees and cradling her head in her hands.

He stood up. It looked as if she could only just support her head, her misery weighed so heavily on her and as he watched, she started to cry. Now her shoulders were heaving and the sound was horrible, worse than that morning after she had been rejected by the Mawsons.

'Fran, don't, please,' he said. 'None of this is your fault.'

He didn't even know if she could hear him above the sound of the crying.

He started to climb down the ladder, checking how she was doing as he went. Not good, judging by the pitiful sounds she was making. He should have just gone to her when she first arrived and apologised like a man.

'Fran, please,' he repeated as he stepped down on to the lawn. 'I understand the reasons you kept it quiet. I had no automatic right to know.'

She still sounded as if she was crying her heart out and he couldn't bear it. Lovely, honest Fran, sobbing because he'd been an idiot. He covered the distance to her quickly and then he was down on his knees, by her side. He remembered how he'd dithered before about how to give her comfort, but this time it seemed natural to wrap his arms around her and pull her into his chest. 'Fran, sweetheart, don't cry.' He wasn't sure whether among those words he'd voiced the deep 'Ahhhhhhh' that he felt as her body nestled into him and he put his cheek to the top of her head.

Fran in his arms. The warmth and the vitality of her.

'Shush, sweetheart, it's all right. Everything's going to be all right.'

She stopped crying and turned her head to look up at him and, instead of blotchiness and tears, there was a wide smile and a deeply mischievous look.

'There,' she said, 'that's how a manipulative woman

would have got you down from the tree.' She laughed and he found his initial surprise turning into something else – something where his head wasn't completely in control of the situation.

'Fran,' he said, suddenly desperate to know, 'those things you said yesterday? The shadow . . . timing . . .?'

She was looking at his lips, even when he'd stopped talking. He was looking at the skin on her cheek and the curve of her brow – breathing her all in.

'I couldn't bear to mislead you, Tom,' she said, softly, 'I wanted to come to you as *me*. And now it's all out in the open between us . . .'

Come to you.

The words ignited inside him – in his head, his chest, his groin – and he had his mouth on hers without registering that he had moved. He was kissing Fran Mayhew, only thinking about how her lips felt and how she was kissing him back, eyes closed. He could smell the grass and feel the breeze, but it was her taste on his tongue.

Deep kisses. Insistent kisses. The kind of kisses where snogging didn't even cover it.

He was laying her down on the jumper, every part of him wanting to please her. And, if he was honest, see her naked.

He could feel her under him, the familiar outline now

taking on a new geography of flesh and muscle and breasts. Her hands were in his hair, one of his had found its way to her thigh.

He had no idea how he was breathing any more, there was just her body and her mouth and his own need to take this further.

More kissing until, as if one of them had spoken some kind of instruction, they pulled away from each other.

'Come upstairs with me, Fran,' he said and she was staring at his mouth again.

'No, I couldn't. That's Hattie's place. I'm sorry, it just wouldn't seem right.' She was kissing him again and it was a while before he felt inclined to pull away and say, 'Not the tree house, the other one. Come on.' He peeled himself off her and stood up.

A hand extended and taken, and she was laughing at her mistake as they were moving towards the back door, but making terrible progress because he wanted to know what it felt like kissing her standing up and because they had to go back for his house keys which were in his bag on the lawn.

Inside, they were Tom and Fran, a gang of two giggling their way conspiratorially past all the normal flotsam and jetsam of his life which suddenly looked magical.

He was hanging back so Fran would go first up the stairs

and he could cup her bottom and she was turning and saying in mock outrage, 'Tom Howard. Really!', her face flushed and her hair awry.

Into his bedroom, with the bed that had never been used for this. But he couldn't get her on to it. She danced away, held out an arm to make him stop. 'Wait.' A giggle and a swoop to lift her dress and pull it up, up and over her head and his emotions rising with it. No agenda, just taking her clothes off for him. Then her bra. Then her knickers, slipped down her thighs, a shimmy of her hips.

And suddenly he was on his knees worshipping her, fingers parting and tasting her until she wouldn't have it any more until he took off his own clothes.

He had only got his shirt off a little way when she was behind him, kissing his shoulders, running her hands over them, turning him round.

'Always had a thing about shoulders, Tom. Powerful shoulders.' Everything came off after that, with only the briefest nag of self-consciousness about what she would think of him, because she was making it very clear what she thought with her hands and her smile and a smoulder that didn't have anything of brisk Fran in it.

The bed still didn't get a look-in. They were on the floor, him learning what turned her on and hunting for a condom, before all logical thought went and it was just actions and sensations. Gentle and slow to begin with and then that point where it didn't matter how he wanted to play this, he was losing himself in her, someone new and unknown yet so dear to him already that it felt like a homecoming. A coming anyway, her arms cradling him and hands soothing him.

And afterwards, in whispers and gentle words, her turn to tell him everything would be all right.

By the time he went to pick up Hattie, he knew a lot more things about Fran Mayhew. The way she arched her back and reached out for his free hand when she came; that she had a graze on her left knee and the fact that her second toes were longer than her big ones.

The last two things he had discovered when they finally made it to the bed and explored those parts that had got overlooked in the first mad dash into each other. Lying face to face, they had talked in low tones as if they had reached a new level of intimacy that was only for their ears – even in a silent house.

He asked her that question that he'd never got an answer to in her kitchen – why had she changed her mind about working for him?

'Because I envied the relationship you had with Rob – it

made the thought of sitting alone in that bungalow quite nauseating.'

'That's all?'

'Well, I felt that you were actually a *Tom*. It's a name I think belongs to a man who has certain . . . admirable qualities. Up until that point you hadn't really lived up to your name, but in the cemetery with Rob, you did.'

He reached a hand over her hip and gave her buttock a gentle pat. 'You mean, you started to fancy me?'

'That's another interpretation.'

'Can I ask you something else? What made you think working for the magazine was going to please Mrs Mawson?'

'Because I am a naïve idiot.'

'Naïve,' he agreed, 'but never an idiot,' and kissed her until he felt her palm on his chest giving him a gentle push.

'*If* I could be allowed to finish . . .' she said with a not very convincing stern look, 'I hoped that if I did a really good job and Mrs Mawson was delighted, she'd think more kindly of me when I went to see her. I'd convinced myself that as my mother had never been in contact, or asked for anything, they would believe me when I said I didn't want anything either.' She paused. 'Actually that's not strictly true, my mother did send Charlie a postcard on the day I was born.'

'From San Diego.'

She looked surprised. 'Monty told you that? Charlie showed it to him? Oh, really, the more I hear about my father . . .' She pressed her lips together and Tom felt he'd lost her until she said, wearily, 'I don't know, I started off hating him for abandoning my mother, then moved on to still disliking him, but feeling sorry he didn't seem to have a happy life. And now? Now I think he wanted the best of both worlds – to be a free-spirited artist but have someone else pay emotionally and financially for it. I'm not sure that he and I would have got along.'

He chanced giving her a consoling kiss.

'So I suppose Monty also told you about Charlie's wife trying to buy my mother off?'

Tom shifted to ensure more of his leg was in contact with more of hers. 'Yes, but that was about the extent of his knowledge. And really, Fran, don't be too hard on Monty. He seems to have kept it quiet all these years. And I did submit him to some fairly intensive water torture.'

Fran looked askance at that, but didn't press him for any more details.

'What happened to your mother after Charlie?' he asked, gently.

'Went home to her parents first of all.'

'To San Diego?'

'Yes.' He couldn't work out what Fran was thinking in the pause that followed. 'The thing you have to understand about my mother,' she said when she spoke again, 'is that she had buckets of pride. She only stayed in San Diego until I was born – that's about as much help as she'd accept from her own family. And accepting money from Charlie's or asking him to acknowledge his child would have been hateful to her, I imagine.'

'Why do you have to imagine? Didn't she tell you?'

Fran wriggled against him as if she too needed to have more of him in contact with her. 'No. Never. Sometime between having the affair with Charlie and marrying Mr Mayhew – when I was about two – my mother re-invented herself as a woman of spotless character. I don't know whether something snapped after Charlie, or she was like that at heart and he'd just snuck in under the wire, but she became very righteous indeed. She got religion, in a big way . . .'

'You make it sound like rickets.'

The way Fran said 'Hmm' told him that she might have preferred that.

'My birth certificate said Mr Mayhew was my father. My grandparents never let on that he wasn't. Only later did I learn that he'd been around when I was born and had stepped up to the plate as far as the legal niceties were concerned.'

'Mr Mayhew – didn't he have a first name?'

'Glenn, but it doesn't seem right to call him that. I didn't know him well – my mother and he parted company about a year after they married. Religious differences, apparently.' She gave a bitter laugh. 'Probably wanted to play the guitar on a Sunday or have a beer without putting on a hair shirt.'

Tom was beginning to build up a picture of Fran's childhood, one that made him want to hold her even tighter.

'As often happens, it all came out after my mother died. I found a neat little file with plastic wallets and in it was the photocopy of the cheque Mrs Coburg had sent. God knows why my mother had kept it – actually, God would probably know. I should think she did it to prove she had the moral fibre to resist temptation.'

Tom felt Fran needed a bit more physical contact – she was starting to look morose.

'In the wallet as well was some kind of contract – accept the money, no further claim on us, etc. A couple of photos of Charlie and my mother on a seat in front of a mountain cafe. Her just "showing", as they say. One or two letters from Charlie. Also a photocopy of that postcard. So typical of my mother, that folder. As if she'd filed her emotions away. But she definitely wanted me to find it.'

Fran stopped and burrowed even further against him. 'Sorry, I'm making her sound very strict and unyielding. She wasn't, not all the time. And really, she was the person she punished the most. I think she never forgave herself for that slip of hers with Charlie. Goodness knows why they clicked. I suspect it may have been because she had a thing about strong men, and he was strong and charismatic. She probably worshipped him and his ego must have responded to that.' Her laugh this time was less bitter. 'There weren't any more romances after Mr Mayhew, but my mother always ended up attached in some way to strong men – priests, preachers. I suppose God was the ultimate one.'

'Poor Fran.' He smoothed down her hair and got her to look straight at him. 'I can understand what a huge shock it must have been, discovering all that.'

Her face seemed suffused with light and she clutched on to his shoulder and gave it a shake. 'Good grief, Tom. No. It was the best thing in the world. When my mother died, I thought I was completely alone. My grandparents were already gone and then I found I had this family. This huge family.' The light dimmed a little. 'Unfortunately that family wasn't as pleased to see me as I was to see them. Apart from Jamie. He's on the outside too, you see. Can't imagine what kind of home life he's had in that bleak house.'

Tom told her what he'd been reading when he waited for the Mawsons to see him.

'How apt. I should have read *Hard Times*. That's what they gave me. They assumed I'd come for money. Accused me of being a fraud, even though I showed them the copy of the cheque and the contract, the photographs – everything. If they wanted me to, I'd take a DNA test.'

'It's all about protecting the family assets and their reputation. And, maybe, if your visit was the first they knew of your existence, it would have been a shock. There's nothing to say that Charlie's wife shared the news about your mother's pregnancy with anyone.'

'I can see that, Tom, but I made it abundantly clear I only wanted to get to know them. I'm not even asking to be acknowledged publicly. I've said I'll keep quiet.' There was a sigh before Fran flopped on to her back and he tried not to let that distract him.

'I really don't know how the world operates, Tom. And now I've provided Natalie and Jamie with a bolt-hole, that's not going to make the Mawsons like me any better.'

'You just let your heart rule your head, don't beat yourself up.'

'That's a kind thing to say, but I should have thought how Deborah would feel.' She turned to look at him. 'I mean, I appreciate how hard this is for her. I'm reminding her of a horrible time in her life – poor woman hadn't been married long and was expecting Edward when Charlie left.'

'I'd have bloody left if I'd known Edward was on the way,' Tom said and Fran burst out laughing and he watched what that did to her body.

'He is particularly unpleasant,' she agreed, settling into his chest again. 'I sensed that even before he shoved me and sent me into the gravel.'

'What? Literally?' Tom pulled away to check on her and saw the quick nod. He thought of the graze on her knee and determined at the first opportunity to do something unpleasant to Edward Mawson. Although he was afraid that when they found out about him and Fran, it would probably be a case of the Mawsons doing something unpleasant to him. Especially if Mrs Mawson suspected that he'd known about Fran's parentage all along.

This bed, rather than the tree house, now seemed like a place of sanctuary – the calm before a great big Mawson-shaped storm.

'We're going to have to try our best to keep this a secret,' he said. 'Hard – Rob and Kath will have to know. My mother. Probably Natalie and Jamie—'

'And Liz. No, really, Tom. If you don't tell her, when it comes out, she won't feel she can trust you about anything again. Oh dear. I've really dropped you in it, haven't I?'

Fran ran her finger along one of his eyebrows and down his cheek. 'First working for you, now sleeping with you. Not the wisest actions, hmm?'

He grabbed her hand and put it to his lips. 'You make me sound like a passive bystander in all this. I wouldn't change anything to be lying here with you.'

'How long before you have to pick up Hattie?' she asked, suddenly.

'Long enough.' He expected there to be more kissing, but she said, very seriously, 'And how long after you pick her up do you have to turn your sock inside out and not see a *play*?'

When, struck with a huge grip of panic, he didn't reply, she added, 'Oh, it's not Thursday, is it? My mistake. It's only Wednesday.' Her eyes were so wide he knew she was mocking him.

'Fran,' he started and she put her fingertips over his mouth.

'Calm yourself, Tom . . . I don't really want to know what you got up to, I just want you to know that I suspect it was not choir practice. Now . . . We're short of time, so . . .' Her hand drifted down his belly and wrapped itself around him. 'Ah, I see that famous "flaccid python" you mentioned is not at home.'

'Thursdays,' he said, fighting his way past his arousal, 'were before you. In the past.'

Her voice had a new edge – he heard it even though what she was doing with her hand was making his brain dissolve, bit by bit. 'Hope so, Tom, otherwise I'm going to have to be quite strict with you. Maybe still ask Natalie to babysit on that night and take you to my bungalow and lock you in. Or just tie you across my bed. Make you stay there while I go and watch the play and write the review.' A low, dirty laugh before she leaned in to him and whispered in his ear, 'Then, when I came back, I'll do exactly what I want with you. How does that sound, Mr Inside-out-sock-Tom?'

'Uh-huh, huhhhhh,' he said and then, 'Ohhhh!'

'Excellent,' Fran replied. 'On we go then.'

CHAPTER 42

Wednesday 11 June

Well, what a lot I've learned. And if I can stop grinning for long enough, I will try to mould it into ten points.

1) It is possible to star in a Greek tragedy, a romance and a sex scene in the space of one day.

2) A man can get hold of the wrong end of the stick so badly that he has to go and sit up a tree.

3) You can be more hurt by someone's opinion of your sponge cake than the fact that he thinks you're the kind of woman who would seduce your half-sister's son. This is probably because I knew his verdict on the cake was correct, while the one regarding my morals was not.

4) I am frighteningly good at manipulation, although I am going to forgive myself and call it acting.

5) The first kiss from a pair of lips that you've been looking at for a long time feels like pain relief.

6) Tom has the most wonderful shoulders. The kind you look at and see protection and strength and quite a few other things that I am not going to write down, but will think about over and over again. He also does kissing very well – no, snogging is a better description, although still not quite there.

7) There is not one part of Tom's body that I don't like. I'm sure in time as I show him that, he will stop sucking in his stomach.

8) Tom is quite, quite bad. He had no scruples about questioning poor Monty and he confirmed my theory about his Thursday evenings. I find that extra edge to Tom very exciting. I look forward to exploring it with him.

9) Telling someone your life story when you are both naked seems to draw the poison out of it. Tom is a good listener, although he does interrupt at crucial points with inappropriate behaviour.

10) It is possible to understand the similarities between your mother's life and your own and still go right ahead and plunge in. Being a methodical person

though, afterwards you write a list of similarities and
fret somewhat.

    A. Falling for an older man. ✓

    B. Falling for an older man who still has a wife. ✓

    C. Falling for an older man who has offspring. ✓

The only one of these I am concerned about is B., and
perhaps as Tom comes to trust me, I will find out why that
wife is still a wife. Until then there is nothing I can do to
prevent the echoes of my mother's life running through my
own. Except ensure we always have plenty of condoms in
stock. And possibly go on the pill.

CHAPTER 43

Tom left the florist's with a huge bunch of flowers wrapped in purple tissue paper.

'For being a tit,' he said to Liz when he handed them to her.

'An aggressive tit,' she corrected him. 'And don't think that this measly bunch gives you the right to do it again.' Her tone was brusque, but when she thought he wasn't looking, she bent her head and sniffed the lilies.

'You feeling better, or do I need to start fashioning these flowers into a wreath?' She was eyeing him suspiciously. 'You certainly look better.'

'I am. So . . . you want to give me about quarter of an hour to get sorted, and then come through?'

Liz's expression showed that she hoped there was a big crisis in the offing. Whereas he was sure his expression said: I am absolutely ecstatic.

He could have run through the office punching the air and someone seemed to have taken away the creaky floorboards and put down soft rubber.

He saw copies of the July edition of the magazine on various desks as he passed. Victoria's copy, he noted, was open at her pages. Had it been like that since its arrival yesterday?

'Is this something new?' She was nodding towards Liz. 'Will all of us who do a good job get a bouquet?'

Nicely done: compliment to Liz while giving herself one too. Tom remembered what Fran had said about her and tried not to let it affect his smile and his cheery 'Who knows?'

In the minutes before Liz joined him, he took a magazine from the pile left on his desk and ripped off the plastic. He flicked through it with an objective eye – until he got to Fran's pages where he lingered and stopped being objective at all. Pride came along first, then regret that this would be the only time her work was featured . . . and then he was seeing Fran's hair around her naked shoulders . . . Well, seeing Fran's naked everything, and feeling her mouth on his neck and hearing the way she spoke to him when they had made love as if his happiness was essential to hers.

There were other lovely images in the Fran Scrapbook too.

The moment he had kissed her goodbye yesterday afternoon, he had wanted to see her again. Which was why, just after he'd picked up Hattie from school, he was indicating right and heading down the track that led to the bungalow.

He'd acted on impulse, but as he parked he knew there were a lot of reasons why he shouldn't be doing this. Would it seem weird pitching up with Hattie? Subtext: now we've had sex, it's time we bonded as a family unit?

He knew that Fran and he should have set some ground rules about how to behave when Hattie was around. No way did he want Hattie to be party to innuendos and whispered conversations.

Another thought hit him as they walked up the path – what if Fran tried some kind of charm offensive on Hattie, just to show how well the three of them might get along?

'Do you know what?' he said to Hattie 'I think I remember Fran telling me she wouldn't be in today. Let's come back another time.'

'But there she is, with a teapot.'

Fran recovered well from the surprise of their appearance. 'Oh! Hello,' she said. 'Long time no see.'

Hattie was frowning. 'Not really. You saw us the other day in our garden. Are you giving the plants a drink?'

'We were just passing,' Tom said, trying not to grin.

'I'm actually giving the plants some tea leaves.' Fran took the lid off the teapot and tipped it so that Hattie could look inside. 'It's very good for them, evidently.'

'We have bags,' Hattie said. 'Can I do it?'

'Can you do it . . . what?' Fran looked pointedly at Hattie.

Hattie considered. 'Can I do it, *please*?'

'Of course, that plant over there, if you could. And try not to get anything on your school uniform; tea stains horribly. In fact, I often stain paper with it – I could show you later if you have time.' Hattie went off to the plant and Fran watched her, seemingly ignoring him.

So much for being over-demonstrative.

'I'm sorry,' he whispered. 'I just wanted to see you again. I should have checked first.'

'Not at all. It's always lovely to have you drop in,' she said loudly, which he realised was for Hattie's benefit. She lowered her voice for, 'I can only get through this, Tom, if you don't look at any part of me below the neck or touch me at all, not even my hand. And if I'm being too ingratiating with Hattie, just give me a sign . . .'

'What kind of sign?'

'I don't know, scratch your ear or something. Right, Hattie, how is it going?' She was striding away from him. 'Ah, on your shoes, well, I think that will come off.'

No ear scratching had been needed. While he really wanted to take Fran into the bedroom and ravage her, he'd had to settle for watching Hattie and her get on with the fish they'd started before he'd stabbed himself. He wondered if he should do it again – Fran and he could end up in the bathroom once more, with his trousers off.

All he got from Fran was a peck on the cheek when they left, but it was a remarkably satisfying peck.

He pushed the magazine out of the way and concentrated on writing the letter he'd roughed out in his head on the drive to work. Just as it chugged out of the printer, in came Liz, notebook in one hand and geared up for a good bit of drama. Well, he wasn't going to disappoint her there.

She'd shut the door behind her, but he went and made sure it was fully engaged with the frame. Liz liked that – the equivalent of a drum roll.

'OK,' he said, handing her the letter. 'I've written out an explanation about Fran, for the staff.'

Liz scanned it. 'Nicely put . . . good and bland. Glad to see you didn't mention banning her from the building.' She handed the letter back. 'Big shame though. We've had some great feedback about her pages already on the website. So what happened?' She nodded at the letter. 'Realised you couldn't win this battle with the Mawsons?'

'Yes. This problem isn't going to go away and . . . there may well be another one . . .'

Liz shifted forward in her seat; she probably didn't even know she'd done it.

'Thing is, Liz, I have to tell you something that must *not* be repeated to anyone. No exceptions. I know I don't really have to labour the point. If you haven't got a safe pair of hands, I don't know who has.'

He told her, as simply as he could, about Fran being Charlie's daughter, although he didn't tell her Monty's part in the story coming out. He watched Liz's new facial display.

'Charlie's daughter?' she said eventually. 'Late-life romance or something?'

He filled her in on how it had happened when Charlie was meant to be having treatment for his drink problem.

Liz snorted. 'I always thought he was a terrible advertisement for that clinic. If that was him *after* rehab . . . Well, that explains Mrs Mawson's extreme reaction to Fran.' Liz darted a glance at him. 'This is all legit is it, Tom? I mean, there's no possibility of a scam—'

'No. I've seen photos, letters. Stuff that links Fran's mother to Charlie and Fran's mother to Fran.'

He had. Another memory from yesterday in the Fran Scrapbook. A knock on the door after Hattie was in bed, and there she was, file in hand. She said she was trying to make up for keeping everything hidden before, but there was a look in her eye that made him waste very little time on the file and a lot on her. They had started off on the sofa, but Tom found that although his desire was driving him forward, the thought that Hattie might discover them was putting the brakes on. They'd ended up making love very quietly, but very thoroughly, on top of his duvet out on the lawn. The back door was locked to halt Hattie's progress and a garden chair wedged against the side gate, just in case any of his family decided to 'pop' by.

'We're sneaking around like teenagers,' Fran had whispered afterwards as they watched the bats swooping over the garden. 'Mind you, that doesn't take much remembering on my part, whereas for you, it's like doing historical research.'

He'd given her a gentle pinch on the arm, but resisted asking her if she really minded about the age difference. The evidence suggested she didn't and besides, what was the point of pulling down all those black clouds on the horizon – the age difference, Mrs Mawson finding out about them, how to play this with Hattie . . .?

'And the Jamie thing was just . . .' Liz asked.

Tom landed back at his desk. 'Her looking out for him. She's his half-aunt.'

He sensed Liz was still catching up. 'Can I just ask why the hell Fran came to work for Mrs Mawson's magazine?'

When Tom explained, Liz said, 'How mad is that? I mean, I like Fran, but did she really think that was going to work? "Here's a lovely paper squirrel, oh and by the way, your dad shagged my mum and we're half-sisters."'

Luckily Liz was shaking her head in mock exasperation so she couldn't see how Tom felt about hearing Fran being talked about like that. He got up and had a wander around the room and wiped a clean patch through the plaster dust on the windowsill and sat down. He remembered the day Fran had ended up with plaster dust on her bottom and slipped into another satisfying memory of feeling that very bottom, not so long ago, naked against his groin.

'OK,' Liz said, 'now I've stopped reeling from that bit of news, what's the other potential problem?'

Tom left Fran's bottom behind and said, 'Fran and I are now . . .' and waited to see how long it would take Liz to fill in the gap.

'I bloody knew it,' she crowed.

He doubted if she had, otherwise she wouldn't have made that 'mad' comment.

This time Liz's head-shaking had something of the 'this will never work' about it. 'Bloody hell, Tom. You couldn't have picked someone else? The sky's going to fall on your head when Mrs Mawson finds out.'

'Yep, kind of figured that out.'

'Is it worth it for something that might not last?'

He was surprised at how irritated that made him. 'I plan

on it lasting,' he said. 'And yes, I should have thought of all the reasons why this was inadvisable, but . . . remember the photocopier guy?'

There was a moment when Liz looked put out, but then she sniggered. 'Oh. Yeah. Good point. He could have been Vlad the Impaler and I wouldn't have cared. Actually, the Impaler part—'

'OK, enough local colour. Thanks. And, Liz, I'm not just asking you to keep quiet about this for my benefit – it means, when the ceiling falls in on me, you'll be able to appear completely innocent.'

They both automatically looked up at the ceiling at that point and Tom wished that he hadn't used that particular expression in this building.

He heaved himself up off the windowsill. 'Right, I'm off to take a great big pin and burst Felix and Derek's balloon.'

That turned out to be a fair description of what happened. One moment Felix was coming towards Tom, holding the magazine and enthusing about the feedback he'd already had; the next he was running through his playlist of expletives and clutching the hair at the nape of his neck.

Tom tried to take the sting out of it. 'She might do some more work for us later in the year. But, as you'll see from the letter that's going to come round, getting this big commission from a supermarket, well, she'd be mad to turn it down for our little bit of work. So it's back to the hunt for someone to fill those pages.'

'That's going to be . . .' Derek said.

'Bloody difficult,' Felix snapped.

On the same day as he gave all but one of his staff a sanitised version of the reason why Fran had to stop working for the magazine, he offered his family the absolute truth: about their relationship, the fact Charlie was her father, the fall-out from her visit to the Mawsons.

He got three very different reactions.

Kath gave him a hug. 'It seems a bit fraught at the minute,' she said, 'but I really like her. She's younger than you, but older, if you know what I mean.'

His mother said, 'You'll be living on takeaways. But she's a lovely girl. Unlike Deborah Mawson. She's as cold as a bitch's tit. She'll never accept Fran.'

He'd been so downcast by that, he hadn't even pointed out that it was *witch's* tit.

And Rob simply said, 'Good on you, mate. But how long do you think you can keep it quiet?'

He hadn't known the answer to that then and he still didn't. The difference was that, right at this moment, he couldn't give a stuff. Fran was curled up next to him in the garden – a colder evening, so a two-duvet job. Next to Tom's head was a baby monitor and there was one up by Hattie's bed too – Fran had arrived with them just half an hour after Hattie had slipped off to sleep.

They were the perfect solution to not being able to make love in the house, but still wanting to hear if Hattie was OK.

How long do you think you can keep it quiet?

Fran had walked over tonight, just one of the ways they were trying to keep their relationship under wraps. His family, once the news had settled in, had enthusiastically suggested others. Friday, when his mother picked up Hattie from school, she was going to take her back to her house so Fran and he could have some time together. On Sunday evening Rob and Kath had offered to babysit.

Tom was worried that it seemed like he was deceiving Hattie, but Fran said he should forgive himself. It was early days yet, wrong to stir her up when they didn't even know what they would tell her.

Tom knew that it *was* early days, but he hated hiding Fran away. He didn't just want to tell Hattie, he wanted to take Fran out for a meal, to the cinema, introduce her to his rugby crowd.

None of that was possible. One whisper and who knew how the Mawsons would react.

He put his hand gently on Fran's shoulder, hoping it might wake her up. Selfish man. When she was awake and talking he could push all the frayed ends of this relationship away. He changed position so that he could see her face while she slept. It was reaching down into him and pulling up a tenderness he didn't know he was capable of any more.

Perhaps he felt especially close to her tonight because she'd talked about her childhood and how rootless it had been until they settled on that island off the west coast of Scotland – the one without the palm trees and with a constant wind.

He wondered what he would have thought of Fran if their timelines had been different and he'd met her then, or at university.

'Oh, university,' she'd said with mock horror. 'It took me the best part of eight months to get used to being around so many people.' A shy glance at Tom. 'So many men.'

Men with flat stomachs, no doubt, but Tom comforted himself that he was the one here naked with Fran tonight.

She had told him how her mother had refused to see her for a while after she'd given up on Ancient History and headed for London and art. Now Fran understood that was because she had been afraid Charlie's genes were coming to the fore.

'I'm sure she was proud of what you achieved,' Tom had suggested and Fran had wrinkled her nose.

'No, she always thought it was frivolous. She would much rather have seen me as a professor.'

Tom had shared some of his own history too, realising as he talked that Fran had thought he was a journalist. When he told her he'd worked in marketing for a multinational, she'd said, 'So you weren't exactly the right person for the job you're in now – kind of overqualified, but in the wrong area?'

He'd agreed. Mrs Mawson had taken a chance.

That had brought a slightly sad, 'She believed in you, at least,' from Fran.

He'd expected other questions from Fran tonight – perhaps about Steph and why they weren't divorced yet. But they never got asked.

He kissed her lightly on her head, now trying not to wake her. He'd forgotten how lovely it was to have someone trust you enough to lie down beside you and just sleep. Someone who wasn't a child.

How long do you think you can you keep it quiet?

How long could they?

In the end, they managed nearly twelve days. Seven more than Natalie and Jamie.

CHAPTER 44

'Typical,' Liz said. 'Flaming June always turns into soggy June and she's not a fun girl.'

She was looking down Middle Street and the cloud was so low it was almost on the pavements. The temperatures had plummeted too. Unlikely that he and Fran could make love outside tonight.

Perhaps he should get the tent out, try to put it up after Hattie went to sleep, take it down before she woke. No, he'd have no energy left for making love. One too many erections.

Liz turned away from the window. 'There is one bright spot. Monty's back.'

Tom nodded, he'd seen a very sad Monty slumped at his desk when he'd arrived this morning. He and Tom had had a quiet word about what had happened, and it was obvious that while Monty knew he'd blabbed about Charlie, he couldn't exactly pinpoint what he'd said. Tom had assured him that what happened in Tynebrook stayed in Tynebrook, but Monty still looked morose. All Tom could hope was that after his holidays in August, he would return in a better mood. And hopefully not with another photo in his wallet.

If Monty was morose, Jamie had perked up. Tom had called him into his office to apologise for his madness – an apology Jamie accepted with grace. 'I'm glad you know about Nat and me,' he'd said. 'She didn't like skulking around not telling you.' He was still doing a lot of flopping his hair about, but he seemed to have a new sense of purpose.

'Was wondering if I could spend a bit of time up in the Finance department, next? It's just, well, Fran told you I have this business? I'm wondering if they might give me some insights into improving my profit margins.'

Tom was amazed. No one had ever volunteered to spend time in the Finance department.

Liz was now doing what could only be described as a chortle. 'And, listen to this,' she said. 'Victoria's fashion shoot at St Mary's Lighthouse? Proving to be a right nightmare. One of the models has vertigo. You couldn't make it up. So . . . can I expect a theatre review or two from you at some point?'

'Look in your inbox,' he said. 'Two done and dusted.' Fran was behind that. She'd been to see two plays on Saturday when he was fully occupied with Hattie. All he'd had to do was listen to her talk about them at the bungalow on Sunday evening and write them up. Amazing how much more rewarding the theatrical experience was when you were lying naked with the reviewer.

'If it keeps you out of Newcastle on a Thursday, that's absolutely fine by me,' Fran had said.

Now he had a closer relationship with the bungalow, it reminded him of the student places he'd lived in. Right down to the horrible mould in the bathroom and the damp patch on Fran's bedroom wall.

'I'll bring something round to shift that mould,' he'd said as he kissed her goodbye.

'You old romantic, you,' she'd replied, before reconsidering and saying, 'You romantic, you.'

'Two done already? That's bloody impressive.' Liz smirked. 'Bet Fran wrote them for you. You're just as bad as Jamie.'

He acted shocked by the suggestion and evicted her from his office. He actually got through some work then, until the phone rang.

'I've just had a most unpleasant visitor,' Fran said.

'Not Vasey?'

'No, Edward Mawson.'

'I'll come round.'

'No,' Fran replied quickly. 'It's all right. I was a bit wobbly at the time, but not now.'

'Was he threatening?'

'When isn't he? It's bad news, I'm afraid. They've not only found out about Jamie and Natalie, but also that they've been coming here. Edward is, as I feared, particularly cross about that. He said I did it to spite them. I didn't tell him the actual relationship had been going on for months before I arrived.'

Tom wondered how much hope Fran had left now.

'He called Natalie some terrible names,' Fran said sadly, before asking if Tom could find Jamie and warn him.

'Too late,' Tom said, looking out into the main office, and he said goodbye and put the phone down seconds before Edward Mawson was at his door.

He expected Edward's opening words to be about Jamie. Instead they were, 'Have you told your staff about that woman?'

'A letter has gone out.'

'I want to see it.'

Tom wondered how long he'd have to wait to shame Edward into saying 'please'. For ever probably.

Edward read the letter. 'That's not the tone my mother wanted at all. And you haven't said anything about her not being allowed into the building.'

'I used my initiative. Your mother said it was a sensitive and personal matter, so sending out a letter that stirred up more questions than answers seemed a bad move. And I doubt if Miss Mayhew wants to come back into the building.'

Edward screwed the letter up and threw it on the floor. He wasn't even aiming for the bin.

What an empty gesture, like stamping your foot.

'Have you found a replacement for Charlie's pages?' Edward barked.

'Not as such.'

'Why doesn't that surprise me?'

'I don't know; why doesn't it?' Tom stitched an ingratiating smile on the end of that and could see Edward wasn't quite sure if he was being rude.

That was when he demanded to see Jamie.

When he appeared, with that beaten-dog stance, Tom wanted to remove him to a place of safety.

'Tom,' Edward said, jerking his head towards the door.

The inference was plain – clear off, I want your office. Tom didn't know how he was going to walk past the guy without barging into him with his shoulder.

He hadn't even made the move to get up when Jamie blurted out, 'I'd like Tom to stay.'

Oh. Poo.

'And I want him to go,' Edward said, moving closer to his brother. There was a look from Jamie that Tom could not, as a parent, ignore.

'As I'm Jamie's employer, at present,' he said, 'I probably need to remain in the room to fulfil my employer/employee safety obligations.' It was complete rubbish and Tom knew he was going to pay for it later.

Edward slammed the door, covering himself in a fine layer of plaster dust.

'Right then, you stupid prick,' Edward said. 'What the hell do you think you're doing screwing the staff? How long has it been going on?'

'A while,' Jamie said, looking towards Tom, almost as if checking he was still there.

'Up in the house? Under our noses? And at that woman's place? Are you deliberately trying to upset Mother?'

'No, I'm trying to have a private life.'

Not a bad answer.

Edward took a step nearer to Jamie, and the way Jamie flinched was unmistakable.

'Her father's in prison.'

'That's not Natalie's fault.'

'The whole family is just one step up from gyppos. The lot of them will be after anything that isn't nailed down.'

'Natalie's worked for us for years. She's never stolen anything.' Jamie's colour was rising.

'And her mother's the town bike, I've heard.'

Jamie looked as if he might respond to that, but nothing came out.

Tom hated the triumphant look Edward had when that happened, but no, Jamie *was* going to speak. 'Uh . . . bringing up her parents?' he said. 'Isn't that like blaming Mother for Charlie's behaviour?'

Oh, well played.

Edward looked as if he might actually hit Jamie, and Tom wondered how many times he'd done it before.

Well, not in his office.

He stood up and hoped that would be sufficient, but Edward barely looked at him. He was back in Jamie's face.

'You *won't* see Natalie again. You *won't* see that woman again. You're to come back with me now. Mother wants you to spend some time looking at our timber operations up in Scotland.'

'No. You can't stop me seeing who I want.'

There was a particularly nasty laugh from Edward. 'If you don't do as you're told, there will be nothing for you. Your girlfriend's going to get fired for a start and you're not earning. Think about that. Is this slut worth it?'

Tom felt the urge to move round the desk, but Jamie,

from a head-down start, lifted both his arms and pushed his brother so fiercely that Edward was caught by surprise and stuttered back before plopping down on to the floor on his backside.

Tom expected a full-blown fight and was ready to put himself between the two men, but Edward had obviously decided to go for the threatening retreat. He got to his feet. 'You're just like your grandfather. A sniff of a skirt and you lose the very small bit of sense you were born with.' He brushed himself down, but Tom was pleased to see it did little to shift the plaster dust. 'I'm giving you one more chance.'

Jamie didn't move.

'Right. When you do come back, you'd better bring your begging bowl with you.'

As the door slammed shut behind Edward, Jamie buckled at the knees and managed to get himself to a chair. 'Oh God, oh God,' he kept saying and his breathing was as bad as Rob's had been in the cemetery.

Tom didn't have long to wait for his punishment. The next morning, when he arrived, he found Liz, Felix and Derek hunkered around his desk. On it were some photocopies of what looked like oil paintings – gundogs, hounds and pheasants.

'Choosing your Christmas card designs?' he asked. He was buoyed up by a sneaky visit to Fran's on his way in. They had simply held each other and kissed, because Natalie and Jamie were in the spare bedroom, but it was worth it.

'No,' Felix said, 'these are what we have to go with on Charlie's pages.'

'Got an email first thing,' Liz said. 'Then Mrs Mawson had these couriered over. Here's the email.'

A friend of the family uses this artist to do portraits of their animals. I feel they are just what we're looking for and, as you've failed to find a suitable replacement for my father's pages after all these months, this is, I believe, a workable solution. Please contact the artist as soon as possible to arrange terms.

Tom's anger was making it hard to think logically. The extra snub of sending the email to Liz was like salt in the wound.

'It's going to be such a backward step,' Liz said.

'They're . . .' Derek shook his head.

'What do we do, Tom?' Felix looked as if all the enthusiasm had been wrung from him.

'They're . . .' Derek tried again.

'You know what this is about, don't you?' Liz said.

'Punishment for you staying in the room when Edward was laying into Jamie. If this is what Mrs Mawson does when something isn't even your fault—'

Tom gave her a warning look and Liz stopped talking.

There was a cheery knock on the open door. 'Hi!' Victoria said, almost bouncing into the room, her hair swinging. 'I just wondered, Tom, if you had time to talk about this lifestyle show that's being held at the Civic Centre. Kelvin thinks it could really raise our profile to sponsor . . .' Victoria had reached the desk. 'Oh, are these what you're going to replace those paper things with? Aren't they lovely?'

Paper things?

Nobody felt inclined to reply, and then Derek suddenly said, 'They're not lovely. They're a pile of old-fashioned toss.'

There was a beat of amazed silence, before Felix clapped a hand on Derek's shoulder. 'Well said, concise and to the point as always.'

Tom saw Victoria's petulant expression and walked her out of the room. 'Yes, Victoria, happy to chat in a few minutes. I'll be as quick as I can with this. OK? Great.'

He turned back to the three forlorn people round his desk and tried to think of a way out of this.

'OK,' he said, 'we're going to go with this guy.' As he

expected, there was groaning. 'No, listen. He can have two of the three nature pages and on the remaining one, plus another page we're going to nick from the travel section, we'll have something different. Felix, get yourself up to the high school. Hattie and I went to their end-of-year show on Friday evening. Lovely stuff – whole display devoted to night predators . . . owls were amazing. See if they'll give permission to showcase some new talent.' He stopped and looked around the faces – yes, they were looking brighter.

'There will be cost implications,' Liz said. 'You're giving one travel page to nature. Might mean a loss of ad revenue.'

'I'm sure we can sort something out. Could you arrange for Kelvin to come see me? Let's give Mrs Mawson what she wants and also keep moving forward. OK, why are you all still here?'

Just before he called Victoria in, he picked up Mrs Mawson's email and ripped it up, before copying Edward Mawson and not even bothering to aim properly for the bin.

CHAPTER 45

They were lying under the kitchen table in that soft, quiet time after just making love, and Tom knew that something had changed in him. He had been quite happy to have sex in the house. He still couldn't get his mind around doing it upstairs, but here they were, under the same roof as Hattie. The baby monitors were in place, and there was a chair against the door so that if she woke up and hurtled downstairs, it would buy Fran a few precious seconds to bolt out of the back door.

Tom was winding and unwinding strands of Fran's hair around a finger, thinking of her running naked into the garden, when she suddenly said, 'Derek told me how clever you were today. Coming up with a way to please Mrs Mawson and your staff.'

'Derek? When did you see Derek?'

'Why, are you jealous?'

He gave her hair the gentlest of tugs. 'Depends what you were doing with him.'

There was a low laugh. 'I was sitting with him in a coffee shop, waiting for Linda.'

Tom stopped fiddling with her hair.

'I'd fixed them a lunch date,' Fran said, sitting up and leaning against the table leg. She had arranged the duvet to cover herself and Tom lazily tried to tug it back down.

'Lunch date? Linda?'

'Yes. I left them chatting happily away.'

Tom sat up too, but as Fran had nabbed the table leg he had to raise his knees to sit comfortably. 'Let me get this right. Derek, the photographer who rarely finishes a sentence, went out on a date with Linda from the Finance department, who never talks, and you left them "chatting happily away"?'

'Well, that may be an exaggeration, but they were definitely talking.' Fran looked smug. 'They've fancied each other for ages, just couldn't put it into words. It's taken some work on my part to get them together, I can tell you. What? Why are you looking at me like that?'

'You do live in an alternative universe, don't you?'

She reached out for him and let the duvet fall. 'Come here, you can live in it too.'

Later, back under the duvet, she said, 'I've stirred up Mrs Mawson very badly, haven't I? Gone about this totally the wrong way.' Tom patted her leg.

'Wise Natalie told me I was wasting my time from the start. Now she says I ought to put up forty-eight sheet posters all over Northumberland saying: "I'm Charlie Coburg's lovechild".'

'Good old Natalie. And how's she doing riding into battle for Jamie?'

'She has a very determined set to her jaw. Oh, and the good news is they're renting a flat – it's been planned for a while and now the secret's out they're going for it. Jamie's got a bit of money from the business, so soon the pair of them won't be in my spare room making the walls wobble.'

'Hurrah,' he said, and squeezed her thigh but felt too sleepy to do anything further. It really was very comfortable in the kitchen with the fridge humming away. He didn't know why more people didn't just sleep on their kitchen floor.

Fran put her hand over his. 'Would you mind if I asked you about Steph?' she said.

Tom felt his dreamy mood die.

'It's just that I know you've lived apart for a long time. But I have to ask this: why aren't you divorced yet? Natalie doesn't know and your mother doesn't.'

'You've asked them?'

'Wouldn't you if you were in my shoes? Were I wearing any at the moment.'

'OK,' he said. The facts were easy enough to tell. 'Steph contested my petition – she instructed her lawyers to file an answer. She hasn't deviated from that standpoint since. And now everything's in limbo unless I fight it in the courts. More money I can't afford.' He slowed down his delivery, it was sounding too rehearsed. 'I keep asking her to just accept the petition and get it underway again, but she ignores me. It's her last bit of power over me. But it'll solve itself in the end. Soon we'll have been apart five years.'

Fran was watching him intently.

'I see. A contested divorce is fairly rare, isn't it? And can I ask on what grounds you're seeking a divorce?'

'Her unreasonable behaviour.' He wished Fran would just be quiet now.

'Ah,' Fran said, settling her head on his shoulder. He didn't like that 'Ah'. What did it mean? He was torn between wanting to ask her and hoping the matter would wither and die.

'You're not telling me everything, are you?' she said after a while, but it wasn't accusatory – it was gentle and sympathetic. 'It's a polished-up version, but that's all right, Tom. It's hard for you, I can see it in your face; hear it in your voice.' She put her hand on his chest. 'Just reassure me I'm not in danger of doing what my mother did, falling for someone who still has a wife and at some point that wife will drag him away?'

He moved so quickly to get her right into his arms that she looked shocked.

'Fran,' he said, 'Steph and I will never get back together again. She has no interest in playing happy families and she dislikes me as much as I dislike her. Real dislike, not one of those love/hate things. If it wasn't for Hattie, I'd never answer her phone calls.'

'All right, all right, Tom. Let's just leave this.'

It killed him that he could see the doubt in her eyes.

The sound of Hattie coughing filtered through the baby alarm.

Upstairs, Hattie was sitting on the edge of her bed looking disorientated. 'I coughed myself awake,' she said, rubbing her eyes.

'Can you cough yourself back to sleep?' Tom handed her the water.

When he was sure she *was* sleeping again, he picked up the baby monitor and went out on to the landing. 'Fran,' he whispered into it, 'you said you were in danger of falling for me. Well, I've fallen already, sweetheart. I love you. And I know you want answers, but I'm not used to talking about this. Just give me time.'

CHAPTER 46

Tuesday 17 June

It's been days and days since I wrote anything; having sex and falling for someone takes up a lot of time. So really, the list below is a total mongrel – bits from different days. My mother would click her tongue and say I only have myself to blame because once you let sex rear its ugly head, everything spins out of control.

In response to that, I would probably say something about a pot calling a kettle black.

So I have learned:

1) Hattie has never used tea leaves.
2) It is not the done thing to turn down the first set of baby monitors brought out by the shop assistants because the 'baby' you're buying them for 'can't stand pink'. It makes them think your child may be a genius or you are mad.

3) Tom has no real interest in drama. I suspect this is because he has had so much in his life.

4) Seeing Edward Mawson at your door is a bad way to start any day. I am actually ashamed to be related to him. His wife must either be:

   A. Very understanding or

   B. Have no understanding at all.

5) Some people think it is acceptable to disown a child because they will not love who you want them to love.

6) It is a big mistake to be horrible to someone like Natalie. Not only because she is very intelligent and extremely tough, but also, as a cleaner, she knows exactly where to find dirt.

7) Sleeping on a kitchen floor is more agreeable than sleeping out in the open. Fewer bats.

8) A man can be as evasive as anything and you still end up feeling sorrier for him than you do for yourself. And, weirdly enough, find yourself falling a little more in love because you can see the struggle going on in him. Perhaps it would be easier if Tom's wife were mad and in the attic, then at least I'd know where she was and why.

9) The urge to go to a coughing child is very strong. Hearing her say 'I coughed myself awake' can have you in tears.

10) Hearing a man whisper into a baby monitor that he loves you is absolutely the most romantic thing, ever.

CHAPTER 47

Tom was watching Jamie being made to walk the plank while Hattie stood 'encouraging' him with the plastic cutlass.

'Does he need rescuing?' he asked and Natalie stopped leaning against the fridge and looked out through the open kitchen door.

'Nah. He's enjoying it. Besides, he's hardly going to hurt himself falling off that, is he?'

She had a point. The plank this time was one of the pieces of laminate left over from the hallway, laid out on the lawn. And Jamie was certainly entering into the game with gusto. He was wailing dramatically in between asking if he could have any last requests.

'Don't think he was allowed to play much when he was little – playing's too common. So . . .' Natalie reached for the bottle of wine by the cooker and topped up her glass. 'Heard anything from Kath?'

'Rang me at work, nothing to report.'

'I think she's gonna be early.'

As Natalie's experience of babies was extensive, he could only agree with her.

He went back to watching the enthusiasm with which Jamie was falling into a watery grave. He seemed little more than a big kid himself.

'You're wondering what I see in him, aren't you?' Natalie suddenly said and he checked her expression. Yup. Even someone like Natalie was vulnerable in love.

He chose his words with great care. 'I did, to start with . . . but now I'm coming round to Fran's way of thinking. She says he's like an iceberg.'

'What? A lettuce?' Natalie said, sharply.

'No. No.' He was trying not to laugh. 'Lots of him hidden. She's right, isn't she? I think the way he seems a bit out of it is a survival technique for when he gets pushed into doing something he doesn't want to. Easier than confrontation.'

'Spot on,' Natalie said. 'Out from under the Mawson clan, he's all right, is Jamie. He'll do.'

Natalie didn't say how long he'd do for, but when she raised her glass to drink from it, she looked down into the wine with what seemed like a fond smile.

Tom topped up his own glass before asking, 'How are your family taking it?'

'Haven't told them yet. Mum will have a fit because I'm moving out and am no longer on tap for childcare duties. My brothers will try to skim him for money. And I'm not letting either of my sisters anywhere near him.'

Natalie took another drink. 'Bloody hell, Tom. Families, eh? Jamie's say they've disowned him – very dramatic. And mine? I sometimes wish *they* would disown me.'

'Disowned? God, it's like a Victorian melodrama. Are you and him, you know, all right for money?'

A cheeky laugh. 'Why, you got any? You would too, wouldn't you, sub us? No, it's OK. Be even better now you don't expect Jamie at the magazine and he can concentrate on his own business.'

Natalie wound herself down into a chair and tucked her legs beneath her. 'Anyway . . . enough of that, how's it going with our Fran? Oh, I see, big grin. That good, eh?'

Tom tried to think what to say to do Fran justice. 'She's . . .'

Natalie raised her hands when he came to a stop. 'Oh, you men! Running away at the mouth about emotions all the time.'

'Uh, Tom . . .' It was Jamie, loitering about on the doorstep. Tom got the idea he always tested the water first to see if it was safe to speak. 'Is it all right if I, you know, fight back? Nothing too physical, but can I, kind of, lift her up, move her around a bit?'

'Yes. No problem. As long as you don't drop her on her head.'

'Great. Uh. Thanks.'

When Jamie went back to playing, Natalie said, 'He has the most beautiful manners, Tom. Asks nicely before he does anything.' There was a raucous laugh.

'Edward didn't inherit them, then?'

Natalie's expression clouded. 'That nobber.' She cast a scornful look at the empty chair next to her as if Edward was sitting there, before giving it another last particularly antagonistic look and saying, 'Don't get me started on those hypocrites. Back to Fran . . . so it's full steam ahead then?'

'Keep your voice down. I've still not said anything to Hattie. I'm feeling bad about it.'

'You mad? That's your only option. Five-year-olds aren't very good at keeping secrets. Shouldn't even be asked to. So . . . shaping up nicely, then?'

Tom got the feeling Natalie was digging. He let her talk, pretending he was engrossed in seeing if there were any letters from school in Hattie's reading bag.

'Only I think she's a bit concerned about Steph,' Natalie said. 'You know, why she's still in the picture.'

Not in the picture. Just a faint outline where she used to be.

'She hasn't said anything, mind. I can just tell—'

'Natalie. Are you trying to find answers to the questions you've always been dying to ask?'

Natalie uncurled her legs and sat up. 'Yeah, OK. But Fran and me are kind of family now, so just watch it, huh?'

Outside there was a huge squeal from Hattie, and Tom saw that she was hanging upside down. Jamie, who was clinging on to her ankles, had the look of a fisherman who was attempting to land something that was too lively. Her squeals changed into, 'Fran, Fran!' and she was trying to turn round to look at the side gate.

Tom headed out of the door, Natalie right behind him.

'Look, Fran, I'm an Australian pirate,' Hattie was shouting as Fran came into view.

'Yeah, hi there, Aunt F,' Jamie said. 'I have my hands full.'

Aunt F?

'I just thought,' Fran said, 'warm afternoon . . . passing the ice-cream parlour . . . happened to have a cool box on the back seat . . . who would like an ice cream? And I said to myself, Natalie and Jamie, and what's that child's name?'

'It's me, it's me,' Hattie shouted and wriggled so much that Jamie had to lower her on to the lawn.

'Oh look! Here's Tom as well,' Fran said, turning to him. 'How are you?'

'Fantastic now.'

'Did you know I've got monitors?' Hattie said. She made it sound like a sub-species of head lice.

Fran looked amazed. 'Have you, really? What do they do?'

'If I wake up and Dad's gardening, he can still hear me. There's one by my bed, and one wherever he is.'

'And does your father do much night gardening?' Fran gave the worn patches on the lawn a critical look.

'Well, I've been putting a lot of work in on the beds recently,' Tom said, before admonishing himself for doing the very *fnarr, fnarr* thing he hated in front of Hattie. He went to deal with the ice creams in an effort to cool off.

'We need some little spoons,' Fran announced and Hattie said she'd show her where they were kept. She held out her hand to Fran. 'Come on.'

Fran looked down at the hand and said, 'Oh!' in a small voice and then caught hold of it carefully as if Hattie's fingers were made of glass.

Tom had to concentrate on reading the information on the side of one of the tubs, because he, like the ice cream, was in danger of melting.

The ice creams had long been eaten and it was just when Natalie and Jamie were talking about leaving, that Tom heard a car pull on to the drive.

'That will be your Auntie Kath,' Fran said. 'She can't keep away.' She was helping Hattie make a caterpillar out of the ice-cream tubs and some string.

The side gate opened and Hattie glanced across and suddenly shouted, 'Mummy, Mummy!'

The four adults looked as if they were frozen into position.

Hattie hurled herself towards Steph and Tom unfroze and stood up so quickly that he felt dizzy.

Steph was down on her knees, arms around Hattie who was now squealing, 'Mummy, Mummy. Look, it's Mummy!'

Tom imagined that anyone who didn't know the person who had just arrived would think what a lovely mother – tears on her face, a huge smile – 'My darling, my darling, it's so lovely to see you.'

But Tom saw a big, showy performance and smelled trouble with a huge T – as big as the Angel of the North with its wings outstretched. His heart was working hard, as if it had just helped him run upstairs.

He checked on Fran. Her face looked fragile, as if she didn't know what to do with it. He couldn't even take her hand and give it a comforting squeeze, she was too far away.

What would she be thinking? Here's the wife back, how long before I'm not needed?

'Look, Dad, look, Dad, Mummy's here.' Hattie was hopping out a dance of celebration. And that was the problem – if Hattie hadn't been there, Tom would have said, straight out, 'What game is this, Steph? You're not welcome here.' But to ruin Hattie's delight . . . akin to kitten stomping.

Steph stood up. If he could be objective he would say she looked great. Tall, narrow-hipped, dressed well – fashion was her job after all. He had no doubt that the shirt that she was wearing, over a pair of linen trousers, had been created by an artisan who survived on candle wax alone in some Parisian garret.

She was not what Rob would call a stunner, and his mother always said her eyes were too small, but there was something exotic and glossy about Steph.

Tom was no longer capable of objectivity, though. He could see the long, graceful neck and the fullness of her mouth, but now everything seemed too polished and her attitude too knowing. She was a woman so used to being the centre of attention that she had come to demand it by right. It was how she defined herself – the body count.

He noticed Jamie taking it all in and Steph do her trademark little flick back of first one curtain of her straight hair and then the other – subliminal sexual semaphore.

Natalie was taking it all in too and there was her vulnerability siphoned into a concerned look Jamie's way. That's what Steph did, zoned in on the one most likely to find her attractive so she could create a bit of discord.

Steph turned her attention from Jamie to deliver a gracious smile. 'Hello, everyone,' she said. 'And, Hattie, darling, what a welcome. She'll have me tumbling over, won't she?'

So we're getting the charming, light-up-the-room version of Steph.

'This is my mummy,' Hattie said.

Tom knew Steph would be trying to work out which of the two women he had fallen for. She came further into the garden, Hattie leading her on.

'Some introductions,' Steph said. 'I'm Steph.' She held out her hand to a blushing Jamie who didn't so much offer his, as plop it into hers.

'Yeah, hi. Uh. Jamie.'

'And I'm Natalie,' Natalie said, taking a big step forward. Steph let Jamie go.

Natalie's little spurt of jealousy would have told Steph that she and Jamie were a couple.

Tom did not know how to introduce Fran, but Hattie did it for him.

'This is Fran. She's one of my grown-up friends. She makes things out of paper. She made me a hat. I was giving it a rest upstairs. Do you want to see it?'

All of this was spoken in constant movement.

'Yes, I would love to see it,' Steph said, and Hattie sprinted away, only to come back before she'd reached the back door.

'You won't go away while I'm upstairs, will you?' she asked Steph. Tom felt his guts twisting on Hattie's behalf and there was a look about Fran's eyes that suggested she was having a hard job keeping them under control.

No one talked when Hattie went, until Fran said, 'Pleased to meet you. As Hattie explained, I'm Fran . . . Fran Mayhew.'

She held out her hand and Steph gave it the slightest shake. 'Yes, good to meet you too. You'll have heard a lot about me, I expect.' Her eyes strayed to Tom.

'I have,' Fran said, jovially, 'but I'm sure it can't all be true.'

Steph's demeanour took the slightest hit. Tom could see her trying to work out if that had been a calculated slight. She obviously decided to ignore it. 'I love your dress,' she said. 'Vintage?'

'It was my mother's and she won't have bought it new, so I guess the answer to that is yes. Not everyone can wear it evidently – or so someone in Tom's office said. Ridiculous, isn't it, those pronouncements people who think about fashion too much tend to make?'

As one of Fran's tactless statements, it was up there with the best.

Steph bridled but did not respond, which in itself was worrying. She turned to him.

'Tom, you're looking well.'

'Am I? What, not looking pole-axed? Like I have no idea why you've pitched up out of the blue?'

'Well I wanted to surprise Hattie. And that's the thing about surprises – you don't say you're coming.'

'Ta-dah!' Hattie reappeared with her hat. It was looking a little worse for wear, having survived many sea battles.

Steph studied it. 'You must be very talented,' she said to Fran, with the smallest of smirks.

'Thank you. I am,' Fran replied.

Natalie didn't exactly push Jamie out of Steph's sightline, but there was a definite rounding-up. 'We're off,' she said.

'None of your family here, Tom?' Steph asked, pulling Hattie in to her when Jamie and Natalie had gone.

'No. Kath's due very soon. Natalie's taken over picking Hattie up from school on a Thursday.'

'It's going to be a boy,' Hattie said, looking up at Steph.

The side gate opened and Natalie came back. 'We're blocked in,' she said to Steph. 'Want to move your car?'

The absence of any 'please' told Tom everything about what Natalie thought of Steph.

'Of course.' Steph gave Hattie a little pat. 'I need to unpack some presents for a special girl, anyway. I've brought you a genuine gondolier's hat from the men who row the boats in Venice.'

'Really? Wow!' Hattie looked towards Tom to confirm that this was the most brilliant news. 'Is it made of paper?'

'Oh no, darling. It's a proper one.'

When Steph had gone, Hattie reached up, took the pirate's hat off and put it down on the lawn.

Tom couldn't bear to look at Fran's face. He went and picked up the hat and placed it on the table.

When Fran said she'd better go too, he assured her that there was no need.

'I'm going, Tom,' she said, softly, 'not leaving. The two things are different.' She turned to Hattie. 'Well, what a lovely surprise for you, your mother popping by? I will see you again soon, no doubt.'

'Uh-huh,' Hattie said, looking towards the gate, and Tom had to remind her about her manners and to say thank you for the ice cream. Fran waved the stilted thanks away and Tom wanted to kiss her, but felt inhibited by Hattie and the prospect of Steph reappearing.

When Steph did return, hands full of carrier bags, her path crossed with Fran's.

'Oh, are you going?' she said. 'You don't need to. She doesn't need to, does she, Hattie?'

Hattie made no reply and Tom saw Steph's smile at that. He looked at the half-made ice-cream-carton caterpillar and the plank on the lawn, and it seemed like they belonged to a different world. Everything had changed now. He remembered that look on Fran's face when Steph had walked through the gate.

Steph settled herself in a chair, Hattie next to her, and arranged the bags. This was what she did best – the Lady Bountiful approach to motherhood. Each parcel offered to Hattie came with a commentary bigging herself up. 'I had to go to a tiny shop on the outskirts of Milan to buy this,' and, 'I spent a lot of time persuading the designer to make this in a child's version.'

Hattie, perhaps sensing that she was required to perform to some specific script, did not do her customary ripping at the paper, but picked delicately at Sellotape and tried to unknot ribbon.

'Good girl,' Steph said. 'We'll save the ribbon for your hair, shall we?'

Hattie nodded enthusiastically and Tom wanted to throw up. If he'd gone anywhere near Hattie with a ribbon she'd have done one of her karate moves on him.

He thought of Fran's face again and picked up the pirate's hat from the table and went into the house.

As he kept an eye on Hattie through the window, he got through to Fran's voicemail. 'Please believe me,' he said, 'I had no idea Steph was coming. Look, if you can, would you pop round after Hattie's in bed? We can talk. Please.'

God, did he sound too desperate?

He went back to the garden and watched the great present-opening ceremony again. Hats, bangles, necklaces, a swimsuit, a T-shirt, a skirt with a frill, a glittery watch, a ceramic pot with a rose on top, some Italian sweets.

He could tell Hattie liked the hat and the sweets best, but there was a 'Thank you, Mummy' after each present. Steph took it as her due, while checking her phone.

He collected together all the wrapping paper and carried it to the recycling bin. When he returned, Hattie was wearing her hat, holding it on with one hand, while she struggled to get into the sweet packet. He took it from her, opened it and doled out a few bits of candy into her open hand.

'Oh come on, Tom, don't be so mean.' Steph swiped the packet from him and poured a lot more sweets out.

'She's already had ice cream,' he said, knowing as he did that he was coming over as Mr Grouch *vs* Ideal Mummy.

'Oh listen to Daddy!' Steph picked up one of the sweets

from Hattie's hand and fed her it. 'It's a special occasion and it's not going to do her any harm, Tom. Lighten up.' She popped a sweet into her own mouth and the two of them did synchronised chewing which made him feel as if he was on the other side of a plate-glass window looking in.

'Now, Hattie,' Steph said, when she had stopped chewing, 'why don't you try the T-shirt on and the skirt?' She pulled them out of the pile of presents. 'Off you go and then come back and give us a twirl.'

With Hattie upstairs, Tom said, 'Your sudden onrush of maternal love hasn't got anything to do with the phone call the other night?'

Steph was collecting up the ribbon, winding it round her fingers. 'Phone call?'

'When I told you I wasn't bothered what you do any more. Where I mentioned someone else?'

'Oh, that phone call.' She stopped winding the ribbon. 'I must say, Tom, she's quite young. How old is she?'

She could stuff her script. He didn't reply.

'And quite . . . individual too. Good hair. Did she ask you if you could remember those dresses the first time they were around?'

Hattie came back and Tom wanted to cry for her. She looked like a half-exploded sausage.

Steph tugged and smoothed at the clothes, trying to make everything look better. 'And we can put your hair up too, darling.' She selected a ribbon and started scraping Hattie's hair up into a high ponytail.

Hattie took it all, enraptured by the attention.

'There, look at you. Tom, isn't she beautiful?'

What could he say? 'No, she looks like a standard-issue Barbie doll'? He wanted to shout, 'Stop it, stop using her like this.' His frustration felt like a belt secured tightly round his chest.

'Where are you staying?' he asked.

There was a shift of her gaze to Hattie and then back to him. 'Shall we tell Daddy?' she said.

'She's staying here!' Hattie shouted. 'She's going to see me at breakfast time and take me to school.'

'We talked about it when you were in the kitchen just now, didn't we, darling?'

He could say, 'No, you are absolutely not staying here,' but that look on Hattie's face . . .

He was heading for the kitchen again.

Fran answered her phone this time. 'Are you all right?' he asked. 'Did you get my message?'

'I'm fine, Tom. And more worried about you. I could see the shock on your face.'

'She's doing it on purpose, Fran. I told her that I'd fallen for someone when we last spoke on the phone. And Steph can't bear to be beaten at anything – she's turned up to have a look at you and try to ruin things. Hattie's her weapon of choice.' He checked on events in the garden. 'And look . . . this is going to sound pathetic, but she's managed to back me into a corner about where she's staying. She got Hattie to agree to it first and . . . I just can't have that fight now. Hattie's beside herself with . . . excitement, happiness. God. It'll just be the one night.'

Fran's reply was a while coming. 'I understand. She has you over a barrel. So, I have no visiting rights this evening?'

'It would just get nasty.'

There was a sigh. 'You're right, and I'm not awfully keen on playing a part in "Two Women Fighting Over a Man". I mean, I would fight for you, Tom, were there a knife-wielding maniac on your case, but not this nails and handbags thing.'

'You're too bloody nice, Fran. Have I told you that? And that I love you.'

'Come and see me tomorrow after dropping off Hattie. Say it in person . . . No, show me in person.'

There were more endearments until he saw Steph coming towards the house with Hattie and he wound up the call.

Steph shivered dramatically as she walked in. 'Getting a

bit cold out there. So, are you going to show me your bed-room, young lady?'

There was enthusiastic nodding and shouting from Hattie and she was pulling Steph by her hand towards the kitchen door. Too late for Tom to remove the designer clothes from the soft toys.

'If you're staying,' he shouted after Steph, 'you can help with bedtime.'

'Of course,' Steph said, slowing down her progress. 'That would be lovely for me. Bathtime first and then we'll snuggle up with a story.'

'She has head lice,' he shot back. 'You'll need to comb those out as well.'

It was the second time Steph's poised demeanour had taken a hit and her hand went involuntarily to her own hair before she put her face back in order and said, cheerily, 'Oh poor Hattie. Never mind. Mummy's here to chase the horrible things away.'

Hattie curled into her mother's body, luxuriating in the contact, and then Steph was chasing Hattie up the stairs, Hattie giggling and whooping.

Tom stood in the kitchen and felt as if the walls were coming in on him. He should be happy that, right now, Hattie was ecstatic – except if this was the *up*, how swift and bad would the *down* be?

Why hadn't he kept his mouth shut during that phone call?

He slowly went up the stairs, listening to the laughing and screeching, but stopped halfway and sat down. He was like the Grand Old Duke of York, neither up nor down, back in a state of limbo once again.

CHAPTER 48

Thursday 19 June

1) For something that started off as a joke, 'Aunt F' does the job. It makes me feel much older than Jamie, even though there is only a gnat's wing dividing our ages.

2) If Edward Mawson were to give me a name, it would probably be 'Aunt F-off'.

3) Having a small child put her hand in yours does weird things to your stomach and your tear ducts. Being ignored by that same child an hour later has the same effect.

4) What comes in through a side gate can kill a party quicker than someone peeing in the punch bowl (no idea where I got that phrase from, certainly not one of my mother's).

5) First impressions can be the right ones. See Thursday 29 May. Point

6) It is to be doubted whether a person who needs to be

the centre of attention all the time is ever going to win prizes for Mother of the Year.

7) It is possible to look at the kind of woman the man you love, once loved, and wonder if you know him at all. Or perhaps you know the person he is now and not the one he was then.

8) Victoria and Steph may have been separated at birth – from any sense of decency and fair play.

9) The likelihood of Jamie and Natalie having had 'words' in the car on the way home is very high.

10) It is very hard to take a step back when you know someone has already broken the people you have come to love and, most probably, is going to have a go at breaking them again. And may even try messing up your life too.

CHAPTER 49

Just before Tom fell asleep, the little red numbers told him it was 01:30.

At 02:04, he was woken by a small finger jabbing his shoulder. Hattie was out of bed and sniffing as if she had either been crying or was about to.

'What's up, big girl?' he asked, trying to jolly her along.

'I went to see Mummy, but her door's closed.'

What, she's not doing twenty-four-hour parenting?

He sat up to let Hattie get in beside him. She was normally like a little hot-water bottle, but she felt cold, particularly her feet which she placed on his leg. She must have been out of bed for a while. He pictured her standing outside Steph's bedroom door and put his arm around her. He clocked the fact that Gummy was in her right hand.

'Going to tell me what you're sad about?' he asked, knowing roughly what it would be.

'What if Mummy's not in her room? What if she's gone?'

'She won't be,' he said, but the sniffing continued and she was starting to gulp. 'Stay there,' he told her and went to look out of the landing window. He came back, going via the bathroom to get some toilet paper. He handed it to her. 'Mummy's car is on the drive. She's definitely in her room, asleep.'

'She will be here in the morning, won't she?' Hattie was running her fingers over Gummy.

'She'll be here in the morning.'

'Can she take me to school?'

'Probably.' Steph was not famous for her early-morning starts.

'Can she stay for ever?'

'We'll talk about it another time, Hattie.'

Gummy was now in the palm of one hand, and she was stroking it with the fingers of her other one. 'I want her to stay.'

'Hattie, let's go to sleep now. I'm tired, you're tired. This is a visit, Hattie. A visit.'

The hand holding Gummy was straying to her mouth and he gently reached across and stilled its progress. 'Have a snuggle up,' he said, 'and just enjoy having Mummy here, don't think about anything else.'

How could you make a five-year-old understand that concept?

'I want to snuggle up to Mummy.'

Steph had been here less than nine hours and had already supplanted him in Hattie's affections. He was trying to take it on the chin, but by God it hurt.

He had continued to sit marooned on the stairs during bathtime and hair-washing and de-lousing, during story-time and tucking-in and felt utterly excluded. 'Mummy will get my drink. Mummy will sit here while I go to sleep.'

Steph would tire of this very soon. Trouble was, what would she have wrecked before she left again?

When Tom woke up next, he could smell cooking. He went downstairs to a scene of domestic bliss. Steph, her hair in a ponytail, was frying pancakes. Hattie, with an identical ponytail, was sitting at the table eating them.

'There you are, Daddy,' Steph said. 'Isn't he a sleepyhead, Hattie?'

'Look, look.' Hattie held up her plate. 'Pancakes.'

'Do you want this one, Tom? It's nearly done.'

'No. Thank you.'

'Oh dear! Daddy's a bit growly this morning, isn't he? Growl, growl.' Hattie's response to that was to giggle and it felt like an early-morning kick in the teeth. Up ten minutes and he was already irritated, particularly by the way Steph talked to Hattie as if her synapses were not yet connected.

'Perhaps Daddy would like some coffee?'

Yes, that was irritating too – talking about him in the third person.

'I'll do it,' he said.

'You used to like me making your coffee.'

He had, he'd liked anything she did for him, to him, with him. He had been besotted and amazed that someone so out of his league would bend down from the heights and choose him.

He let her make his coffee – watching her move easily around the kitchen. Today she had on some jeans and a white T-shirt and managed to look sophisticated rather than as if she was off for a trip round B&Q.

When she turned off the heat under the frying pan, she retrieved a silver bangle from the table and slipped it back on her arm.

'Here you are,' she said after she had poured the coffee and as she walked away, she ruffled his hair. It was done so quickly, he couldn't stop her.

'You always had lovely hair, Tom. Doesn't Daddy have lovely hair?'

Hattie had her mouth full, but nodded. He couldn't take this at breakfast. He told her what time they had to leave and that they couldn't be late because he had two meetings early on (only he knew one of them was with Fran) and then went into the sitting room to check his emails.

This was a remarkable charm offensive and, worryingly, it not only seemed to be targeted on Hattie, but also him. Steph hadn't even mentioned the way her presents were adorning the soft toys.

When breakfast was over, the logistics of the trip to school reminded him of that old riddle – how to get a fox, a chicken and bag of corn over a river safely. He didn't know who was the chicken or the corn, but the cunning fox was definitely Steph.

His plan had been for Hattie to come in his car and Steph to follow on behind. But Hattie wanted to go with Steph. Tom reluctantly agreed, but Steph couldn't find her car keys.

He didn't want them all to go in his car like some happy family. *And* it would mean coming back to drop Steph off before he went on to work.

They all looked for the keys until they had to go or they would be late. He wanted to say, 'You did this on purpose,' but there was Hattie watching him. This was how it went – Steph using his fear of upsetting Hattie to trap him into doing what she wanted.

In Tom's car, Steph played the role of perfect mother and as they passed the turning for Fran's bungalow, Fran walked up the track and to the main road. She had her back to them and although his impulse was to beep the horn and get her to turn round, he suddenly didn't want her to see them all together like this. He said nothing and kept on driving hoping that Fran would only see the car after it had gone past.

Steph was opening the window. 'Fran! Fran!' she called. 'Look Hattie, there's Fran.'

Fran turned and Tom saw her take in everything that he hadn't wanted her to. She raised her hand in a stiff wave.

In the playground, Steph sought out Josh's mother and Hattie's teacher and schmoozed her heart out.

'I'm taking you back home,' he told her after they left Hattie. 'You can have another look for those car keys.'

'But I want to come along to Tynebrook. Maybe we could have a spot of lunch together?'

Tom pulled over to the side of the road, not even bothering to wait for 'his' lay-by. He put on the hazard-warning lights. 'Steph, I'm pleased you've come to see Hattie, but let's get this straight – I don't want to have lunch with you, tea with you or any other bloody meal. I don't want you staying in my house and I'm not particularly happy being in the same car with you. For the last three and a half years, you've dragged your feet to wield some kind of power over me and take advantage of the fact that I don't want anything to hurt Hattie. I can live with that, but I'll never forgive you for the way you've messed Hattie about too. And now you're Mother of the Year suddenly?'

He didn't need to look at her to know that she was crying.

'I'm sorry, Tom,' she said, between the tears, 'I know how much of Hattie's growing up I've missed. I'm just trying to make up for it.'

This was 'sincere Steph', the one he'd believed for years.

'Really? And how long can we expect this masterclass in mothering to go on for?'

'I'm staying till Tuesday, Tom, if that's what you mean. Then I'm going to see Mummy and Daddy. I can go to a hotel if you want – although I think that will really upset Hattie—'

'Have you told her when you're leaving?'

There was no answer to that, just a prolonged period of crying.

Tom took that as a 'no'. Fantastic, so if he turfed her out and made her stay somewhere else, Hattie was going to be upset now and again when she left on Tuesday.

He looked at the clock on the dashboard. Damn, this was eating into his Fran time. He took off the handbrake and pulled out into the road and there was the blare of a horn behind him and the sound of someone trying to stop and he managed to get part of the way back up on the verge before there was a thud, a jolt and the noise of a car hitting them.

CHAPTER 50

Tom stood by the dent at the back of his car and looked at the piece of paper in his hand. On it were the name and contact details of a very irate guy whose only other communication with him had been to shout, 'You bloody idiot! Hazard-warning lights on, no use of indicator, sharp right turn into the road. What kind of fuckwit are you?'

He remembered Fran's accident up in the forest and looked at Steph sitting in the passenger seat rubbing her neck. She said she had whiplash, which was possible. After all, there must be the odd thing that came out of her mouth that was true.

It was too late to go to Fran's now, and if he took Steph home, it would make him late for his other meeting, the one at work.

He got back in the car. 'How's your neck?'

Steph winced. 'Quite painful. Is there a doctor in Tynebrook?'

'Yes,' he said, dully, aware his own shoulder was aching,

and this time he checked the mirror before he pulled out into the road.

Once Steph was out of the car, he rang Fran. Damn voice-mail again. He told her what had happened and apologised for not coming round. Next he called his mother and filled her in on Steph's arrival.

She swore so badly that he wondered what the rev. thought of that.

Like Tom, she wanted to know what Steph was after. The two women had never bonded, and after Steph had more or less absented herself from Hattie's life, Joan had little time for her.

'It's jealousy about Fran,' Tom said. 'But there must be something else going on because she's being nice to me too. So, just warning you, Hattie will be fairly hyper when you pick her up from school later.'

'Poor, poor Hattie,' was his mother's closing remark. 'She'll be over the moon.'

Tom decided not to tell Rob and Kath that Steph was around; Kath's blood pressure was high enough as it was. He didn't tell anyone at work about his visitor either, although he half expected her to put in an appearance.

As he worked, another potential worry surfaced. Up until Steph's arrival, there had been six people who knew about him and Fran. Now there were seven. How could he ask Steph to keep quiet when that would alert her to what a very juicy piece of information she had hold of?

There were few points of light in his bleak day. One was that Felix and Derek had scouted out some good images from the end-of-year show. Another, that Kelvin had sweet-talked some new advertisers on board. After he'd told Tom that news, he continued to sit looking out into the main office at Victoria.

'I've still got quite a bit to do,' Tom hinted and Kelvin nodded.

'Yeah, me too.' And then, 'What do you think of Vicky?' *Vicky?*

'Well . . . she's talented and determined and she's got a good eye for what does and doesn't work in a magazine—'

'Yeah, but her and me? Think we could make a go of it?'

Kelvin did something enthusiastic with his eyebrows.

'I have no answer to that,' Tom replied and Kelvin agreed that it was 'a bloody curly one'. When he left, he made his usual detour via Victoria's desk. Tom was still no wiser about what 'make a go of it' meant. And now his shoulder was really aching.

Just after school had finished, his mother rang back.

'We're home,' she said, 'and so is *she*. And I've got a bone to pick with you: why didn't you mention you were in an accident? Madam is lying on the sofa, says she's got slap-dash.'

'Mum, it's . . . yeah, whatever.'

'She's not injured so badly that it's stopped her shopping though. Looks like Hattie's getting a whole new wardrobe.' There was a sniff that said it all. 'Don't be too late, will you, Tom? You can imagine the lovely chats we're having.'

Tom checked his mobile again. The Steph effect was already kicking in – Fran hadn't contacted him when she knew he'd been in an accident, so she must be really hacked off. He stared at his phone as if he could hypnotise it into ringing.

Once home, he found that his mother had summoned reinforcements. Rob and a very uncomfortable-looking Kath were sitting, arms folded, watching Steph like sheep-dogs.

Steph was lying on the sofa, Hattie with her, and they were going through a fashion magazine. His mother, mouth drawn into a cough-drop suck, was in a straight-backed chair brought in from the kitchen.

'Does your neck hurt too, Dad?' Hattie asked and he said 'No, my shoulder is just a bit sore.' She didn't reply and went back to pointing out what she liked in the magazine.

It was obvious that Hattie's sudden interest in fashion was to keep her mother's attention. She was modelling another T-shirt and skirt, and although these fitted her better, the outfit was still some way off the coast of her personality.

'We've all been having a nice chat, haven't we?' Steph said looking around Tom's family. 'Catching up.'

'A nice chat' didn't seem to sum up the mood of the party. Kath's expression was stone-like.

Now it seemed incredible to Tom that there had been a time when he had absorbed Steph's views of his family – provincial, limited and limiting – and his trips north had grown infrequent.

'Make you a cup of tea, mate?' Rob asked and jerked his head towards the kitchen.

'What the hell is she doing here?' he said as soon as Tom joined him. 'It's not right her turning up like this. And then what? Bugger off again and leave you to pick up the pieces?'

'She has a right to see Hattie, Rob.'

'Yeah. Doesn't use it much though, does she? When I think how casual she is about having a child, when some of us . . .' Rob took his feelings out on a teabag.

'Take Kath home,' Tom said gently. 'This isn't helping her. I appreciate the support, but please, take her home.'

Rob and Kath *did* go not long after that, Kath telling him

she was just on the other end of the phone if he needed her. Steph had given them a gracious goodbye from the sofa – 'My neck, you see. I won't get up.'

Tom knew where this neck injury was now leading. There would definitely be no move to a hotel – that would be a nice image for Hattie to savour: her father ejecting her injured mother on to the doorstep.

When his own mother left, she said, 'Let me know if there's anything I can do to shift her, won't you?'

'The rev. doesn't do contract killings, does he?' Tom replied.

As the sound of his mother's car faded away, he felt alone and trapped. Steph was already wrong-footing him and fate and road accidents seemed to be helping her.

He was in the kitchen thinking what to have for tea, when he heard the side gate squeak and shot out into the garden again.

Please let it be Fran.

He barely had any time to smile before she had her arms around him.

'Oh, thank God you're all right. I saw the dent in the car.' She had pulled back and was looking at him and he reversed the action and kissed her.

'Your lips didn't get damaged, I see,' she said when he'd finished.

He just held her close and felt the warmth and energy that was Fran. 'Oh God. I am sooo glad you're here,' he whispered into her hair. 'I thought you were hacked off with me – seeing us all in the car, me not turning up when I said I would. When you didn't answer my calls . . .'

'Oh, Tom,' she said, sadly, 'when are you going to learn that I'm not like . . . well, other people?' She disentangled herself from him. 'It's wearing the way you always think I'm going to strop off at the slightest thing.' She shook her head at him, but it was in a 'What am I going to do with you?' way and not an 'I'm so angry I'm going to throw you on the floor' one.

'I've been out shopping for bits and pieces with Jamie and Natalie for the flat,' she explained. 'Goodness me, so much time taken to decide on an ironing board. Anyway, I had my mobile, but it was right at the bottom of my bag and the shops are so noisy. Otherwise, my little wounded soldier, I would have been here like a shot.'

She administered some more mouth-to-mouth resuscitation which was disturbed abruptly by Hattie saying, 'Why are you kissing Fran?'

They leaped apart to find Steph standing behind Hattie.

'Perhaps she has something stuck in one of her back teeth,' Steph said and there, just for an instant in the look she gave Fran, was undiluted vindictiveness. Tom would have been quite happy not to have seen that look ever again.

'I'm very sorry to hear about the accident,' Fran said. 'Were you hurt, Steph, or just shaken up?'

'Both.'

'Mummy's hurt her neck,' Hattie explained, looking sad.

Tom nodded. 'Earlier she could barely get up off the sofa.'

'Well you *should* take it easy,' Fran said. 'Get plenty of rest.'

'I intend to. My bedroom here is very comfortable. The bed especially.'

Fran kept smiling and did not respond to whatever point Steph was trying to make about sleeping arrangements.

'We were just about to play a board game, weren't we, Hattie?' Steph announced. 'Does Daddy want to play? I thought Monopoly.'

'Please, Daddy, please!' Hattie was jumping about.

He saw Steph's smug smile.

'Monopoly's too old for her,' he said.

'Well, you'd like to try it, wouldn't you, Hattie?'

Hattie would, although Tom guessed that ten minutes in, she'd rather be playing Snakes and Ladders.

'Perhaps Fran could play too,' Hattie suddenly suggested and Steph's smile faltered.

'Oh that's kind.' Fran bent down to Hattie. 'But I have to go back. I'm working on a new animal. Just to see if I can.'

'What is it?' Hattie asked.

'It's a hedgehog. I've found one living in my garden. He has a little bolt-hole there.'

'Bolty what?'

'Oh, sorry, Hattie. It means somewhere you can go where you know you'll be safe. Him and his fleas are curled up in a burrow under an old tree stump.'

'Are we going to play this game?' Steph held her hand out to Hattie and clicked her fingers. Hattie went like a shot.

'I'd better go,' Tom said, morosely, when Steph had taken Hattie in. 'This is bloody purgatory, Fran. And I can't turf her out now, not when she's meant to have whiplash. I've got a whole weekend of this to look forward to.'

'Hmm. That whiplash, comes and goes, doesn't it?' Fran leaned over and kissed him. 'Perhaps you could try and sneak over and see me sometime this weekend, when Hattie goes to bed. Leave Steph to babysit.' She was very close to his face and he felt her scrutinising him, but before he could give an answer, she provided one herself. 'No, that's not going to happen, is it? Now, why is that?'

He knew she was waiting for something from him and when it didn't come, she said, 'Well, you have no choice then. You'll have to let her monopolise you.' There was a laugh. 'Ah, see what I did there. *Monopolise* . . . very good. Off you go then, Tom. Go directly to jail, do not pass Go . . .' She patted him fondly on the backside and walked away.

He wasn't taken in by Fran's cheery tone – he knew she was frustrated that he would not open up to her about Steph.

He walked back into the house feeling as if he *was* being packed off to jail. Perhaps next time Fran came she would bring him one of her cakes. He didn't care how dreadful it was, just as long as it had a file in it.

CHAPTER 51

Pulling back the curtains on Sunday, Tom saw the rain and knew that things were going to get rough. Rainy days and an active five-year-old were enough to test even the most patient parent.

He had no hope that today would be as 'successful' as yesterday.

Saturday morning had been particularly good, largely because Steph spent the morning in bed, suffering with her neck, but when he'd suggested that he take Hattie out so that she could continue to sleep in the afternoon, she made another miraculous recovery. Within minutes, she had appeared in the kitchen, ready to go. He had looked at her white trousers and slate-grey cashmere jumper and decided on a farm tour.

Apart from a little pull down of her mouth when they arrived and she'd had to walk over the mud and straw, Steph had powered up her mothering act. She agreed with a dad in the hen barn that it was indeed hard to get your children to eat eggs and chatted with another mother about how important it was for every child – a sweep of her arm to gather up Hattie – to be out in the fresh air.

Hattie had responded to all this by walking between them, catching hold of their hands and asking to be swung back and forth.

'This is lovely, isn't it?' Steph had said. 'Just the three of us.'

Unable to face the prospect of a cosy evening in, he'd driven on to Newcastle for pizza. Steph had assumed her natural place in the spotlight, charming the waiters with exactly the right degree of mummy flirt and trying to charm him too. Her enthusiasm as she helped Hattie with the wax crayons and colouring pad the restaurant provided was something to behold.

But the day had not all been Steph's. When Tom had gone to bed, his mobile had rung and it was Fran. After listening politely to his tale of woe, she'd said, 'Well that's all very fascinating, Tom, but I've been doing some research into telephone sex, and I'm sitting here in only a very small pair of black satin panties and wondered what you thought about that?'

He had thought: *Way hey, let's bloody go for it.*

As he watched the rain slashing down, Tom tried to dig

back into that lovely memory, but he could already sense trouble brewing in the kitchen.

Hattie was asking if she could have pancakes again and Steph told her that she needed to get the Sunday newspapers first.

'It's a long walk in the rain,' Tom said and, in response, Steph tossed her keys up and down in her hand and said she'd just found them.

'Where were they, Mummy?' Hattie asked and got told, sharply, to be quiet.

'I'm sorry,' Hattie said, her lip looking a bit wobbly, and Tom put his hand on her shoulder and said to Steph, 'It was a perfectly reasonable question.'

He saw Steph's urge to snap something at him, but she reined herself back. 'Yes, Mummy's sorry, Hattie darling. She didn't sleep very well. She's the one who's a bit growly this morning. Why don't you lay the table while I'm out and we'll have those pancakes as soon as I get back?'

Hattie set to with a will and they put a tablecloth on and used the better china and sat and waited for Steph to return. And waited. The nearest paper shop was a ten-minute drive there and back. After half an hour, the sight of Hattie repeatedly going to the window to check for Steph's car sent Tom to the frying pan and he started making the pancakes himself.

'Do you think Mummy's all right?' Hattie asked as she watched him and he said she'd bumped into someone and got chatting. So much for not doing Steph's PR any more.

When Steph did return, an hour and a half after she'd left, Hattie was hunkered down on his lap. He was trying to read to her, but her misery kept making him lose the thread.

'Oh well done, you've had the pancakes,' Steph said, looking at the dirty frying pan. 'I was desperate for a coffee after the night I had. Naughty Mummy had an almond croissant too. Here, Hattie, look, I bought you some comics.'

As if she sensed that Tom was going to have a go at her, she added, 'Come on, Hattie. Sit with me and I can read my newspapers and you can read your comics. Girls together.'

Hattie was like a little wave throwing itself against a rock, working extra hard to engage Steph and chat. Steph kept saying 'Lovely' and 'Excellent' while rarely taking her eyes from the Lifestyle sections.

By evening, Steph's neck was hurting too much to do bath-time and de-lousing, and as Tom watched Hattie splashing about half-heartedly, he knew she would be thinking this was her fault. It had to stop. He had to have the argument he should have had on the first day – Hattie was upset now anyway, how much worse could it get?

Just as he was wrapping Hattie in a towel, Steph wrong-footed him again. 'OK,' she said enthusiastically, 'who's for loads and loads of stories?'

Off Hattie trotted, in heaven once more.

Downstairs, Tom opened a bottle of wine and drank a glass straight off as he was ironing the school uniform.

'Good idea,' Steph said as she came back down and poured herself a glass.

When he went to say goodnight to Hattie, she was smiling.

'What are you looking so happy about?' he said.

'It's a secret.' She put her finger to her lips and the smile grew even wider under it. He could get no sense from her.

In the sitting room, Steph was sitting on the sofa checking her phone when he walked in. He saw she'd brought the wine bottle and the glasses in from the kitchen.

'Why's Hattie so happy?' he asked, sitting down in the armchair furthest away from her.

She put her phone back in her bag. 'You've made this really nice in here, Tom. English cosy. God, do you remember that first flat we had in Barnes? That carpet!'

He drank some more wine. 'I'm presuming you haven't told her about leaving on Tuesday, then?'

Steph smiled. 'We had to take it up in the end, didn't

we, that carpet? Smelled of cat's pee. Nice little flat though, Tom. Often think about it. We could lie in bed and only see tree tops.' She smiled at him, all the power of her charm in that smile. 'Happy days, Tom.'

'When are you going to tell her?'

Steph finished off the wine. 'Tell her what?'

'That you're going on Tuesday.'

'I have told her.'

He put his glass down. 'Steph, what have you done?'

'I told her I'm going, but that I'll be back. I'm planning to move here. That's why I was really so long this morning – I was looking in estate agents' windows.'

'You've told her what?' he said slowly, hearing the tremor in his voice.

'That I'm moving here.' Steph's smile was chilling. 'It's something I've been thinking about since I arrived. I'd forgotten how lovely it is in this part of the world.'

That might have been believable if she hadn't repeatedly told him how 'dull' she found the place. But she was getting into her stride.

'I could be based anywhere near a good airport, so why not here? I don't want to miss any more of Hattie growing up, Tom.'

'Steph, this is a fairy story,' he said, sharply, thinking of Hattie upstairs, blissfully happy.

'No, it's the truth. I've left you with all the hard work and it's time to take some responsibility now.' There was a self-deprecating laugh. 'I know I don't often show it, but I think you're a wonderful father.'

He felt as if he was being caught in a sticky web.

'I'm not saying that I expect any reconciliation.' Her hands came up as if that was a definite. 'But as you said on the telephone, the divorce will happen of its own accord soon, and in the meantime there's no reason why we can't be amicable for Hattie's sake.'

She gave him a look that before would have had him on his knees in front of her. She did sincerity so well. Sometimes she even meant it.

'Steph,' he said, finding it hard not to shout that word, 'you can't tell Hattie you're moving up here when you have no intention of doing it. And what about Alessandro? Is he going to move here, too?'

'But I do intend to move here, Tom.'

It was as if anything he said was just bouncing off her. He got up and closed the door. 'This fantasy of being more involved with Hattie? You want to think back to when you were completely involved with her?'

'I was younger then,' she said, quickly. 'Hattie was younger. I've really enjoyed this visit—'

'Being here for a few days is not the same.' He felt his

temper start to flare. 'You have to put her first when you're tired, when you're irritated, even when you're ill. I don't see any evidence of you committing to any of that, even in the short time you've been here. Are you really telling me you'd change? Give up the parties and the late nights, your friends, taking off at the drop of a hat when a good job crops up?'

'You used to enjoy that life, Tom.'

'Yes. But my priorities changed when Hattie came along. Yours didn't seem to.'

'That's not kind, Tom.' Steph pouted and these days it just looked ridiculous to him.

'What's this really about?' he asked.

'Why do you think I always have an angle?'

He sat down again and found himself dramatically rubbing his forehead with the palm of his hand, feeling as if he couldn't think straight. He tried to be calm but firm.

'Steph, please see sense. Be honest about what kind of relationship you want with Hattie. If all you can offer is to see her now and again, that's fine, but stick to what you promise. And don't tell me you want more responsibility for her, because I don't think you're capable of handling it.'

Here were the tears. 'I just made a few mistakes, Tom.'

'You're not listening to me, Steph. You lose interest in her after a while. Or, because she's not exactly as you want her to be, all ribbons and dimples, you try to change her. When it doesn't work, she irritates you. Then you get angry.'

'I was under a lot of stress at work, Tom.'

'And I wasn't?' he shot back.

'You can't judge me on that. It's not fair,' she said, sulkily. 'Things are different now. I want to be a proper mother to Hattie.'

She could lie so well it made you forget what the truth was. Did she actually believe this stuff herself?

'We've been through this,' he said, 'so many times. She just gets too much for you.'

She turned away from him and the curves and lines of her face still had the power to move him. But what he felt now was pity, not love.

'It's not your fault, Steph,' he said. 'But lying about it *is*. Just be honest. Let's bring an end to all this bloody acting.'

She was still turned away.

He waited for her to say something and when she didn't, he stood up, suddenly too weary to keep going. 'I've got work tomorrow. Sleep on it, Steph, then we'll have to think about how the hell to unpick what you've said to Hattie.'

Another night where it took him ages to get to sleep, his shoulder painful and his mind refusing to switch off. And then he was woken up by Hattie again, slipping into bed with him.

'What's up?' he mumbled and she put her hand on his arm and he was wide awake. It was a grown-up's hand.

'Tom,' Steph said. 'We're still good together.'

In the light from the landing, he could see the gloss of her hair and her breasts and he thought of all those times with her. Different hotels, different beds.

The smell of her.

A body he knew so well inside and out.

Her mouth was on his and it would have been so easy to just go under and drown, but he was struggling up into the air, rolling to the other side of the bed.

He didn't want to be a slave to all that again – a bit player in the Steph show. He wanted Fran.

He stumbled to Hattie's room and stayed there a long time, staring at the baby monitor.

When he went back to his own bed, Steph was no longer in it.

CHAPTER 52

Sunday 22 June

Another mishmash of what I've learned, I'm afraid.

1) Baby monitors are rubbish. If they were really useful they'd work over longer distances. Then I could just put one in Tom's house and one in mine and hear what's going on. Although, now I think about it, that's probably called bugging not monitoring.

2) When you hear that the man you love has been in an accident you worry. And it seems such bad luck – he is already being held hostage.

3) A woman can click her fingers at a child and make you instantly want to stop being reasonable and adult.

4) Tom should spill the beans and share the load – if that's not too much of a mixed metaphor. Whatever he's afraid of, it cannot be as bad as the torture he is enduring now – trying to please a tiger.

5) As regards point 4, I do not know if that is exactly the situation, but I have learned that secrets are corrosive. And they do have a habit of turning round and biting you on the bottom.

6) Telephone sex is much to be recommended, although it would be easier if I could work out how to use the speakerphone on my mobile and therefore be able to operate hands-free, as it were.

7) I am becoming wanton. Fran Mayhew, a while ago, would never have written point 6.

8) Steph has very small eyes. I am just picking on them as everything else about her is damn near perfect. Except her personality.

9) Hedgehogs are harder than they look. By that I don't mean they turn up at your back door demanding money with menaces. What I mean is that creating a realistic set of spines that don't look like

   A. A load of frills, and

   B. A toilet brush, is very difficult.

10) Creating a blood-sucking vampire bat is much easier. Especially as you do not have to spend much time on the eyes because they are so small.

CHAPTER 53

Steph did not join Hattie and Tom for breakfast the next morning, and he was hoping to get out of the house without seeing her, but just before they were leaving, she arrived downstairs.

'Hattie, darling,' she said, 'Mummy won't come with you this morning, but I'll be here when you get home. Big hugs.'

She did not speak to Tom at all then, but when he had got Hattie and her karate kit into the car, she called him back.

'I've decided not to move up here. You've put me off, so *you* can tell Hattie. You always leave the nasty jobs to me so you come out of it looking like Dad of the Century. Well, not this time.' She looked him up and down. 'Going to work via Miss Vintage?'

The gloves were off again and it was back to everything being his fault.

On the drive to school, Hattie was still high on the belief

that Steph would be coming to live near her, which then grew into questions about why she couldn't just move in with them. He wondered what story Josh would get at school.

'You look lovely,' he said to Fran when she opened the door and she said he was a flatterer and led the way into the sitting room.

'So, nothing to report?' she asked.

'Just that I still love you . . . and you seem to be wearing more than you were on the phone the other evening.' He pulled her to him and kissed her and felt some of the tension that Steph and the accident had put into his shoulders unknot.

'I meant,' she said, when he stopped kissing her, 'anything to report about Steph?'

'Do we have to talk about her now? I've got to be at work very soon.' He reached for her and must have winced because she nodded at his shoulder and asked, 'How's it doing?'

'Aching a bit. Could do with a rub.'

Fran obliged and it felt bloody good. 'My penis is aching a bit too,' he told her. 'Any chance of a quick rub for that?'

'Tom Howard,' she said, 'that's awful,' but the atmosphere had changed and when they went back to kissing it felt different. Deeper kisses, hotter. Hands starting to roam and explore.

'Let's get you out of that dress,' he said.

'No need.' She broke away from him and lifted up the hem. No knickers – thighs, pubic hair, belly.

'Oh, God,' he said, 'you were waiting for me,' and then they were down on the floor.

'You'll be late for work,' she panted as he pushed into her.

'I'll be quick,' he said and then, 'sorry, that's not much of a turn-on. I meant, oh God, I don't know what I meant.' And it felt great, an urgent coupling, his pants and trousers down, her dress up round her waist.

Afterwards he said, 'I needed so much to be that close to you again.'

And she placed her forehead against his and agreed.

Putting himself back together he said, 'Thank you for being so understanding about all this, Fran. Not being stroppy or going into battle with Steph.'

'Well, I hope above all things I'm a grown-up, Tom. It's best to stay objective.' It was said with conviction, but Tom thought she looked preoccupied and the way she was standing in front of her work table reminded him of how she'd been when she'd trapped her jumper in the boot of her car.

'What have you got behind you, Fran?'

Her attempt at an innocent face was rubbish.

He gently moved her to one side.

She was working on a sculpture of a vampire bat hanging upside down from a tree. It had great black wings and white fangs from which droplets of blood were dripping. Its eyes were very small.

'It's Steph, isn't it?'

She looked very guilty. 'Well, I'm only human.'

He found it funny, but less amusing was the way that it reminded him of how vindictive Steph could be. Would she go quietly tomorrow, or draw further blood?

'Tom.' Fran's tone alerted him that she was about to be serious. 'You look like you have the worries of the world on you and I wish you'd realise that you don't have to face all these things on your own. You *can* trust people with your secrets – as I've done with you.'

He felt the warring impulses to tell her or to be quiet. 'Maybe once Steph's gone,' he said, 'then I can think straight.'

Fran was giving him that grave look of hers and when she reached for his hand, he thought she was going to kiss it, but she placed it on his chest.

'Remember that day we met?' she said, patting his hand and then pressing down on it with her own. 'You were like this, trying to hide the llama spit?'

He nodded.

'But when I first saw you, I actually thought something different – one of those back-of-the-brain thoughts that only comes out later.'

'That I'd hurt my arm wrestling?' He laughed, but she cut across it.

'No, that was my second thought. My very first impulse was that you were protecting your heart. And I think you're still putting up a barrier, rather than opening up and trusting that someone will catch you if you fall.'

'I really do have to go now, Fran, sweetheart.'

She removed her hand. 'Well, off you trot then. But it really would make everything easier if you confided in me.'

'What can I say, I'm terrible; a typical, uptight Englishman.'

They both laughed at that, but later, when everything was falling round his ears, he wished he'd laughed less and listened to her advice more.

CHAPTER 54

Liz didn't need hand signals or words to convey that something was wrong – her eyes said it all.

Mrs Mawson and Edward Mawson were sitting in his office.

Awkward so soon after he'd been with Fran.

Who was he kidding? It would have been awkward even if he hadn't just seen her. This was too mob-handed for a cosy chat.

Careful, Tom.

'Have you been offered coffee?' he asked them as he closed his office door. Mrs Mawson gave a curt nod. She looked more strained than the last time he had seen her.

'Let's cut the small talk,' Edward said. Tom figured that usually when Edward was as pumped up as this, he got to kill whatever he was pursuing.

Mrs Mawson smiled and it was the one she used for Jamie. Not a good sign. 'We wanted to discuss the nature pages with you,' she said. 'You have, I believe, not only gone against my wishes, but also did nothing to stamp on negative comments from your staff about my choices.'

And how would you know that?

'I'm not quite sure what you mean,' Tom said, trying to keep it amicable. 'We are featuring the artist you suggested.'

'Alongside some amateurs from the local comp,' Edward cut in. He seemed to be channelling a 1950s sitcom, possibly based at Eton.

'My email could not have been misinterpreted,' Mrs Mawson said. 'I wanted the paintings by the artist I recommended to replace my father's work.'

'You said nothing about *only* using him.'

Edward made a noise like air escaping from an uptight git. 'It's the action of a man who hasn't got the balls to be openly defiant, but still wants to take a pop at us.'

Tom looked at the two incredibly rich people sitting in his shabby office and said, 'I find that reading of the situation really insulting. I've tried to give you what you want, while fulfilling my remit – one you agreed on – to take the magazine forward.'

Edward was trying to engage Tom in one of the Mawsons' stare-offs, but Tom wasn't having it. He looked at Edward's receding hairline.

'I did flag up last time we met, that interference in my

editorial role would create problems such as this. Even so, I've tried to accommodate you—'

'That's big of you,' Edward snapped.

'Despite,' Tom pressed on, 'the fact that I feel this particular artist's work is, I'm sorry to say, not up to the high standards expected of us.'

'Ah yes, high standards,' Mrs Mawson agreed. 'Which brings me to my next point. How long have you been having an affair with Fran Mayhew?'

Tom would not have been surprised if some more of the plaster fruit fell off the walls. There it was – the real reason for this visit.

Damn, damn, damn. This had to happen now?

'We paid you the courtesy of ringing your home this morning to tell you we would be coming in,' Mrs Mawson explained. 'A woman who said she was your wife informed us that you were at Fran Mayhew's bungalow. When I enquired why, she told me. At great length.'

Tom imagined the relish with which Steph would have spilled the story. She'd have been even happier if she'd realised that she wasn't simply getting him into trouble for fornicating on company time.

Mrs Mawson looked pained. 'So now we're dealing with misconduct as well as incompetence.'

'Uh, excuse me,' Tom said, 'where do those two things come into it?'

Edward spelled it out for him. 'Failing to find a proper replacement for the nature pages. Expressly going against my mother's wishes regarding artist selection. Rubbishing her judgement by tearing up her correspondence and leaving it on open display. And now this Mayhew lark.'

'I might simply have tackled the incompetence with a formal warning,' Mrs Mawson said. 'But it's unlikely we can rebuild our working relationship following this latest . . . development. She, presumably, has told you who she is—'

'Who she *says* she is,' Edward corrected his mother.

Mrs Mawson did not acknowledge that correction, which made Tom suspect that she believed Fran *was* Charlie's daughter. Had she always known there was a half-sister out there who might turn up one day?

'You must see,' she went on, 'that I can no longer trust you with anything that is commercially sensitive? You could simply relay it to her.'

'Why would I do that, and why would Fran want it?' Now he was getting angry for Fran as well as himself.

More air escaped from Edward. 'To obtain money from us. Why else is she here? You must think we're idiots.'

Edward was right about that.

'I'm extremely disappointed in you,' Mrs Mawson told

him, and she certainly looked it. 'Up until recently, we had what I thought was an amicable relationship. But now? Well, I'm afraid I'm going to have to relieve you of your duties.'

'Just like that?'

He was feeling so angry it was making his legs shake, even sitting down. He'd done a bloody good job, better than their other crappy candidates could have done.

'People have employment rights,' he said, forcefully, 'you should know that, you employ enough of them. And my personal life has no bearing on how I do my job. If you think it does, you're going to have to prove it. I'll be taking legal advice on this, *Deborah*, and I don't think you've got a leg to stand on.'

'Got deep enough pockets for that?' Edward's sneer was farcically exaggerated.

'And do you have a thick enough skin for when the papers get hold of this?' Tom said right back to him.

The Mawsons exchanged a brief look.

'This conversation is over,' Mrs Mawson said, standing up. 'Please clear your desk and leave now.'

Tom picked up the phone. 'Liz, could you come in here, please.'

'Go ahead, you tell her,' he said to Edward when Liz arrived. When Edward did, she looked at Tom as if she wanted to hear him say it wasn't true.

'Because?' she asked.

'Incompetence and misconduct,' Edward replied. 'We'll tell the staff presently.'

Tom stood up, which was when what had just happened really hit him. He set about gathering up his things, sorting out what was his and what he should leave.

'Liz,' he managed to say. 'I'm sorry you've been landed with all this.'

'You do know that we're already in week two of the four-week lead-up to publication?' Liz said to Edward. She got as much response as she would from telling a wall, but Mrs Mawson said, 'We have a safe pair of hands to steer us towards publication.'

Liz looked vaguely embarrassed as though, even now, she wasn't at ease with things going her way. Tom went on opening drawers, taking out pens, notepads, an old address book.

'Shall I call Victoria in?' Edward asked his mother.

She nodded and with that nod, Tom understood who'd been feeding the Mawsons information. He thought of Victoria admiring the gundogs and Derek's comment about them, of having her in for a chat straight afterwards and the ripped-up email. He recalled Fran's verdict on her. He'd seriously underestimated her ambition.

Tom wondered if Liz had got to the punchline yet.

Victoria arrived, not looking at anyone but the Mawsons.

'There you are.' Mrs Mawson shook her hand. 'As discussed, you'll be taking over the role of editor. Effective as from today.'

'What the hell?' Liz said.

Victoria did not display even a trace of embarrassment.

'Anything to say to me at all?' Tom asked her.

'Well, I have enjoyed working for you, Tom. But really, people allowed to stay off sick for so long, Monty falling apart, hiring unsuitable freelancers. It's not fair on the other staff.'

Tom continued collecting his things together. It was all becoming slightly unreal . . . Liz standing at the corner of his desk looking stunned, him filling his bag.

'We want you to leave the building before we make the announcement,' Edward said, while Victoria surveyed his desk as if already planning where her things would go.

Tom had a final check around. He was going to miss those bloody plaster fruit. He closed his bag, picked up the paperweight of Hattie and put it in his pocket and walked out of the office. He got some quizzical looks as he passed, but who would imagine he was leaving and not coming back? Going down the stairs, he met Linda and Derek coming up, hand in hand. They weren't speaking but they had that intimacy about them that suggested they didn't need to.

He went to the ice-cream shop, stood in the queue and came out with two cornets, then sat on the steps of the market cross. Not many tourists today – too likely to rain.

He licked his vanilla ice cream and looked at the other one.

And out of the door of the magazine office stormed the woman who was going to eat it. He saw Liz hesitate and then come over.

'What the fuck just happened?' she said to him.

'We both got shafted,' he replied and handed her the ice cream. She stared at it as if unsure what to do.

'Sit down and eat it,' he said.

'Why?'

'Because I think you need to cool down. You've stormed out and you're planning to tell them to shove their job because you won't work for Victoria.'

Liz sat down but the ice cream remained un-licked.

'You become a mind-reader?' she asked.

'Yes. I'm thinking of doing it professionally now my most recent choice of career has crashed and burned. Come on, eat and listen. You have to go back in there.'

He thought she might shove the ice cream in his face. 'You're kidding. Can you imagine?'

'You have kids and a mortgage and you love what you do, Liz. And I feel responsible for this happening.'

She tentatively licked at the ice cream. 'It's coffee. You

got me coffee.' She took another lick and only stopped to say, 'Responsible. How?'

'This isn't about my competence or conduct. It's about Fran and you got caught in the crossfire.'

'I'm not going back, Tom. I'll end up running everything, but Victoria will get the glory. And the higher wage.'

'No change from normal, then.'

'Come off it, Tom. On a good day, you knew what you were doing.'

'Yeah, so much so that I'm sitting on these steps with the contents of my desk in my bag. And my pocket.' He patted Hattie to make sure she was still there. 'If you don't go back, I'm going to stage an intervention and march you in.'

'You're banned, you can't. God, it's like being a serf, working for the Mawsons. It makes me so mad. I hope you're seeing a lawyer? And that Victoria! What a two-faced cow. Did I ever take to her? No.' Liz seemed to have forgotten her ice cream.

He nudged her arm and the cornet wobbled. 'If you're going to go, at least keep working there while you look for something else. But I'd sit it out, I can't see Victoria lasting. Now, get that ice cream down you.'

He had to buy her another one before she saw sense.

CHAPTER 55

Tom didn't know what the newly sacked did. His first instinct was to go to Fran, but he needed to think about how to break the news to her first. She'd be distraught knowing that he'd been punished because of her.

It was a novel experience to worry about someone being too caring after spending years working around someone who didn't care enough.

He decided to deal with one crisis at a time. First he'd get Steph off his back and out of his house and then speak to Fran. And all the other people he'd need to tell. Including the bank – how long would he be able to keep going without a wage? That was another question for after Steph.

As he drove away from Tynebrook, he felt a slew of emotions. Anger at his treatment, sadness that he wouldn't be working with people like Felix and Liz again, regret that someone else would be stamping their personality on a magazine he'd grown to love.

In the end he went into Newcastle and sat in a coffee shop

with his computer and registered with some recruitment sites. It took him two hours and a couple of cappuccinos. That would have to stop – they were too expensive. Depressed by that thought, he went for a pint, which seemed much better value. And then, when he really didn't expect it, a moment of sheer happiness hit him as he realised that he and Fran didn't have to skulk around any more. They could go for a drink just as he was doing now. He could tell people what she meant to him. Here he was, newly sacked, with a daughter who was going to be miserable again very soon, a brother who needed serious support to get through fatherhood and an estranged wife dedicated to causing him grief, but he loved Fran Mayhew and she loved him back.

He took out his phone to ring her, but figured a text would be safer. Fran was too perceptive and would hear something was up in his voice. He sent the text and finished his pint and had a walk around the city. In another spike of happiness he went into one of the department stores and bought some books for Fran and a pair of dungarees with a tool loop for Hattie. Better make the most of it while he still had some money.

When he got home, Steph's car wasn't there.

No, you cannot leave without saying goodbye to Hattie.

He rushed upstairs and found her suitcase still open on the floor.

Enjoying how the house felt without Steph in it, he made a cup of tea and lay down on the sofa and then woke with a start when the back door opened. As he scrambled up, he nearly kicked over his cup of tea, now quite cold.

'You're home early,' his mother said, bustling in, the bag with Hattie's karate kit under her arm.

'Yeah, thought I'd make the most of the weather.'

His mother looked out at the grey clouds, but didn't comment.

Hattie came in behind her. 'Mummy's car isn't there—'

'She's still here. She's just gone out somewhere.'

Hattie nodded, but after he'd given her a hug, she went upstairs and he heard her go into Steph's bedroom.

'Poor little thing,' his mother said. 'She still off tomorrow, then?'

When he nodded, she said she wouldn't stay around to say goodbye and was out of the house with the speed of someone much younger.

When the back door opened again, it was Steph. She'd obviously been to the supermarket.

She looked at him coldly. 'You're home early.'

'I thought as it was your last evening.'

'Oh, I'm sure. Might have been nice if you'd arranged something special, I've had to go out and buy food.'

He ground several layers of enamel off his teeth, not

responding to that. His role tonight was to maintain the peace and try to keep Hattie from getting too upset. He felt the chances of that were nil.

'Have you told her yet?' Steph snapped, unpacking some cartons of Chinese food from the bags. 'About me not moving up here?'

'No. I couldn't tell her on the way to school—'

'*Wouldn't*, you mean. Such a coward, Tom. Always have been. Howard the Coward.'

He walked out of the kitchen and nearly collided with Hattie running in. 'Mummy,' she shouted. She had on a T-shirt and skirt and Tom wanted to march her upstairs and give her the dungarees.

He listened from the other room. 'There she is, Mummy's little helper. Shall we get all this yummy food cooked? Have a little party? Oh that's a lovely hug. OK, enough now. Don't spoil things by being all droopy. That's it. Take the lids off those.'

Hattie in clingy mode and Steph as vindictive wife – it was a toxic combination.

He went back into the kitchen and helped Hattie with the lids.

'Oh, someone rang this morning,' Steph said with a little slide of her gaze. 'I told her you were at Fran's. Hope I didn't get you into trouble.'

'Not at all.' He purposely kept concentrating on the cartons of food.

When he heard a noise, he did look round and she was opening the back door. There was a bottle of wine on the side with the top off. He was going to pour himself a glass when he thought about needing to stay on top of however the evening unfolded.

'Do you want a drink?' he asked Hattie and got her some lemonade in her plastic cup and knew as he handed it to her, she'd head for the garden too.

'I'll cook the Chinese meal then, shall I?' he said to the cooker and started to work out the timings. He set the table while keeping an eye on Steph and Hattie in the garden.

In a lull, he remembered the text to Fran and wondered if she'd replied. Quick check. No. He felt a bit disappointed at that. He could have done with some kind of contact, but then the timer went and he was back to dealing with spare ribs and beef in black bean sauce. Outside, Hattie was showing Steph how fast she could climb up to the tree house and back and Steph watched her for a while before she turned towards the window. She drank her wine and smiled. She must have known he was watching and that smile made him uneasy. There was something triumphant about it.

'OK,' he shouted, 'it's ready.'

Hattie came in holding Steph's hand and Steph said, 'Just let me go a minute, will you?' and topped up her wine glass.

'I want to sit next to Mummy.'

'No problem,' Tom said, 'sit where you like, love. Right, mind this dish, it's hot.'

'Thank you for this, Mummy,' Hattie said when everything was laid out on the table. It was followed by the sweetest smile to which Steph replied, 'My pleasure, darling. Enjoy it.'

'Where will you live when you come back?' Hattie asked, as she spooned sauce over the beef on her plate.

Steph did a pincer movement on a prawn with her chopsticks. 'Oh, Daddy wants to talk to you about that, don't you, Daddy?' There was a dramatic bite through the prawn.

When Hattie looked to him, he said, 'Later on. Gosh, I'm hungry! I could eat all this food and then the plates. So . . . come on, Hats, tell us who you overpowered at karate today.'

Hattie was distracted enough to enable him to give Steph a warning look which she responded to with an exaggerated tilt of her head. Her 'like I give a damn' look.

Tom could feel the tension around the table and Hattie must have too because she became extra clingy, thanking

Steph again for the meal, asking her if she could have more of this, the last of that. He could see Steph becoming increasingly irritated. When Hattie dripped some black bean sauce down her T-shirt, Steph lashed out with, 'Look what you've done. That was very expensive.'

Hattie tried to rub at it with her finger and he got in before Steph could say anything else. 'It's OK, just nip upstairs and take it off. Bring it back down and I'll soak it. No harm done.'

He waited until she was out of earshot and turned on Steph. 'Just stop it. She's trying her best to please you and she's sad because you're going. Can't you just put her first for *one* fucking evening?'

'Don't tell me what to do. Don't lecture—'

'If you go on like this, I'll take her to Mum's and we won't come back till you've gone.'

'No you won't, it would upset Hattie too much.' Steph looked so sure she'd got him where she wanted him.

'Use your brain, Steph. She's going to be upset anyway very soon and at least at Mum's she'd be free of you and your drip, drip of torture. So, ball's in your court. Hey, hey, here she comes. Good girl, hand me that T-shirt.'

For the rest of the meal, Steph behaved – even trying half-heartedly to teach Hattie how to use chopsticks.

'Everyone finished?' Tom asked and set about clearing

the table, wondering when he should ruin Hattie's good mood. Was it best to do it tonight? Before Steph went? Or tomorrow, early? He wouldn't be going anywhere after all. He could take his time and if she was upset she didn't need to go to school. He could have a whole day of delivering bad news to people.

'Would you like a drink, darling?' Steph asked, picking up Hattie's empty cup.

'Yes please, Mummy.'

Steph opened the fridge and reached for the orange-juice carton.

'She's not over-keen on—'

'You can't let me do one thing, can you?' Steph snapped and seeing Hattie's worried face at her mother's tone, Tom just said, 'Sorry. Good point. You go ahead.'

He pulled down the front of the dishwasher and started to load it. Then he heard a text come through on his phone. It was Fran.

Call me.

He closed the dishwasher again. 'I'll finish that in a minute.'

In the garden, he rang her while looking back into the kitchen. Hattie was putting the serving dishes on the draining board. Steph was drinking some more wine. Great. That was going to help.

'Hello, gorgeous,' he said when he heard Fran's voice. 'Get my text?'

'Yes.'

One word and he knew immediately that something was wrong. 'Have you got a minute?' she asked in the way people do when it's an order and not a question.

He instinctively turned his back on the house to get some privacy. 'Fran . . . are you all right?'

'Well, it depends what you mean by all right,' she said. 'If all right means, "Are you happy?", then no. If it means, "Do you feel as if someone has treated you like an idiot?" then the answer is yes.'

Tom was trying to get a foothold on the conversation and so her harsh, 'Aren't you going to ask what's wrong, Tom?' came back before he could speak. 'Or perhaps,' she said, 'you've already guessed what I'm talking about?'

'No, no, I haven't,' he stuttered out.

'Well, I've had another uninvited visitor, Tom. A woman who told me that the man I love and trust had sex with her the night before. And that she is moving back up here to be with him. Can you guess who that was?'

Steph's smile made sense now. She'd drawn blood. He spun round and looked back into the kitchen. Steph was standing at the sink actually doing some washing up and talking to Hattie who was going for the tea towel. He turned away again.

'Listen, Fran,' he said, his heart racing, 'you cannot believe anything that comes out of Steph's—'

'I don't believe it, Tom. Not a word of it.'

'You don't! Oh!' He took a deep breath. 'Thank God for that.' He turned and gave Steph the finger, even though she wasn't looking in his direction. 'Fran, she's just a piece of—'

'I don't want to discuss her. I want to ask you some questions.' Tom's heart didn't start racing again, but he sensed it might have cause to in a moment.

'When Steph said you had sex with each other, is this just something she plucked out of the air?'

'Uh, well . . . Look, Fran—'

'Tom, if you don't answer the question, I'll ring off.'

There was a noise behind him and a poke to his thigh.

'Mummy says, do you want the leftovers thrown away?'

'You tell bloody Mummy she can take them and—' He stopped, but only because he saw the shock on Hattie's face. 'Sorry, look. I don't mind what she does with them, Hats. This is an important phone call. Can you just leave me for a couple of minutes?'

She looked towards the kitchen and then back at him, anxiously. 'But she wants to know.'

'Hattie, please. I don't want to get cross. I will be back in soon. Now, don't disturb me again. I mean it.'

He watched her walk off, shoulders hunched. Oh damn. He felt he was being pulled in so many directions he was going to snap.

He put the phone back to his ear. 'Fran? Look, I went to bed last night and I was asleep . . . Fast asleep. Steph got in beside me. And she tried to kiss me and I got out of there pretty quick.'

There was silence, before Fran asked, 'And she was naked?'

'Uh-huh.'

An unmistakable sigh. 'Second question. Her plans to move up here. Again, is this something she just fabricated?'

'Well, she came up with that news, out of the blue, last night. And she told Hattie. But it was never going to happen, Fran, and I reminded her why . . . And so, by this morning, she'd changed her mind.'

'So let me get this straight, Tom. When you came to see me and I asked you if there were any developments, all these things had happened the night before. And you didn't think to mention them?'

'I didn't want to worry you.'

'Even though I've told you how much I hate secrets. Even though I have tried and tried to get you to see that you *have* to trust some people and open up? I had to stand there completely clueless while she hit me with one piece of news after the other. But if you'd confided in me, I could have said, smugly, "Tom's told me everything – he says you tried to seduce him and also, that thing about moving up here? You've already changed your mind." Why did you put me in that position, Tom?'

'Fran, I'm really sorry.' Should he say that again because she wasn't speaking? His heart *was* racing now. 'Fran, look—'

'No. I've always said I'm not a person who flounces and sulks and stomps off.' She sounded as if she was fighting to keep her voice under control. 'Well, I've changed my mind. You've made it clear that you won't trust me as I've trusted you. So I suppose we'd better call it a day. Goodbye, Tom.'

She had gone, but he kept jabbing at the buttons trying to get her back.

He looked towards the kitchen and saw the quick turn of Steph's head back to the washing up. Even if she couldn't hear what he was saying, his body language must have told her that he was reaping the results of her mischief.

He tried to ring Fran back, but it went through to voice-mail. He had to get round to the bungalow and hope she was ringing from there. He walked quickly towards the house, stress twisting his stomach, and the phone rang again. Thank God.

It was Rob's number. 'It's happening,' he said, 'she's gone into labour. She's at the hospital.'

It was the only news that would have halted his progress to the house, and in that instant he wasn't thinking of Fran or himself, he was thinking of Kath. Natalie was right, she was early.

'That's great,' he said, 'really, really great news.'

He looked towards the kitchen – he could shout to Hattie and tell her, but Rob was speaking again. 'Sorry,' Tom said, putting the phone to his other ear, 'didn't catch that. Is everything, you know, going all right?'

'That's what I was saying, everything's fine. She's not far on, but it's definitely underway.' Rob sounded breathless. Well that wasn't a surprise. 'They're monitoring her . . . all that.'

'You're doing great,' Tom said. 'You're so nearly there, Rob. Proud of you. In a few hours you'll— Rob, where are you? That music is really loud.'

Tom was sure women didn't give birth to techno-rock.

'It's coming from one of the shops.'

'What, in the hospital?'

'No.'

That stress was suddenly twisting in him again. 'So . . . you just nipped out for some fresh air?'

All Tom could hear for a few seconds was the music and

Rob's rapid breathing and then he said, 'I went to have a pee and, standing there in the Gents, I knew I couldn't hack this, Tom. I'm going to the railway station. I'm getting on a train and I'm sorry, but Kath's better off without me in the way.'

Tom had turned his back to the house again. 'Rob, stop walking right now. You get back there, you can't leave Kath on her own . . . Ask for a slug of gas and air or whatever it takes and hold her hand and get through it with her. Rob! *Rob!*'

Everyone was hanging up on him today. He tried to ring back. Voicemail. What if Rob didn't get on a train, but chucked himself under one? He knew he was pacing back and forth across the lawn. He turned and looked towards the kitchen. Hattie was sitting at the table, her cup in one hand. She was talking to Steph.

He rang his mother. Got the rev.

'It's Tom. Joan's son.'

'Uh-huh. Is it your mother you want? Well, I'm sorry, she's not free at the moment.'

'I'll try her mobile—'

'Is it urgent, then?' That was a definite change of tone. 'Hang on.'

Oh God, what had he interrupted?

When his mother said, 'Hello,' he was straight in with,

'Listen, Mum. Has Rob rung you? Kath's gone into labour, yes, it's brilliant, but we've got a problem.' He told her the story.

'I'll find Rob,' he said. 'Will you go and keep Kath company? I have no idea if she knows Rob's missing yet. Keep in touch, yes?'

He walked quickly up the garden and saw Hattie was no longer in the kitchen. He so needed to talk to Fran.

Steph was mopping up something from the floor, Hattie's plastic cup in one hand. She looked at him and quickly glanced back down at the spillage. He wasn't going to give her the bloody satisfaction of saying anything about what she'd wrecked with Fran. She'd be expecting a big fight, well let her bloody stew.

'I've got to go,' he said. 'Kath's in labour.'

He expected a sarcastic comment, but she just said, 'Right. OK.'

'I'm taking Hattie with me.'

A quick nod.

He saw her hand go to her face, the unmistakable brushing away of tears. That figured, bringing out the tears because she'd thought he was going to shout at her about Fran. He left her and went through to the sitting room.

He called up the stairs. 'Hats, Auntie Kath is at the hospital – the baby's coming and we need to go and get Rob from the station and take him there. The railway station in town. Quickly.'

He'd shouted that last word even louder, but no response.

'Hattie, love, come on, quick as you can.' He tried not to be tetchy with her again.

What was she doing up there? He expected her to be wherever Steph was.

He stood, halfway up the stairs, and listened. No noise at all.

'Hattie?' He ran up to the landing and opened doors, checked the bathroom. He felt his stomach twist tighter.

'OK, Hattie, come on, stop messing about,' he said, and went back down the stairs.

Steph was in the sitting room, moving the magazines around on the table. She was still making little crying noises.

'Where did Hattie go?' he asked her.

She shrugged.

'Well, where was she going when she left the kitchen? Did she say?'

'Upstairs, I think.'

'I've looked up there.'

He left Steph staring down at the pile of magazines.

He went through to the back garden. Perhaps she'd come out when his back was turned?

'Hattie! Hattie!' he called.

The twisting in his stomach was constant now, and his throat felt tight.

He climbed up the ladder of the tree house and looked in at the door. Empty, just some small plastic figures in one corner. They looked abandoned and that thought hiked up his anxiety.

He walked quickly around the garden calling her name and went back in the house. He darted through the kitchen, past whatever had been spilled and the empty cup on the draining board. Back in the sitting room, Steph looked up as if she hadn't heard him until the second he'd walked in and he got an unprepared face, an involuntary reaction. She looked scared. No, more than that. Guilty.

The spillage on the floor clicked into place. Hattie's empty cup in Steph's hand.

'What did you do?' he said.

She didn't answer.

'What did you do?' he asked again, louder, closer to where she was sitting.

'She wouldn't drink her orange juice. She's been difficult all evening.'

'What did you fucking do?' he roared. He forced himself to stay on this side of the table or he didn't know what he would do to get that information.

She wasn't speaking, just sniffing.

'You hit her, didn't you?'

'She wouldn't drink her orange juice,' Steph shouted back. She was starting to cry again, her breathing irregular. It was proper crying. The stuff in the kitchen had been proper too; he just hadn't picked up on it. 'She wouldn't drink it. I asked her to and she wouldn't drink it.'

He had to get out of there or he would hit a woman who had just hit a child. He went along the hall to the front door. It wasn't closed properly.

He wrenched it open, starting to panic. Steph had hit Hattie and she'd run off. He'd been on the phone and he'd told her not to disturb him. Hadn't he always said she came first? Before Fran or Rob or Kath? But when she really needed him . . .

It would be all right. She'd just run out of the garden. He'd find her on the lane, maybe she'd even be coming back by now.

By now? How long ago had she gone? When had he last seen her? Before he'd rung his mother? No, she was there when he'd been talking to Rob. He returned to the house. Steph was still in the sitting room, on the sofa, the knuckle of her thumb held to her lips.

'Did you hear her go out of the front door?'

She nodded her head and moved her thumb. 'She wouldn't drink her juice,' she said again.

'How long ago?' he bellowed at her.

'Five minutes. Ten. I don't know.'

In the kitchen he picked up his mobile and was out the back door, through the side gate.

He was shouting, 'Hattie! Hattie!' He couldn't see her on the lane.

He rushed up next door's drive, fumbling the bell. No answer. He went round the back, shouting. The garden was empty.

He looked at his watch and felt the twin pulls of Rob and Hattie. On to the next house. They were in and he gave them an edited explanation. They would keep an eye out. He wrote down his mobile number. All along the houses he went. A couple of dads said they would walk up the hill and have a look around. They told him not to worry; they'd ring him when they found her.

Kids, eh?

Rob.

He kept walking while he rang his mother. He was nearly at the end of the lane and it felt like the completion of the first phase of something. It would only have been a little thing for her to go out on to the lane, but beyond it? On the side road leading down to the busier one?

'I'm not there yet,' his mother said in the distracted tone she always had when the phone rang as she was driving.

'I can't go to Rob,' he told her. 'Hattie's missing. She's run out of the garden.'

'It's all right,' his mother said straight away, 'it's all right. Children wander in summer all the time. I'll ring George and get him to go and find Rob. She'll not be far, Tom.'

He tried to look in the verges, see if she was lying down, hiding, but the bloody cow parsley was too high.

When should you ring the police? How long had it been now? He was at the end of the lane. There were no more houses, just the road with a plantation of trees on one side, fields on the other. He stood on the stile and looked over the field. Only sheep.

He went to the fence bordering the plantation and called her name and only the birds called back.

If she was upset she would be hiding. *If.* Of course she was upset.

But she'd still come to him if she heard him calling, wouldn't she?

If she was able to.

He shoved away that thought and quickly stored it with the last tetchy thing he'd said to her. His breathing sounded deafening and he knew he was in the grip of panic; he felt light-headed, but his lungs were full of lead.

He shouted into the evening, 'Hattie! Hattie!' Now he was down on the main road, crossing over and back, over and back, parting the cow parsley on both verges, trying to look over the fence into the fields that led down to the river.

No, don't think about the river, it was slow-moving and shallow this time of year.

Unless they've let a load of water out from the reservoir.

A car came past him, slowed and halted. 'You all right?' the guy in it said when he wound down the window. A guy in a suit – he used to be that normal just a few minutes ago.

Tom explained, trying to make full sentences, but his fear was affecting his speech.

'How old is she?' the guy asked and when Tom told him, an expression skimmed over his face. Was it worry, or thankfulness that this was happening to Tom and not him?

'I'll keep an eye open,' he said, 'as I drive. You rung the police?'

Tom did then. It had been half an hour. What was it they always said in the papers? The first hour was crucial. Another thought to shove away.

He walked as he phoned, still hitting at the hedgerows, trying to make them give her up. 'OK, sir, take it slowly,' the person on the switchboard said. Tom answered questions and stumbled on the one about what she was wearing, not because he couldn't recall, but because he was spooked remembering news reports where bodies were identified by their clothing. What if she'd got to the road and someone had dragged her into a car? Or knocked her over and driven off?

'Where are you now, sir?'

They would send a car straight away. The fact they took it so seriously made him realise how bad this was.

Please God, I don't believe in you, but please let her walk along this road now. Let me find her.

He thought of Kath labouring away in Newcastle – please, not one in, one out.

He remembered every time she'd asked him for a pet and he'd been mean and only offered her the one choice. If he got her back he would fill the house with whatever she wanted – rats, scorpions, anything.

He stopped walking. He needed to use his brain. She could have just run anywhere, blindly, too upset to care. But what if she ran *to* somewhere. To *someone*.

Fran. He rang her number and prayed for her to be there. Voicemail. 'Hattie's run away. She might have come to you.' He didn't know what else to say and finished the call. He rang back. 'She's run away because Steph's hit her. She can't cope with things not going her way. No . . . she

can't cope with being a mother for any length of time . . .
she loses interest or loses it completely.'

He had to stop and get his breathing under control
because he wanted to tell her everything. He gabbled it all
out. 'She's always been volatile, but it got worse when
Hattie came along. And then we were both working long
days, travelling. I tried to cope with it, but I couldn't be
there all the time, the nanny couldn't be there all the time
. . . And although I could never be sure, I think she might
have done it before. Lashed out. I didn't know definitely,
but things got worse and in the end I left with Hattie.'

He had to stop to get things in the right order. 'Steph
will never accept that's what she's like and I . . . I've kept
it to myself because I didn't want Hattie ever to know. Tell
one person, they tell another and then she'd find out and
think it was her fault. That's what happens – kids keep on
loving the person who hurts them. And I was ashamed too
. . . that I'd agreed to start a family, even though I knew
Steph was . . .'

He didn't know if the voicemail was still running. Had
it finished? He rang off and rang back again. 'Oh, Fran, I
thought I could keep all the plates spinning – let Hattie
still have a relationship with Steph as long as I was always
there to keep an eye on her. But Steph's got more and more
twisty. She contested the divorce because she won't accept

she's ever been at fault. And . . . and she still wants that control over me. If I wanted to move it along, I'd have had to go to court and spill out everything.'

He paused and then sprinted to the end. 'But you're right, I should have told my family, friends, let them help me through this. It's come back to bite me because I've kept quiet and given Steph the upper hand. And now I've failed at keeping Hattie safe. I was wrong, Fran, and I love you and I'm so bloody scared.'

He couldn't remember ending the call that time, only that he was looking at his watch and thinking where else Hattie could be. Natalie? No, she had no idea where Natalie lived now.

Josh, but they were miles away. He still rang. Josh's mum didn't waste any time. 'I'll get the car out and we'll look. It'll be all right, Tom. I'll ring you.'

It would not have taken much to make him sob. More cars passed, some slowing. 'A little girl,' he said if they asked who he was looking for. 'Blue top, pink skirt, red sandals. Five years old.' He didn't look to see what their faces did when he told them.

He just kept walking and looking and telling himself this was his fault, for being on the phone, for not telling Steph to go, for not telling everyone what she was like, for not telling Hattie.

He saw the police car coming. Two young constables got out, one a woman with her blonde hair back in a neat bun; the man carrying too much weight. 'All right, sir, let's go over some things,' the woman said. 'You've searched your house thoroughly? The garden? Anywhere you can think she might have gone? Has she done it before? Was she upset?'

Tom said she'd had a disagreement with her mother – he didn't mention anything about hitting, not because he gave a damn about defending Steph, he just didn't want them sidetracked.

Shouldn't they stop talking and start looking?

His mobile rang and he grabbed at it. 'Any luck?' his mother said and he told her there hadn't been and rang off.

'Shouldn't we be looking?' he said and the woman constable asked a few more questions and then her colleague got back in the car. 'Spreading the word,' she said. 'Come on, we'll go this way. When Darren's finished, he'll go the other. Lucky it's summer, plenty of daylight left.'

They walked. How long? Calling. Looking.

She was out there somewhere on her own and everything that had looked so familiar now seemed sinister. The woods and fields, outhouses. Lanes that were overgrown.

He was living his worst nightmare.

How long now? Nearly an hour.

He wanted to grab back that time. It was getting too long since she'd disappeared. Missing for hours was so different from barely been gone fifteen minutes.

His mobile rang again. Please God, please God.

It was Fran and the whole evening stopped – the birds, the cars, the policewoman next to him.

'She's here, Tom,' Fran said. 'I'd just set off for Newcastle when I got your message, so I came straight back and there she was, sitting under the garden table. She's fine, Tom, very, very distressed, but fine. Take a breath, Tom. She's safe.'

CHAPTER 56

The world turns, Tom thought as he lay on the floor in Hattie's room. It turns and you can go from happiness to despair and back to happiness again in the space of twenty-four hours. You can have a job and lose it. Lose a daughter and find her. Have a lover, lose her and get her back again. Welcome a nephew (Hello, Patrick Tom George Howard) and wave off a wife (Goodbye, Stephanie Bartlett).

You can also gain a vicar. Retired.

If Tom turned his head and put his ear to the floor, he might be able to hear George downstairs talking to Joan and Rob. Whisky made people very talkative even at – Tom slowly lifted his arm and looked at his watch – 3 a.m. Well, George could talk till the cows came home, whenever that might be, because he had played a blinder.

Like some ecclesiastical Superman, he'd hared to Newcastle Station where he had stopped Rob before he could board the train to Penzance. There were many other trains Rob could have caught before that particular one, but he had decided he needed to go somewhere a very long way away.

Tom had asked George how he had managed to get through the ticket barriers without a ticket and he had just winked and said being a vicar gave you special privileges. Tom didn't know if he believed that, but he did know that somewhere between Newcastle Station and the maternity unit, George had put steel in Rob's backbone.

'You were right, Tom. He's done a lot of counselling over the years,' Joan said. 'Bereavement, post-traumatic stress, divorce. I should have taken your suggestion and got him to talk to Rob weeks ago.'

The result was that Rob made it into the operating theatre in time to see his son born by Caesarean section. He did faint later and spent some time in A&E, but by then he'd held his son and counted all his fingers and toes and everything in between and pronounced him perfect. And Kath, wise Kath, had not mentioned the two hours it had taken him to go to the toilet, but had included 'George' among her son's names.

Tom liked the idea of George as Superman and hoped that image would supplant the one that had lodged in his brain since Joan's fuck bunny revelation – that of him pleasuring Joan doggy-collar style.

Suddenly George seemed part of the family – Joan was

calling him 'dear' and doing hand-holding in public. Or had Tom imagined that? He'd had a couple of drams himself to wet the baby's head.

And was the Steph problem finally solved? He dared to hope it was.

He and Hattie had been brought back to the house in a police car, along with Fran, and although Hattie had not told the police her mother had hit her, they had come in to satisfy themselves that they weren't delivering her back to a place that she'd want to run away from again. They hadn't stayed long, but Steph had gone to pieces afterwards. That was partly due to the fact she'd been genuinely scared that Hattie had gone missing, and partly because of Hattie's reaction when she'd tried to say sorry.

Tom had expected his daughter to take all the blame on herself for the incident, or make excuses for her mother, but while she had mumbled, 'It's all right,' she had kept on clinging to Tom and would not let Steph touch her.

Fran had already told him that Hattie's first words to her had been a wailed, 'But I only said I didn't like orange juice,' and he guessed that alongside being upset, she was also outraged.

When Fran finally managed to persuade Hattie to go upstairs and sit in a hot bath, Tom had watched Steph cry herself out. As she cried, he suddenly thought of all her phone checking and how she had not answered his question about whether Alessandro would move with her.

'He's dumped you, hasn't he?' Tom said and Steph nodded and many things about her visit became clear.

'I didn't mean to hit her, Tom. Honestly I didn't,' she said, over and over again.

He believed her and told her that, but it was the only comfort he was prepared to give her. And then he rang Geoffrey and Caroline to come and collect her – he gave them directions to the Tap & Badger. She could stay there until they arrived, he wanted her out of his house.

On the journey to the hotel, he spelled out to her that now Hattie knew the worst, there was nothing preventing him from going to court to get a divorce. She said, straight out, that it wouldn't be necessary.

'And I'm not taking any crap with Hattie any more either,' he said. 'The first time you break a promise . . .' He didn't go on. Steph had a keen understanding of manipulation and knew that Tom no longer had any reason to keep her sweet.

'I did try, you know, Tom,' she said, before he left her in the pub lounge. 'I tried hard to be a perfect mother.'

'I don't know any perfect mothers, who wants that?' he told her. 'If you just keep your promises, that would be a start.' He had no idea whether that went in or whether, when her parents arrived, she would bemoan how unfair he had been. It was only while driving back home, that he realised he hadn't had it out with her about her visit to Fran.

Tom sat up slowly, shuffled over to the bed and watched Hattie. Exhaustion had carried her off eventually, rather than a wish to sleep. Tomorrow she might wake up and want Steph back. Who knew? But at least tomorrow she had a baby cousin, a pair of dungarees and a day off school to sweeten the pill a little. He bent and kissed her on the cheek, taking in the smell of the bubble bath and toothpaste and Hattie.

He couldn't bear to run her route back in his head and think how easily she could have dashed out into the path of a car.

He lay back down and heard the bathroom door open, the light go off and footsteps coming towards the room.

'Budge over,' Fran said and lay down beside him under the duvet. She reached for his hand and squeezed it and said, 'Sweet dreams.' She must have understood that the emotions of the day had flattened him and he felt unable to cope with anything other than tenderness and sleep.

But it wouldn't come.

'You're only twenty-four,' he said, 'you shouldn't have to deal with all this. You should be out partying.'

There was a snort. 'Who are you to tell me what I want, Tom Howard? What I want is right here in this room – these one and a half people. A different family than I came to find, but my goodness, you've grown on me.' Another squeeze of her hand. 'When Hattie looked at me from under that table and said it was her "bolty hole", I tell you, Tom, I had to go and have a discreet howl in the kitchen.'

Now it was him doing the squeezing. 'Only twenty-four,' he mumbled, 'and you put the stake through the vampire's heart.'

'It was a scalpel actually, Tom, and I do wish I hadn't done it. I ruined a perfectly good piece out of petulance. Did it the moment Steph left my doorstep.'

'What a bloody day, all round. But those people tonight – neighbours, drivers, the police, all of them just wanting to help . . .'

'Uh-huh. But you have to ask for it first, the help. Confide in people.'

'Point taken,' he said. 'Tomorrow I'll tell you the whole Steph story. And something else, about my job.'

'You got the sack?'

That did make him open his eyes.

'Liz phoned me,' she said. 'And Natalie had warned me that my lovely relations would do that to you, eventually.' She laughed, a most un-Fran-like laugh. 'But don't worry, Tom. Close your eyes. Clever, tough Natalie has a plan.'

CHAPTER 57

'I could have beaten him,' Hattie said.

Tom eyed up the large teenager punching his fist into the palm of his other hand, and his opponent who was lying on his back and trying, unsuccessfully, to get up.

'He's got a weak leg,' Hattie said with a dip of her chin. 'I'd have gone for that.'

Hattie had taken the news that there was a lower age limit for the Cumberland & Westmorland wrestling well. Eventually. She had told Tom that she would spend the years before she was allowed to enter studying the opposition. He did not point out that by the time she was twelve, the opposition would not be the opposition. Still, if it made her happy, he was OK discussing blind sides and weak legs.

She was also, Tom suspected, not as bothered as she might have been, because her schedule for show day was already hectic. There was the karate display in the main ring in the afternoon and they'd been up early getting Alfie the rabbit ready for judging in the fur and feather category.

Plus she had a major entry in the Home Crafts marquee. They were going there next to see how she'd done.

They already knew how Alfie had done. He had not covered himself in glory, but he had covered his back legs in something else and Tom had returned him home already. He was thankful there had not been any competitions that Hattie's rat or terrapins could be entered for.

'Seen enough?' he asked and she nodded and they were off. He remembered last year's heat and preferred today's weaker sunshine and lively breeze.

It wasn't only the weather that was more to his liking. Every other single thing was too. He was no longer like a sad hamster going round and round on his wheel. Everything felt familiar but fresh.

He remembered too how last year he had to keep up with Hattie dashing ahead and taking an impromptu part in the wrestling. She still skipped along with enthusiasm, but there was no straying. He didn't think that was due to the many lectures he'd delivered about the dangers of running away, more to do with how he had grabbed her on arrival at Fran's and sobbed that he'd been so, so scared.

She had diverted to a jewellery stall and was poking around among the earrings.

'Could I buy Mummy these?' she asked and he said, 'Of course, got any money?' She did, but not enough and so he handed her some of his and she went to pay. She came back with them in a little paper bag.

'Shall I keep them safe?' he asked.

'I'll hold them for a bit.'

He wondered if they'd survive, but let her carry on. Hattie's emotional state regarding her mother was hard to read. Nearly a year after the incident, he had no idea if it was an injury healed in Hattie's mind or the pain was just being worked around. In the days that followed that evening there had been a fair amount of 'It won't happen again, I'll be a good girl' alternating with: 'I don't like Mummy any more. No, I won't come to the phone and talk to her.'

Tom had been completely honest with her afterwards, but trying to explain a complex and volatile personality to a little girl was hard. Fran said to boil it down to two messages: 'Steph is like this with everyone, it is not because *you* have done anything wrong' and 'Love is kind. If someone says they love you but in among the hugs and kisses they make you feel bad, or hurt you, that's not right.'

Fran said that was an especially important message for a girl to learn.

Things had eventually stabilised; these days she rarely clutched Gummy to her as if it was a talisman.

Steph had kept her word about the divorce and recently

there had been some meet-ups – neutral territory, a day maximum, no pressure. It was not ideal – Steph still liked to feel hard done by, but it was a million times better than what had gone before. On the last occasion, Caroline and Geoffrey had come along too and so Tom had brought Fran as wing man. Fran told them about being taught arithmetic by a martial arts expert, which had distracted them beautifully.

'This will all get so much easier as she gets older,' Fran said and then paused. 'When Hattie gets older, I mean. Not Steph. That's actually going to make things worse – she's not going to like ageing. She'll be even more needy. Hey-ho.'

Hattie stopped walking.

'Something up?'

'I've got no money left for Fran's present.'

'What's it to be?' He looked around at the nearby stalls. 'A lawn-edger, something to get hair out of the shower plug or a picture of Elvis on a velvet background?'

He realised he'd learned nothing about parenting when she looked excited by that last description.

They bought the picture and Hattie insisted on carrying that too, but when she spotted Josh and his parents, he had the picture and the earrings shoved at him and knew he was going to spend the day carrying it around as people questioned his taste.

'Nice picture of Saddam Hussein,' Josh's mother said.

When Hattie and Josh could be peeled apart, the meandering route to the craft tent continued and included a detour for doughnuts.

Tom was chewing his way through one, trying to win a game where you weren't allowed to lick the sugar from your lips, when he saw Mrs Mawson with her granddaughter. There was the briefest of eye contact before Mrs Mawson steered the granddaughter away.

He couldn't blame her for not wanting to see him. He would always be linked to Natalie and how she had unpicked her elder son in front of her eyes.

Natalie's 'plan' was a massive unveiling of dirty laundry. Tom had been off the magazine for three weeks when she rang and said they were off to Mawson Towers. He would have rather gone to Hades, but she was insistent.

During Tom's three-week 'rest', he had realised how hard it was to get a job and how much he missed the magazine and the staff. Although he didn't miss them as much as he could have done because a few of them were on the phone to him regularly. Liz told him everything was pants, Felix complained that he was working for an 'artistic philistine' and Derek said, 'It's not as enjoyable as when . . .' and then fell silent.

In addition, he'd bumped into Stan who said mysteriously,

'It's turning into a soap opera,' and had given Tom a manly slap on the back.

Tom took the grumbling with a pinch of salt until the day that Liz rang and said Kelvin had actually had a fists-out roll-around-on-the-floor fight in the main office with a freelance writer who had been a bit too flirty with Victoria.

When he told Fran, she said, 'Consumed with jealousy, of course. Tragic how some men are taken in by highlights and veneers.'

He had laughed in disbelief and got a pitying look. 'Oh, Tom, did you notice nothing in your time there? Kelvin adores her.'

'Adores? No, he was just being Kelvin.'

'Absolutely smitten. Thinks she's the love of his life. Of course, she's playing him along. Eyes on a bigger prize.'

'What, bigger than her hedge-fund-manager husband?'

Fran gave him an enigmatic look. 'My lips are sealed. Which is more than you can say for Victoria's.'

So off they went to Mawson Towers, he and Fran sitting in the back of the car, Natalie driving and a carrier bag full of paperwork on the front passenger seat.

'No Jamie?' Tom asked.

'He's not going back till they invite him, or they'll think he's angling to be "forgiven". Besides, the flat's full of tin soldiers and he needs to get them packaged up and sent off before we can get to the bed.'

Fran's grip on Tom's hand became tighter the closer they got to the house and when they parked, she seemed loath to leave the car.

'They know we're coming, do they?' Tom had asked and Natalie said, 'Yeah. Proper letter saying we'd rather discuss these matters with them than go through other channels.'

Tom feared that they would be greeted by a pack of baying hounds, but it was a housekeeper who answered the door and had a chat with Natalie as she showed them in.

This time it was a high-ceilinged, wood-panelled room Tom was in and it seemed to serve as an office. A partner desk dominated one end of the room, a wide, polished table the other. Natalie made them sit one side of it and plonked the carrier bag of papers on the spare seat next to her.

'Glad I don't have to polish this bugger any more,' she said.

They had a long wait.

'Amateurs' trick,' Natalie said, sitting back and folding her arms.

Fran looked completely ill at ease.

'It will be all right, sweetheart,' he told her. 'Nobody's

going to hurt you while I'm here.' It seemed a dumb thing to say and Natalie uncrossed her arms and took all the papers out of her carrier bag and passed it to Tom.

'For Fran. She might be sick.'

'I meant it, Natalie, don't take the piss.'

Natalie blinked at him. 'Yeah, I know you did, it was lovely. The bag's 'cos she looks like she might heave. Nerve-racking for her coming here – she's gonna get a lot of chat about how she's grubbing for money. Get a grip, will you, Tom?'

When the door opened, Mrs Mawson walked in followed by Edward and another man wearing a suit that was not made of tweed or corduroy. Tom guessed he was some kind of legal bod, which was confirmed when he introduced himself.

The atmosphere was glacial and there was no eye contact from the Mawsons, who sat either side of the lawyer. Tom almost felt sorry for him being the filling in that cold sandwich.

'Your letter, Miss . . .' The lawyer looked down at the piece of paper in front of him on the table. 'Woodward. Perhaps only just the legal side of threatening.'

Natalie looked delighted. 'Good. That's the tone I was aiming for.'

'Oh for God's sake,' Edward said, shifting in his chair, 'am

I really meant to sit and listen to these people? Someone who used to be our cleaner, someone who used to run our magazine and someone who says she's a relation.'

Edward brought his hand down on the table and gave the impression of a man who had been told to sit and be quiet, but was damned if he'd take orders from anyone: 'Didn't take you long to try a little blackmail, did it?' he said directly to Fran and Fran looked down at the carrier bag.

Tom was going to say something, but he felt Natalie's foot press on his very firmly.

The resolute way that Mrs Mawson was staring out of the window suggested that she too had been 'persuaded' into this meeting.

'So,' the lawyer said, putting his hands together and then splaying them apart again. 'What can we do for you?'

Tom had no idea if Natalie's performance was based on her observations in court or of TV legal dramas, but she was concise and forceful and the presentation of her 'evidence', as she called it, had something of a machine gun about it.

She went over the reasons for Tom's dismissal and said that this was hypocritical in the light of information that had come to her regarding Edward Mawson and Victoria Ellington, the woman who had been selected to replace

Tom. She pushed a piece of typed A4 paper towards the lawyer.

'Dates and times and durations of, well, let's call them meetings between Mr Mawson and Mrs Ellington on Thursday evenings over the last year at a flat north of Aln-wick. Rented in the name of E. Morton – very imaginative. Thursdays are the evenings, I believe, that Mr Mawson attends a meeting of the Landowners' Association in that town.'

Edward Mawson's jaw seemed as if it was falling away. Mrs Mawson was no longer looking out of the window.

Natalie had another piece of paper in her hand and Tom thought of Liz's paper hand grenades.

The lawyer was still reading the first typed sheet when Natalie said, 'I'd also like to point out that the attitude to Fran Mayhew is a little hypocritical too. I know no one can force people to accept what used to be called "illegitimate" children into the family – although some don't seem to care.' Natalie grimaced and Tom guessed she was thinking about her own home life. 'But it might be useful to set Miss Mayhew in context, should anyone at this table wish to reconsider their attitude in years to come.'

Natalie left the perfect amount of dead space before saying, 'I have details here of a child born in Newcastle General on June 16th 2012 to one Lesley Ryhope.' Mrs Mawson's chin shot up even further than usual which made Natalie say, 'Yes. She is *that* Miss Lesley Ryhope, the one who used to do the catering for your parties. So . . . the birth certificate says the father is Michael Ashford, who by the way now lives in Dumfries with another partner, but I have evidence that suggests the baby is actually Edward Mawson's and bank statements to prove that he makes regular payments to Miss Ryhope.' That piece of paper was pushed towards the lawyer too.

'Fuller details are here,' Natalie said, patting what had been in the carrier bag. 'Happy to leave them with you.'

Edward had the look of a man whose ribs have dissolved.

Mrs Mawson said, icily, 'And how much money do you want in return for all these grubby bits of information?'

'They're only grubby,' Natalie shot back, 'because they're about your son, so don't try and make me out to be the guilty party here. And, actually, it's not money we're after. It's a form of justice. We'd like Tom's job back, otherwise we'll have no choice but to include this information about Victoria's horizontal job interviews in his defence case at the tribunal. And we'd like Fran Mayhew to be given first refusal on the lease of the shop – currently an art gallery – in your building in Tynebrook, if it ever becomes available.' Tom turned to Fran and raised his eyebrows and she gave him a weak smile.

'I'm not going to say anything will happen if you don't agree to that latter request,' Natalie said, reasonably. 'We're not the kind of people who'd talk to the papers or leak anything on to the Internet when it involves a child. But it would be an act of goodwill, wouldn't it? And it would stop me looking at a payment Edward Mawson made for a car in November of 2013 that is now registered in the name of one Penny Michaels, who I believe is the wife of a livestock feed merchant not far from Morpeth.'

Edward's neck muscles wilted.

'I think it would be beneficial,' the lawyer said, very precisely, 'if we leave this here so that I can consult further with my clients. I'll be in touch – the address on this letter?'

Natalie nodded and as none of the Mawsons were moving, she and Tom stood up.

Fran rose unsteadily and had a voice to match. 'I wanted to say something about how sorry I am that this has happened and that perhaps one day we can come to terms with each other. But all I can think of is a terrible pun about how a man who likes to chase and kill small furry animals has been trapped by a load of beaver.'

The Mawsons seemed to sink further into themselves, while the lawyer tried to control his face.

After that, Tom remembered getting out of the front door and Natalie and him hanging on to one of the huge stone urns, bent over with laughter, while Fran said, 'Oh Lord. What possessed me?'

In the car on the way back, they were high on adrenaline. When Tom asked Natalie how she had found out all that stuff, she said it helped to have a dad in prison and left it at that.

Tom thought back to Edward Mawson telling Jamie that he was as bad as his grandfather where women were concerned. A hypocrite indeed. No doubt Mrs Mawson had picked up on the similarities between her elder son and Charlie too – while underrated Jamie seemed to be doing very nicely under his own steam and with one woman.

As Tom absent-mindedly licked the doughnut sugar from his lips, and Hattie shouted that she'd won the game, he had another go at wondering what the conversation had been like between the lawyer and the Mawsons when they'd known they were beaten. One week after they'd been Natalied, the Mawsons notified him that he was reinstated at the magazine and Victoria left to spend more time with her veneers. A couple of months after that, they sold the magazine to a guy who'd made a lot of money out of software and had a stable of other publications. So far he was proving to be a better employer than they had been.

The Mawsons sold the building to him too and Tom

feared that would be that as far as the art gallery was concerned. But when it became vacant, the new owner offered the lease to Fran first. He said that had been one of the stipulations when he'd purchased the place.

While Tom was hopeful that some refurbishment might now be carried out, he was not so hopeful that anybody's relationship with the Mawsons would ever be repaired.

'OK,' Tom said as they neared the marquee, 'let's see how you did, Hats,' but before they actually got in, Kath and Rob came out, pushing Patrick in his buggy.

'Ooh, I wouldn't go in there,' Kath said, doing some dramatic eye-rolling. Hattie was already in her usual position with Patrick, down on her knees by his buggy, pulling faces. He was kicking about and looking happy under his hat.

'Not another baking incident?' Tom asked with mock horror.

'Worse than last year,' Rob said. He looked tired – Patrick wasn't a good sleeper – but under his floppy sun hat, his brother also looked happy. It was a hat that was exactly the same colour as Patrick's and that made Tom indescribably pleased.

'See you in the food tent?' Kath said. 'His highness needs something soon or he'll start wailing. And so does Patrick.' She gave Rob a fond poke to the stomach.

Arrangements to meet were made and Tom watched them set off, then Rob was coming back. He took Tom to one side, 'Patrick's a bit red on his cheeks, a bit grizzly.' Rob was looking at Tom expectantly. 'I'm thinking teeth, but it could be anything—'

'Is he generally happy, apart from that?'

A nod.

'And he hasn't got any rash? No funny cry when he moves his head?'

'No.'

'Teeth then. Get me a beer in.'

Rob bounded off again with a 'Cheers, mate.'

Inside the tent, Tom headed for the vegetable animals and before he got there, saw that Hattie had won by the way she was doing karate moves and shouting, 'Take that!'

He read the judges' comment:

An imaginative and skilful interpretation of a fox and her cubs executed in sweet potato and butternut squash. The use of samphire as grass is a particularly charming touch.

Hattie was still karate-chopping, so he said, 'Hey. Tone it down a bit. Ever heard of being a "good winner"? You have to be modest.'

'What's modest?' she asked, making an L for Loser hand gesture at the less-successful animals.

And then he didn't care about her being modest because Fran was coming towards him. They grinned at each other. They'd talked about this earlier, how weird it would be to be back at the start. Now he thought about that, he felt choked up and so he checked Hattie was occupied and put down the picture and the earrings and placed his hands on Fran's waist and kissed her on the lips. He felt her arms come up round his neck and she was kissing him back.

French-kissing in the craft tent, near uncovered baked goods; they were probably contravening all kinds of Health and Safety rules.

He stopped kissing for long enough to say what had just come to him, 'I am so glad I bumped into you here that day. I love you, Fran. You caught me when I had such a bloody big fall, and I adore every bit of you from your brilliant hair to your long second toes and all the beautiful places in between. I can't believe my bloody luck.'

'You've practised that,' she said. 'It makes my speech seem completely lame. I can only think to say that I love you, Tom. You feel like part of me, somehow, grafted on but in a good way. I would fight lions to save you.' She paused. 'Can I also ask you why you're carrying a picture of Saddam Hussein?'

'Hattie brought it for you. And it's Elvis.'

'Ah. An energetic interpretation.'

He went back to kissing her.

When he opened his eyes, he could see Mrs Egremont, of the sharp elbows, having a set-to with the baked goods' judging panel.

'Trouble up?' he asked.

'Indeed. Someone has beaten her in every category. She's not taking it well. Oh, Hattie, darling, thank you for Elvis, he's so . . . individual. And may I congratulate you on your magnificent achievement.' She got down to Hattie's level and gave her a hug and they looked at the fox family and the rosette propped against them.

'I think you should wear that rosette,' Fran said and pinned it to Hattie's T-shirt.

Hattie examined it. 'Next year I might do something prehistoric.'

'Oh yes.' Fran was screwing up her eyes. 'I'm seeing some major battle between a tyrannosaurus and some velociraptors?'

Tom walked over to his mother.

'Don't ask,' she said, pushing air with her hand. Tom didn't and went to look at the entries and came back.

'So who's this Mary H. W. Fane then?'

His mother shrugged. 'No idea. Taxi driver delivered the

entries, along with all the proper forms. Whoever this Mary woman is, she obviously wanted to be androgynous.'

'Anonymous.'

His mother didn't respond, she'd been dragged back into a confab with the other judges.

'It's not legal,' Mrs Egremont was saying. 'The rules state that entries must be delivered in person.'

Fran had joined him. 'Oh, I think you've just made that up, Mrs Egremont. Having to deliver in person would count against anyone who is housebound, but a good baker.'

'Sweetheart, I'd just stay out of this,' Tom said.

The judging panel had obviously come to a decision. His mother said, 'Well, our marks stand, but Mary Fane will have to put in an appearance. I mean, she could be a professional chef or such like.'

'Yes, she bloody could,' Mrs Egremont said and several of the judging panel murmured, 'Language.'

'Oh all right then, mystery over,' Fran said, cheerily. 'It's me. I'm Mary H. W. Fane, it's an anagram of Fran Mayhew, you see. I've been practising and practising. I wanted to show you, Joan, what a very good teacher you are.'

'Oh, Holy Crap,' Joan said, which Tom did not think was a very good thing for a woman married to a vicar to say.

'You!' Mrs Egremont snarled at Fran. That got a lot of heads turning. 'You! But you're her son's fancy woman.'

'Oh what a lovely way of putting it,' Fran said. 'Did you hear that, Tom? *Fancy woman.*'

'Fran dear,' his mother was saying, 'this is very awkward—'

'Not to mention suspicious.' Mrs Egremont looked as if she was gearing up for some head-butting.

'But why?' Fran asked, her eyes wide. 'I used an alias so you and the judging panel wouldn't know who I was, so you couldn't be accused of favouritism.'

The judging panel smiled at her until they saw Mrs Egremont's expression and then they busied themselves with tidying up their table.

'But it might not be interpreted by others like that.' His mother did a not-very-subtle head jerk at Mrs Egremont.

'Oh,' Fran said as if a penny had just dropped.

Tom leaned back against a table and watched events unfold. He was smiling, he couldn't help it. Just another example of how Fran did not always understand how the world worked. There had been others, there would be more, and in the future it might even mean court cases, but he didn't care. Her straight-down-the-line view of life was one of the things he loved so much about her.

'All right, all right,' Fran said when there was the smallest of lulls in Mrs Egremont's complaining. 'Why don't we take one category, say, rock buns and re-judge it?

And honestly, Mrs E, I'm quite prepared to taste your entry and you can taste mine and we'll be brutally honest and see what happens.'

Tom watched Fran's enthusiasm trying to ignite the others. 'So,' she said, clapping her hands. 'Come along. Rock cakes.'

Fran was moving to the relevant table, Mrs Egremont grudgingly going with her.

'Right, here we go,' Fran said. 'I'll take first bite . . . Oh!' She was looking down at the plates on which her entry and Mrs Egremont's were displayed.

Mrs Egremont's plate was empty.

'That's not right,' Fran said, 'who's . . . ?'

Hattie was standing just behind the table. She looked like a hamster and you didn't really need an X-ray machine to see that it was one half of a rock cake that she had in each cheek.

There was a lot of talking and some shouting then, but Tom just stayed leaning where he was.

'My girls,' he said and his vision started to blur, 'my bloody wonderful girls.'

ACKNOWLEDGEMENTS

Thank you to the following for generously letting me pick their brains – Emma for insights into the logistics of magazine production; Sally for advice about pregnancy and maternity care; Mo for information regarding police procedures; Victoria for briefing me on the legal aspects of divorce and Penny for updating me on what small children eat, read, think about and play with. Any inaccuracies in the book on these subjects are down to me and none of the above!

Seeing Helen Musselwhite's stunning paper sculptures gave me the inspiration for Fran's work. Thanks to her for making the time to chat to me. Any grumbles I gave Fran about her work schedule were definitely not Helen's and you can see her lovely paper art at www.helenmusselwhite.co.uk

I'm extremely lucky to have objective, kind people reading my work as I write. Thanks to Chris Marples, particularly for her sound plot advice, and to Sara and Ruth.

A rousing cheer for my Agent, Broo, whose calm hand on the tiller and laugh at the end of the phone has got me through an 'interesting' couple of years.

And, of course this book would be nowhere without Quercus. I am hugely grateful to the whole team, from designers to sales and marketing people and especially to Kathryn who had the dubious job of overseeing the editing stage and Jo Dickinson who started it all off by ensuring the book was in the best possible shape.

Lastly a big hug to my sisters for their continuing merriment and support and more gratitude than I can put into words to Matthew, Kate and Becky for being so damned lovely and always one hundred per cent on my side. Girls, I'm looking forward to the brand new chapters that are about to unfold in your lives.

And of course, grateful thanks to you, the reader. Don't forget to let me know what you think of the book.

Hazel Osmond has been an advertising copywriter for many years. In 2008 she won the *Woman & Home* short story competition sponsored by Costa. In 2012, *Who's Afraid of Mr Wolfe?* was shortlisted for the Romantic Novelists' Association's (RNA) Romantic Comedy award. While she is a southerner by birth she now lives in Northumberland and, thirty years after first arriving, has finally taken off her vest. The county has been the inspiration for two of her books and she hopes, in turn, that they will inspire readers to come and discover Northumberland and its people for themselves.

Find out more about Hazel at
www.hazelosmond.co.uk

Also by Hazel Osmond

Who's Afraid of Mr Wolfe?
The First Time I Saw Your Face
Playing Grace

The Mysterious Miss Mayhew